BEAST

NEW YORK TIMES AND *USA TODAY* BESTSELLING AUTHOR

JASINDA WILDER

BEAST

ISBN: 978-1-964892-52-8

BEAST

Prologue

A Chance Collision

JAKOB

PIGEONS SWARM AND FLUTTER, COO AND STRUT. The pistol is a heavy, cold, unfamiliar presence at the small of my back—I have never much cared for firearms. They are a necessary tool, at times, but I dislike them as a general rule. They are impersonal. Any idiot with a finger can use a gun; it takes intent, training, and determination to kill someone with a more...shall we say, personal...method.

I reach for my mobile, and for the umpteenth time in the last hour, I am annoyed to remember I do not have it. I curl my hand into a fist and let out a long sigh.

My contact is late.

I scan Central Park again, and see only the expected: couples canoodling on blankets, pairs and trios and quartets of women in Lululemon leggings and Patagonia cross-body slings power-strolling along the path, runners puffing, dogs chasing balls and frisbees, kids shrieking.

While my attention is fixed on a pair of older men walking together without talking, I feel the bench shift as someone sits beside me.

She's the female version of a Gray Man: absolutely

forgettable, intentionally so. Dishwater blond hair in a ponytail, dressed in jeans, sneakers, and a plain T-shirt. Average features. Neither beautiful nor ugly. Just...a woman. Middle-aged, maybe, although she could be younger than she appears...or older. She could be from nearly anywhere there are white people. Her bag rests on her thighs, a large leather tote, the kind of thing a soccer mom would carry. She reaches into the bag and produces an insulated lunch bag, unzips it, and withdraws a clementine, which she begins peeling in a single careful spiral.

"Roberto Pugli was last seen on CCTV footage in Rochester, New York." She says this in a low, conversational tone, without looking at me.

"What is he doing there?" I ask.

"Not within the purview," she says, setting the peel aside and popping an orange wedge into her mouth.

"Right. Of course. When was this?"

"Seventeen hours ago."

"Was he alone?"

"Yes."

I sigh, grinding my molars in irritation—with these intelligentsia types, you have to ask very specific questions, and you only receive answers to those specific questions. "Did you learn anything else about the target that you can share with me?" I swear, it's like dealing with a djinn from 1001 Nights.

The phrasing of my questions gets me a twitch of her lipstick-free lips—a slight smirk of amusement. "He made several phone calls to a burner phone. I was able to ping the burner off of a tower in Queens." A pause, as she places another wedge in her mouth. "Also, you're being followed."

Fuck. I thought I saw a face more than once. "You're certain?"

"About the calls, the cell tower in Queens, or your rather clumsy tail?"

"Yes."

A snort. "Yes, I'm certain. There were three calls over twenty-four hours, but only one lasted long enough to get a ping. After that last call, the phone was ditched." She eats another wedge. "After I leave, wait ten minutes. Exit the park, cross the street, and go into the bodega next to the cellular shop. Buy a burner and some minutes. When you exit, you'll see a man across the street pretending to buy food from the street vendor. He's short and chunky, has a big bald spot, and he's wearing a black track suit with yellow stripes."

"And then?"

A shrug. "And then nothing, as far as I'm concerned. We're even—I don't owe you anything anymore, after this. Don't ever contact me again."

She produces a felt-tip pen and writes something on the inside of the orange peel, which she then discards on the ground as she stands and walks away, taking the rest of her clementine with her.

Within seconds, she's gone as abruptly as she appeared. With another annoyed sigh, I retrieve the peel. Stand up and head for a nearby waste bin, glancing at the inside of the peel—she had written down a set of coordinates. How helpful.

I tear away the section with the coordinates, surreptitiously tuck it into the hip pocket of my suit trousers, and discard the rest. I sit on the bench again and make a long, slow production of eating the gyro I purchased from the street vendor on the way here; fifteen or so minutes later, I'm ambling out of the park and across the street to the cellular store, where I buy a mobile and a minutes card. The cellular device has a GPS app, which is important, as coordinates don't do much good without a way to pinpoint where they lead.

I exit the store, inserting the disposable SIM card. While I'm powering on the phone, I cast a glance across the street: exactly as she indicated, there's a short, stout man in a black tracksuit standing in line near a street vendor. He's pretending to read the menu while watching me.

I shuffle to a waste bin and toss the packaging away while the off-brand device powers up; my tail is next in line, making a big show of counting cash. I pull up the GPS app and input the coordinates; as I suspected, they're for an address in Rochester. A random house in the suburbs, it appears. A safe house, most likely, knowing Pugli.

Why Rochester? There's no answer to that—Pugli is unpredictable, paranoid, and an old hand at these spy games.

To most of the world, Roberto Pugli is an upper-level executive for INTERPOL—a suit whose work is done in a corner office at INTERPOL headquarters in Lyon. To some, he's a master manipulator, an organized crime kingpin too careful to let himself be connected to any of his nefarious dealings.

But to a very, very select few, Roberto Pugli is just his most well-known alias.

You see, before he became Roberto Pugli and climbed the ranks suspiciously fast, he was an analyst and operative for an intelligence agency... until his predilection for using his position to commit crimes became too obvious.

He vanished, resurfaced years later as Roberto, and continued to be devious, cunning, and cruel…just with the might of INTERPOL as his smokescreen.

It's an open secret in many intelligence circles that he is a kingpin responsible for a truly shocking amount of awfulness around the world, mostly to do with arms dealing and human trafficking. It's just that he's too damned clever to leave any actionable evidence tying him to anything concrete.

Which is where Nicolae comes in…the man otherwise known as Lash.

But that's for later.

Right now, alarm bells are jangling in my gut. The fact that Pugli is Stateside and in New York is worrisome. After the events in Vegas, I'd have expected him to return to Europe.

If he's still here, it means he intends to personally make sure business is dealt with—said business being me.

More specifically, said business is what I know, and what Lash knows. What we have evidence of. What I personally witnessed several years ago—there are many reasons for my intense secrecy, and fear of Pugli's retaliation is only one of them, and a minor one at that.

I put Pugli out of my mind for now—he's not going to be at that location by the time I get there, and I have a feeling there are much more pressing matters at hand. Those three calls to a burner, plus the thug tailing me, equal bad things for me.

I'm tempted to call Inez—Sophia, I should say. But then I think about all she's been through, and how she's just now finally found peace. Rafael is dead. She's free. All of my Arrows are free.

I don't call anyone. I know Lash is unlikely to simply let things be—he has even more reason to hate and fear Pugli than I do. Which means he's out there, somewhere, hunting Pugli.

That's good enough for me; Pugli is as good as dead.

But those three calls.

More than likely, he was putting together a hunting party.

The quarry?

Me.

A Yellow Cab squeals to a halt a few feet away, and a portly man in his sixties wearing an expensive suit emerges, phone clamped between ear and shoulder, jabbering angrily into it as he juggles shopping bags, a briefcase, and a paper Starbucks cup. I slide into the backseat before he can even let go of the door; he gives me an annoyed, puzzled glare before waddling off down the street, still awkwardly juggling all of his belongings.

"Go around the block," I tell the driver, handing him a hundred-dollar bill.

The driver, an old man wearing a Sikh turban, bobbles his head with a soft, "Okehhh, okehhh."

I twist in my seat as he pulls away from the curb—my tail takes a big bite from the gyro he just bought, sees me getting into the cab, and drops the tinfoil-wrapped sandwich into a bin and sprints after me. For a moment or two, I think I've gotten away. But he has his phone to his ear, and seconds later—as we're squealing to a halt at the next intersection—a black Suburban halts beside him, and he gets into the front passenger seat.

These bastards.

The light turns green, and we reach the corner. My

driver trundles around, and we're stopped by an unloading cube van and oncoming traffic.

"Goddammit," I mutter. "Go, go, go."

"I cannot," The driver says. "Car come."

Oncoming traffic finally clears, and he guns it, the rattling old Impala groaning in protest. We swing around the cube van an instant before the arrival of another clump of oncoming traffic.

"Faster, please," I say.

"Okehh, faster. Yes, okehh."

I glance behind us again—the Suburban is three cars back. We reach the next intersection and turn right again. I pull another hundred out of my pocket and shove it at him. "Get me across the intersection as fast as possible."

He frowns at me in the mirror. "Impossible. I will crash."

"Just go. Into traffic, on the sidewalk, I don't care. Just go."

He snatches the bill from me, pockets it, and then, muttering under his breath in his native language, guns the engine again. We squeal into oncoming traffic, garnering a chorus of honks, squealing tires, and shouted curses from angry, impatient New Yorkers. My driver curses in a complicated mix of what sounds like half a dozen languages or dialects, jerking the wheel this way and that to dodge cars as he weaves diagonally across the thoroughfare toward the far-left corner. I glance behind, hand on the door handle—here comes a bus. The Suburban is trapped momentarily by a cluster of stopped cars left in the wake of our reckless bolt across the intersection.

The bus halts behind us as the driver brakes in the fire lane.

"You get out, crazy man," the driver says. "I keep the money."

"Good. If that black SUV keeps following you, take them on a ride."

He doesn't answer, not that I expected him to. As the bus rumbles behind us, blocking us from sight, I slip out of the car and duck behind a parked UPS vehicle with its flashers blinking. The taxi takes off, followed by the bus. It's a pretty shitty hiding spot, but it's all I've got at the moment. I see the Suburban slide past. I'm about to breathe a sigh of relief when the SUV's brake lights flick on as the vehicle angles toward the curb. The rear doors fly open, and four men emerge, two from each side. They're dressed in worn blue jeans, solid-color T-shirts, and black body armor. They're carrying fully-automatic subcompact short-barrel assault rifles.

And they see me.

I hear shouts, but I'm already sprinting. I cross the street, back the way I came, and cut through an alley to the next numbered street. I bump into an old man, sending him bowling into a cluster of passersby. Knock a caricature artist aside, pencils, sketchbook, and easel scattering.

Damn this arrogance of mine. I assumed my wealth and secrecy would protect me. I assumed even Pugli couldn't find me—I am dead, after all.

I assumed a lot of things that have turned out to be incorrect. And now I'm on the run myself, after years of helping my Arrows escape their pasts.

The other facet of my arrogance that has hamstrung me is my refusal to ask for help. I know Sol and the boys would come for me in a heartbeat if I asked. But they've just been through too much. I can't ask them to risk their lives again...for me.

I know, that sounds like I'm being nice. But really, it's just that I've invested way too much into those men to risk it all falling apart, now. Pugli wants me—and Lash. The others were just collateral damage.

My heart is pounding, and sweat pours down my face, making my shirt stick to my back. The next several minutes are a blur as I push through my exhaustion, dodging and weaving and ducking and sprinting block after block, turning at random, cutting down alleys.

My pursuers are relentless. And younger than me, fitter, stronger, faster.

Catching up.

I slam into a brick wall and stumble into an alley. I reach the far end when I hear the CRACK-CRACK-CRACK of an automatic, and brick dust showers me as the rounds chew up the wall just behind me.

I round the corner, slippery-soled Italian leather dress shoes skidding on the sidewalk. Trip over a stroller pushed by a pregnant woman, crash into a businessman with a cell phone in each hand.

Curses follow me as I stumble into a run yet again; this is untenable. I'm not fit enough to lose them. At some point, they're going to catch up with me. And knowing the sorts of men Pugli hires, they won't be overly worried about collateral damage. If innocent bystanders are hurt or killed, none of them will care.

Left here, right there. Cut through another alley. I don't know where I am, nor do I have a destination in mind. If I'm being honest with myself, I'm running on blind panic.

I don't want to die.

I'm no weakling; I'm no pacifist. I've hurt people. Shit, I've even killed people before. But gunfights? No. I know myself, I know my strengths, and I know my limitations, and I will absolutely lose a gunfight with four highly-trained operators.

That's the irony of the whole situation. I've spent the last decade seeking redemption for my past sins by rehabilitating people who've fallen through the cracks. Any of those men—and Scarlett and Inez—could handle this situation with ease.

And I'm too damned stubborn and proud to ask for their help.

I'm flagging, now. My legs burn, my lungs are on fire, and I'm dripping sweat. I've come I don't know how many blocks, and I can only be grateful that the one time I can ever quiet my mind is on the treadmill, slogging out mile after mile. Lifting is for stress management, to exorcise the anger that has been a constant companion and demon on my shoulder. Running? Running is meditation.

I just don't usually do it in loafers and a bespoke suit, through the crowded streets of Manhattan, for my life.

I recognize a few things as they flash past in a blur—a cafe here, a specific bodega there, and then I'm wading through the infinite crush of humanity thronging Times Square, knocking over a short, skinny person in a terribly ill-fitting Spiderman costume and then rebounding off of a six-foot-tall topless woman clad in nothing but a top hat, steampunk goggles, a bikini bottom, and glitter.

I can't go much farther at this pace.

I glance behind me as I leave Times Square behind, hoping I've lost them in the chaos.

No such luck.

They're closer than ever, if anything. Even more problematically, they seem barely winded, as if they can keep this up all day.

I think it's time to think beyond outrunning them, then, since that's clearly not going to happen. I bolt across the road abruptly, earning blaring horns and squealing tires; I react instinctively as a blaring horn and flashing brights bear down on me too fast, leaping and doing a Starsky and Hutch-worthy slide across the hood. I hear my pursuers shout in startled irritation, more horns blaring, more angry New Yorkers cursing as they follow me across four lanes of traffic.

And then I hear it again: the unmistakable crackling chatter of automatic gunfire. Something whizzes past my ear, and then a horde of furious wasps buzzes over my head. I slam into a parked car, setting off the alarm. Caroming back onto the sidewalk, I hear the guns go again, rattling and cracking. Glass shatters, people scream. I glance over my shoulder to see that stray shots have shattered a restaurant's windows, scattering patrons and sending them running in hunched, screaming clusters.

My blood boils—who does that? Who fires blindly across a crowded street? I suppose it's illogical to assume that someone willing to kill someone else for money would have ethics, but still.

I round another corner, shoes skidding. Shouts and screams echo behind me. I'm a block or so away from the busier thoroughfare, now. The sidewalk, while not empty, isn't clogged with tourists, and the road is still crowded with cars but not at a standstill.

I glance behind me, still sprinting.

Nothing. Maybe shooting at me like that wasn't such a great idea, huh? Assholes.

I look forward again, and that's when I see her.

Time stops.

I desperately attempt to halt myself before I crash into her—the process of stopping seems to take a million years. I feel her soft body slam into mine as I crash into her, send her flying. I manage to snag her wrist in a desperate attempt to prevent her from hitting the ground.

I yank her hard and she lands against my chest.

Her scent is the first thing I notice. Vanilla base, a hint of floral overtones, and citrus undertones. God, it's an intoxicating scent. And then I notice her eyes—hazel, technically, but I've never seen eyes like hers before: she has a ring of startling blue around the outside and a ring of brown-green on the inside surrounding her pupils. It's a shocking effect, freezing me in place for a moment.

I hear my pursuers closing in, booted feet slapping on concrete, snapping at each other in accented English—more of Pugli's seemingly endless supply of hired goons, albeit these goons are all former spec ops, I think.

I lift the woman, pivot, and walk her backward until she catches up against the brick wall of the alley.

"Play along," I growl, hoping they'll think we're just a couple of lovers stealing kisses in an alley.

Her back is bare—I steal a glance at her, really seeing her for the first time.

Somewhere around 5'9", she has more curves than a Formula One track—something I should know about, as I used to own an F1 team, before I died.

She's wearing a dress that is little more than a sheath of silver sequins contoured to the stunning lines of her lush body. The hem hits at mid-thigh, cups her plump, round ass, tucks in at her waist, and plunges down between the biggest natural breasts I've ever seen in person. I say natural because nothing silicone moves the way those monsters do—jiggling like Jell-O in an earthquake with each startled breath.

Fuck me.

My stomach falls out of my body, my heart twists into a pretzel, and my mouth goes dry.

I must have this woman.

It's the first thing I think, once I regain some semblance of mental clarity—the shock of her eyes and then the breathtaking curves of her incredible body rendered me briefly insensible.

"HE'S GOT TO BE AROUND HERE SOMEWHERE!" I hear a rough voice say, faint, distant.

The woman shivers—I doubt she's even aware of it. I shuck my jacket and settle it over her shoulders.

"OVER HERE!" A voice shouts nearby.

A tendril of honey-blond hair drifts across her face, sticks to her lips. She's stunned, still, and scared. "What's going on?" It's a confused breath, and I'm not sure she's aware she spoke.

"You're saving my life, that's what."

Her mouth opens, pink lips parting. "Saving your—"

I wasn't planning on any of this. Certainly not being chased across Manhattan by gun-wielding assholes, let alone literally running into a gorgeous woman.

With stunning technicolor eyes...

Hair like a summer sun...

The body of a goddess, the curves of a siren...

When I woke up this morning, my only concern was getting a bead on Pugli's last known location.

Now?

For a split second, the whole world fades into the background as she gazes up at me with shock and anger and confusion and fear…and arousal, attraction…

Her lips are soft and plump and pink, open to speak, glistening where her tongue slid along them…

She tastes like red wine. For a microsecond, she's frozen. But then her lips soften against mine, the tension in her body ebbs, and she presses her breasts against my chest and her hips against mine, soft thick thighs sliding against mine. I slide my hand over the bare warm expanse of her exposed back and find the swell of her ass, dig my fingers in; I caress her cheekbone, taste her breath, and never in my life have I felt such an intense reaction to a mere kiss.

Not even when I kissed *her* for the first time did I react like this.

With an immediate erection, yes.

But with a mindless ravaging desperation—not to possess, not to own…but to worship.

It's insane.

It's immediate and wild and gutting.

A single kiss, a momentary touch of lips, a brief press of her curves against me, and I'm destroyed.

I feel the blitz of a light on our faces.

"Do you fucking *mind*?" the woman snaps, and either she's a world-class actress…or she's not faking the annoyance at having our kiss interrupted.

I'm not thrilled either, but then, I know who these men are and what they want.

Which is when my heart sinks down to my toes—they've seen her face. And Roberto Pugli doesn't take any chances. Anyone who could even *possibly* identify *anyone* even remotely connected to him is eliminated. Quickly and brutally.

And these men have seen her face.

Chapter 1

A Barnacle Attached to a Very Fine Backside

BRYS

"Wait," Jakob says. "Just...wait." He presses me flush against the wall and peeks around the corner. "Okay, we're good. Go, go."

I feel silly, scurrying barefoot toward my door like I'm sixteen and late for curfew all over again. If it wasn't for the very immediate and very visceral memory of gunfire still ringing in my ears, I'd think this whole thing was a big joke or prank. It's the type of idiotic, over-the-top bullshit my idiotic brother Bryan would pull because he thinks it's funny. Only the fact that the armed men chasing my mysterious companion were absolutely firing live rounds convinces me that even Bryan isn't stupid enough to hire men to fire live rounds at me. I know Bryan doesn't like me, but I don't think he's malicious enough, or clever enough, to pull off an assassination attempt like this. Never mind the fact that if this is an assassination attempt on me, it's a very roundabout way of going about it. And he is exactly that stupid, admittedly, but even for him, this would be a cockamamie way of trying to get at me.

All of this runs through my head in the space of fifteen

seconds, and convinces me that this situation is most likely exactly what Jakob is claiming—Occam's Razor and all.

Which means creeping cautiously up to my door and trying to unlock it silently feels a lot less silly. There could be killers on the other side of this door.

I pause with my hand on the knob, look over my shoulder at Jakob. "I'm scared to go in."

He doesn't say anything, and his expression doesn't change—stony, impassive. He pulls me away from the door and pushes it open from one side; when we aren't immediately cut down in a hail of gunfire, Jakob enters the condo.

"Wait here," he says, once we're both over the threshold.

I hang back just inside, perfectly content to let him sally forth boldly into possible danger, closing the door and putting my back to it as Jakob moves through my home. He peeks into the powder room off the kitchen, then vanishes into my bedroom suite.

"I don't see any sign that anyone has been here, but take a quick look yourself. You'd know if anything is out of place or missing."

"Missing? They're thieves now, not just killers?"

"No," he says, sounding nearly amused. "Not to my knowledge."

I do my own quick assessment and come to the same conclusion. "Everything is as it should be."

Jakob goes into my kitchen, spotting my drying mat cluttered with upturned coffee mugs and juice glasses. He grabs a glass and fills it from the faucet, gulping it down in two swallows before refilling it and drinking again, this time more slowly. "I find it hard to believe we lost them that easily," he says. "I've been running from them for..."

he shakes his head. "Halfway across Manhattan, let's just say that."

"I have an idea," I say. "How about I get in bed and go to sleep, and *you* go away and take your killers with you? This has nothing to do with me."

"I wish it were that simple, Brys, truly I do." He goes to the window and peers out without putting his body in front of it.

"But they saw me for, like, six seconds. What are they going to do, Jakob? Sit down with a sketch artist?"

"Or CCTV footage," he says. "Those four men were hired to find and kill me. They're just the stooges. The one who hired them has world-class computer techs on his payroll, the kind of people who can ID you based on a single still from grainy CCTV footage from an ATM across the street, feed that image into an algorithm, and track your movements across the city."

"That's Hollywood bullshit. Fictional computer magic." I really, really want this to be true.

"Unfortunately, it's not. It takes longer than they make it seem on TV, but it's definitely real. And I guarantee you that there's some nerd clacking away at a keyboard somewhere, tracking our journey across Manhattan to this address. Or, more likely, IDing you, pulling up your address from public records, and sending a team here."

"Why me?" I ask, more out of petulance than anything else.

"Pure bad luck, Brys, and that's pretty much it. I ran into you, they saw me with you, and now you're in the crosshairs."

"*Whose* crosshairs, though?" I snap. "Who wants to kill you? And why? And who are *you*, for that matter?"

"I'll explain...well, maybe not everything, but some of it. For now, though, we have to keep moving. Which means you need to change into practical clothes, and fast." He eyes me. "Do you, in fact, have anything so prosaic as jeans, sneakers, and a T-shirt?"

I huff an annoyed but amused laugh. "Yes, Jakob, I do."

He shrugs. "You never know. I've known quite a few women who wouldn't be caught dead in denim."

"So, seeing as this is my first time running for my life from murderous cretins, should I pack a bag, or...?"

He arches his eyebrow. "No. You should not pack a bag. You should leave your cell phone here. You should grab as much cash as you have available. No ID, no wallet, no phone, no purse. No lotion, no hand sanitizer, no lipstick. Just you, comfortable, practical clothes, and sturdy, sensible shoes in which you can run if need be. If I were you, I'd do something with your hair. Braid it. Put in a bun, tie it back, put on a hat, something. Because as gorgeous as your hair is down, it's gonna be a problem loose like that."

I do my dead-level best to ignore the way the word "gorgeous" makes my heart pitter-patter. "You've got a lot of experience running for your life from murderous cretins, do you? With innocent women in tow, especially?"

He sighs, pinching the bridge of his nose. "Just go change, Brys. You can be witty and sarcastic at me later."

"Fine. Just...stay here and make sure the murderous cretins don't walk in on me naked." I glare at him. "You either, mister."

He holds up both hands, palms out in surrender. "Of course not."

I head into my room. The first thing I do is sit on the

closed toilet lid and use a wet washcloth to scrub my blackened feet clean. Remove makeup. Braid my hair.

The thing I didn't say to Jakob is that his comment about not being caught dead wasn't all that far from the truth; I was just too embarrassed to admit it. I *have* jeans and sneakers; I just... well, to be perfectly honest, I have in fact said out loud that I wouldn't be caught dead wearing jeans in public. Desperate times and all, though, right?

I peel out of my slinky little dress and the barely-there undergarments required by such a revealing garment.

At the exact moment in which I stand facing my closed but not locked bedroom door, buck-ass naked, the door slams open inward, revealing a wired and intense-looking Jakob. "They're here!" He stops in his tracks, mouth ajar, eyes wide. "Shit. Um. Apologies. But get dressed as fast as humanly possible."

Another instant passes, in which he blatantly stares at me before ripping his gaze away from me and lurching out of my room. The whole thing occurred in under ten seconds, and I haven't even had a chance to be pissed off.

I step into plain black granny panties and a sports bra, my best—and only—pair of jeans, and a pair of ungodly expensive hiking boots my idiot brother gave me for Christmas one year, even though the closest to hiking I've ever come in my life is cutting across the grassy part of Central Park. Which I did in a pair of Jimmy Choos. Fortunately, he managed to get them in the right size, so at least there's that.

I spend a precious moment waffling between my favorite comfort hoodie—a men's XXL Rangers pullover that belonged to Charles—and my leather biker jacket. I opt for the leather, mainly because some possibly misinformed voice in my head says it will provide some sort of protection against...something. I'm not entirely sure what.

I exit the room and find Jakob at the window, peering down at something from the edge of the frame. He snaps his fingers and points, indicating that I should join him at the other side of the window.

When I do, and look down, what I see makes my heart sink into my boots: not one, but two large black SUVs, disgorging men in jeans, tees, and body armor who carry machine guns like this is Iraq circa 2004 instead of Manhattan in 2026.

"What the fuck did you *do*?" I snap at Jakob. "Kill a warlord's daughter?"

"Worse. His dog." When his comment only gets him a puzzled look, he sighs. "Clearly you haven't seen *John Wick*." He eyes me. "I don't suppose you own a firearm? Or some other weapon?"

"Unless you count my Wüsthof knives as weapons, no."

He shakes his head. "Yeah, no." Another speculative glance. "Why on earth would you have a professional chef's knife set?"

I arch an eyebrow. "For cooking with." When he merely stares at me without expression, I sigh in irritation. "I enjoy cooking, alright? It relaxes me. It's my hobby."

"You don't seem like the hobby type, to be perfectly honest with you," he says. "You seem like the type who works evenings, weekends, and holidays and orders in because you don't have time for anything else."

"Judgmental much?"

"Am I wrong?"

I don't answer, because he's not. I huff. "I don't get to as often as I'd like, but I *do* love to cook. And I do it well, I'll have you know." I gesture at the cluster of killers below, who are, literally, huddled together receiving instructions. I mean, there are eight of them and two of us, and we're unarmed. How much strategery could possibly be involved? "What's your plan for getting me past them?"

"Getting *us* past them, you mean?" he asks.

"No, I mean *me*. You dragged me into this mess; it's your responsibility to drag me all the way back out of it unharmed. So I do mean *me*. I can't claim to care overly much what happens to you, Jakob. You're the one they want. I'm just collateral damage to them."

He eyes me again. "I see."

"I'm a bottom-line kind of girl, Jakob. I'm practical. Efficient. I am generally unconcerned with silly things like sentiment. And the bottom line here is that you're now responsible for me."

He nods as if this makes perfect sense. "I see." A pause. "Any useful skills? Knife throwing? Kung fu? Crazy, long-lost uncle with an underground bug-out bunker?"

"I have a purple belt in Brazilian Jiu-Jitsu," I tell him.

He tips his head to one side. "That's not nothing, and you very well may need it before this is all over."

"That's reassuring." I watch as the men below do their macho, about-to-kill-an-innocent-unarmed-woman huddle of manly manfulness. "Should we consider escaping now, Jakob?"

"Yes. We should." He notices my attire, now. "There we go. Nice jacket. Excellent choice." His eyes go to my boots. "And very nice boots. Didn't take you for the type to hike the Appalachian Trail."

I snort. "I'm not. My brother is an imbecile. He figured that because I like shoes, I'd like *any* shoes as long as they're expensive. So he bought the most expensive pair of hiking boots he could find in my size."

He blinks. "That's shockingly bizarre." A shrug. "But you'll be grateful for them before the day is out."

"Do they know we're here?" I ask, following Jakob away from the window and out into the hallway.

"Unlikely. Follow me and stay close."

The injunction to stay close feels unnecessary. The presence of murderous cretins who want me dead merely for existing near them is enough to turn me into a barnacle attached to his very fine backside.

We pause in the hallway as Jakob seems to debate between the stairs and the elevator.

"Why would we take the elevator?" I ask. "As much as I don't relish the idea of a dozen flights of stairs."

"Because they'd expect us to take the stairs." He eyes me. "But I'm only guessing. I'm used to staying off-grid, but being hunted like this is new for me, too."

"So, elevator?"

He nods. "Worth a shot."

Right as the elevator doors open, I hear the stairwell door crash open. Jakob hustles me on, stabs the close button repeatedly, and then the button for the ground floor. The door slides silently closed; as the view of the penthouse floor narrows into a thin vertical slice, I catch a glimpse of bodies crouch-walking past, machine guns tucked against shoulders.

I can only hope they didn't see me. The elevator lurches gently into motion, sinking toward the ground. The silent wait is awkward—on one hand, you're afraid that when the doors open, some asshole with a machine gun is going to shoot you to death, but on the other hand, it's hard to maintain active terror when you're idling around waiting for an elevator to stop.

The lift slows, settles; Jakob nudges me into the corner against the bank of buttons and presses back into me, physically shielding me with his body as the doors whoosh open.

"Fuck." Jakob's curse is a startled growl.

It's followed by a sharp, deafening bark, and the back wall of the elevator sprouts a hole.

He charges through the door, and then I can't see anything, can only hear grunting, grappling, curses, fists on flesh.

There's another blast of a firearm, this one muffled.

Silence.

I may not exactly *like* this mysterious Jakob, but he's my ticket to not dying, so I'd like him to not be dead, please.

I hold my breath and wait to find out.

Chapter 2

Unknown, or Unknowable?

JAKOB

For a few moments, all I can do is lie there, gasping, hurting, and amazed that I pulled that off.

I think of Thomas, and the many, many hours we spent sparring and wrestling together, before his heart attack. God, that was a loss. Thomas wasn't just a driver—or just a bodyguard. He was my friend. One of two humans on this earth I've ever truly, totally trusted. Thomas went behind my back to help *her* against my wishes, because he knew I'd lost myself to obsession. He was protecting me from me. He knew my secrets. He knew me when I was still Jakob, before Caleb Indigo ever existed. Thomas, in fact, was the first person I ever hired as a full-time employee. At that point, I had a lot of liquid capital and a burning passion to reinvent myself. My new persona would be bigger, better, richer, more powerful, more cunning, and more unstoppable than Jakob Kasparek ever was or could be. What I didn't have was an office to work out of, or much of a concrete plan besides getting into commercial real estate and keeping my businesses largely on the right side of the law.

I bought a used Escalade, contacted a headhunter, and conducted roughly a hundred interviews before hiring

Thomas. It was something in his demeanor that got me. He was calm, polite, stoic, well-spoken…and underneath all that was a subtle but definite air of do-not-fuck-with-me hardness. For almost eighteen months, I lived out of a hotel and worked out of that SUV with Thomas as my sole employee. He was my constant companion for nearly twenty years, and when he died so unexpectedly, I wasn't sure I'd recover. He's the only reason I emotionally survived walking away from *her*, from the life I'd so carefully constructed.

"Jakob?" A tentative female voice shakes me from my possibly concussed reverie.

"Yeah," I groan, sitting up and dislodging the body.

My belly is soaked with hot, wet blood—his. I look down at myself as I get to my feet; I'm stained with blood from chest to belt, and my black button-down is soggy and sticking to me. Yeah, I'm gonna need a change of clothes.

I hear shouting from the stairwell, and adrenaline sizzles through me all over again. I snag the dropped pistol and shove it into my waistband, rifle through the dead man's pockets—I take the two spare magazines for the pistol, a rubber-banded roll of twenties, a cell phone, and a folding pocketknife. Last, I strap the dead man's assault rifle across my chest and the single spare magazine for that.

"Let's go." I march away from the elevator in the direction of the stairwell to the parking garage.

Brys follows me. "Not to question your capabilities or anything, Jakob, but do you know what you're doing with that machine gun?"

"It's an assault rifle, not a machine gun," I correct. "And more or less, yes."

"Cool, I don't care what it's called. It's just that you didn't seem to be too accurate with that pistol. And, like, you threw the gun after it was empty. Now, I know I'm not, like, super knowledgeable about guns and whatever, but the only time I've ever seen a good guy throw a gun at a bad guy is in satire."

I open the door to the stairwell, poke my head, listen for a moment, and then creep in, Brys on my heels. "No, I do not have any formal training in the use of firearms. You've had the bad luck to fall in with the one person in my entire social circle who's *not* an operator—and that's me."

I've watched plenty of training videos, however, and I have some idea of what I'm doing. I'd never say that to my Arrows, of course, because they'd laugh me out of the room. I tilt the rifle over the railing, peer down, listen, and then put my shoulder to the wall and slide around the stairwell, keeping as wide a field of view as possible on the way down. We reach the bottom, and I push the door open from one side, exposing as little of myself as possible, gesturing for Brys to stay well out of the way of any lines of fire, should anyone shoot at us.

The garage seems quiet and empty but for the rows of parked cars. I'm not one to take such things for granted, however. I glance over my shoulder at Brys, who is scanning the shadowy corners with wide eyes, gnawing on her plump, pink, kissable lips.

Wait, what?

I growl at myself for the errant, idiotic, unhelpful thought. Sure, we've kissed twice in the two hours I've known her. Sure, those kisses have left my pulse pounding, my blood sizzling with a superheated effervescence, and my long-suppressed libido on a rampage.

There's no space in this situation for me to be distracted by said plump, kissable lips. Or by her plump, round, spankable ass. Or those big, bouncy, kissable breasts.

The sound of a door opening echoes throughout the stairwell above us, shocking me out of my horny reverie.

It feels like my thoughts are being broadcast for all the world to see on a chryon running across my forehead: *Man who claims to be dead thinking perverted thoughts about woman he's supposed to be rescuing. More at eleven.*

I inch forward through the door and into the garage, scan the space, and dart out into the open, dropping into a crouch between a thick, square concrete pillar and a Range Rover. "I don't suppose you own one of these, do you?" I whisper.

"No," she whispers back. "Do I look like I know how to drive? If I want to go somewhere, I call a driver like a normal person. I live in Manhattan, for fuck's sake."

"Normal people can't just call a driver."

"You've never heard of Uber or Lyft?"

"That's not what you meant," I point out. "You meant a private chauffeur."

"Shut up, asshole. Don't judge me."

I snicker. "I'm not. Up until last year, my driver was one of two people I actually trusted."

"What happened last year?"

"He died of a heart attack."

"Oh." She gently nudges my arm with her shoulder. "I'm sorry. No one knows us like our driver, huh?"

"No kidding. The secrets that man carried?" As soon as those five words leave my mouth, I silently curse myself for being seven kinds of an idiot.

I don't recognize myself around this woman. My dignity, my poise, my restraint, my intellectual sophistication?

The traits I've long prided myself on? Farts in a windstorm, when Brys Bennett is around, it would seem.

"Have a lot of secrets, do you?" She sounds amused—she probably knows I didn't intend to say anything quite so revealing.

"I mean, I conducted a lot of business in the back of a car, before I was able to lock down office space, early in my career." I feel good about this save. "Thomas was privy to the details of a lot of very sensitive deals."

She snorts. "Uh huh. I'm sure that's what you meant." She nudges me again. "What's the plan here? Hide in the garage until the bad guys find us? Have a nice little shoot-out down here? I don't know about you, but reenacting the movie *Heat* doesn't sound like my idea of a good time. Especially not when the guys after us are trained killers and you, by your own admission, are not."

"I'm not an operator, no," I tell her. "But I'm not helpless. And you're still safer with me than on your own. Unless you're lying to me and you're actually a secret spy or something."

"Nope, no secrets here. Just little ol' white collar me, no combat skills of any kind except BJJ, which I do primarily for exercise, and so I can break a mugger's arm if I had to."

"You may need that before the day is out," I say. "This is where knowing how to hot-wire a car would come in handy." I glance at her, the question in my expression.

She splutters. "Don't look at me, Jake."

My look turns into a glare. "Jakob. My name is *Jakob*."

It's weird to introduce myself as Jakob; I haven't been Jakob Kasparek for more years than I care to count. I was Caleb Indigo for nearly all of my adult life; I was twenty-five when Jakob vanished, and forty-three when Caleb died in a car bomb.

"Alright," I whisper. "Let's find the exit."

"You mean that big bright thing over there?" She points at the door that's rolling up as we speak, admitting a resident.

"Has anyone ever told you how much of a sarcastic pain in the ass you are?" I mutter.

She just snorts. "Repeatedly. It's a feature, not a bug."

The resident pulls down into the garage, makes a wide circuit, and parks in a corner away from the elevator and stairs; perfect. I cut across the garage and creep between the front bumpers and the wall. The resident is an older woman with silver hair in a Karen bob, driving a new Mercedes S-class.

Brys snags my arm an instant before I reveal myself. "Jakob, no," She hisses. "She's an old lady. You're not carjacking an old lady."

"You're right, I'm not carjacking an old lady. I'm… aggressively borrowing."

I step out into the light as the woman straightens from the back seat, her arms full of paper bags laden with groceries, a Birkin worth as much as her car hanging from one elbow. "Hello, ma'am," I say, keeping my tone level and conversational, the rifle slung across my front, my hands gripping the strap rather than the grip and handle. "I'm afraid I'm going to need to borrow your vehicle."

She blinks at me, her gaze flicking over my shoulder. "Is this man bothering you, dear?"

Brys appears beside me. "No, ma'am. He's actually doing the exact opposite."

"When you say borrow, I assume if I get it back at all, it won't be in one piece?"

Brys steps forward, putting herself between the woman and me. "Ma'am, I live in this building myself. And you have my word that no matter what happens, I'll see that either your car is returned in the same condition or replaced."

She sighs. "It was an anniversary gift from my husband," she says. "But it's far too big for me. If you could find a way to replace it with something smaller and easier to park than that behemoth, then we have a deal."

Brys laughs. "That can be arranged, I believe."

The older woman sets her paper bags on her trunk, rummages in her purse, and withdraws a key fob, which she hands to Brys. "If anyone asks, you stole it."

Brys tosses the fob to me. "If anyone asks, *he* stole it."

The sound of a crashbar and the slight squeal of hinges echo through the underground garage.

"That's our cue," I say, taking the fob. "Ma'am, if I were you, I'd take the elevator straight up to your house, lock the door, and don't open it for anyone."

Without a backward glance, the woman scoops up her groceries and hustles for the elevator. By the time she reaches it, I'm behind the wheel, Brys is beside me, and we're backing out of the parking space.

I glance in the rearview mirror as we angle up and out of the garage, the door opening automatically; a cluster of men swarm out of the stairwell.

The last thing I see is muzzle flash as they fire at us; their rounds thunk low into the trunk, and then I'm skidding out into traffic, horns blaring and brights blinking and voices cursing from open windows.

Beside me, Brys is twisted in the seat, watching out the rear window as her condo building falls away. When I turn, and her view of it vanishes, she slumps back around, sighing. "Now what?"

I shrug. "I don't know, Brys. That's the honest truth. I don't know. I guess we get out of the city."

"And go where? Where can we go that these goons won't find us?"

"That's a good question. For now, we just get off the island of Manhattan and ultimately out of New York—it's the most heavily surveilled city in the world. I'm hoping once we're out of the city, it'll be harder for Poo—" I cut myself off before I say his name. "For my enemy's computer nerds to find us, and thus hopefully harder for him to send his goon squads after us."

"Your enemy is poo?"

I sigh. "No, Brys. I'm keeping the details from you. Hopefully, the less you know, the safer you are."

She snorts derisively. "The shit is out of that elephant, Jakob. You may as well spill the whole sad truth."

For a moment, I actually consider it. What would that be like? To tell someone the whole sad, strange, toxic, sordid truth of my life?

Now that Thomas has passed on, there is not one person on this earth who knows all of me. *Her* knowledge of me stops at the day she saw me die. Inez knows who I am now and likely suspects who I used to be, but I've neither confirmed nor denied anything.

I am unknown.

But am I unknowable?

I can't claim to be proud of who I've been, or of some

of the things I've done. But not being proud of your past isn't the same as telling someone all your secrets.

"Wow," Brys says, jarring me out of my thoughts. "You really have to consider that one, huh?"

I brake to a stop at a red light, still mulling over the notion of unburdening myself of my many awful secrets. My gaze, naturally enough, wanders from the left corner of the intersection to the right.

Black hair, glossy and raven-dark, razor-bobbed at her sharp chin. Bug-eye Chanel sunglasses cover dark eyes. Black leggings hug strong, curvaceous legs. Shopping bags hang from an elbow. A cell phone is pressed to one ear.

You smile, nod. Laugh. Turn with an absent-minded glance, look over your shoulder—they're ten, now. One with hair the color of the sun, the other with hair the color of the night. Tall. Attractive. Well-dressed, well-groomed. Calm. Full of poise and elegance, of course; they're your children, after all. Beside you? Him. And he's aged damnably well. Lean and muscular, flat of stomach and with all his hair, nary a trace of silver in the golden strands.

My fingers go to the silver staining the temples of my own hair.

What would you think of me now, Isabel?

A horn blares twice, but it's Brys's voice that brings me back to life. "Jakob?"

I accelerate away from the intersection.

Away from you.

When the crowd of pedestrians obscures you from view, I am released from your grip on my psyche, and I suck in a bolt of oxygen.

I squeeze the steering wheel with both hands to hide the way my fingers tremble.

It feels like I've passed a test of some kind.

"Jakob?" Brys's voice is soft, concerned, lacking any trace of her usual sarcasm.

"I'm not a good person, Brys," I murmur. "I never have been."

Chapter 3

A Question For A Question

BRYS

I'm not sure what just happened, but Jakob is white as a sheet, shaking, and looks shell-shocked. The phrase "looks like he saw a ghost" comes to mind; I always assumed that was an exaggerated statement, but Jakob really does look like he's seen something beyond the pale.

I don't think he's even aware of me for a moment or two.

"I'm not a good person, Brys," he says, his voice low, distant. "I never have been."

A block slides past, two. What does one say to something like that?

His fist is white-knuckled on the steering wheel, his brow furrowed.

I have a billion questions.

"Who was she?" It's the one that tumbles out.

"Someone from a past life." His eyes flick to the rearview mirror, but we're stuck in traffic, and the flow of pedestrians on the sidewalks is a surging river. Whoever she was, she's long gone.

"You look like you've seen a ghost." Again, it just sort of pops out unbidden.

He snorts at this, for some reason. "An ironic turn of phrase, considering." His speech pattern, here—his tone of voice, something indefinable about him—shifts.

Tightens.

Hardens.

Formalizes.

"I don't know what that means," I say.

"No, I don't suppose you would. How could you? You'd have to be privy to some deep, dark, dangerous secrets if that made any sense to you."

"Another delightfully cryptic statement," I say. "But then, all I know about you is that you claim your name is Jakob, and someone named Poo is sending gaggles of killers after you, and now me simply for being seen with you, which only happened because you tried to hide behind me."

"There are several incorrect elements to that statement," he mutters.

"So enlighten me."

He makes a turn, and then we're joining a merging line of cars headed for a bridge to the outer boroughs. "I wish it were that simple."

"It is," I say. "You open your mouth and start talking."

His gaze is incendiary. Burning with a glut of emotions too complex to comprehend. "If I gave you even a fraction of the truth about myself, Brys Bennet, you would jump out of this car and take your chances with the killers."

"That sounds like an exaggeration," I say.

Those dark eyes cut sideways, land on me, and then flick away, back to the slow-moving traffic. "It is not."

"You may as well just start talking," I say. "I'm not going to give up until you do."

He exhales softly, a short puff through pursed lips. "Brys..."

I lean an elbow on the console and stare at him. "Yes, Jakob?"

"This really is a situation where the less you know, the better."

"Bullshit. We were past the point of culpable deniability when you took me home to change clothes so we could go on the run. You owe me answers, mister." I pause for effect. "Plus, I simply do not believe that lacking information is ever a net positive."

We inch closer to the bridge—at this point, we'll get there sometime tomorrow.

Jakob says nothing for a long time, and I let him wallow in his silence. Every once in a while, he glances at me, but I can't parse his expression. Speculative? Considering? Wary? Scared?

I think there's a bit of fear in there, but I know a man like he seems to be would never admit to fear, even to himself. Or maybe especially for himself.

"I wouldn't know where to start, to be honest."

"Why are there men trying to kill you, and thus, by association, me?"

"I know something...incriminating...about someone who doesn't like to leave any loose ends lying about."

I huff. "If you're just going to be vague, you might as well not say anything at all."

He groans—either annoyed, regretting opening his mouth, or both. "The details would do you no good."

"But it would assuage my curiosity, which is starting to feel like an existential rash."

He eyes me, amused. "An existential rash?"

"Yeah, you know. Itchy and burny to the point of obsession."

"I suppose I do know a bit about obsession." Another sigh. "His name is Roberto Pugli. On paper, he's a high-level executive for Interpol."

"The international police force?"

"They're an investigative agency, not an enforcement one, but yes."

"And in reality?"

"He's one of the most violent, notorious, dangerous, and impossible to convict criminal kingpins on the planet. He's a drug trafficker, an arms dealer, a human trafficker, a murderer, and one of the most sociopathic and evil human beings to ever live."

"And he wants you dead?"

"He has for a long time."

"Because you possess incriminating evidence of his nefarious deeds?"

"Correct."

"Is he cold and calculating but charming, or impulsive, erratic, and emotionally reactive?" I ask.

He glances at me. "Psychopathically, then, if you wish to split hairs on the man's specific mental disorder." Again, I'm detecting a distinct shift in the way he speaks. It's subtle but noticeable.

"If, as you say, he's wanted you dead for a long time, why is he just now attempting to render you deceased?"

"I was out of reach until recently."

"How can you be out of the reach of a supervillain?"

"By being dead." He doesn't even have the decency to look at me when he drops this bomb.

"Excuse you?"

A sigh. "It's a long story."

"We've been over this, Jakob."

"I answered your question, Brys." His tone is hard, sharp.

Good thing I'm used to dealing with men with overblown senses of self.

"And in so doing raised, ohhh, at least a hundred more."

"A quid pro quo, then." He shoots me a look, dark eyes as unreadable as ever. "One question for one question."

"You have a deal, sir," I answer.

We've moved six inches in the last twenty minutes. Good thing this isn't a car chase.

"You may start," he says.

"The only caveat I'll put in here," I say, "is that your answers must be thorough and complete and direct. No vague nonanswers."

He growls softly. "Fine."

"The woman back there," I say—he immediately tenses, his shoulders lifting toward his ears, his jaw turning to granite, "your entire demeanor shifted the instant you laid eyes on her. Who is she to you? And don't say 'just an ex' because it's obviously way more than that."

He huffs—technically a laugh, but really just a wordless noise of irritation. "Right for the jugular, is it?"

I shrug. "How'm I supposed to know? You saw some lady on a street corner and turned all tense and angry and formal."

He glances at me. "Formal?"

I nod. "Yup. Until you saw her, you were...looser. Not just in terms of tension, but...speech patterns. Mannerisms. You're all..." I sit up straight enough to make Miss Manners proud. "Uptight...Erect." I point at him. "No crude jokes."

He narrows his eyes. "Crass humor is the purview of the simple-minded."

I laugh. "See? Like that."

He frowns thoughtfully, scratches his jaw. "Her name is Isabel Maria de la Vega Navarro Ryder."

"That's a mouthful." I blink as my mind summons bits of memory. "Wait...Isabel Ryder. She founded the Minnie Centers and A Temporary Home...she's a philanthropist, isn't she?"

"Something along those lines, yes. I doubt she would refer to herself as such, however. She's far too humble for that." When I offer no remark, he eyes me. "There. I told you who she was—is."

"I obviously meant who is she *to you*."

"That is not what you asked."

I laugh. "It's like that, is it? Squabbling over wording?"

He hangs his head for a second. "She's an ex."

"Jakob. Stop stalling."

"You're asking me to..." he shakes his head. "You don't know what you're asking."

"No, obviously not. Thus the reason for the question."

Another long silence—the line of cars has moved several whole feet and is creeping along steadily, now. The bridge is in view.

"I don't know how to explain who she is to me. There's a lot of...context...that's required."

"So contextualize me, hot stuff."

He arches a wry eyebrow at me. "Hot stuff?"

I shrug. "Just go with it."

A shake of his head. "Isabel is...was..." Another head shake. "No. It's impossible."

"Jakob."

"You're pulling on a single thread, but that thread is part of a Gordian knot. There simply isn't a single, pat, easy answer."

"She's really not just an ex, is she?"

His gaze, when I meet it, is heavy. "No, she isn't." A frown crosses his features, then. "I don't have anything so prosaic as *just an ex*."

"What a strange thing to say."

He shrugs. "I'm not a simple man, Brys."

"So I'm gathering." I sigh. "Fine. I'll take pity on you for now. I'll ask a different question. But you're not off the hook forever. I'm going to ask that question again. So, you know, be thinking about the answer."

"It's my turn." He shoots a sideways look at me, thoughtful and deep. "Why are you single?"

"Who says I am?"

"You haven't so much as mentioned a boyfriend, fiancé, or husband. I feel like it would have come up if one existed, especially after that kiss."

"Which one?" I mumble.

His answering grin is superheated. "Exactly." The grin fades a bit. "So. Why are you single, Brys Bennett?"

"Because I don't have a boyfriend."

He snorts. "Remember your caveat? No vague nonanswers."

"You want the deep, uncomfortable truth?"

"Clearly."

"What was it you said about going right for the jugular?" I shift in my seat, starting to regret this game already. "Because I'm just not girlfriend material."

He looks at me without speaking for a long moment, absorbing my answer. "What does that mean?"

"Ah-ah," I say, wagging a finger at him. "One question, one answer."

He rolls his head on his neck and then nods. "Yeah, yeah. Your question, then?"

I consider. "You don't have anything so prosaic as just an ex, you said. Elaborate on that."

"My life has not lent itself to dating, as you'd know it. For the most part, it's simply due to the fact that I've been too busy. I've been an entrepreneur my whole life. I was worth almost twenty billion dollars at one point."

My mouth goes dry. "*What*?" He's wearing expensive clothes, yes, but…worth *billions*?

He just shrugs.

"Okay, but *at one point*? Did you lose it in a game of cards or what?" I stab a finger at him. "And don't give me the one-question-one-answer bullshit."

"I gave almost all of it to the woman we saw back there." He pauses for a beat. "Before I died."

"That's the second time you've said that. What does—"

"Why aren't you girlfriend material, Brys?"

"Because I'm a self-centered bitch who's always been more focused on my career than anything else. I'm sarcastic as fuck, as you've learned, I have zero time or patience for fools, and I'm nearly always the smartest person in any room I'm in, which makes the vast majority of men deeply insecure around me. I don't have a submissive bone in my body. I like to be on top. I prefer to sleep alone. I don't like sharing my space. Need I go on?"

"What I'm hearing is that you're unapologetically yourself, and successful, and weak, small-minded men are threatened by that."

My heart flutters in my chest like a bird fluffing its feathers. "That's...quite a take."

"It's the truth. Only little boys with minds and wills as small as their penises like a submissive, easily controlled woman." He states this as a fact, as if my worldview wasn't tipping on its axis.

Despite the fact that traffic seems to be barely moving, when I next glance forward, the bridge is much larger and closer. "You're seriously going to dodge the question?" I say. "No details at all? Just gonnna drop the little bomb that you were once worth twenty billion, with a B, you gave it all away to some woman, and also you died. Not *almost* died, but *did* die. And then you just dodge my questions like a politician caught on camera with his dick in the wrong place?"

He shakes his head slowly—less a denial and more a *can you believe this shit?* sort of thing. "It's a long, painful story that I've never told anyone. I'm not sure you'd believe me if I did tell you the whole thing, and even then, assuming you *did* believe me, you would *absolutely* think much, much less of me than you already do."

"I don't think less of you, Jakob. I don't know you well enough to think much of anything about you. I know you're absurdly gorgeous. I know that even if you gave away most of the twenty billion, the clothes you're wearing are expensive and bespoke, and indicate you kept enough money to be comfortable. I know some crazy bad guy from

Europe has a hard-on to murder you, and me by extension, since I had the misfortune of being slammed into by your giant ass. Which, by the way, was actually pretty good timing. That dinner was interminable and fucking awful, and I'm rather grateful it got interrupted, although I could have done without the machine guns, and, you know, the whole running for my life thing. I also know you're not a very good shot, but you can and will fight for your life—and mine." I shrug. "That's about all I know about you, Jakob Kasparek."

He remains silent for so long that I'm left with no choice but to assume he's done with the conversation. He steers with his left hand, thumb tapping arrhythmically on the wheel; his right hand rests on the console between us, fingers drumming idly—also in a rhythmless pattern.

The temptation to slip my hand into his is nearly overpowering. It's a silly, stupid impulse, and it's so wildly out of character for me that it makes me irrationally irritated at myself.

A penny flashes in the air, bounces off my thigh, and lands on the floor of the footwell.

I retrieve it and shoot Jakob a look. "I don't need your money, you know."

His lips twitch in an almost-smile. "Noted. That penny was for your thoughts."

I roll my eyes at him. "Smooth move, Exlax."

He snorts. "My Motorola Razr is ringing—it's the nineties, they want their comebacks back."

"Wait, was that...*a joke*?" I gasp, hand fluttering at my chest like a scandalized Victorian lady. "Well, I *never*."

"I don't think that's how that phrase is used," he says.

"If you're not going to share your thoughts, give me my penny back."

I turn the penny over in my hand—it's a new one, bright and shiny. "I can't tell if you're joking or not."

"I never joke about money," he says, deadpan and serious.

I sniff, handing him the penny back. "My thoughts are worth far more than a mere penny, I'll have you know."

"Very well, then." He lifts his hips up, digs in a trouser pocket, and comes out with the roll of cash—the roll is wider than a roll of quarters, fastened with a thick, fat rubber band, the heavy-duty kind used for fresh produce. "That enough?"

I undo the roll, straighten the cash, and make quick work of counting it—it's all twenties, but because the paper is rolled up, it only adds up to $160. "Huh. I'd have expected more."

"Rolling cash gives the impression of more than there is," Jakob says. "Back when I was young and dealing with various nefarious types, I saw it often. usually, there'll be a hundred or two on the outside, a couple of twenties, and the rest nothing but ones, but when you whip out a fat roll of cash like that, it's an effective illusion."

"It's empty posturing."

He snorts. "To those familiar with true wealth, yes. But in a world where image and reputation are everything, it can be important." He juts his chin at me. "So. Does that buy me what you were thinking about?"

My cheeks flame. "No."

The twitch of his lips is very nearly an actual grin. "Ah. I see."

"You see nothing."

"I see that you're refusing to answer a simple question, which means you were definitely thinking about me."

"How very egotistical of you," I say, not looking at him.

"But am I wrong?" he asks, now fully smirking at me.

I look away rather than outright lie, because I'm a terrible liar; I'm *fantastic* at omission, obfuscation, and diversion, but if called upon to bald-faced lie, I can't do it without giving it away via my expressions. It's a personal failing of mine.

"Come now," he cajoles. "You know you want to tell me."

"Fine, I'll tell you, but you have to trade me."

He nods, glances at me. "Okay, I'll play. Trade what?"

"A piece of equally damning, personal, or otherwise revealing information about yourself. Not 'I've never been to a Mets game' or 'I once shoplifted a candy bar and got away with it.' I'm talking real intel. Something no one else knows."

"Hmmm," he hums. "Not sure I want to know what you were thinking *that* badly. Must have been pretty damn personal." A pause. "How do I know the intel I give you will be of equal value?"

"You don't."

"You drive a hard bargain, Miss Bennet." He extends his right hand toward me—the one I was looking at, wanting to hold. "But you have a detail. I'll share mine first, as a gesture of good faith."

He lets out a long, slow sigh from puffed out cheeks and pursed lips. "I once ran a...hmmm. I suppose the most accurate term would be escort service."

"You were a *pimp*?" I sound horrified, scandalized, and fascinated—all equally accurate.

"No," he snaps, his tone sharp. "I was *not* a *pimp*."

I hold up my hands. "Okay, my bad. Didn't know there was a difference. I'm not exactly experienced in the sex work industry."

He closes his eyes, sighing. "I apologize for my tone. I have strong feelings on the topic."

"By all means, Jakob, say more."

"You first." A hard look at me. "The truth, if you please."

I swallow hard—this man has a strange way of pulling things out of me. Like the truth. "I was thinking about holding your hand."

Chapter 4

A Sin-Blackened Soul

JAKOB

That's it?

That is what all the fuss is about? Holding hands?

My impulse is to snort at her, but one look at her face tells me that for her this is no laughing matter. She's gnawing on the corner of her lower lip and glancing at me sideways, assessing my reaction, waiting for it, nervous for it.

I honestly assess myself—it's an interesting idea. And that's when it occurs to me: I've never in my life just…held someone's hand. Touch has always come with a purpose. Never just because. Never just for comfort or pleasure. I don't mean ill intent or always out of manipulation, but… for a reason. To accomplish something, to communicate something.

This woman, though. She draws things from me. Elicits reactions I didn't know I possessed, elicits feelings I didn't know I was capable of. I say things I shouldn't, find myself feeling things I didn't think I could feel.

All sorts of weird feelings keep cropping up in the atrophied remains of my sin-blackened soul—nascent seedlings of hope, tiny green shoots of tenderness, fragile sprouts of protectiveness.

All of them regarding her.

There's tension in her brow, written in the furrows and carved in the lines. Worry eats her.

"This means something to you," I murmur. "The hand holding."

She nods, but otherwise doesn't reply.

"Why?"

"I answered your question. It's my turn again."

We're finally crossing the bridge—albeit in fits and starts, like glugging molasses. "Alright," I say. "What's your question?"

"Why did you kiss me?" She looks at me, her expression too complicated to read. "In the alley, after you plowed into me and then used me as a human shield."

Irritation rifles through me. "I did not use you as a human shield, Brys."

"Close enough, and you know what I mean." She holds my gaze, hers unwavering and clear—but full of emotions in a chaos of conflict. "Why did you kiss me?"

There is no option but the truth. "I wish I knew," I speak over her protest. "It's the truth. I didn't plan it, didn't intend it. I just...you were—" my utter inability to articulate any manner of logical explanation irks me to the point that I bite down on my stammering, my teeth clicking together audibly.

"I was what, Jakob? You're an educated, articulate man. Surely you can explain yourself."

"You kissed me back," I point out. "Thoroughly."

She acts offended. "I did not. And that was *not* a thorough kiss. Wasn't even a top ten."

My lips curve into a facsimile of a grin. "Is that so?" My voice is a predatory purr. "Noted."

"That wasn't a challenge!" she protests. "You don't have to prove me wrong."

"I had to," I say after a moment; it's the god's honest truth, too. "I had to kiss you. I didn't have a choice."

"I don't know what that means," she says.

I frown at her. "You've never felt that way?"

"I have never felt the urge to shove my tongue down a stranger's throat, no."

"I don't believe you," I say. "You have. You may not have ever acted on it, but you've felt it."

We're stopped again, three-quarters of the way across the bridge; I feel antsy, feel the unsettling prickle of being watched, even though I know we've lost our pursuers for the moment.

She's looking at me, staring at me hard, her unique, intense eyes piercing mine. "Absolutely not."

With traffic halted, I put the car in park and turn to face her. The lie is written all over her face. "You're a bad liar, Brys."

"Fine—I've had the impulse. And no, I've never acted on it. Because I'm an adult with impulse control."

"In almost every aspect of my life, I possess an iron will." I roll a shoulder. "Kissing you like that was extremely out of character."

"Kissing you back was extremely out of character for me, as well," she says. "I don't even really like kissing all that much, for the most part."

This makes me pull a face. "You don't?"

She shrugs. "No, not really. It's...wet, and weird. It's awkward. My nose gets in the way, and I don't know what to do with my tongue, and it feels weird when someone tries to French kiss me." A sigh, a shake of her head. "I don't know. I just...I don't know."

"Felt to me like you liked it just fine."

Her cheeks turn red. "It was okay."

Moving slowly and deliberately, I reach out and take her hand. I'm not sure why. Just like when I kissed her, she resists at first, stiff and tense and unyielding. And then, gradually, by degrees, the stiff tension in her hand ebbs, slackens. Her blue-green-brown eyes search mine, flicking and sliding this way and that, hunting, darting, intense.

"Why?" She breathes. "Why mock me like this? I answered the question honestly."

"Mock you?" I echo, frowning. "Who's mocking?"

"Then why?"

"I'm curious," I answer—truthfully, I realize. "I've never held hands before."

Brys snorts. "Oh, bullshit. Everyone holds hands. My first 'boyfriend', and heavy quotes on the term boyfriend there, all we ever did was hold hands. Granted, we were twelve at the time, and it felt pretty daring."

I shake my head. "I never experienced that."

"What, were you super sheltered or something? One of those 'no touching girls till marriage' situations?"

I lick my lips, put the shifter into Drive, and follow traffic forward once more; we are still holding hands. "My upbringing was...nontraditional, at best. And whatever childhood I may have had came to what one might accurately call a rather abrupt halt. I was not a child at the time, technically, but..." I trail off, the rest lodged somewhere between my esophagus and stomach.

Isabel is the only one I have ever told the whole story

to, and I just do not know how to put the story out into the world again, how to trust anyone else with the truth. With the sordid reality of who I am—who I've been, perhaps more accurately. I'm losing my sense of self, somehow, lately. If I'm not Caleb Indigo anymore, and I'm not sure who Jakob Kasparek is anymore, then who am I?

Brys stares at me for a moment, then frowns when it becomes clear I'm not offering any further information. "You really aren't going to say anymore?"

I rub my forehead with a fore knuckle. "Sorry, but I'm not exactly raring to divulge my whole life's story to someone I just met."

She wrinkles her nose. "I suppose I can sympathize with that a little. I don't go around telling people all my secrets on the first date either." She winces, eyes widening and darting to me, then away. "Not that this is a date, or anything like it. I just..." She sighs. "Never mind. I'm shutting up before I eat my whole entire foot."

I chuckle. "I know what you meant."

"You're still holding my hand," she points out.

"No, *you're* still holding *my* hand." I smirk at her as I say this.

No snarky comeback, just silence. But she also doesn't let go of my hand, and neither do I.

And so we cross the bridge and begin the trek across the outer boroughs in a strange silence—not awkward, entirely, but not easy exactly or companionable either. It's a unique silence, one I've never experienced before. I am comfortable with silences of all kinds. I use them to great effect in interviews, negotiations, and interactions. But this is...different.

I tend to wield silence like a weapon, or perhaps

merely a tool. Silence can be a device for eliciting a desired response. It's basic psychology. But with Brys, it's a silence without intent. We are each laden with things to say, but aren't saying them. Yet despite the weight of all the unsaid things, it's bizarrely easy to say nothing. To simply sit beside her and ruminate on all the things I've never told anyone, not Isabel, not Inez—sorry, Sophia—not anyone. It's bizarrely easy to just hold her hand and weave my way through the Bronx northward toward Yonkers, leaving behind the glass and concrete jungle of Manhattan. It's not silence with a purpose; it's just…silence.

At some point, I realize the silence is because she's fallen asleep.

Yonkers. White Plains. Sleepy Hollow. Ossining. Peekskill. Barely an hour outside the city, but it feels like a different world. For all the years I spent in NYC, I rarely ventured beyond the confines of the five boroughs.

I don't have a destination in mind. I'm just getting out of New York, away from the crowds and surveillance. Out here, I can spot a tail—so far, so good.

I do need a change of clothes—these are crusty and stiff with blood; we also need to switch vehicles. And I need a fucking nap.

I know we're not off scot-free—whatever the hell that means—but we've bought some time to come up with a plan, at least.

For now, I keep driving north. It's not until a construction detour takes us westward that I realize where I'm taking us: Rochester. Pugli's last known location.

Beside me, Brys continues to sleep, mouth slightly ajar, head tipped against the window, one hand curled beneath her chin. Her eyelashes are thick and dark, swept against her cheeks. Her lips are plump and pink—she took her makeup off, and is all the more beautiful for it. She was a sophisticated bombshell when I ran into her—wrapped in an expensive dress, wearing unutterably rare and expensive shoes, carrying an equally unutterably rare and expensive handbag, hair done just so, makeup perfect—smoky eyes, dramatic red lips, delicate, skillful contouring. Breathtaking. A sleek, lovely, elegant New Yorker through and through.

But this version of her? Jeans that hug her generous hips and ass, a simple tee, sturdy boots, a biker jacket, no makeup, hair braided? She's real. Still elegant and breathtaking, but…I don't know. The polish and hauteur of a wealthy white-collar executive are gone. In her place? A woman who, despite the unexpectedness and terror of the whole situation, kept her head and stayed calm. This is a woman who doesn't panic when shit hits the fan.

My mind wanders as I drive steadily north and west.

She wanted to hold my hand.

I'm still not sure what to do with that, how to feel about it. It was strange, at first, holding her hand. I wasn't lying or making things up when I told her I'd never held a woman's hand in that fashion before. I never had a childhood girlfriend. I was educated at home by a dour, hard-faced, unforgiving, cold-hearted tutor. I had no friends—my social circle consisted of my mother, father, nanny, and my tutor. I was, in a very real sense, isolated from the world. Looking back, I've often wondered why—what were my parents hiding me from? I'll never get an answer, I know. Doesn't stop me from wondering.

And then my mother died. My father killed himself.

And I was sent here, to America, to NYC. When you're a sheltered rich kid from Prague, to call America the New World doesn't feel all that archaic or anachronistic. It feels accurate. It is a whole new world. A strange and scary one. And I was here for about five minutes before I was thrown to the wolves by my father's cousin.

God, why am I maundering through all that old, awful mess?

Because Brys wanted to hold my hand.

Why?

Comfort? I'm the reason she's in this situation, so why would she expect me to comfort her? Why would holding my hand be that comfort? Yet, despite the questions ricocheting around my brainpan, I can't help but acknowledge that holding her hand was...pleasant—more than pleasant. Simply holding her hand made me feel grounded. Connected, somehow. To her, to something indefinable.

I'm overthinking the whole thing, probably. She was scared and reached for the only source of comfort available—me.

But that doesn't explain the kiss. The tension—sexual, emotional, psychological. It doesn't explain the way she looks at me sometimes—with heat, with interest, with... I'm not sure. She's got a hell of a poker face, for the most part, and it's not always easy to read what she's thinking or feeling from her facial expressions.

Passing through a midsize town—the kind of place that's almost indistinguishable from pretty much any other midsize town anywhere in the US, with identical strip malls and department stores and fast food restaurants and gas stations—I spot a Kohl's set back from the highway that runs through the town, the out-lots packed with the usual suspects.

When I pull into the yawning lot and park near the back, Brys stirs. “Mmm?”

Watching her stretch and yawn is distracting—but then, everything about the woman is. “Where are we?”

I shrug, shutting off the motor. “Not sure exactly. Upstate New York somewhere.”

Brys scrubs her face with both hands. “Kohl’s?”

I tap the front of my shirt, and my fingernail clicks audibly against the dried blood. “Need some new clothes.”

She makes a disgusted face. “Ew.” Then a concerned face. “I just realized I assumed none of it was yours.”

I snort. “It’s not. But I appreciate your concern.”

She gives me a sheepish look. “Sorry, my first time running for my life.”

I wave her off. “Forget it. What you can do is take that cash I gave you and go buy me some clothes. Jeans, tee, maybe a hoodie, and some sneakers. Cross trainers, running shoes, I don’t care.”

“A hundred and sixty bucks isn’t gonna go all that far, Jakob.”

I shrug. “Then scour the sales racks. Do the best you can.”

She pauses with her hand on the door handle and looks at me with fear written on her features. “What if they find me while I’m in there by myself?”

“I can see the door from here,” I tell her. “I’ll be watching. And you keep your head on a swivel. Watch for lone adult males.”

She snorts. “I’m a single woman who lives in Manhattan. I’m *always* watching out for lone adult males.

There's no creature on this earth as dangerous as a lonely adult male."

"Lone and lonely are slightly different," I say, "But point taken. Just keep your eyes open, and if you feel like your gut is telling you to run, you listen."

She grins at this. "Oh, I know. I've made a career out of listening to my gut."

"Sounds like the start to an interesting conversation," I say, "considering what I know about your father."

She frowns. "Not sure what you mean by that."

I wave her off. "Forget it for now. I haven't seen any signs of our pursuers, so I think we're good, but I want to keep putting miles between them and us."

She exits the car and heads into Kohl's. To my shock, she emerges barely twenty minutes later with a big plastic bag in one hand. Yet, instead of returning to me, she heads toward Target next door.

"Really?" I say out loud.

I'm less annoyed, however, when she comes back to the car with her purchases, pushing a red Target shopping cart—jeans, socks, underwear, a 3pack of T-shirts in black, white, and gray, a black hoodie, a ballcap with the Yankees logo, and a pair of sneakers all from Kohls; From target she got snacks, an emergency medical kit, a case of water bottles, and a case of Diet Coke.

I watch her toss the items into the back seat, return the cart to a corral, and buckle back in beside me. "Not gonna go that far, huh?"

"There was a sale, so the clothes were all like fifty percent off, and the last time I wore these jeans, I apparently left cash in my back pocket." She shrugs. "That was actually kind of fun."

I look at her, bemused. "What was?"

She gestures vaguely at the stores. "That. Shopping like that."

"Not following."

A sigh. "I'm embarrassed to explain."

I snort. "Brys, I think of all the people in the world, I'm best positioned to understand what you might mean. I once bought an entire company just so I could fire one person."

She laughs. "You did not."

"I did. I went into a store in Dumbo, and one of the employees was incredibly rude. Even for New York."

"That's really saying something," she mutters."

"Exactly. Instead of complaining to the management, I bought the company with a single phone call while standing in front of the woman who insulted me. Signed a few documents via email, and fired her on the spot. And then got her blacklisted from everywhere I knew in all of New York."

"Damn. She must have really pissed you off. That's some next-level vindictiveness."

"I've never been of the mind that the customer is always right," I say. "It's a toxic mindset. I *do* believe the customer should be treated with respect; however, this woman was snarky, sarcastic, and rude. When I called her on it, she got in my face, called me names, and was generally just a massive bitch. So yes, I taught her a lesson."

"Sounds valid to me." Brys reaches back, twisting in her seat, opens the case of soda, and snags one, opening it with a *crack-hiss*. "I don't shop like that," she says after taking a sip. "Just...go into stores like that."

I cover my amused smirk with a hand. "So then how *do* you shop?"

"Personal shopper. Private offerings from my favorite designers brought to my home or office."

"And for plebeian things like food and non-clothing essentials?"

"Delivery service. I send them a list of what I need, and someone gets it, brings it to my place, and puts it away while I'm at work."

I shake my head. "I see."

She eyes me. "You were a billionaire, as you like to point out. You're telling me you just went into a department store and bought your suits off the rack at Macy's?"

"God, no. My tailor came to me. But I do enjoy spending money, and I'm quite good at it. So I do, in fact, go shopping. I like twenty-four-hour supermarkets. I do my best shopping at three in the morning when I've got the place to myself."

She frowns at me. "Sorry, I just have a hard time picturing you pushing a cart through the aisles of a supermarket."

What I'm not saying is that since I'm technically dead—Caleb Indigo is dead, and Jakob Kasparek legally vanished long, long ago—I have to be extraordinarily careful about appearing in public. Caleb Indigo was a public persona. My face is out there—Jakob was less public, being who and what I was. During the years I was building Club Sin and recruiting my Arrows, Inez handled almost everything I needed from out in the world, allowing me to stay hidden in my penthouse above the club. But then things got spicy, Pugli and that fucking bloodthirsty monster Mercado sent men to assault my home, and I had to go on the run.

And then it was just Thomas and me. I couldn't have him do *everything*. I had to learn how to disguise myself without looking like I'm wearing one, how to avoid showing my face to cameras, and how to shop like a normal person while staying incognito.

"I feel like that silence said a lot," Brys says.

"I'm not judging, I promise," I tell her. "I get it, believe me."

We leave the nameless town behind, and Brys alternates between staring out her window and giving me curious looks.

"It's tempting to think this is just a road trip," Brys says, eventually.

"It is," I agree. "Until we stop paying attention and wake up with guns in our faces."

"Assuming we wake up at all."

"Exactly." I reach over and pat her thigh. "That's not going to happen."

"You can't promise that," she says.

"No, I can't. All I can promise is that I'll do anything and everything in my power to keep you safe and return you to your life as soon as possible. And I really am sorry I got you involved in this."

"I suppose that's as much as anyone could ask for, under the circumstances." A glance at me. "I do appreciate the apology, though."

"You should. I do not dole them out easily or often."

"Shocker."

I manage another hour behind the wheel before my eyes start to burn and feel heavy, bathed in grit. "I think I need to take a break," I say, eventually. "I've been up for forty-eight hours at this point."

Brys looks at me with concern. "My god, Jakob. It's not safe to drive in that state."

I roll my eyes at her. "I'm taking a break now because I am beginning to feel the need to rest."

She nods while shrugging. "I suppose that's valid." A pause, a curious glance at me. "Do you have more cash stashed somewhere? Because I do watch enough TV to know we can't use cards."

I grin at her. "Unless you have a card linked to a bank account owned by a Gordian knot of LLCs, subsidiaries, and shell corporations, a thousand forensic accountants can't trace that back to me in a thousand years."

Instead of commenting on my financial resources, she tilts her head and gives me a strange look. "You really oughta do that more."

"Do what?" I ask, frowning in confusion.

"Smile like that. You're a damnably attractive man, Jakob, but you're so serious all the time. You're super hot when you smile."

"A man who worked in one of my offices was fired for making a comment like that about a female colleague," I point out.

Brys looks at me with a straight face for a long moment before bursting into laughter. "Oh god, oh wow. That's rich, buddy."

"I fail to see the humor," I say.

She snorts. "I'm sure you do."

"Elaborate, will you?"

"You, a man, are telling me, a woman, about sexual harassment in the workplace? I'm the CEO of a major company, Jakob. Yes, my father founded the company, but I worked my way up on my own merits. I started in the proverbial mailroom. I was an unpaid intern to a mid-level manager, working eighty hours a week, and I recognize my privilege in that I was financially cared for by my parents in terms of living expenses while I was an unpaid intern, and I recognize that most people aren't so lucky. Which is why one of the first things I did as CEO was to abolish unpaid internships across the company. All interns are paid a fair wage. Not a CEO salary, obviously, but they are paid a fair wage for their work. Unpaid internships, in my opinion, are a toxic system that should be illegal. If you perform a job, you deserve financial recompense, even if it's part of an educational process. You're still doing work that the company is profiting off of."

I hold up a hand as I take an exit and head toward the Best Western sign. "Hey, you don't have to convince me. I never utilized unpaid interns. I am the farthest thing from a saint, but I do believe work deserves fair compensation."

We reach the hotel, and I secure us a room under the false ID connected to my card—despite my claims to Brys, using the card is still a risk; Pugli is not an enemy to underestimate.

I go back out to the car and inspect the trunk out of curiosity—there's a blanket in there, along with some other emergency supplies. I take the blanket, wrap the assault rifle in it, and load myself up with some of the drinks, snacks, and the bag of clothes, so the suspiciously shaped bundle isn't quite so conspicuous.

Once back up in our room, I dump a can of Diet Coke down the sink and balance the empty can on the lever that is the door handle.

Lying on the bed with her boots and socks off, Brys frowns at me. "What's that for?"

"Low-tech alarm," I answer. "If anyone tries to enter the room, we'll know."

"But it's locked."

I snort. "Those keycard lock systems are child's play to bypass."

"How reassuring," she deadpans. "And the best solution is an empty soda can?"

"If you have a better idea, I'm all ears," I say.

To her credit, I watch her consider the problem for a long time, turning various ideas over in her head. Finally, she sighs, throwing up her hands. "Fine, you win. There are other solutions, but they all require things we don't have and cannot easily find. Your solution is elegantly simple and relatively foolproof, using something readily on hand."

"I can't take credit. Saw it in a movie, once."

I remove the long gun from the blanket and lean it against the side table, near at hand. Next, I give the handgun to Brys. "I'm going to sleep. If that can rattles, you wake me up. If someone knocks on the door claiming to be maintenance or housekeeping, say no thanks. If someone comes through the door, shoot first and don't bother with questions because anyone coming through that door is gonna try to kill us both."

She holds the pistol in both hands, palms up, as if it were a sacred object or alien artifact. "Um. No thanks?"

I show her the safety. "The safety is on. You can't accidentally fire it unless you turn the safety off. I'm a light sleeper, Brys. If that can rattles, I'll hear it. But you need to be ready and willing to protect yourself, if need be, if we're ever separated." I place it on the side table on her side of the bed. "Just leave it there. If you hear anything, grab it and just hold it, finger outside the trigger guard, safety on. If it sounds like someone is trying to get in, turn the safety off, but keep your finger like this." I show her my finger along the trigger guard. "If someone starts coming in, point at the center mass and squeeze the trigger. Hold it with both hands, arms out straight in a triangle, like this." I show her the beginner stance.

To her credit, she pays attention and shows me that she understands and can replicate what I'm showing her.

Finally, I think I've prepared her as much as I can, and shuck my filthy, blood-stiffened button-down, and my sweat-stained, dirt-caked, blood-splattered suit slacks.

An odd tension in the silence has my eyes flicking to Brys as I stand beside the bed in my underwear. She's pink-cheeked, eyes everywhere but on me, fingers twisting and twining and knotting on her lap. She's not panting, exactly, but she is taking noticeably deep, affected breaths.

"Problem?" I ask.

"Nope."

The fact that her gaze flicks around the room, lands on me, lingers, roams up and down, and then hastily flickers away again tells me all I need to know. Too bad I'm far too exhausted to do anything about it.

I toss back the blankets, climb in, roll away from Brys, and close my eyes.

"Jakob?" Her voice is low, quiet.

"Mmmm."

"What am I supposed to do while you're sleeping?"

I crack an eye open, snag the remote for the TV, and hand it to her. "Just keep the volume low."

A moment later, I hear a laugh track and conversation as she watches some sitcom.

Sleep pulls me under, then, but even as I drift under, I feel her. I'm hyperaware of her breathing, her body heat.

More than anything else, I'm aware of my own intense attraction to her.

If I weren't more exhausted than I've been since my days as a homeless street kid, I'd be entertaining her in a rather more…vigorous…manner.

If I could get her to let go of her inhibitions, I bet she'd be a real wildcat in bed.

That's my last thought before sleep claims me entirely.

Chapter 5

Challenge Accepted

BRYS

I JOLT AWAKE, EYES FLYING OPEN, AND MY HEART crashing in my chest.

For a moment, I'm utterly discombobulated; I know I'm not at home, but where am I?

Lying on a man's chest, his heart thudding gently under my ear, his hand slung over my hip to rest on my lower belly.

But. . . I broke up with Charles.

Which means this isn't Charles.

Charles is a wonderful man. He's smart, successful, kind, driven, and handsome. Our breakup was mutual and relatively painless—as much as a breakup can be—because we simply realized we weren't compatible, romantically. We're excellent friends, we're supportive of each other, and we're happy to celebrate each other's successes, but our competitive, Type-A, hard-charging personalities just do not mesh romantically. The sex was hot and cold, also. It was either passionate and quick or lackluster and performative. There was no in-between.

I can honestly say without any prevarication or pretense that Charles is one of my nearest and dearest friends.

That said, I do sometimes think that perhaps Charles may, deep down, still harbor some kind of feelings for me. My position on that topic is to ignore it and hope it never comes up, because that ship has long since sailed and shall never return to harbor.

Since that breakup, I've been far too busy with work to date. I did scratch the itch, so to speak, with a hunky young buck from the temp pool—he brought me my coffee and mail for a few weeks, and shot me white-toothed grins and flexed his gigantic, rippling, twenty-four-year-old biceps at me. I rewarded his valiant, if rather obvious, attempts at flirtation and seduction with a couple of brief but satisfying after-hours trysts in my office. I have a standing brunch date with several other high-ranking female execs, one of whom runs the temp agency that supplies my office with grunt-work drones, which made it easy enough to make sure Shawn F. got assigned elsewhere on the down-low without him being any the wiser. It's best for everyone that way, you see. No point in making anything awkward for the guy; he was nice, pleasing to look at—especially naked—and fun to fool around with a couple of times to relieve the tension, but that's all it was going to ever be, and I just don't have time for that conversation, so I had Alicia finesse his assignments away from my office.

Such is the train of my thoughts as I lie with my cheek on Jakob's firm, bare chest. And my god, what a chest it is. For a man who must be nearer fifty than forty, he's in better shape than twenty-four-year-old Shawn F., and that's really saying something. Shawn F. is only moonlighting as an office temp while his career as a fitness influencer takes off, or so he said… repeatedly. The sexy young lad did have a set of abs so deliciously sharp and shredded you could cut your finger on them, you might think.

Jakob is built differently. His shoulders are broad and thick, his chest is dense and hard—it isn't the bulging, rounded chest of a bodybuilder, but the flat, hard-as-steel chest of someone whose fitness is functional versus aesthetic. His abs are defined, certainly, but they're thick and hard blocky rather than ridged and sharp.

His arms are thick and dense.

His thighs are corded with muscle.

I feel my cheeks flaming as I think about the far-too-brief glimpse of his body I got last night before he collapsed into bed and promptly passed out.

Tight black boxer-briefs left very, very little to the imagination—his bulge was prominent, the outline of his penis pressed clearly against the stretchy material… and imprinted vividly on my brain.

Shawn F. was several months ago, and while I may cultivate the reputation of being a cold, hard, demanding, sharp-tongued, venomously sarcastic ice queen to my employees, I am an intensely sexual woman. I need sex regularly, and I haven't had any in so long my vagina is considering a permanent shuttering of the offices, so to speak.

The tension within me is intolerable.

Jakob is ferociously attractive. Those glittering, hard, cold brown eyes that pierce and scrutinize, razor-sharp with intelligence, boiling with cunning. Thick, black hair perfectly and expensively cut, and even the silver at his temples does something to me.

His body.

His hands.

But more than anything, it's the mystery of him that

has my attention. His arrogance—confidence, yes; the inevitable assurance of self that comes from being the master of all you survey, yes. But it's also just arrogance.

And it's hot.

Mainly because so far, he's proven that he can back the arrogance up with action.

Being defended and protected is sexy.

I know, I know: I wouldn't need protection in the first place if it weren't for him, but I also recognize that it wasn't his fault I got sucked into his orbit; it was pure chance.

Jakob shifts beneath me, making a small, soft, growly noise in his throat that is oddly endearing. His shifting rolled me against his chest, and his hand slips away from my belly and rests on my thigh.

I'm in my T-shirt and panties, because I can't sleep in jeans. Which means his hand is hot and rough against my bare thigh. My stomach tightens and my heart pitter-patters.

It's nothing, I tell myself. But it doesn't feel like nothing. It feels like I'm being held by a strong, powerful, attractive man who has literally killed to protect me; that's not nothing.

I rub my nose. Stretch and yawn; Jakob remains asleep through my yawning and stretching. The yawn is prodigious, the kind where you shudder, and something flutters in your eardrums, the world goes black, and a frisson of energy ripples through you, leaving you momentarily helpless and spastic. My hand, as the yawn ends, comes to rest on his belly. My eyes open and roam his bare chest. I like the coarse black body hair coating his chest and abs. It's masculine. Speaks of brawn and power and a lack of concern for the opinions of others. This is a man with no time for shaving or waxing for aesthetic purposes, and to me, that's sexy.

I can't help but trail and swirl my fingers over his chest and stomach. My lower lip catches in my teeth at the warmth of his skin, the firmness of his muscles. I swallow hard. For a moment—or maybe two or three—I forget our circumstances. I forget how and why we met, why we're in this hotel room together—very easily the cheapest hotel I've ever stayed in. For a moment or two or three, I'm just a horny girl in bed with a hot guy...

A horny girl who hasn't gotten laid in almost an entire fiscal quarter.

As I feel the roiling of my libido in my blood and gut and bones and organs and brain and soul, Jakob stirs again. He makes that soft, growly, grumbling sound again. His eyes flutter, close again. The hand that's not clutching my thigh skitters to his belly; pauses, scratches compulsively. And then dives under the waistband of his underwear to grab his—oh. Oh my.

Wow.

He has an erection.

A very, *very* impressive erection. The length and breadth and girth of his penis boggles my mind—it stretches his underwear to a comical degree, and the tip protrudes, pink, above the elastic.

Sleepily, unthinking, he squeezes and shoves his erection this way and that—adjusting, seeking relief from the tension.

My teeth tighten on my lip as I stare unblinking at the beautiful beast within his boxer-briefs.

My god, what a lovely penis that is.

I want to help him relieve the tension.

I want to touch him.

I squeeze my eyes shut and tell myself no.

No.

Absolutely not.

But...why not?

Why on earth should I not enjoy what's on offer here? I don't think he'd reject me if I were to make a move on him. Obviously, we both know it wouldn't be a thing, or what-have-you. Just a mutual enjoyment of each other's bodies. Scratching an itch. Dealing with stress and adrenaline.

I've heard that adrenaline can make you horny; maybe that's all this is between us—adrenaline.

My hand rests on his abdomen, palm covering his navel. His breathing is uneven, now deep, now shallow, now fast, now slow.

He stirs. Shifts. His hips drive upward, relax back down, thrusting against nothing.

Arousal burns inside me like wildfire—my belly is hot and tight with need, my panties soaked with the leaking essence of my desire to touch and be touched. To be seen not just as a CEO and boss, but as a female. A woman. Someone to be touched, caressed, teased, taken.

Shawn was fun, but I was in charge—and let us be crystal clear, here: *I* seduced *him*. I allowed him to think it was his idea, naturally; rutting young bucks like that need to think it's their idea or they get weird about the power dynamic. Let him think it's his idea, and you can lead him around by the balls. Get him wanting you so bad he's damn near feral by the time the office is emptied out, and he will all but attack you when you haul him into your office and tint the electrochromatic glass. It's fun and hot. Distracting and bad for productivity, so best reserved as an occasional treat rather than a regular habit.

But sometimes, a girl just wants to be ridden hard and put away wet, as it were.

Used.

Dominated.

Taken.

Controlled.

It's a secret fantasy of mine, one I've long harbored. It's the fantasy I go to when I'm masturbating: I'm the plaything of a man powerful enough to dominate even me. And to be quite clear, my entire career is predicated upon the exact opposite—I am where I am because I refuse to let any man even *think* he can exert any kind of authority over me. I'm violently allergic to commands, obedience, or authority of any kind. Despite my grades—and I was valedictorian at my elite prep school as well as Yale and MIT—I was constantly in trouble because I was so violently opposed to doing what I was told, especially if the one trying to tell me what to do was a male.

So yes, my secret fantasy of being dominated by a man is exactly that—a fantasy. An impossible fiction.

I feel Jakob stirring again, and my eyes flick to his face.

His eyes are open, heavy-lidded, sleepy, unfocused, unguarded. "Should be a law against being that beautiful in the morning," he murmurs.

I don't bother even trying to keep my gaze from wandering south and locking in on his erection. "I agree, wholeheartedly."

"Brys," he says, his voice rough and raw with sleep, with arousal. "Don't."

"No?"

His brow furrows. "I am complicated. My life is complicated. And that's putting it as mildly as possible."

"I am not asking for commitment," I say, waspish and tart and prim. "I was merely admiring your penis."

He coughs a shocked laugh. "Oh. I see." The humor fades as fast as it appeared, and his dark eyes search mine. "I am a complicated man sexually, too, Brys. Start something with me at your own peril."

"At my own peril? Why? Are you violent?"

His gaze crackles with intensity. "No, Brys. I am not violent. But I am most definitely not your average, easily manipulated office-tryst boy-toy."

My cheeks burn—it feels as if he's read my thoughts, somehow, which is wildly disconcerting. "If I wanted an easily manipulated office-tryst boy-toy, I'd have one. They're a dime a dozen." I shrug. "I *have* had plenty of them, if we're being honest with one another."

The gleam in his eyes is dangerous. I can feel it. This man is not to be trifled with—not in the boardroom or the bedroom.

As a girl, I was a bit of a pyromaniac. I loved playing with fire. I'm not an idiot or crazy, so I wasn't going around starting housefires. I'd just burn things in a metal trash can in the backyard, just for the rush of watching fire consume things—leaves, pinecones, grass, paper, cardboard, whatever I could get away with burning, or trying to burn. That rush-seeking behavior never left me—the rush I seek now, however, is success in business and the pursuit of excellent sex.

My point is, I still like to play with fire. Tell me I can't do something, and watch me try, and likely succeed; tell me something is too dangerous, and watch me jump in headfirst. I *might* have a touch of obstinate defiance disorder.

Case in point: Jakob is dangerous. He's telling me as much without saying so in so many words.

He's warning me. Too bad a warning only makes me try harder.

I hold his eyes, slide my hand down the hard, flat liminal space between navel and erection. An instant before I can curl my fingers around his cock, Jakob snags my hand, his grip hard and unforgiving. "Be careful what you wish for, Brys Bennett. If you open that door, you cannot balk at the monster that comes through it."

"You're saying you are a monster?"

His eyes glitter like black marbles in the early morning light. "I am who I am."

"Would you hurt me?"

"Physically?"

"Correct."

"No. My depravity is of a different nature."

"And emotionally?"

He stares at nothing. "Not...intentionally," he says after a long pause.

Every warning bell my psyche possesses is clanging and clamoring like a klaxon, warning me that this man is dangerous; the fire and fury of his complicated, mysterious, arrogant persona is beyond anything I've ever known. I will not play with this fire without getting burned.

The hunger for physical connection, for release, for relief of the ache of need is too great to resist.

And I'm not interested in resisting it anyway.

Having given his warning, Jakob releases my hand, threading his fingers together behind his head. The invitation is clear; I have his consent, as long as I understand that I am also giving him my consent—tacitly, if not explicitly.

"What shape does your depravity take, Jakob?"

His answering smirk is the only response I get; it's barely a smirk, to be honest. A ghost of a smile. An almost-grin. Secretive, mysterious, heated, dangerous. A predator has his prey exactly where he wants it.

Joke's on him, though—I welcome the chance to be that kind of prey.

I trap my breath behind my teeth and fix my eyes on his erection, burgeoning against the cruel confines of his underwear, the pink tip sprouting above the rim of his boxer-briefs.

I slip my hand under the elastic, palm sliding over skin, scraping against the coarse scratch of his pubic hair, and then I curl my fingers around the thick, hard heat of his erection.

His sharp inhalation at my touch is a soft hiss of tongue tip against teeth, followed by a hollowing of his stomach and a tightening of his abs. His gaze is hard and inscrutable, impossible to read, impossible to fathom the depth of thought and emotion. His whole body is tensed now, flexed and iron-hard. His jaw ticks. His hands are curled into fists at his sides.

This isn't for him, it's for me. I am touching him for my own enjoyment, not out of any desire to bring him pleasure. That is merely an incidental by-product.

Watching his face for reactions, I caress his length, once, slowly, in a loose, soft grip. His eyes narrow and his jaw ticks, but that's it.

Clearly, if I want a reaction out of him, I'm gonna have to bring my A-game.

The subtle, mischievous spark in his eyes is a gauntlet thrown at my feet:

Challenge accepted.

Chapter 6

Action and Reaction

JAKOB

HER HAND IS TINY.

I am, I admit, rather improbably well-endowed; more than one previous sexual partner has stated that I ride the cusp of too big for comfort, and one woman, memorably, took one look at my erection and left without a word. I have assumed she did so out of fear, and since she offered no explanation, that's the answer I'm going with.

Which means that Brys's small, soft, delicate, elegant hands make my already-large organ seem even more disproportionately enormous in comparison. My ego most assuredly needs no inflation, but it *is* a nice feeling, looking down and seeing her little hand wrapped around my cock, the size of my dick making her hand look even smaller and my dick even bigger.

The urge to take over is all-consuming. I deny myself that relief with vicious self-control. It means not moving at all. It means barely breathing. It means every muscle is tensed, every fiber of my being straining against the confines of my control.

I need control over *something* at all times. If not her,

then at least myself. Control is an integral part of who I am. My urge is to control her; use her; take her.

She's got her hand wrapped around my cock, yet she's barely touching me. I want to knot my fists in her honey-colored hair and feed her my cock, inch by inch. Watch her lips stretch around me, struggle to take all of me. Watch her eyes widen as I fuck her throat, watch her try to swallow around me.

Fuck, it's been a long time.

"Do dead men fuck, Jakob?" she asks, apropos of nothing.

"Yes."

She smirks. "Interesting."

"You probably don't want to know."

"I do, though."

I cast a pointed glance at her hand, wrapped around me. "Is that *really* what you wish to discuss at this particular moment?"

"No," she murmurs. "Not really. But I will want to, later."

"Perhaps."

Her thumb roves lazily over my tip, the pad sliding delicately over the slit; her eyes flick from me to my cock and back, assessing me, scrutinizing my reaction. She wants my expression, I realize. She wants my reactions. She wants to get something out of me.

I don't want to allow it. I can't. I can't let anyone see the truth of me, can't let anyone see who I am—who I was. I don't know that I know who I am—not anymore. Maybe I never have. I can't give this woman any part of me, not even an honest reaction. It's dangerous—for her. I am not a safe man, and not just because of this current situation. Who I am is dangerous. My need for control, my need to dominate, to own, to master...it is obsessive and all-consuming.

I died to set Isabel free of my need for total control.

I spent a decade in near total isolation, hiding from the world and my own destructive nature.

This woman threatens to undo all of that with a single touch.

Yet here I am, offering myself to her like a lamb to the slaughter. Albeit, I am a wolf in lamb's clothing, to be sure, and I have to believe she's smart enough to know that.

I can't hold back another hiss of pleasure as her hot, small hand glides down my shaft, where she squeezes, pulses her hand up and down a few times, and squeezes again at the thick root of my cock.

She bites back a little smirk of victory at the hiss. Her tongue slips over her lower lip, vanishes. Her gaze fixes on my cock as she slides her touch upward, pulses another series of short, soft pulsing strokes at the top, twists a few times, and then gives me another plunging caress.

I have to close my eyes and breathe carefully to restrain my reaction, which is in itself a reaction, I suppose.

Another slow stroke, and then another, and now my stomach hollows out, my heartbeat slams in my chest, and my hips want to move, to push into her touch. My fists tighten as every impulse I have is screaming at me to flip her beneath me and make her scream my name until she's hoarse.

Instead, I hold absolutely still, barely breathing as she caresses my length slowly and steadily, the liquid-smooth caresses of a woman who knows what she's doing and enjoys doing it.

"You're toying with me, Brys," I say. "You play a dangerous game."

She inches my underwear down past my hips with her free hand, one side and then the other in turn, back and forth, until I can wiggle them lower and kick them off.

"Considering how we met, I'd say courting danger is rather appropriate," she says.

I grit my teeth, catching a groan before it can escape, but my hips betray me, lifting on their own, pushing me into her hand.

"It's okay to like it." Brys shifts upright, sitting beside me with her legs crossed; I catch a glimpse of black panties between her thighs, and my gaze catches there. "I *want* you to like it."

I say nothing, molars grinding around a growl as she feathers several swift, shallow, loose-gripped strokes around the head of my cock, and my eyes close of their own volition. Instantly, my mind's eye is awash with images of Brys standing in front of me in her bedroom, nude and sensual and startled. Enormous breasts sway with her shocked gasp, mini-quakes shivering fat and flesh. Thick pink nipples stand on end, turgid and plump and begging for my mouth, surrounded by wide areolae a few shades of pink darker than her nipples.

I knot my fists into the blanket at my sides in an increasingly vain attempt to stop myself from tearing her shirt open so I can bury my face between those monster tits of hers.

"Tell me exactly what you're thinking right now, Jakob," Brys smirks at me, licking her lips, glancing at my cock, and then back at me. "I may just decide to have mercy on you if I believe you to be genuine and honest in your answer."

"I was thinking that I'm approximately twelve seconds away from ripping that fucking shirt right off you so I can sink my face between your breasts."

"It's the only shirt I have at the moment," she says. "So maybe don't literally rip it."

"I was thinking that I've never seen tits as incredible as yours."

"You saw them for two seconds. And I have a hard time believing that, Jakob. A man like you surely must have a Rolodex full of women with silicone G-cups on speed dial."

"I do not have a Rolodex at all, and I certainly do not have any such list." I swallow hard and pause to catch my breath as Brys slides her fist down my length, her touch skating down further to cradle my balls in her palm. "And while I do not discriminate against women who choose to augment their bodies as they see fit, if I did have a list, women with silicone G-cups would not be on it."

"What about natural G-cups?" She licks her lips again. "Mine aren't that big, so don't get too excited. I'm just asking."

"I couldn't care less what letters or numbers one uses," I say, "it's about aesthetics. I personally prefer to look at natural breasts, no matter the size or shape, rather than obviously fake ones. Vaguely gelatinous basketballs do not do it for me, I'm afraid—though I am not judging anyone who possesses or appreciates them."

"Typical man," she mutters. "Nothing on the brain but tits."

"You're jerking me off, Brys." I arch an eyebrow at her. "I'm supposed to be thinking about loss indices?"

"If you're thinking about loss indices while I'm jerking you off, Jakob, then I'd take it as a compliment."

She cradles my balls in one hand, massaging them gently, rolling them in her palm, scratching delicately with her fingertips, tracing veins, and making my cock pulsate with tight heat; her other hand glides in slow rhythm on my shaft, thumb smearing over leaking precum.

Fuck.

I can't control myself much longer.

"I'm not following," I say through clenched teeth. "How is that a compliment?"

"It means you're trying not to come, which means I'm doing a good job jerking you off."

"Hard thing to do wrong."

"Want me to show you what a bad handjob feels like? I can try."

"No, that's alright, I'll pass."

Brys brings her hand to her mouth, and then the next time she jacks my length, it's smooth and slick and hot and wet with her saliva, and the intensity of the pleasure rockets through the stratosphere. I hiss, the sound a ragged sigh from the back of my throat. "*Fuck*."

My curse elicits a wide, pleased grin. "Is that so?" She gnaws on her lower lip. "You like it nice and wet, do you?"

"Brys." It's a warning. "My control is fading quickly."

Her grin only spreads, eyes lighting up with eager glee. "Is that so?" She speeds the slick strokes of her hand down my shaft, pausing to pulse at the root, twisting short jerking strokes around the tip. "I'm utterly terrified, Jakob. Just petrified. Whatever shall I do?"

The heat in my belly and the pressure in my balls are unbearable. The desperation to reach release is crushing and chaotic and maddening. I've never had much self-control, sexually. In business, yes. In bed? No.

As Brys is about to find out.

I reach up and cup her cheek—her skin is softer than silk, delicate and warm, clear-complexioned and blemish-free. She's perfect. Her hair is loose, hanging in honey-blonde waves to her mid-back, kinked from the braid of yesterday. "Brys, I warn you again. I'm going to come in a moment." I brush my thumb over her lips. And it will not be your hand that receives my release."

"Is that so?" She smirks yet again.

Perhaps she thinks I'm playing a game. More the fool, her.

I don't bother to hide my feelings, now. I let her see my need. I buck into her fist, let myself groan as she slowly caresses the aching length of my cock.

I shut my eyes again, focusing on holding back as the heat and pressure become intolerable, building to a frenzy inside me, eradicating the last vestiges of my control. I see her again, the way she was in her bedroom. I see her pussy, a shadow of a V between her thighs, glazed with closely-trimmed pubic hair in a narrow triangle. I see those tits again.

Stroke after stroke, Brys's delicate, gentle touch brings me closer and closer to release, and now I'm tensed and flexing as I actively clamp down on the release threatening to explode out of me.

"Brys," I snarl. "I'm going to come."

"So come. That's the whole point."

"Give me your mouth."

"What if I say no?"

"Are you?"

"No, but what if I did?"

"I am in no mood for hypotheticals, Brys. Put your mouth on my cock." I fill my gaze with the hard glitter of authority. "Now."

She just grins at me, slowing her strokes to the point of teasing, torturing. "I dunno. Maybe, maybe not."

I cup the back of her neck, sitting upright and forward, and put my lips to her ear. "In ten seconds, I'm going to put my cock down your throat, Brys."

She inhales sharply, a shocked gasp. "Jakob!"

"Ten."

She wraps both hands around my cock and plunges a slow slide down my length. "You're really going to count?"

"Nine."

She nips at my earlobe. "Let me help—eight-seven-six-five-four-three-two-one." She says it all in a rush. "Now what?"

Chapter 7

Yes, Jakob

BRYS

FOR A FRAUGHT INSTANT, I'M ACTUALLY AFRAID of Jakob. The look on his face is so intense, it leaves me shaking all over.

I wonder if perhaps I've miscalculated. Misunderstood the man I'm with.

His upper lip curls in a silent snarl, and he pulses in my hand, swelling as he nears the edge of climax. God, his cock is incredible. Fucking enormous, thick and long and hard as a rock in my hand, silky soft and straight as an arrow.

I should give him what he wants—but I want to see what he'll do. How else can I prove to him that I'm game to take anything he can give? Within reason, of course.

He's utterly still, frozen except for his deep, rapid breaths and the helpless pulse of his cock.

He flops backward to his back, and his spine arches up as I caress his throbbing length. For a man who has warned me repeatedly and professes to be an instant from coming, he seems rather intent on holding back.

I like to think it's because I'm making it feel so good, he doesn't want it to stop. I don't *want* him to control himself; he seems like a person for whom control is paramount, and I like to win.

Without warning, Jakob jackknifes upright, rolling off the bed with me in his arms. I'm airborne, my legs cinching around his waist automatically, and I feel his massive cock probing my slit through the barrier of my panties. And my god, I want him inside me. A cock that big? He'd rip me to pieces in the best possible way. He's too big, perfectly so, and I want him.

I can't help but grind against him, whimpering as he walks away from the bed with me in his arms. He cups my face, peers at me, stopping in the middle of the room.

He kisses me. It's soft, all wet lips and searching tongue, and I open for him, taste him, whimper into his mouth, soften for him. Rub my slit against him. "Jakob," I whisper against his mouth.

"I did warn you," he growls.

I hit the floor—he's dropped me abruptly, only slowing my descent at the last second. I land on my knees almost by accident, and now he's towering over me, six feet and four inches of massive, powerful man, brutally built, dark and dangerous. For a moment, all I can do is gaze up at him, cowed by his vicious male beauty. His massive cock stands upright against his hard abs, the tip glistening with precum, my saliva dripping down the sides. Veins stand out purple, and for an instant, my mind fills with visions of running my tongue over those veins.

But before I can turn the vision into reality, Jakob winds my hair around his fist, pulling it tight until my scalp stings. He grips his thick shaft in his other hand and tilts it away from his body. "Open your mouth, Brys."

Oh, fuck.

He meant it.

He really, actually meant it.

His tip nuzzles my lips, and I taste him—salty, tangy, not quite sweet but almost.

"Open, Brys."

I hesitate, but I know I'm going to do as he asks—commands. Hesitantly, I part my lips. Just a little bit.

It's all he needs.

I taste his flesh and his essence, and my mouth is forced wider by his cock—it's that or scrape him with my teeth, and his cock is too pretty for that. I earned this, after all. Fair is fair. He warned me, and here it is.

I expect him to thrust down my throat all at once, and mentally prepare for it.

That rough thrust never comes. Instead, he only gives me a little bit. Enough to fill my mouth, to taste him, to feel my jaw stretch.

And then he's gone, and my eyes fly open—just in time to see him reach down and gather a handful of my shirt and yank upward. I have no choice but to lift my arms and wriggle out of it or be throttled by the garment as he drags it upward.

The shirt is tight around my breasts, dragging them upward as the garment lifts, and then they drop heavily as he rips the shirt free, leaving me naked but for panties.

I lock eyes with him for a moment—and then lose his gaze as his eyes wander down to my bare breasts. I'm breathing hard in anticipation and no little amount of fear—I realize I don't actually know this man at all, and I'm baiting him to lose control. I like to take risks, yet I can't help but wonder if this one is foolish.

Too late to go back, now.

He wraps my hair around his fist again. Stares down at me with a hard, inscrutable expression. "Take it, Brys." I reach up with both hands and grasp him, but he grabs my wrists and pulls them wide. "No hands."

He releases my wrists, makes a loose pile of my hair on top of my head, and holds it there with both hands, clutching my head.

It's been a while since I've gone down on a guy. I don't do it very often—not because I don't like it, though. I do. But it's an act that a man must earn, for me. A hunky twenty-four-year-old from the temp pool has no chance. He gets to eat me out and like it, and if he's lucky and excels at cunnilingus, I'll let him fuck me.

The tables have turned.

It's me on my knees, now. My heart is pounding, but I'm secretly excited.

I like this.

I want it.

It's a secret fantasy I've never even committed to a diary, let alone out loud to another person, but it's very real, and very powerful.

Jakob hasn't earned this—he isn't asking. He's in control. He's *taking* it.

I'm so turned on my pussy is dripping.

"No," I murmur, and I know my eyes can't hide my arousal or my anticipation.

His lips curve in a predatory grin. "Very well, then."

He touches my lips with a thumb, and my eyes go heavy-lidded. His thumb hooks over my lower lip, tugs down. "Open up, Brys. You want it. I can see it in your eyes." His thumb fills my mouth, salty against my tongue. "Open your mouth and take my cock. *Now.*"

The snap of authority is sharp, icy, and hard. His thumb presses my jaw down.

I gaze up at him from under my lashes, my mouth opening slowly. Without looking away from his hard, blazing black eyes, I lower my mouth toward his cock. He has my wrists again. Brings my hands around and places them on his ass—which is bulbous and harder than steel and warm. I groan at the feel of him in my hands, and I can't help but clutch his ass cheeks, grip and claw into the muscle and fat and flesh.

And then I taste him again, salty skin sliding over my tongue, smoky precum mingling with my saliva.

His eyes burn, hot and wild. "Take it, Brys. All of it." His hands tighten around my skull. "Take my cock. Now. Take it all."

"I can't," I whisper, and then wrap my mouth around him for a second before pulling away again. "It's too big."

"You're going to try anyway."

"I'm scared." I'm only partly playing.

I am, honestly and genuinely, more than a little frightened.

"Open." He tilts my head backward, so I'm looking up at him. "Open wide, Brys."

I open for him as wide as I can.

He fills my mouth, but he's so big I have to stretch my jaw to accommodate him. "Take a deep breath for me, now." I suck in a breath through my nose, gaze up at him with unfeigned fear so intoxicatingly arousing that my panties are soaked through. "You're gonna take it, now, Brys. Are you ready?"

"Mmm-mmm," I hum a wordless negative.

"Too bad. Hold on tight and remember to breathe."

My fingers dig into Jakob's ass as he slowly drives his hips forward, thrusting his hot, enormous cock to the back of my throat. I hum a shrill whimper that ends in a ragged, gagging gulp. And oh god—oh dear lord, his cock is too much. Too big. I can't do this. It's too much.

I cast my gaze up at him, trying frantically to swallow around the thick, hot intrusion filling my throat.

"Good girl, Brys," he murmurs. "So damned sexy, watching you take my cock."

Oh…fuck.

Fuck, that's hot.

I never thought I had a praise kink, but I legitimately almost had an orgasm just now, so perhaps I do.

"You like that, don't you?" His growl is dark and hard and roiling with power. He knows I do. "You do. I can see it in your eyes, Brys. You love this. Don't you?"

I whimper again at his words.

"Don't you, Brys?"

"Mmmm-hmmm!" It's all I can manage, and that just barely as his cock slides deeper and deeper, millimeter by millimeter, and I have to breathe through my nose and gulp and gag for breath around him, and I'm on the cusp of panic.

As if able to read me like a book, Jakob withdraws, a string of saliva connecting my lips to his cock. His thumb caresses my lips. "Good girl, Brys. You take my cock beautifully."

"Thank you," I whisper, gazing up at him through lowered lashes, chest heaving, desire pooling between my thighs.

His grin is searing, pleased and aroused, blazing with

erotic glee. He *really* gets off on this whole power trip thing. Why that's so fucking hot to me, I am unwilling to examine.

I know how freaky it makes me, wanting to be controlled and dominated. And by the way, I'm not using the word "dominated" in the BDSM sense, but rather in the more literal, mental and emotional sense. I'm not into leather gimp masks and ball gags and being hogtied like some sort of fly caught in a nylon spiderweb. I just want a man to take away my control, my power, my authority. To use me. To take away the decisions. And I want this on my terms, safely and consensually. I want my agency back the moment we leave the bedroom. I want it to be private between the two of us because I have a reputation to consider, one that is the foundation of my authority as CEO of Bennet Development, Incorporated.

Jakob's breathing is slow and deep and even—tightly controlled. His abs are braced. Thighs bunched and iron-hard. Jaw clenched.

He is at the ragged edge of climax and desperately fighting it back. My god, the man's control over himself is honestly very impressive.

He grips his cock in his fist, paints my lips with precum beaded on his tip. "Ask for it, Brys."

"Please, Jakob," I breathe, stomach fluttering and pussy clenching around nothing as desire howls inside me like a hurricane. "I need your cock."

Who am I, right now? Begging for a penis? Yet I can't stop myself. I really do want it. I want him to take my mouth and use it. Not that I'd ever say as much in so many words, even under threat of death.

"Open."

I part my lips and gaze up at him. "Are you going to come in my mouth, now, Jakob?"

He feeds his cock into my mouth, hot, firm flesh sliding over my tongue, nudging the back of my throat. He knots my hair in one fist, keeping a firm grip on me as he pumps gently, nuzzling the back of my throat with his soft, springy tip. "Is that what you want, Brys?"

"Yes."

"Say it. Tell me what you want."

"I want you to come down my throat."

"Beg for it."

"Please, Jakob." I stare up at him, caress his thighs with my palms, his hips, his ass. Gather his cock in my hands and stroke his length with both fists. "Please, *please* come for me. Give it to me. All of it. Right now. Fill my mouth. Make me choke on your cum."

Jesus, I'm a depraved woman. *Make me choke on your cum?*

Really? *Really,* right now? What the actual hell is wrong with me?

Why is *that* what I want more than anything? With this man, especially, the one putting my life at risk—this man who blazed into my life, literally crashed into me and turned everything upside down and inside out while offering very little by way of explanation.

And now I'm on my knees in front of him, playing with his cock and begging for him to come down my throat.

But I'm nothing if not honest with myself—when I want to be—and the honest truth is that as fucked up as this is, I'm thrilled. I'm seconds from orgasming without him so much as touching my tits. I'm so turned on by this reversal of power dynamic that I could come from a stiff breeze blowing across my clitoris.

Jakob's grin is feral. "I don't believe you." He frames the back of my head in his hands. "Show me that you mean it, Brys. Show me how badly you want my cock. Show me how badly you want my cum."

I lock eyes with him, caressing his thick, hot length with both hands. I watch his jaw tick and pulse, feel his cock throb in my hands, watch his abs tighten until he's harder than a cinderblock wall. So close. I speed my strokes. Curl my fingers around his cock-head to form a cup, drip saliva, and smear it down his shaft so my strokes slide slick and quick. He sucks in a sharp inhalation through his nose, lets it out slowly, brow furrowing, jaw grinding so hard I swear I hear his molars creak under the titanic pressure.

Faster. Faster. On one hand, pumping furiously at his root, the other fluttering and twisting around the glans.

His eyes slide slowly closed, and he hunches forward, and for the first time, he bucks helplessly into my fists. "Fuck," he snarls. "Give me your fucking mouth, Brys. *Now.*"

"Yes, Jakob," I whisper.

I clasp his ass in one hand and cup his balls in the other, and take his cock into my mouth. Swirl my tongue around his glans, over his tip, taste his precum, feel him throb against my tongue. And then I open my throat and take him.

All of him.

In a slow, intentional slide, my eyes never leave his.

God, it's been a *long* time since I've given a man my throat like this; I'd nearly forgotten how my eyes water, how I have to close my throat around him and gulp air through my nose.

I fucking love it—this helplessness. It's so perversely thrilling to upend my Type-A Boss Bitch Ice Queen persona and let myself be used like this.

Jakob watches as I slide my lips down his length, swallowing frantically around him. His lip curls and his eyes flutter shut for a moment or two as my nose nudges his belly. He hunches over me, and his hands tighten around my head.

Yes. Yes. Please, yes—take me. Make it rough.

I catch his hooded stare and wait, wondering if he really can read me as clearly as I suspect. I'm breathing carefully, one hand on his ass and the other cradling his plump, heavy balls. Waiting for him.

"You want to be used, don't you, Brys?"

I nod and whimper an affirmative sound.

"You want me to fuck your throat, don't you?"

I nod and whimper again. *Fuck yes, I do*—it's unspoken but obvious.

He's unleashed a hitherto hidden, buried, secret version of Brys, and she is feral with need, seething with primal, filthy, uninhibited feminine sexuality.

He draws back until I'm kissing and licking his tip, mouthing it the way I would the first bite of an ice cream cone. He cups my cheek, strangely gentle and affectionate. "Get ready, Brys. I can't hold back any longer."

"Fuck my throat. Please. *Please,* Jakob. I need your cum. Please. *Please.*" I cup his ass in both hands and stare up at him.

Open my mouth wide, tongue out, ready and waiting.

"Such a greedy little slut, aren't you, Brys?"

"Yes, Jakob."

"What are you?"

"A greedy little slut."

"What does my hungry little slut want?"

"Your cock."

"Say please for me. Once more."

"Please?"

He feeds me his cock again, letting go once he's partway down my throat. But this time, he gives me a thrust. I gag on him, catch my breath, gulp, and gasp. Once I've caught my breath, he does it again, deeper, harder. I whimper as he fills my throat, whimper when his balls tap my chin. I cup his ass in both hands and pull him toward me on his next thrust. He growls like a wolf, savage and wild. I take this as a compliment, as encouragement. Gaze up at him as he fucks another slow thrust down my throat.

I pull at him again, and he thrusts. Another pull, faster. Faster.

His breathing is ragged now, his lip curled in a snarling rictus as he fights back his release. God, the man just doesn't know how to let go, does he?

I'll have to show him how. I'll have to make him.

I don't wait for his next thrust—I take it from him. Gag as I take him, inch by inch, tongue working against his length, fingers clawed into the tensed muscle of his ass. Whimper in delight as I take him and take him, backing away and slamming all the way down, hard and rough.

"That's how you want it?"

"Mmm-hmm!"

"Very well, then. So you shall have it."

He takes over, then, and it's the beginning of my deepest, most secret fantasies coming true. He clutches my head in his hands and fucks my mouth, hard and fast and brutally unrelentingly, and all I can do is gag and gasp and take his cock and try to breathe, relishing each brutal thrust down my throat.

"So fucking gorgeous, Brys," he whispers, "taking my cock like such a good girl."

A long, rapturous moan escapes me at his praise, and his eyes light up at the sound. "Ah, fuck, Brys. You really love this, don't you? You love it when I praise you, don't you?"

"Yes!" I gasp, as if the tip of his cock is a microphone. "More. More."

"I don't want to come," he murmurs, giving me shallow, gentle thrusts for a moment or two. "I want to fuck your mouth forever. You have such a pretty mouth, Brys." He caresses my chin with a thumb pad. "Feels so good. So hot, so wet, so tight." He thrusts deep, then. "Suck."

I suck and drive deeper, tongue extended out of my mouth so I can lick him while I work him with my throat; this makes him snarl and thrust helplessly. Fuck yes—I love those helpless little thrusts. I back away and suction my lips around his glans and swirl my tongue around his tip, now leaking precum in a steady seep, and I lick it all away greedily.

"Fuck." His voice is ragged and breathless.

I cup his balls and massage them with both hands, sucking and suckling and bobbing shallowly around his glans, teasing and scratching his root where balls and shaft meet, raking my fingernails along his taint. And then I grab them in a tight grip and squeeze until he grunts in surprised almost-pain as I use my grip to pull him toward me, deep-throating him all at once, without warning.

I feel his balls pulse an instant before he unleashes a flood of cum down my throat. He shouts, raw-voiced, snarling and lupine, and adjusts his grip on my head and thrusts hard. I gag, gulp, swallowing desperately, but he's down my throat and coming, releasing rocket after rocket of hot, salty, thick cum. I pull back so he falls out of my mouth, gasping and panting, cum dribbling down my chin and throat, eyes watering.

"Fuck, you're beautiful," he growls.

I can't stop. I need more. I stroke his slippery, sticky, dripping cock, wrap my mouth around his head, and lick and suck, cheeks hollowing, and he spurts onto my tongue. I pull away so he flops free, bouncing and drooping heavily, swallow the mouthful of his cum, and lick my lips and gaze up at him; I am all too aware that my expression must surely border on adoring.

For a moment, then, Jakob stares down at me, brow furrowed, expression unreadably intense. "Good girl, Brys." He cups my jaw, applies pressure, indicating that I should stand up; I do, and he wipes my lips and chin with his thumb, showing me the glistening liquid.

I open my mouth dutifully, and he presses his thumb onto my tongue. I taste him, and his essence, and nothing has ever tasted sweeter.

"Such a good girl," he says again, whispering, almost dazed. "Such a lovely little slut. You sucked me dry, Brys. Like the obedient whore you are."

My heart flutters and crashes in my chest. "Yes," I whisper. "I'm a good little whore."

He grins, and it's utterly devastating. "You know what happens to good little whores who suck my cock like that?

"No," I admit. "Tell me, Jakob. Please."

"Good cock-sucking little whores receive their reward." He sidles closer to me, until there's no space left between us, my tits crushed against the anvil of his chest, his drooping cock nudging my thigh. "Do you want to be rewarded?"

"Yes, Jakob."

"I thought you might." He brushes his thumb over my lip. "Take off your panties."

I shimmy out of them and stand naked, pussy weeping desire, my entire being quivering, shaking in anticipation. "Are you going to fuck me, Jakob?"

He leans into me, nuzzles my ear with his lips. "Is that what you want?"

"Yes."

"Yes, what?"

"Yes, Jakob. I want you to fuck me."

"How?" he breathes. "Tell me exactly how you want me to fuck you."

I swallow hard and say the first thing that comes to mind—the raw, unadulterated truth. "I want to be bent over my desk in my office and fucked from behind," I answer. "I want it bare. I want to feel your cum dripping down my thighs while I'm inspecting quarterly reports."

"I'll keep that in mind," he rumbles. "But we do not have a desk available at the moment, and it isn't safe to go back to your office." He presses his palm to my belly, fingers pointing to the floor. "Try again. How do you want me to fuck you, Brys?"

"On all fours," I answer immediately. "I want you to spank me."

The lascivious gleam of desire bathing his expression is blindingly intense. "Mmmmm. Yes." Heat billows off of him in palpable waves. Primal, sexual fury drips from his every pore. "But not yet. I don't think you've earned that just yet, Brys. But you *do* deserve...something."

I stand, shaking, silent, waiting, arousal rampaging through my veins. "Please, Jakob. I need—I need..."

His mouth slants over mine, silencing me. "I know what you need." He puts his lips to my ear. "Go to the window and stand facing it."

Trembling with nerves and anticipation—and mostly the latter—I do as he says.

He rips the curtains open, letting in blinding morning sunlight. Below, the parking lot is dotted with parked cars. A couple checking out early loads their luggage into their sedan. A man stands under the portico near the entrance, smoking a cigarette.

His glance shoots up this way, locks on me. Surprise washes over his features, then curiosity.

My heart slams madly behind my ribs—an exhibitionist I am not. Or, haven't been...until now, apparently.

Because I don't shy away. I don't close the blinds. I don't protest. I stare back at the man without flinching. We're close enough that I can read his expressions. He puts the cigarette to his lips and inhales, holds the smoke, spews it out his nostrils, never looking away from me.

I feel Jakob behind me. I stop breathing.

His hands carve over my belly. He cups my sex with one hand; the watching smoker freezes, hand to mouth, cigarette framed between index and middle finger.

"Let's give the man a show he won't soon forget, shall we?" he whispers into my ear, sliding a long, thick middle finger inside me.

"Yes, Jakob."

Chapter 8

Beyond the Edge

JAKOB

My god, what delight she is. I want to reward her until she can't see, hear, breathe, or move. I want to fuck her into the next millennium. I want to watch her tits shake as she takes my cock in that plump, pretty pussy.

Yes, plump.

She's not a slender woman. She's curvy. Soft. Thick thighs, bell-curve hips. Huge, teardrop breasts. Silky, pillowy, tender belly. A big, juicy, round ass. And a pretty pussy with plump, pink lips.

Fuckable.

Kissable.

Mine.

I feel my predilection for obsession taking hold—I try to wrestle it back into its prison and lock it up and bury it down deep.

I nearly destroyed one woman with my obsession; I will not do so to another.

Not this woman.

She's brave, she's smart, she's successful. She wields authority like a whip, and that is utterly intoxicating. She's the master of her world, in control, arrogant, cold, and powerful. It's fucking addictive.

The fact that she very obviously craves submission is a fantasy come true. Isabel had to be taught. I had to wrest control from her, and she fought me at every turn. Victory, then, was all the sweeter because it was so hard-earned, it is true, and I do not deny it. But in retrospect, that was not consensual, and I like to think I have grown as a human since then.

Brys wants to give me what I want to take. She wouldn't admit it—she can't, I would guess. But it was clear she was willingly giving me her submission at every turn.

And I am lost to her. She doesn't know it—can't. She may never know, as I am incapable of that kind of vulnerability. But it's true. And if she continues to crave the power play that just occurred, she will own my very soul.

She stands at the window, naked and lush and goddamned breathtaking.

Bold and fearless and unashamed and proud.

Submitting to me does not dim her energy, does not crush her spirit, does not deflate her pride.

It energizes her.

The light in her eyes as she looked up at me with my cock down her throat was brilliant and full of glee and arousal.

I didn't know such a woman could exist, that anyone could want to give the very thing my fucked-up psyche demands I take.

I hold all this within myself and keep my face composed into the mask of indifference I have worn every moment of every day of my life for so long that I no longer know how to remove it.

I am the Man in the Iron Mask.

God, I need to fuck her. I need to own her pussy. I need to own her asshole. Her mouth. Her words. Her gaze. Her hands.

I want to paint her face and tits with my cum.

I want to put a vibrator in her ass while I fuck her sweet, tight, plump pussy.

I want to hold her all night long and whisper words of adoration as she tumbles into sleep.

I want to protect her.

Shelter her.

Keep her locked up in a tower because she's MINE.

I savagely shove that line of thinking away; I am no longer that man.

"Jakob. Please." Her whisper jolts me back to the present, and I realize I've been lost in my thoughts for who knows how long, while she stands, waiting, needing, and watched by a stranger.

"What do you want, Brys?"

"Let me come, Jakob. I need to come." She leans back against me, turns her face to mine, whispering. "Please."

I wrap my hand around her throat—cupping, holding, not squeezing. Her breath catches on a shudder at my touch, making her tits jiggle. God, she's going to be so fucking gloriously beautiful when I let her come.

I shuffle backward a touch, keeping my hold on her throat, forcing her off-balance so she has no choice but to lean against me, to trust me to support her weight. I'm ravenous for her, but I keep a savage grip on my need.

"Jakob? Please. Touch me. Please." Her voice is a ragged hiss. Desperate. Her hips buck forward, seeking touch.

One hand cupping her throat, my thumb on her

pulse-point, I at last gather the satin weight of her breast in my other, and I cannot hold back a groan at the glory of it. Hot and heavy and so soft, the tender globe fills my palm and spills over it. I tweak her nipple, and she gasps sharply.

The smoker has lit another cigarette, watching shamelessly.

I release her breast to fall heavily, bouncing and swaying. Cup the other, tweak her nipple, getting another sharp gasp.

"Sensitive, aren't you, Brys?"

"Yes, Jakob. Very sensitive."

I flick her nipples, scrape my thumbnail over the turgid tips until she whimpers. "You like that?"

"Yes, Jakob."

I slap her breast—sharp, with a loud smack. She screams, a shrill, wordless cry, more out of shock than pain. "Jakob!"

"How about that? You like that?"

"I…I don't…"

I smack her other tit the same way, and she dips at the knees. I caress them, then, tenderly, gently, until the tension in her body eases…and then I smack her breasts again, right then left, hard. Her knees almost give out, and she whimpers, biting her lip.

"Jakob!"

"Do you like that, Brys?"

"No!"

"Liar." I do it again, right then left. Caress, smack. Caress, smack. And each time, she gasps louder, sharper, more shrill, more breathless. "You do like it. Don't you?" I nip her earlobe. "You don't want to like it, but you do."

"Yes. I like it."

"Just like you secretly like letting that man down there watch."

"Yes, Jakob. I do. It's hot."

"You know you'll never see him again. It turns you on knowing he's watching this. Knowing it's not for him. It's for us. Yet there he is, watching." I slide my hand down her belly and drive my middle finger inside her pussy. "He's watching me finger your tight...hot...wet...little...*cunt.*" I emphasize the 'c' and 't' sounds, just to shock her. She gasps at the word, at the intensity of my pronunciation.

"Yes!" she gasps. "I like it."

"You want him to watch. You want him to see your naked body and wish it were him up here. Don't you?"

"Yes, Jakob." It sounds like her words are being dragged out of her by a team of horses. "I want him to watch you make me come. I want him to go home and fantasize about us. About me. Knowing he'll never have me, not like you do."

I slick my finger in and out of her pussy. "Hear that?" I add a second finger, my ring finger, and my thrusting fingers make a loud, wet squelching sound. "Hear how wet you are for me?"

"I hear it."

"What are you going to do when I make you come, Brys?" I demand.

"Scream as loud as I can."

"Scream what?"

"Your name."

I drive my fingers inside her, gather her dripping essence, and smear it over her clit, making her jump, buck, and quiver. "Scream for me, Brys."

She whimpers instead. "*Jakob*—oh...*god.*"

I drive my fingers inside her, curl them, and scrape the pads against her inner walls, and she gasps, mouth dropping open and shuddering; a soft, breathless cry escapes her throat when I drag her juices over her clit again, and this time, I keep touching. Circling. swiping. Flicking. Bring her to shuddering and bucking, and then plunge my fingers inside her and fuck her with them until she's shuddering all over again. Then her clit again. Back and forth, never letting her find a rhythm until she's grinding and gyrating and snarling like a wildcat, desperate and feral.

"Jakob!" she cries, "Please! Fuck, please, just make me come."

"Not yet. I don't believe you want it."

She lets out a soft sob. "I need it so fucking bad, Jakob. Please. How can I convince you I need it?"

I grin at the way she begs. "Fuck yourself on my fingers."

Her arms sling up around my neck, and she tangles her fingers together around the back of my neck and hangs on to me as she sinks onto my fingers. I bring my other hand down and press a delicate touch to her clit while she rides my fingers. Her movements are slow and hesitant at first, but as she finds the rhythm and balance, she gains confidence and speed. Soon, she's grinding on my fingers with everything she's got, whimpering and gasping. Within seconds, I feel her shudder, trembling all over with a building climax.

"Jakob!" She pants. "Oh—oh god. Oh god. Yes. Please, please, don't stop."

"I'm not doing anything, Brys. You are."

She loses the rhythm, then, when her legs buckle, and her balance gives out. "Please, Jakob. I—I can't. I need you to—" even her voice gives out, then. "Please." It's soft, breathy, and desperate.

"Ask." I drive my fingers inside her, plunge them deep, fuck her with them. "Ask for it, Brys."

"Make me come. Please, Jakob."

"Be specific."

"Anything, goddammit. Fuck me. eat me out. Finger me until I come. Anything, Jakob, just please fuck, let me come."

"You have to ask for what you want, Brys."

"Eat me—fuck, please, Jakob. Please. Eat me out. Fucking...*devour* my pussy. Let me ride your face. Please. I'm begging, Jakob. I'll suck your cock again. I'll do *any*thing you want, please, just—just please fucking god eat my pussy."

I drop to my knees with my back to the window—this is a Best Western, tragically, so the windows are waist-high. The effect is far more dramatic when she's pressed up against floor-to-ceiling windows with all of Manhattan spread below her. But this...it's almost hotter for the fact that we're three floors up and a hotel patron is watching us from the parking lot.

I put everything but Brys out of my mind, then; she is a goddess, and she deserves worship.

I wonder if she is cognizant of her own majesty, her intoxicating beauty, her seductive eroticism.

I extend my tongue and drag it along her seam, making her shudder deliciously. "Ahhhh god, Brys. You taste like fucking honey."

She groans. "Jakob. Oh god."

I taste her slit again, dragging my tongue over her

plump, delicate lips, which glisten with her dripping desire. Again and again, until she's quaking and panting.

"Have you ever tasted yourself, Brys?"

"No, Jakob."

"Look at me." Her eyes drop to mine at my command, her brow furrowed with wide eyes, mouth hanging open; I hold her gaze without blinking as I drive a finger inside her channel, withdraw it dripping and slick, and then lick it clean like a kid with a bowl of brownie batter. "Your turn."

It amuses me that this makes her cheeks flame. But yet, she obeys. Hesitantly, her hand drifts to her core. I carve my hands up the backs of her thighs and take this moment to enjoy the broad, round wonder of her perfect ass. She pauses, one finger at the apex of her seam, and then she's got her finger in her pussy, pulls it out, hesitates again… and then pops it into her mouth. Her face goes through multiple expressions in a quick sequence.

"Oh." A blush, a shy smile. "Oh, wow. I…Oh."

"My turn."

"Oh god, yes, please." Her hands feather through my hair as I bring my face between her thighs, and she whimpers when my tongue drags up her seam. "Jakob!"

No more games. It's time for Brys to come.

I drive two fingers inside her pussy without warning, and she jerks, panting. slow thrusts of my fingers at first, and then I taste her slit, lick away the juices coating her lips. Find her clit, a hard, erect little nub of nerve endings—more than ten thousand of them, to be precise. I devour her as if trying to lick each individual nerve fiber. That is to say, greedily, ravenously. She's quiet for the first few minutes. Gasping, panting, whimpering, all sotto voce.

But then, when she begins to shake and tremble, and

I give her a third finger and thrash her clit with my tongue in a relentless barrage, she begins to wail and sob, and then to cry out, shrill and breathy.

I feel her pussy clenching around my fingers, feel her belly go taut, and she hunches over me while dipping at the knees and thrusting against my face. She slaps a hand on the window to brace herself, clutching my head between her shaking thighs with the other, and she rides my face, grinds against me rabidly, desperately.

Her grip on my head is fierce and powerful—holding me where she needs me as I ravage her with my tongue and fuck her with my fingers. "Yes! Oh fuck yes! Oh god, oh god. Jakob, please. Please. Oh god, please. I'm—I'm gonna come, Jakob. Oh god, I'm gonna come so hard."

"Give it to me, Brys," I demand. "Now. I want you to come for me *right now*."

"YES!" It's a scream.

She comes.

She screams again, wordless and breathless. Her legs give out all at once and I barely catch her in my arms before she collapses. I guide her to her back on the floor. She's quaking, shaking, spasming, panting.

"Jakob! Oh god, oh god, oh my god." Her eyes are wet and wide and wild. "That was—holy shit."

I brace above her, a fist planted beside her ear. Dip and claim a kiss.

I wish she knew, I wish I could explain to her the significance of a kiss to me. But where would I begin the telling of that tale?

Brys lifts to meet me, one hand clasping my nape, and then her fingers trail through my hair and trace the shell of my ear.

The delicate affection in those small, simple touches savages my soul, leaving me gutted and unable to draw breath. My eyes burn, and I turn to the only means of expression I know.

"I didn't say you could stop coming, Brys." I glide down her body, cup her heavy breasts, and twist and pinch her nipples as I settle in the sweet, soft, warm cradle of her thick, strong thighs, and I mate my mouth to the lips of her pussy, and I taste her essence, and I devour her with a ravenous fury that shocks her.

"Jesus Christ, Jakob!" she screams, jackknifing forward and then collapsing to her back and bucking her hips upward, hands clutching my skull fit to crack it.

She fucks my face, holds me where she needs me, and writhes against my hungry, eager tongue, and she bucks and thrusts and writhes and screams until she has no breath left in her lungs. Her mouth opens in a silent cry, head thrown back, hips frozen in an upward thrust, trembling, she comes and she comes and she comes, tits jiggling and swaying, thighs tensing to push her ass off the floor.

She sucks in a ragged, shocked, shrill breath, like a scream in reverse, and her whole body contorts in a jackknifing spasm, and her thighs crush my head and neck with unbelievable power as the waves of climax smash through her like an onrushing flood-tide.

"Stop," she pants, legs suddenly going slack. "Please, please—Jakob, stop, stop. Please, oh god, I can't take any more. I can't—I can't take any more."

Greed for her ecstasy makes me merciless. I rise up over her and drive three fingers into her clenching wet channel, and she grips my fingers like a hot, slick vise, and I fuck her like that, fingers in a delta inside her pussy, smashing and driving and thrusting and demanding and taking more and more from her. She cannot even scream, can only tremble beneath me with tear-stained eyes wide, searching me with a complex array of emotions as she climaxes beyond her mind and body's ability to tolerate or comprehend.

And then she shatters.

I feel the wet rush flood my hand as she gushes around my fingers, a tight wail scraping out of her throat, eyes disbelieving and even afraid as her orgasm wrenches her apart. She curls forward again, gasping a shriek as she continues to detonate, spasming wave after wave all over my hand and the floor.

At long last, with Brys writhing and panting and whimpering and trembling, naked curves sheened with sweat, I take pity on her. "*Now* you may stop."

Her eyes, when they open, are stunned. Tear drops cling to her lashes like liquid diamonds. Her lips quiver as she struggles to breathe past shuddering sobs. "Jesus," she whispers. "Jesus fucking Christ, Jakob. What did you *do* to me?"

"When you please me, I reward you." I lean on an elbow, half on her, half on the floor beside her. I idly trace the outline of her areola. "*That* was your reward for being a good girl."

She shakes her head, at a loss for words. "I feel half paralyzed." She levers upright and scoots back, patting the thin, industrial carpet between her thighs. "Um. So I sort of soaked this."

I grin, and I know it must look predatory and arrogant and supremely self-satisfied. "Yes, you did." I caress her breast, trail a fingertip along the tender underside, purely for my own pleasure. "Have you ever squirted before?"

Her cheeks blaze scarlet, and she covers her face, shakes her head. "No." It's a tiny breath of a word.

I pull her hands down. "Why are you embarrassed, Brys?"

"I..." she shrugs, refusing to look at me. "I don't...I..." she dares a peek at me from the corner of her eye. "I peed on the floor like a bad puppy."

"There is some debate as to the precise composition of the substance, but I am of the opinion that it doesn't matter if it's pee or not." I squeeze her nipple until she gasps and flinches. "It's the natural result of a particularly intense orgasm. It is a *beautiful* thing, Brys. You are not to be ashamed of it. You are to celebrate it. Be proud. Many women are unable to achieve even a fraction of such ecstasy."

"Being able to climax is *not* an *achievement,* Jakob." Her tone is sharp and hard. "To say that orgasm is an achievement is to say that a woman who struggles to reach orgasm is a failure."

"I stand corrected. That is not what I meant, and I take your point. Thank you for correcting me, Brys."

Her gaze is suspicious. "Is that sarcasm?"

I frown at her. "No. I am not prone to sarcasm."

"You are actually, truly thanking me?"

"Yes. Why is this surprising?"

She snickers. "Um, because men generally don't take correction well. Especially not billionaire CEOs who can buy companies on a whim just to fire some rude bitch."

I clear my throat. "I am not a billionaire anymore."

"Perhaps not financially, no, but your attitude and demeanor are one hundred percent billionaire-coded."

"Is that a bad thing?" I ask.

She frowns, shrugs. "Not necessarily, no. It can be, but it is not by nature a criticism. Just an observation." Brys climbs to her feet, grunting as she wobbles, arms windmilling as she finds her balance. "Geez, my legs don't work." She traipses to the window—peering out from the side, now.

"Is our friend still there?" I ask.

She shakes her head. "Nope. He's gone." She yanks the curtains closed and turns to face me; I'm still seated on the floor, legs crossed. "We need to talk about some of what just happened, Jakob."

I rise to my feet and go to her. Press a finger over her lips. "I will never cause you real pain. If something crosses the threshold from pleasure into discomfort, simply tell me and I shall stop whatever I am doing immediately."

"Like a safe word?"

I shrug. "If you wish. Or simply tell me to stop. But you must be certain you want to stop. I do not play games in that regard, Brys."

"I told you I couldn't take any more, yet you kept going," She points out.

"I stopped doing that particular thing, did I not?" I say. "And when I put my fingers inside you, did you want me to stop?"

"I…"

"*Did* you?"

"No."

"I know you didn't. You didn't tell me to stop because you didn't think you could take any more, Brys; you told me to stop because you were afraid of that edge. You could feel yourself reaching a breaking point which you have likely never had the courage to go beyond on your own, and which no one else has had the knowledge or skill to get you past."

Her mouth opens and closes a few times. "I was scared of it."

I inch closer. Hold her eyes. "I know. You trust me to keep you alive out there, yes?" I gesture at the window.

"So far, yes."

I point at the bed. "Then trust me to know your limits there, as well."

She shakes her head, pushes past me. "You don't know what you're asking, Jakob."

"Oh, but I do."

She whirls. "No, you don't!" She's in my space, angry and wild, eyes blazing fury. "You don't know *anything* about me or my past. You don't know what I want. What I like. What I don't like. You don't know what I'm afraid of. You don't know what I fantasize about."

"Yet." One syllable, emerging from my lips unbidden.

It reveals truths I am terrified to examine within myself.

At that moment, tires squeal outside.

Chapter 9

Dangerous to My Heart...Or Just My Lady Bits?

BRYS

JAKOB IS IN MOTION INSTANTLY, BOUNDING TO THE pile of his clothes and dressing so fast it defies belief. I'm not far behind, and by the time I'm shoving my feet into my boots, Jakob has the machine gun slung across his chest, handing me a bag laden with clothes and rattling cans of soda.

My heart is in my throat as I follow Jakob out of the room less than ninety seconds after the first sound of squealing brakes and skidding tires. We beeline for the stairs, but Jakob pauses just inside the stairwell, listening—male voices.

"De ja vu," I whisper. "This feels all too familiar."

Jakob doesn't answer—he's hesitating. The elevator worked last time, sort of. But will it work a second time?

"Come. I have an idea. I don't like it, but I don't see an alternative." He exits the stairwell and jogs to the tiny alcove containing the ubiquitous ice machine. He presses me into the corner and gives me his back, crouching just out of sight, the gun held awkwardly across his middle at a diagonal angle.

We wait.

"What's the plan?" I ask, hissing.

"Wait till they come out of the stairwell and shoot them, then run like hell."

"Oh."

The sound of a crashbar echoes through the hallway. Jakob peeks out, sinks back. Waits. Leans forward to peek again. "Four of them. Cover your ears."

I huddle back as deep into the corner as I can get, shrink into as small a ball as possible, and clap my hands over my ears. And even then, the noise of the firearm in the small space is beyond deafening. *CRACKCRACKCRACK!—CRACKCRACKCRACK*] Time slows. The rifle slams against Jakob's shoulder in slow motion, and I can see his finger squeeze and retract with each burst. Something craters the wall and rips a chunk out of the doorframe above Jakob's head, and then he's throwing himself backward inside the tiny alcove as a hail of bullets pepper the air where he'd been an instant before.

He recovers, catches his breath—I don't think I was supposed to notice the way he releases his death grip on the barrel and shakes his hand, or that his hand is trembling.

He exhales forcefully, re-grips the barrel, and then leans out and fires off a burst, ducks in, and pauses as rounds thud into the floor and doorframe.

The next time he leans out and fires off a burst, he lets out a triumphant grunt. "Last one. Come on, you ugly fuck." It's muttered, more to himself than to me. He leans against the inside of the splintered frame, breathing deeply and slowly. Licks his lips. Shakes out his trigger hand, wiggles a finger in his ear, wincing.

He twists out and fires a burst, only for his rifle to buck up abruptly, his last round going wild as he scrabbles back in with a yelp, one hand clapped to the side of his neck.

"Jakob!" I cry, leaving my corner and scrambling over to him.

"I'm fine," he snarls, glancing at his hand, which comes away painted red.

My medical expertise is limited to what one can learn from watching *9-1-1*, *Chicago Med*, and *The Pitt*, but it looks to me like the round merely creased the outside of his neck.

The abrupt cessation of gunfire leaves a deafening silence in its wake.

Jakob frowns thoughtfully into the unexpected quiet, peeks out cautiously, one hand still pressed to his neck. "Huh. I guess I got him." He sounds surprised. "Come on. We need to get out of here *fast* before the cops or more of Pugli's thugs find us."

He rolls smoothly to his feet, glances at his hand—his neck is still bleeding, but a trickle rather than a flood. I follow hard on his heels, trying not to look at the four dead bodies.

Turns out I can't *not* look. And they're not all dead. One, at least, is still alive, with red holes in his chest pumping blood everywhere. His breath whistles—my idiot brain helpfully supplies a memory of an episode of *Chicago Med* where the heroes deal with a similar wound. Too bad I don't want to help this man stay alive, even if I had the time or supplies, and I'm also quite well aware that watching medical shows on TV does not make me a doctor any more than an actor playing a doctor is one.

His eyes are frightened as he glances up at me, gasping past the whistle.

I step over him.

The next body my eyes land on is dead, his throat a red ruin. My stomach revolts; again, seeing gore on TV doesn't prepare you for the grisly reality of it right there in front of you, seeing a real human with his eyes open and vacant, blood everywhere.

The third body is alive as well, but barely. He's writhing in agony, clutching his belly with one hand and his thigh with the other. A sickening, nauseating stench of fecal matter fills the air around him—pierced intestines, I would guess. But it's his thigh wound that's his death—the pool of blood under him is massive and spreading quickly. And even as I watch, his thrashing slows, and his hands fall away; his leg twitches one last time, and then he goes still, and his eyes stare sightlessly at nothing.

The last one is the worst. He's slumped against the door frame, the door partly closed on him, stuck against his legs. His head lolls to one side. His brain paints the wall, the floor, the carpet…

I lurch over him into the stairwell and promptly vomit onto the landing. Strong hands guide me down the stairs, but I barely see anything. White spots dance in my vision, occlude the edges. My chest is caught in a visegrip, and I can't pull in a breath. I stumble, trip on a stair. Gravity vanishes for a moment, and then I find my feet and manage to half-walk, half-stumble down the stairs. Jakob hip-checks the crashbar of the exit and hustles me through, an arm around my shoulders.

Instead of the Mercedes, however, he lifts me bodily into the front passenger seat of the idling black Ford

Explorer the attackers drove, parked at an angle near the side exit, all four doors hanging open. Tossing the rifle into the back seat, he takes the bag of supplies from me, and it joins the gun on the back seat.

I expect him to take off like a bat out of hell, but he does the opposite, exiting the parking lot at a sedate, unremarkable pace. A line of squad cars with howling sirens and flashing lights streams past us on the main road, and then we're back on the freeway.

For a minute or two, silence hangs between us. I cast a look at Jakob; his neck is still seeping. "You're still bleeding."

He juts his chin in the direction of the glove box. "Is there a first aid kit in there?"

"WIth the stuff from Target in the back seat. One sec while I grab it."

I twist in the seat and crawl—supremely awkwardly, and hyperaware of the enormous target that is my giant ass—between the seats to the back row, and then peek into the trunk. "Got it!" I snag the red plastic case with the white cross on it and crawl back to the front seat.

Opening the case, I rummage through it, find what I need to clean the area, rinse the wound, apply some Neosporin for good measure, and then tape a bandage over it.

"Thank you," Jakob murmurs. A glance at me, then. "Are you alright?"

I shrug. "I'm not the one who got shot."

Jakob waves a hand. "It's scratch. Barely counts."

"It counts."

"Fine, it counts," he says, "but I'm not talking about

that. I'm talking about your anxiety attack back there. Are you alright?"

I let out a shaky breath. "Yeah. I mean, no, but yeah."

He snorts. "That clarifies things."

"I thought you weren't sarcastic?"

"You're rubbing off on me."

I cackle. "I think it's the other way around. You rubbed off *in* me."

His glare is so intense that I realize he doesn't appreciate my joke *at all*. "Brys."

"Yes, Jakob?" I keep my voice quiet, soft.

He shifts in his seat uncomfortably. "Don't."

I hold up both hands, palms facing away. "Okay."

"You haven't answered my question."

I sigh. "Yes, I am alright. Shaken up, scared, and I'll definitely have bad dreams about all that at some point, but I'm okay. I'm a New Yorker—I've seen dead bodies before. Just…not like that. Not that close. And…I…I've never watched anyone's last breath like that." I shudder. "The brains on the wall. Ugh." I shudder.

This silence possesses a razor-sharp tension, a fraught intensity radiating from Jakob. "It isn't a pretty sight, is it?"

I peer at him as he navigates around a slow-moving semi. His face is carved from granite, the sharp angle of his jaw shadowed with thick dark stubble. His glittering dark eyes are fixed on the road ahead, but seem to see more than the blacktop and white and yellow lines. His brow is furrowed, jaw pulsing and ticking.

"Hey." I touch his shoulder. "What's wrong, Jakob?"

He shakes his head. "Nothing. I'm fine."

I snort. "I'm a woman, Jakob. You think I don't recognize a fake 'I'm fine' when I hear one?"

His expression softens a hint—a subtle expression of amusement, or perhaps merely recognition of my attempt at humor. "It's…" Another shake of head, a sigh. "Nothing."

"Jakob."

"Brys." He glares straight ahead, anger clouding his features. Anger? Pain, more likely, because as my therapist tells me, anger is merely a byproduct of pain. It's a secondary emotion, growing out of unexpressed pain.

"That isn't the first time you've seen brains splattered on a wall, is it?" I'm tossing out a guess.

"No." His growled response is a deep rumble, quiet and heavy with old pain.

"Tell me about it?"

The lines of decades-old agony carved into his face deepen. He's silent for several miles, but I see his mind working, considering.

"My father." His voice is sepulchral and gritty, gravel rattling at the bottom of a deep well. "I was sixteen."

"Why?" I ask, whispering, because reverence feels natural in this context, as if to speak too loudly might disturb the dormant monster of his grief.

"Because my mother died. To this day, I do not know exactly what…what happened. What she had. One day she was fine, the next she was in hospital. She was dead a week later. My father became mad with grief. It shattered him." He swallows hard, audibly. "The day she died, my father left the hospital, walked home, went into his office, shut the door, and shot himself. I never went into the office. I never saw…" he shakes his head. "I have seen violence. I have killed before. But seeing that man like that, something about it made me think of my father. How it must have looked like that. I keep—I keep seeing—" he shakes his head, cutting himself off.

My heart breaks a little, especially when his features shut down again, closing up the momentary glimpse of the man beneath the calcified armor.

"I'm so, so sorry, Jakob. To lose both parents in one day?" There's no hiding the tenderness in my voice. "I know what it is to lose your parents. But like that? *God,* Jakob."

He glances at me, and he appears almost...confused. He doesn't reply, but shakes his head and grits his jaw.

That's all the emotional vulnerability I'm going to get out of him for now, I think.

I let it go; if I know anything about men, it's that if they don't want to talk about something, they're not going to.

I doze off, eventually.

When I wake up, Jakob is still driving, still pensive. He glances at me as I stir upright. More silence.

The silence and the lulling hum of the tires turn my mind inward, and I can no longer keep my thoughts away from what happened in that hotel room this morning.

It just sort of...happened. I don't remember how it began. I know I'm attracted to Jakob, because who wouldn't be? The man is objectively gorgeous. But mere attraction can't explain...all of that. I barely know him. It's been less than twenty-four hours.

And I deep-throated him.

That's not that big of a deal, not in comparison to

my behavior. My instant submission to his commands. My *desire* to obey him. I barely recognize myself; I *don't* recognize that woman. Obeying his commands, *Yes, Jakob* this and *Yes, Jakob* that. The begging. The wild desperation.

I all but worshipped his cock. And, to be fair, it *is* a cock very much worth worshipping, it must be said. But I don't worship anyone or anything. I don't give *anyone* authority over me. I don't even allow myself to be in personal financial debt. I own my Manhattan penthouse outright. I own my condo in St. Pete outright. I have zero credit cards. No student debt. Nothing. Mainly because I refuse to allow anyone to have any kind of hold over me.

There are reasons for that.

But my good lord in heaven, the orgasm he gave me? My face gets hot just thinking about it. And the squirting? Jesus. I thought that was a porn thing. Fake. Or maybe not fake but…a specialty thing specifically for neckbeards jerking off in their mom's basement. Sorry, that's judgmental. I just didn't think it was a real thing.

Apparently, it very much is real, and it is the most intense physical sensation I've ever experienced. Like a regular orgasm, but on PEDs. It felt like something inside me just…broke. Shattered. And to be totally honest, I'm not sure I'll ever be the same.

I think back to sex with Charles. Even the most intense and passionate sex was…staid and demure and quiet. He came with a shudder and a grunt, went still above me, tensed, and then collapsed onto me for a moment or two, and then set about attending to my needs—he always came before me, but it never bothered me because he always made sure I finished. He was good with me using toys, too, which helped.

But the more I think back with brutal honesty, the more I realize how unsatisfied I was, deep down. I mean, I knew I didn't love him. I cared about him deeply and still do, but I wasn't *in love*. Not the point. The point is that I let the fact that I cared about him and wanted the relationship to work cloud my true feelings.

I was unsatisfied, sexually. Emotionally too, yes. We were intellectually matched, it is true, but that's not enough for a relationship.

He never instigated sex. He hinted, broadly. He'd plan elaborate dates—helicopter rides, hot air balloon rides, sailing trips, candlelit dinners on multimillion-dollar yachts, things of that nature. Which was wonderful, please do not misunderstand. It was romantic, exciting, thrilling. But when the end of the evening arrived, it was always up to me to get things going in bed. He was an eager participant, but I was in charge.

And that's the problem I have always had in any romantic relationship: I end up with men who are either content to let me be in charge, or who are arrogant, narcissistic, chauvinistic fuckboys with high testosterone, low IQ, and zero interest in me as a person.

Neither works for me.

I glance at Jakob, and I can't help but wonder if he's the exception.

I felt safe with him. I mean in bed—metaphorically speaking, since none of the fun stuff this morning happened in a bed at all. He saw me. Instinctively seemed to understand my limits and carefully pushed me past them.

I never felt degraded or used—involuntarily, at least. He was firmly in charge, yet at the end, I was taken care of.

Jakob glances at me. "Do I have any credit left?"

I frown at him. "Pardon?"

"When I gave you $160 for your thoughts. Do I have any credit left from that transaction?"

I feel amusement tugging at my features. "Meaning you want to know what I'm thinking about."

His head tips to one side. "I'm pretty certain I know what you're thinking about, generally. What I want is to know the specific contents and tenor of your thoughts."

"I hardly know where to begin, Jakob. It's tempting to open with a statement along the lines of 'I'm not that type of girl, normally,' which *is* a factual statement."

"What type of girl would that be, Brys?" Ah, there it is—that tone. His voice—already deep—goes deeper and darker and syrupy-smooth, crackling with seduction. It makes my core throb, makes my hormones go haywire. Makes me want to beg for his cock. I'm not going to, but when he uses that voice on me, my reaction is instantly and viscerally erotic.

The intense heat in his eyes when he looks at me tells me I've delayed my answer too long. "What kind of girl, Brys? I expect an answer."

"We aren't doing that right now, Jakob. There is a time and a place and a context for such behavior, and this is not that."

He quirks an eyebrow at me. "Do what, Brys?"

"Use that voice on me."

He seems puzzled—genuinely, or he's a very good actor. "Voice?"

"The seductive voice."

His smirk is a fascinating thing. "Oh. I see. *That* voice."

"You know you're doing it, Jakob. Don't play dumb with me." I give him a pointed glare. "We can discuss terms for engaging in...consensual and mutually agreeable adult activities...but do *not* insult my intelligence by pretending you don't know *exactly* what you're doing, or that I'm unaware of what you're doing."

Jakob snorts. "Engaging in consensual and mutually agreeable adult activities. Is that what we're calling it now, Miss Bennett? Shall we circle back to this later? Put a pin in it? Work together for greater synergy? Should we try and take a more holistic approach?"

I wince. "Jakob, stop. You know what I meant."

"I do. But I believe in saying what you mean. I hate corporatese. I hate vagueness. I hate dancing around the subject." He checks his blind spot before swinging around a slow-moving tractor-trailer hauling gravel or something like that. "If you have something to say, say it. If you can't discuss your own sexual preferences openly and honestly in plain terms..." he trails off, leaving the 'then' portion of his statement unspoken. It's obvious enough what he means, however.

I glare out the window, equal parts annoyed and angry at him for calling me out and embarrassed that he's right. "I have never done anything like that. The...submissive...stuff, I mean. Obviously, the sexual acts I have. It's the..."

"It isn't submission, Brys."

"Not in the dom-sub way, no. I know that."

"In *any* way, Brys. You did not submit to me. You played a part. Look at it like role-playing."

I shake my head. "Absolutely not. I despise role-playing. When I was an intern starting at the bottom of BDI, one of the middle managers was *obsessed* with role-playing games as a team-building exercise. Drove me insane. So that's pretty much the worst thing you could have said."

He scrapes his hand through his thick, glossy, wavy black hair. "I'm sorry."

"You couldn't have known."

A shrug. "No, but still." A beat passes, his expression shifting as he thinks. "My statement stands, however. I don't like to think of it as dominance or submission. Those have specific meanings, even outside of sexual kinks or whatever. What we did was…it's about control, Brys. I require control. In business, in everything, but especially in sex. I…" he shakes his head. "And you…you do too. But I think you don't *want* to be in control all the time, do you?" He holds my gaze as long as he safely can while driving on a freeway, his eyes darting to the road and back to me every few seconds. "Can you answer that honestly and bluntly, Brys?"

"No," I whisper. "I don't want to be in control all the time."

"I know. You readily, willingly, and I would even dare to say eagerly handed me the reins, metaphorically speaking. No, I'm not calling you a horse, it's merely a turn of phrase."

I roll my eyes. "I understand, but thank you for that clarification."

"You *enjoyed* giving me control, didn't you?" His question feels like a leading statement by a prosecutor.

"Yes," I breathe. "I did enjoy it. It was...it was a relief." My face heats and my belly twists, but I plunge onward with the truth. "It's something I...something I have..." I can't get it past my throat.

"Say it, Brys."

"It's something I've secretly fantasized about for a very, very long time. I've just...I've never trusted anyone with that secret. How do you go about finding someone to fill that role? What I want and need is very specific, Jakob. I will not be led around on a leash. I will not sit by, demure and silent, while the men speak. I am who I am. Out in the world, in business, in day to day life, I am who I am—a businesswoman, a boss, a CEO...I'm type-A. I'm competitive. I like to win. I am driven to succeed."

"Sounds familiar."

"I'm sure it does. But I've struggled with relationships. I naturally take charge in most, if not all, situations. Which means the men I end up dating are...how do I put this kindly? The type of men who are okay with that. My most recent ex, Charles, is a wonderful man. But our relationship didn't work...for a lot of reasons, really, but at least in part because I wanted something from him he wasn't geared to give. And that's the repeating pattern."

"Why do you need to be in a relationship?" he asks. "You can find what you need to fill that part of you without being in a committed, monogamous relationship. I would suggest perhaps it may be the only way *to* get what you need."

"Unfortunately, I am too complicated for that. I don't have the time, if nothing else. When I need sexual release, I seduce one of my temps. It's convenient, and has a built-in shelf-life. But that's...it's just sex. It's just plain old scratching-an-itch fucking. What I fantasize about is much, much deeper than that. It requires trust—*emotional* trust, emotional vulnerability." I glance at him. 'Which makes it so fucking weird to me that I went there with you without batting an eye. I don't know what to do with that, and it's not even really about the sex."

Jakob doesn't answer for a long time. "I understand more than you can know, Brys."

"Do you?"

He nods. "Yes. I do."

I wait, but he doesn't seem inclined to elaborate. "And? How?"

He sighs, chews on the inside of his cheek. "Brys, I..."

"Oh, I see. I can unload my baggage on you, but yours is too heavy."

"It isn't that."

"Oh no?"

His look is thoughtful, confused. "Perhaps it is, at that." He pauses for a long beat. "When you have lived a life in which you have zero control over *any* aspect of your existence, including sexually..." he swallows hard. "It does something to you. My need for control goes beyond sex. Far, far beyond."

I hear pain in his voice. I see it on him before his features shut down again, the expressionless granite mask once more in place.

"Jakob," I whisper. "What happened to you?"

"That is a tale I have only told once. I do not know

that I have the wherewithal to tell it again. Certainly not in this context."

"What context is that?"

"Being hunted? Running for my life? Having an innocent woman's life in my hands?"

"Oh, that context. I suppose that's fair." I look at him, but his face gives nothing away, nor do his eyes; he scratches his jaw with his right hand and then rests his hand on the console, and for the life of me, I can't seem to stop myself from folding my hand into his. "You don't have to tell me anything."

He glances at me, relief softening the granite mask. "Please do not take my reticence to discuss that personally. It's…it's not something I care to dwell on or bring up."

"No explanation necessary. We all carry our trauma differently." I hesitate. "Let's just agree that the control business is a whole separate thing that only applies to… that. To sex."

He nods. "Very well." A glance at me. "Thank you for understanding."

I get the sense that the amount he's told me about himself, little as it is, is likely far more than he's ever told anyone, with the one exception he mentioned.

Isabel?

Curiosity burns inside me, but I have trauma in my past I don't care to have unearthed, and questions only beget questions.

Best to stick to staying alive, first and foremost, to getting back to my life, perhaps find time to enjoy some more…activities…with Jakob.

I hedge even in my own mind, apparently.

What I mean is, I want more. I want Jakob. I want to feel him inside me. I want to taste him. I want to lay down my control at his feet and blindly trust him to make me feel good.

Put plainly, I just want to hide away with him and spend a week straight exploring this weird thing we have. Maybe it'll get it out of my system, and I can finally have a normal relationship.

Or maybe I'll end up craving something only Jakob can give.

And where will that leave me? He's very obviously not a man you hang onto. There is something indelibly primal about him. Untamable. Wild and hard and mysterious and frightening.

Yet intoxicating, too.

Addicting.

Fascinating.

Problematic.

Dangerous.

Jakob is dangerous; that much is obvious.

To my heart, though? Or just my lady bits?

I suppose I'm bound to find out

Chapter 10

The Devil in the Details

JAKOB

THE HOUSE AT THE COORDINATES I WAS GIVEN—what feels like a lifetime ago, already—is an extremely ordinary colonial in an extremely ordinary suburb in the southwest section of Rochester. It's gray brick with dark blue siding on the upper story, and twin dormers with shutters painted a truly garish shade of purple. A colorful profusion of zinnias lines the walkway leading from the sidewalk to the front door; the lawn is in need of mowing, and the flower beds up against the house need weeding. There are no cars in the driveway or parked on the street, but that's no indication it's empty; the blinds are all drawn and the garage door shut. This is a quiet suburb, the purview of working families. It's the perfect place for a safehouse.

I park on a corner a few hundred feet away and settle in to watch. Beside me, Brys has dozed off again—I'm rather jealous of that ability. Sleep has never been my friend. In fact, I'm shocked at how well I slept last night. I didn't expect to sleep more than a couple of hours, as usual, especially not with a woman I barely knew, even as exhausted as I was. I possess the fairly rare genetic mutation that allows me to function normally on an average of four hours of sleep, and I can function on one or two, as someone else might on four.

Waking up with her nuzzled up against me, her soft thighs bare against mine, those strange, hypnotic blue-ringed eyes hazy and lazy and hot with arousal—frankly ravenous, they were...I don't know what came over me.

I could literally smell her arousal wafting up from beneath the blankets; that heady scent sent me into an aroused frenzy I could barely contain, even with my iron will.

What is it about her that makes me feel so... off-balance, out of control, and disoriented within myself? Physical attraction alone cannot account for my reaction to her. Granted, my attraction to her body is a raging inferno of an intensity I simply do not know how to explain or understand. It's not about body parts, no matter how magnificent hers are. It can't be about who she is as a person, either, because we don't know one another at all, and I don't see myself being able to open up to her.

Isabel stole my soul nearly twenty years ago, and with it my heart. I may have died as far as the world is concerned, but my heart never fully caught on. Time has certainly played its part. The vicious agony of separation and loss has dulled. The feverish madness of obsession has dimmed and cooled, to a great degree, but she affects me still.

Seeing her yesterday was...brutal.

She never saw me, thank god. But I saw her. I saw her face. I saw her husband, her kids—my son.

My son.

No. *Her* son, *his* son. He may have my DNA, but he will never know I exist, and nor should he.

I have lived a decade without Isabel, yet that mad, turbulent time when she met Logan, discovered herself, and came to understand what I'd done to her is still ravaging my psyche.

I cannot forget; I cannot forgive myself.

I glance at Brys again. Thick, dense black lashes rest against her cheeks. Her hair is back in a thick braid, but a few tendrils have come loose to drift around her cheek and chin. At rest, she looks barely thirty, if that, although I know she has to be at least five years older based on her statement about the timing of my near-deal with her father.

She's a fascinating, complicated woman, resilient and brave. She's dealt with everything that has happened with remarkable adaptability, calm, and practicality, especially for a woman who, by all accounts, grew up wealthy and privileged. She hasn't complained; she has made it clear she's unhappy about the whole situation—understandably—but I think she also knows that I didn't want to and wasn't trying to pull her into my mess. She just gets on with the business of surviving, of doing what has to be done. She vomited at the sight of the dead man's brains on the wall, and then pulled herself together. I admire her resiliency, if nothing else. It's shocking to see such things in real life, right in front of you. Television doesn't prepare you for the scent of death, the stench of gore.

Inevitably, of course, my mind wanders to this morning—again, and again, and again.

So eager, so willing. Ravenous. Insatiable. Immediately willing to play along with my fucked-up mind games, my need to control…well, everything. God, she was fucking magnificent. Giving me what I demanded and somehow making it seductive, yet somehow...elegant.

Sex is not an elegant thing, usually. It's wet, messy, noisy, strange, intimate. Baring your body to another person, touching their most erogenous places, inciting such intense sensations...it's a highly personal thing, yet we engage in it with strangers. Perhaps we do so because of how vulnerable a thing it is—a stranger's judgment and criticism of our bodies, of our sexual performance...in a way, it is less frightening a thing because they do not know us, cannot, will not. After the heat has abated, we go our separate ways, feeling a little better for having gotten off, and for the most part, never think of that stranger again.

The same act with someone you know well, someone who knows your mind, your heart, your soul, someone who has seen you sick, clumsy, at your worst? That is frightening.

Brys made sex elegant. Graceful, beautiful. Her hunger was rapturous. She took my release with erotic delight, and if I had wanted her to, she would have kept going; kept giving; kept taking. When it was her turn, she gave me her body with utter trust. She let me take her past her threshold and into a release so intense she was left sobbing—that requires courage, especially with a man she scarcely knows.

My eyes slide shut for a moment—over the past decade of isolation, whenever I close my eyes, it has been Isabel I see. When I grip myself in the shower and bring myself to climax, it is memories of her I have turned to, time and again. Even when availing myself of the services of the girls who lease rooms from me down in Hel, it is Isabel I was with, in my mind. Unhealthy, I know. Toxic.

Obsessive. Yet I couldn't ever banish her from my mind, couldn't untangle her from my soul.

Eventually, I spent a year in total celibacy—not even pleasuring myself—in an attempt to exorcise her from within me. I learned to meditate. I journaled and dream-journaled. I did anonymous, voice-only therapy. I threw myself into exercise, lifting massive amounts of weight and running on the treadmill to the point of insanity.

It worked.

Mostly.

I no longer think of her almost at all. I never went back to hiring girls from Hel; it felt...wrong, somehow, in ways I could never articulate. I provide those girls with a comfortable, safe, protected place in which to practice their chosen profession. They are there willingly, of their own free will and choice. My lease terms are generous in their favor. I ensure that Hel is a drug-free working environment; I even provide referrals to drug, crisis, and sexual assault counseling. I have a whole onboarding presentation that Inez—Sophia—now has prepared for potential new hires, listing the benefits of working for me.

I am not a pimp; I do not take a percentage. I merely provide a safe place for them to do what they're going to do, anyway. It's the only ethical way to approach sex work.

I realize I may be an outlier on this topic—in the States, at least; sex work has existed since the dawn of human civilization, and I think it probably occurred in some recognizable capacity before we developed civilization. It is going to happen, and if it isn't regulated and the workers and clients protected, violence and exploitation become the means of control of supply, and those who suffer the most are the sex workers. To me, this is wrong; I have experienced it firsthand. Society and government exist to provide structure and support for *all* members. A wild, dangerous notion, I'm sure, especially in this age.

My rumination is disrupted when the garage door of the safehouse trundles upward—a blacked-out Lincoln Navigator approaches from the left, slows to turn into the driveway, pulls into the garage, and halts. The brake lights glow red for a moment and then shut off. The driver's door opens; the driver is a suit-clad young man, brawny and lithe—obviously a former operator. He opens the rear passenger door for the occupant—a leg emerges, khaki-clad, with loafers. Fucking loafers: obnoxious, pretentious, impractical footwear, and uglier than sin. Loafers are to shoes what the Pontiac Aztek is to automobiles.

I digress.

The rest of the person unfolds—a black polo tucked in just so. Dark hair slicked back. Clean-shaven. Khakis pressed, the cuffs hitting just right. The polo is fitted, likely tailored. Preening, arrogant peacock of a man with the soul of a cornered pit viper. I would gleefully, and with great relish, watch that man's brains paint an alley wall. If I had my way, he would spend the rest of his short life at the bottom of a cobalt mine, and his death would be slow and excruciating.

Alas, the privilege of his murder belongs to Nicolai.

At the very least, I can facilitate that process.

The two figures enter the home, and the garage door rolls quietly back down, and all is still and quiet once more. You'd never know that this sleepy little Rochester suburb harbors one of the cruelest, most bloodthirsty monsters on the planet.

I pull the cell phone I took from the dead guy from my hip pocket, power it on, and dial a long string of numbers; it rings three times, and then there's a digital beep. "It's me. Quarry is in Rochester, New York. Coordinates to follow. Send Lash ASAP." I recite the coordinates and then end the call. That done, I power the phone off, remove the battery, and pocket both pieces.

"Who is Lash? And why send him?" Brys's voice is slow and sleepy. "Who did you call?"

I glance at her; she stretches, yawns, and then watches me expectantly.

"It was an answering service—basically a voicemail box that forwards the message to predetermined recipients." I weigh how much to tell her. "Lash is an employee. He possesses...certain skills that will be invaluable in this situation. More importantly, he hates Pugli far more than I, or anyone, ever could."

"Jesus. What did he do to him?"

"Not only is it not my story to tell, but you also do not want to hear it. Suffice it to say that even the devil would be horrified."

She blinks. "Dear god. I think you're right—I don't think I want to know."

"Trust me when I say that you do not."

"And Lash, what is he like?"

"Complicated. Mysterious. Scary. Kind."

She frowns. "How can he be scary *and* kind?"

I shrug. "They are not opposites. He is scary to those on the receiving end of his skills, but if he is your friend, there is no one kinder."

"So we're glad he's on our side?"

My grin at her statement is probably a cold, frightening thing. "Oh yes. Very, very, *very* glad."

"How do you come to have an employee like that?" she asks.

I let out a long, slow, cheek-puffing sigh. "If you'll recall, Brys, not long after we met, I told you that if you were to know the truth of what manner of man I am, you would take your chances with the killers in there," I indicate the safehouse. "That is still true. I am not a good man, Brys."

She stares at the house for a long time. "I don't know that I believe that, Jakob. I have seen no evidence supporting this claim. Perhaps, in the past, it was true. But I like to think people *can* change...they just have to want to." Her eyes cut to me. "Listen, Jakob. I just need to know where we stand, okay? If you want the sex stuff to be strictly physical and we keep our pasts and our emotions out of it, I can do that. Most of my liaisons for the past few years have been of that nature. If you'd rather keep things strictly try-not-to-die and eliminate the sex altogether, that's fine too. Like I said, I just need to know the score so I can adjust my expectations accordingly. Just be honest with me, Jakob, even if you're being honest that you can't or won't engage with me emotionally."

I look at her as a dozen responses bing-bong through my mind, as if someone had sent too many balls into a pinball machine. "I must consider this, Brys. I will not give you a dishonest or disingenuous answer."

Her smile is shockingly tender and understanding. "I appreciate that answer more than I can say, Jakob. Take your time. I'd rather a truthful and genuine answer tomorrow than a lie or a half-truth now." A long silence ensues. "So...is this what a stakeout is like?"

I shrug. "I don't know. I have never been on a stake-out before. I have been many things in my life, but never law enforcement."

"Like what?"

I glance at her. "Hmm?"

"You said you have been many things. Like what?"

I should not trust her. I should not divulge any of my many sordid truths. It should stay physical—for her sake, if nothing else.

"I was a victim of sex trafficking and forced into prostitution as a teenager."

Into her stunned silence comes the unmistakable sound of gunfire.

CHAPTER 11

NOT LIKE THAT

BRYS

JAKOB REACHES BACK AND SNAGS THE STRAP OF THE rifle, kicks open his door, and is jogging across the intersection an instant after hearing the gunshots. Which comes from the house we are obviously watching—I assume because 'the quarry' is inside, the quarry being this Pooly guy, whoever he is. Although who is shooting at whom, I do not know.

A nasty, vindictive bastard, by the sound of it—he did something so awful to Jakob's employee Lash that he won't speak of it. *The devil would be horrified* is a pretty incredible and damning statement.

I don't know what I'm supposed to do—sit here and wait? What if there are more of those maniacal murder-thugs out there patrolling the neighborhood? What if—

Glass shatters in conjunction with a deafening series of cracking gunshots from very close. Before I can so much as scream, a gloved hand reaches in through the shattered window, wielding a tool of some kind; its purpose is revealed when the person uses it to slice my seatbelt apart. The door is wrenched open before I can react, hands grip my arm, and yank me bodily out of the vehicle like a rag doll. I land in a heap in the grass, my head bouncing off the hard earth, my shoulder screaming in protest at the way I was yanked.

I've never been one to go down without a fight—*NOT LIKE THAT*, get your mind out of the gutter—so I log roll away from the hands, onto my back, and start screaming, kicking, thrashing, and flailing like a madwoman. My limbs connect with someone, and I'm rewarded with a pissed-off masculine yelp of pain. Thus encouraged, I kick and thrash and fight all the harder, and again my efforts are rewarded with a thump of my foot against flesh and another wordless expression of pain, followed by what sounds like cursing in some European language I can't place.

A loud *crack* accompanies a flaring burst of agony and a splintering, coruscating flash of lights; my cheek throbs with flaring pain, and the world spins.

Something cold and hard touches my forehead. "Kick me again, and I paint the street with your blood, bitch-woman." The voice is rough, accented, and vicious.

I go still. "You are making a mistake."

"Oh, you think your precious Caleb Indigo will save you?"

"Who?" I blink away the dancing dots; the face above mine is wide and round and dotted with the scars of a severe chicken pox infection.

The gun, a comically colossal silver hand-cannon, waves at the house. "Him. Indigo. Now—you stand up very slowly and do as I say, or I hurt you more." He uses the gun to gesture for me to stand up. "I do not like to hurt women, so do not give me a reason."

"I don't know who you're talking about," I say, even as my memory niggles at the sound of the name.

"It does not matter what you know or do not know about the man." He stares at me with small, dark, porcine eyes set deep in a fleshy face, and that cold, wicked gaze is all the convincing I need to play along, for now. "You are to come with me." Once I'm on my feet, the man presses the gun to my forehead again.

Never let a kidnapper take you anywhere. Fight like hell. Once they get you into a car, your chances of survival plummet. My father's voice echoes in my ear—this was advice given to me the day he dropped me off for my first day of university at Yale...along with other fun nuggets of wisdom, mostly to do with how not to get raped, kidnapped, murdered, or scammed. Fun guy, my father.

The gun, making an O-shaped indentation in my forehead, however, is a pretty convincing argument for picking the right moment for my resistance. Fight now, and this moon-faced fuck will go all Jackson Pollack with my brains on the concrete. Which doesn't sound like a good time to me.

I keep my hands up and visible. "Okay. Okay. I'll cooperate."

More gunfire echoes from the house—a single *crack* followed by a short burst from an automatic. Another automatic burst rattles, and another single crack, a second crack, a third, all in short order.

That's not good. At all.

The man's big, fleshy, strong hand clamps onto the back of my neck as if I were a recalcitrant child wandering off in public. It's a bad move because it pisses me off. I am easily annoyed, especially by stupidity. But to truly piss me off? Like actual anger? That takes a bit more effort. And just for the record, I am an almighty unpleasant bitch when I'm pissed off. I'm talking unmitigated cuntery. Viciously irrational. My normal sarcasm seems like High Tea pleasantries.

"Take your hand off of me," I snap. "You will regret this no matter what," I tell the man, glaring up at him with naked fury carved into my features, "But if you put your hand on me again, your regret will be compounded."

He smirks at me derisively. "You think much of yourself, little woman." The gun twists into my forehead, and he clamps down all the harder with his fist around the back of my neck. "Tell me what is *or what,* hmm?"

If not for the gun, his wrist and elbow would be broken by now. I hold his glare but remain silent, not allowing the pain of his grip to show on my face.

He gives me a little shove as he releases me. "Go. Walk."

"Where?"

He gestures toward the house. "That way. Indigo should be dead by now. You will not enjoy what is next for you, but I will."

Oh dear, I do not like the sound of that.

And *who the fuck* is Caleb Indigo?

Clearly, he must mean Jakob. But why does that name ring a bell?

I almost owned BDI, a long, long time ago, in another life. Jakob's words from the day we met echo clearly in my memory. He almost owned BDI? As far as I know—and I'm CEO, so I have access to our records, as well as my own memory from being part of the company from the age of fourteen—BDI only ever came close to being sold twice. Once to a corporate raider from Hong Kong who thought bribing my father was a sound business tactic, and once to...Indigo Enterprises, Incorporated. The first time was when I was in high school, a freshman, maybe a sophomore. I only vaguely remember any of it other than overhearing my father ranting to my mother about some shady Chinese asshole who thought he could bribe Father into selling at disadvantageous terms.

The second time, I remember much more clearly. I was home from Yale, and Father held a business meeting in his home office on a Sunday morning. This was unusual because he tried very hard, especially after Mother's death, to be at home with me on the weekends, and even after I left for college, he kept the habit of not working weekends. He wore sweats and ratty old shorts, played squash with his friends, and barbecued. He never, ever took meetings at home. So when he came down in a three-piece suit, saying he had an important meeting and could I please keep quiet for a couple of hours, I knew something was up.

I eavesdropped, obviously. I heard Father's voice, and another. A deep, smooth, powerful, and cold voice, carefully accentless, polished, elegant, and sophisticated. I'd never heard a voice like that. I remember thinking, *I could listen to that voice read the phone book.*

I could only catch snatches and fragments of the conversation, but I heard the name Mr. Indigo and Indigo Enterprises several times.

Now, I mentally overlay the voice from my memory against Jakob's, add in his own claim that he nearly owned my father's—and now my—company, and I can only come up with the reality that Caleb Indigo is Jakob...and I am only now realizing I don't know his last name. Or his real name. Or much of anything about him at all.

Except for a few interesting tidbits, I suppose. He used to be worth billions—and, assuming he is or was Caleb Indigo, that tracks. Indigo Enterprises was a massive company in New York, with holdings across the five boroughs, as well as a finger in NYC telecom infrastructure, data management, corporate acquisitions, and who knows what else. I vaguely remember reading an article in...oh god....Business Insider? Barron's?—something like that—about Caleb Indigo and his mysterious persona and freakish success rate in business gambles. He had a penchant for knowing which way the wind was going to blow when almost no one else did, the article said. So it would make sense that he'd be worth billions. And I also remember the shock that rippled through NYC—and the wider business world as a whole—when a car bomb took his life so unexpectedly...and randomly. The speculation was that a disgruntled corporate owner whose business had been acquired, dismantled, and discarded by Indigo Enterprises had taken revenge on Caleb Indigo; no one had ever been able to find a single scrap of evidence linking anyone to the explosion, however. A perfect murder, one might say.

Now it is much clearer—Caleb Indigo faked his death, gave away the bulk of his massive fortune to the woman from the street—Isabel de la Maria Vega Navarro Ryder. Philanthropist, queen of the Manhattan socialites, and Jakob's ex. Or Caleb's ex? Is Jakob his real name or Caleb? Neither? Why did he fake his death? Indigo Enterprises was on the rise when he "died," showing no signs of slowing or stopping. He could have been bigger than Musk, Buffet,

Bezos, all of them. He faked his death and vanished off the face of the earth...why? Gave his fortune to his ex...why?

Some things regarding Jakob's reticence to discuss his past make more sense, but on the whole, I'm left with far more questions than answers.

As Moon-Faced Fuck frog-marches me toward the house with one hand clamped on the back of my neck and the other pressing the gun into my kidney, I mentally rehearse various BJJ hold-breaks, throws, take-downs, and arm- and wrist-snapping disarming techniques. I visualize a moment of distraction when the gun wavers and I have an opportunity. I visualize myself twisting in place, breaking his wrist and arm in several places, and maybe even going so far as to shoot him with his own gun. I'm not a violent woman, generally. Brazilian Jiu-Jitsu is as much about fitness and mobility as it is about self-defense, though for a single woman who frequently walks the streets alone at night, the self-defense aspect is important. And I have used it on would-be muggers more than once, to wonderful success. It's pretty amazing how fast "give me your purse" can turn into "please stop breaking my bones." Typically, the pleading starts when you've turned his elbow inside out.

But again, I'm not violent. I don't relish such things. I just work too damn hard for my stuff to let some jobless, stinking hobo take it from me. Come for my Chanel, bitch, and you'll be jerking off left-handed.

Okay, fine. Maybe I do relish it, just a little. You *do* get a pretty intense rush of power and satisfaction watching some yoked, mouth-breathing caveman who thought he could grab your ass with impunity scream for mercy as you turn his wrist the wrong way around.

I won't start a fight, but I'll damn well finish one.

All that is to say that I've never had to fight for my life. My possessions and my honor, sure—and by honor I mean staying un-raped, because you never know when a mugger might decide he wants more than just your three-thousand-dollar clutch. If I'm capable of snapping bones over a purse, what will I do when my life is on the line?

You guessed it: I'll murder a motherfucker.

I feel it; I know it; I know myself well enough to know I can do it.

I'll just have to set aside some money for the therapy bills.

Moon-Faced Fuck, for reasons I'll never understand, uses the keypad to open the garage instead of taking me inside through the front door. This is his mistake. He shoves my cheek against the frame of the garage door and jams the gun into my neck, awkwardly using his off-hand to reach around me and input the code—wrong, once, twice, and a third time, eliciting a series of ugly-sounding words that are surely curses in whatever language this Shrek-looking jackass speaks.

My heart pounds in my throat as I realize my moment has come. He growls wordlessly in frustration, then is forced to switch hands so he can use his dominant right to enter the code correctly. I make my move in the split-second that his attention is diverted and the gun isn't pointed at me.

I stomp my heel down with all the force I can muster onto his instep—a classic opening move. He howls, enraged, hopping and dancing backward. He takes an angry swipe at me with his big, heavy, hamhock fist, which all but whooshes audibly past my nose. I grab his wrist and twist his hand around upside down, forcing his elbow against the bend. Unfortunately, I've grabbed his empty hand, not the one with the gun. As I'm an instant from crashing my elbow against his joint, a deafening concussion erupts beside my ear, leaving the inside of my skull ringing like the bells of Notre Dame. My left side screams in pain at the junction of underarm, breast, and ribcage, a burning sensation unlike anything I've ever felt. And now it's my turn to be even more pissed off.

"You *shot* me?!" I screech. "Oh *fuck* no."

He jabbers at me in Moon-Faced Fuck-ese, trying to use his greater bulk and strength to dislodge my grip on his wrist, which I'm using to keep him in an arm-lock. He fired the last time blindly, and either he got lucky, or I did, depending on your point of view. Given the unevenness of the fight—considering he outweighs me by roughly a metric ton of ugly-fuckness—I need to end this posthaste.

I twist his wrist and put more pressure on his elbow, which only makes him howl and thrash all the more, firing his gun blindly again. This time, he misses completely, the round going who-knows-where. I jam my knee into his ribs as hard as I can, and feel something crunch like eggshells. I drive my elbow down against his upturned elbow joint, and that snaps. He's sagging against my hold, and I let him flop to his back…

And come face-to-face with the round O of his pistol.

Time slows to glugging treacle. I see his finger tightening on the trigger. I swat at his hand, but I'm going to be too slow.

A hot, wet mess splatters all over me—a pinkish-red mist liberally sprinkled with chunks of something gloppy and awful and warm.

BOOM!

The report hits my ears a split-second *after* the mess bathes my face.

What just happened?

I use the back of my wrist to clear my eyes of the pungent mess. Look down: Moon-Faced Fuck is nearly headless—what is left of his skull is a cratered bowl of bone splinters and gore.

Um.

"Thanks?" I say to no one.

"RUN!" It's a distant voice, a faint echoing shout. "RUN *NOW*!"

I can only assume the voice is the source of my all-too-timely salvation, and so I opt to listen. I bend, grab the slippery handle of the pistol, step over the oozing—and, horrifyingly, twitching—corpse, and then break into an all-out sprint in what I hope is the direction of the voice.

Another thing no one tells you is how weird and awful it smells when someone's brains go sploot. Sort of like bleu cheese, and let me say, I've never liked the stuff, but I'm going to have a Pavlovian barf response if I ever smell it again.

I hear a *crack* from behind me, and a bee buzzes around my ear. Another crack is followed by a weird snapping sound.

BOOM! This sound is farther away, the sharp cracking echo rolling over me like thunder. Unable to help myself, I crane my neck to look behind me while running: I'm just in time to see a figure topple to his knees, handgun dangling from a finger, and then dropping to the ground; the figure's head is a misshapen lump.

Jesus.

Nausea lurches up my gullet, and I trip, spewing bile to the side. Another sharp *crack* echoes behind me, and that stupid bee hums past my ear again. I wave a hand to shoo the thing away, even as I keep tripping and stumbling back into a run.

Where are the bees coming from? And why now?

What did I do? I don't know what's going on. I can't identify anyone, let alone this Pooly bastard. Why does everyone want to kill me? It's really pissing me off.

And where the *hell* is Jakob? I haven't heard his rifle chattering in too long.

I trip over a curb, stumble across a narrow grassy verge, a sidewalk, and onto a soft green lawn. Expecting more gunshots and more of those awful buzzing bees—which I am beginning to suspect are not in fact bumblebees at all—I duck as I run, deking and juking this way and that. I stumble over a child's toy and go sprawling into grass. I roll a few times, none the worse for the trip except the fear that the next shot will see my brains painted on this very well-kept lawn. I'm in a backyard, now, open to a miniature suburban forest bordering the back of the subdivision.

I glance left as I scramble to my feet; a sliding glass door affords a glimpse into the living room of the home, and I get a rather unexpected vignette: a woman with a Karen bob on her hands and knees on the living room floor, getting plowed from behind by a burly man wearing the brown polo of a UPS driver. And now that I think of it, there's a UPS truck parked on the curb. You'd think the driver would know better—those trucks have telemetry and their every movement is tracked, including how much time they spend at each address. So unless my guy is a two-pump-chump—and I'm watching evidence to the contrary—he's gonna get in trouble for this little stunt.

None of my business—and to be honest, you go, girl, get that porn-plot sex on. Fucking the UPS guy in your living room on a Thursday afternoon? Bold move, Cotton.

This whole aside lasts for the length of time it takes me to get to my feet.

I lurch unsteadily into the trees, spitting sour bile. Once into the shadows of the trees, I slump back, gasping raggedly, against the trunk of a towering maple. I have a straight line of sight to the safehouse from here, and my heart sinks into my stomach as I watch the garage door open, showing Jakob's slumped form being hauled between two men, feet dragging behind him. They toss him into the trunk of the Navigator like a sack of rice and then return inside to escort another figure. This one, I assume, is the Pooly bastard.

Before I know what's happening, I'm stepping out into the light and gripping the blood-slick handle of the pistol, and it's bucking in my hands. A window shatters high above the garage, and concrete sprays from the driveway apron—clearly, I'm a terrible shot. To be fair, however, it's a pretty far distance for a pistol, and I've received zero firearms training. I've never even shot a gun before now.

A hard brown hand clamps onto my wrist with unbelievable power, easily stripping the gun out of my hands. "You risk hitting The Boss." The voice is low, silky smooth, with a lilting accent. "That is not the way we shall recover him, my dear lady."

The man beside me is clearly a wizard or a vampire or a ghost or something, because he apparated from nowhere. He is about my height but built like a firetruck, with improbably broad shoulders tapering to an improbably narrow waist. His hair is jet black and short, combed neatly to one side, not a hair out of place, with a Van Dyke goatee coming to a precisely trimmed point below his chin. I do not know how to explain his eyes—dark and black and glittering, at once hard and cold, yet when he meets my eyes, they communicate kindness, even though I can feel and sense the violence radiating from him in palpable waves.

"You must be Lash," I say. "At least, I hope so."

His frown is puzzled. "How do you know me, madam? I have been staking out this safehouse for a week, waiting for Pugli to arrive." He says the name with a different pronunciation than Jakob; Jakob said it "Pool-ee" while this man says it "Pool-yee." It's a subtle but distinct difference.

"You *are* Lash?"

He nods once. "I have been called Lash, yes. These days, however, I prefer the name my mother gave me—Nicolai. Nico, if you prefer." He gives a sweeping bow: elegant, courtly, and archaic. "You have the advantage of me, I fear. An unusual turn of events. You are?"

"Brys Bennett." I watch with a heavy heart as the Navigator disappears from sight. "They have Jakob."

Nico's eyes lose any hint of warmth or kindness. "Not for long. I have tracked Pugli all over the globe. He will die with my blade in his heart before the week is up."

"Do you know where they're going?"

He pulls a smartphone from a back pocket, wakes it up, and shows me the screen—a blinking dot traveling away from us. "I placed a tracker on the car last night."

"So let's follow them."

Nico eyes me, nodding. "As you say. My vehicle is on the other side of these trees. Please follow."

I touch him arm. "Nico?" I say, and he stops, looks at me expectantly. "Jakob said Pugli did something terrible to you. He wouldn't say what, as it's not his story to tell. It's none of my business, but I just wanted to say I'm sorry for whatever happened. Based on what Jakob did say, it must have been awful."

Nico lets out a long, rough sigh. "Yes, it was. I appreciate…Jakob's…tact and respect, but it is no secret. I was married. I had children." The pause before speaking Jakob's name is interesting; I wonder what that's about.

He turns and walks into the woods, compelling me to follow; once I've caught up, he continues. "Ileana was my wife. Leanora and Leander were my children, a son and daughter, twins. Precious children. Just babies. The whole story is too long for the telling at this moment, but suffice it to say that Pugli trapped my wife and children in our home, dragged me outside, set fire to the house, and forced me to watch as they burned alive. All because I had evidence of his crimes."

I shudder. "Jesus. And he didn't kill you?"

"Not for lack of trying."

We emerge from the trees a few minutes later, on the far side of a municipal park. The trees form a border along one side of a soccer pitch, with a baseball diamond beyond it and an elaborate play structure area farther yet, nearest the road. A battered but serviceable compact pickup is parked up against the treeline a few feet from where we're standing, and Nico heads for it with me in tow.

He opens the passenger door and produces a package of wet wipes. "I think you will like to clean some of the mess away."

"God, please, yes. Thank you."

He has a long, black, military-issue bolt-action rifle hanging from a shoulder, and he lays it on the rear bench of the truck while I clean up, then whips a handgun out from the small of his back, and checks the magazine with the smooth swiftness of a man who has done so countless times.

He also cleans off the pistol I took from Moon-Faced Fuck, checks its load, and then disassembles it so rapidly it looks like prestidigitation, cleans it using supplies he took from a small backpack that had been on the front seat, and reassembles it—again so quickly it looks like sleight of hand.

He hands the weapon to me. "I will instruct you in its use at a later date and safer location. For now, keep it, but do not use it. The safety is on. It is loaded, and thus live and dangerous."

"Jakob gave me the same run-down. I could use some target practice, though. . .clearly."

"Jakob. That is still a strange thing to me, to use his name."

I frown. "It *is* his name, isn't it?"

He shrugs. "So I have been told. I do not know—I have never met the man."

"But he's your boss."

"It is a long story. I shall tell it while we drive."

As if to prove that the bow wasn't just for show, he opens the door and hands me in as if the truck were a coach, I'm an aristocrat, and he's a footman. Chivalry isn't dead, after all, huh?

Nico clicks the cell phone into a holder, plugs in a cord—the GPS screen pops up on the dashboard, and we're bouncing across the soccer pitch to the main road.

"Nico?" I say, after a few minutes.

He glances at me. "Yes, Miss Bennett?"

"Well, first, my name is Brys. Second, thank you. I'd be dead if not for you."

He merely smiles. "Of course. You fought him most bravely."

And that's how I find myself in a *different* car with a *different,* strange man. Now, though, we're not running for our lives.

We're embarking on a rescue mission.

Stay alive, Jakob. I'm coming.

No, not like that.

Yet.

CHAPTER 12

BAIT IN THE TRAP

JAKOB

I AM A FOOL.

Pugli is a wily old fox. You don't stay ahead of international law enforcement for as long and as completely as he has by being easy to find. If it were possible for one untrained civilian to find and capture him, it would have happened by now.

Yet that's what I thought was going to happen. La-la-la, I'm Jakob Kasparek, I'm so cool, I can find Pugli's safe house, bypass his security detail, and make him pay for his crimes all by my-untrained-self.

That is most assuredly *not* what happened.

I got into the house, cleared the living room and kitchen, and made it as far as the stairs to the upper story. Which is when I tripped a silent alarm via a hidden laser tripwire. I was immediately attacked by gunfire from the top of the stairs, which clarified for me that I'd walked right into a trap. Also, I'd forgotten the basement; guess who had *more* guards hiding down there, ready and waiting for me to do exactly what I did? Thus, I found myself pinned down by gunfire from two directions with only one magazine for my rifle.

Maybe an operator like Lash could've fought his way out, if not accomplished the mission. Alas, I am not an operator. I took a round high on my left side; it went straight through, which I think is a good thing as it means I don't have a bullet lodged inside me somewhere, and it also didn't bounce around a lot. Now, whether it hit any organs or not, I don't know. I know I'm losing blood, but they did pack the wound and cinch a bandage around me—none too gently, I might add.

I'm not feigning anything—I'm in a lot of pain, and I'm weak from blood loss. I'm just playing it up a bit, acting more severely wounded, weakened, and out of it than I am. It's the only play I have, at the moment. My worry is for Brys. She's impulsive and braver than she has any right to be, so I can see her trying to come in after me once she realizes something is amiss. I wish I'd called in Lash and the guys sooner, now that I'm shot and captive in the back of an SUV. Hubris prevented me.

We round a long, tight curve—a freeway onramp. I'm rolled against the side and onto my wound, which rips a long, low groan from my chest, not at all faked or exaggerated.

Getting shot fucking sucks, it turns out.

I know, I know, I'm Jakob Kasparek, I should be above such vulgarity. I usually am. I trained Isabel to speak with fluency, eloquence, and elegance, without swearing, because profanity is the mark of a small mind, and all that.

I'm starting to think I may have been full of shit.

We hit a massive pothole, which sends another jolt of agony through me.

"FUCK!" I snarl. And wouldn't you know it, a good curse does seem to help me manage the pain.

In the row ahead of me, Pugli chuckles. "Hurts, eh? Relish the suffering, Mr. Indigo. I have plans for you. Plans which shall make your current pain feel like the sweetest pleasure."

I ignore him; I believe him, but I'm just banking on the situation resolving...otherwise. In my favor, of course.

Pugli really does do an excellent job of filling the 'maniacal supervillain' role, though. Because he can't just leave it there. He has to monologue at me.

"You're not my primary target, of course." He twists in the seat, putting his back to the car door so he can direct his dead, zero-Kelvin gaze onto me; I've detected more humanity and warmth in the eyes of a reptile at the zoo. "You are merely bait."

This gets my attention, against my will. I let the momentum of a lane change roll me over so I can look him directly in the eye. "*I'm* bait?"

He smirks, an insidious and maleficent glitter in his eyes. "At this point, Mr. Indigo, you are merely a loose end. You possess evidence of my crimes. I do not debate this. But the evidence you possess is minor in comparison to the evidence your elusive compatriot Lash has in his possession."

Ah. Now I see. It's about Nicolae—it always has been. My Arrows have spent weeks hunting this asshole, dodging his thugs, getting in firefights...my club was destroyed, my home assaulted and compromised.

Because of this man.

Because whatever Nicolae knows about him is just that compromising. It's worth expending the time, effort, and manpower to hunt down not just Nicolae but all of us. My Arrows. Sophia. Me. Even Brys, who knows nothing.

Makes one wonder what Nicolae knows.

I thought he'd met with someone in Europe regarding his evidence, but that debrief was cut short by the discovery of Pugli's agents on my trail after I bolted following the assault.

"Nothing to say, Indigo?" Pugli pops a Zyn pouch into his mouth, which makes me nauseated. It's a disgusting habit.

I summon a lazy, unconcerned grin, sprawled against the hatch like Dr. Ian Malcolm in the back of the Jeep. "Not really. Your time on this earth is measured in hours, now, Roberto. Enjoy your sense of superiority while it lasts."

"You think you're going to fight your way free and kill me in the process, do you?" The derision in his eyes is wickedly sharp. "How amusing."

Inside, I'm freaking out—mainly about Brys. It's tempting to bring her up and see what he says, but I hold my tongue. No point in baiting him on that topic, in case she's gotten away or has slipped his mind.

"Your friend," Pugli says conversationally, immediately dashing my hopes. "The curvy blonde. CEO of Bennett Development, yes? Miss Brys Bennet? I imagine you'd like to get her off the hook. Or perhaps 'off my radar' would be a more accurate way of putting it."

I can't stop fury and hate from bubbling up inside me, but I do my dead level best to keep it from showing on my face. I'm sure my eyes betray something, however. "I'm listening."

"Give me Lash, and Brys Bennett is free to live her life. She'll never see me or any of my *friends* again."

"You overestimate my influence on Lash," I say, truthfully. "Especially as regards his antipathy toward you."

"Oh yes, his hate burns most brightly, I know. I'm counting on it, as a matter of fact. I have you, and he owes you his loyalty. He hates me—not without reason, I suppose." So flippantly, so casually does he reference his evil acts. "It's a perfect setup for an ambush. He won't be able to resist. If I could add your Miss Bennett to the trap, I'd be happier, but things got rather exciting as we were leaving. If it wasn't Lash himself out there, it was another of your damnably effective Arrow friends." A shrug. "No matter. Death comes to us all, but to you and Lash rather more immediately."

I hold his gaze silently, and it becomes a staring contest, which is, I understand, patently ridiculous and utterly childish. It's not a don't-blink-or-you-lose contest, though. It's a don't-look-away contest. It's like trying to stare down a cobra, though: there's just no life in his eyes, not a scrap of humanity, no warmth, no light.

We're saved from having to declare a winner when our driver slams on his brakes, cursing angrily in Bulgarian, drawing both Pugli's and my attention at the same time.

I'm thrown painfully around the trunk as the driver swerves while cursing; I brace against the hatch and sides with splayed arms and legs, snarling through the pain.

Dizziness washes over me, which isn't good. I close my eyes and sink into my mind, pushing aside the pain, Pugli, chases, gunshot wounds, everything.

What fills the void of my thoughts is Brys.

The hot, bright gleam of arousal in her exotic, blue-ringed hazel eyes. The small softness of her hands. The hunger in her as she swallowed my cock, the way she gazed up at me, begging for more. Obeying me so willingly, greedily.

The way she collected herself and kept moving despite the horrific gore of dead bodies.

The gleam of humor as she doles out wicked, cutting sarcasm.

I sink deeper into the darkness of quasi-consciousness, letting Brys fill my mind and overtake my thoughts.

Inevitably, however, Isabel ghosts through my awareness—the Isabel that was: Madame X. The woman locked in my tower, nameless and without a past. Mine to create, to control. She was a study in grace, elegance, and understated perfection. She moved through the world like a dancer, even as a coltish sixteen-year-old.

I was her world. My word was all there was. I had but to speak, and my will would be carried out.

She was a living doll. Almost a golem, a barely animate thing without a will of her own.

For years, I worked tirelessly to create a perfect vessel for my will, a creature I could bend to my purposes. For someone with an undiagnosed but very real obsessive disorder—or whatever is plaguing my brain—she was my ideal possession.

And a *possession* she was. I didn't see her as a person, an individual. I stopped seeing her individual qualities, her sense of self. I knew who she was and where she came from, even if she didn't…I just stopped caring. The pursuit of ever more finely-tuned control over her behavior, her decisions, her thoughts, even her needs—that was all I cared about.

She was all I wanted, all I needed.

And then she met Logan. Her eyes were opened. She began asking questions. Began wondering.

And so the house of cards I'd built came crashing down around my ears.

And I realized, sitting in the balcony of a cathedral watching her marry Logan, that I had formed my entire world around her.

My businesses, my billions...none of it mattered without her. I could have lived out my days as Caleb Indigo, building my corporate empire, raking in billions upon billions until I was worth more than many third-world countries. But without her, to what end?

No one knew me. No one cared about me. No one knew Jakob Kasparek. No one knew Caleb Indigo, not really—because Caleb Indigo was fake. He was a fraud. A creation, a fiction as carefully crafted as Madame X.

Without Madame X propping up my psyche, I had nothing. Caleb Indigo, as an entity, collapsed. I hadn't consciously intended it at the beginning, but when I vanished and returned as Caleb, it was entirely with the purpose of finding Isabel and carrying out a plan to possess her. How that seed of obsession was planted, I do not know.

I'm sure if I were to trust a psychologist with the whole sordid truth of my life, I could find out the root cause of my tendency to fixate and obsess. Something to do with my mother's death and my father's subsequent suicide, I think, and my time as a prostitute—although sex-slave is a more appropriate term. I had no control over any aspect of my life—not even my thoughts. When you're living in a drug-induced fog, your thoughts are not your own; they belong to the drug. You're easily manipulated, coerced, tricked, and strung along. Whispers in the ear become truth under the chemical guidance of heroin. My body was not my own; I was not my own.

Once I was free, I didn't need to make some sort of teeth-gnashing, fist-clenched vow to never let anyone control me ever again—it was self-evident. My existence, after that, was bent toward total control over my thoughts, over my body, over my finances; over my whole world. I dedicated myself to physical perfection—eat right, lift weights, run, box, swim, row. Carve my body from marble, etch each line, build each muscle. Control my thoughts—do not be lured or enticed, never be upsold, never be undercut. I must be the one to manipulate, never the one manipulated. Control sex—how long I last, when I release, and where. Do not let lust control me. Love, of course, is a fiction, a fantasy.

I did not love Isabel; I cannot love.

Can I?

Love requires trust; trust requires vulnerability; vulnerability is the ultimate lack of control.

I have been owned before, and I nearly lost myself to it—I do not mean mere death. How can I open my soul to someone, now? I've been shuttered, battened down, impregnable for so long I don't know any other way.

And it's thinking of love, and the impossibility of it, that brings my mind back to Brys.

Kissing has always been a deeply personal thing for me. Sex is not. When you have been bought and sold and used and discarded like a piece of machinery, sex loses its meaning. But kissing…

I can't say why. I don't know. I've never examined it too closely. It's just…intimate. It feels like giving something away, and nothing in life is free.

So why did I kiss Brys in that alley? It was a compulsion, something I could no more control than getting an erection in the morning, or blinking, or breathing. Yet even now, after the delicious things we did together, it's not oral sex I'm thinking of, or the taste of her pussy—as sweet as it was—but her mouth on mine. The delicate touch of her lips. The way she quested against my mouth and then delved in, seeking and probing. The warmth of her mouth, the pillowy softness of her lips, the ache in my soul as she melted against me...those moments, those sensations are imprinted on the very fabric of my soul in a way not even Isabel can hope to compare with.

It's disorienting.

I think of her constantly, but I am not thinking of how I can craft this part of her, change her speech, alter her wardrobe, fine-tune her manners, perfect her diction.

I do not want to change Brys. I do not want to own her or control her.

She is a wild horse, meant to run free. To control her, to bring her to heel, would be to break her, to ruin her.

I won't do that.

More to the point, I have no desire to.

And *that* is the most disorienting thing of all. I am not so blind or unself-aware as to think I am fixed, that my obsessive tendencies have been solved; I am the king of control freaks.

So what is different about Brys?

Why am I different around her?

I told her things I never talk about. She has only to look at me with those strange, hypnotic eyes of hers and she can pry out of me all my secrets—or so it seems. I have kept much back, so far, but if I were to spend more time with her—as I so badly crave—I know all would come out.

And if she knew the whole vile truth of who I am and

who I have been, she really would take her chances with the monster in front of me.

Because I am realizing one awful fact: I am a monster as well.

She deserves someone who is capable of softness, of affection, of gentleness. Love. She's willing to play the game, to give me her body and her obedience as long as I do not demand her heart if I am not willing to give her mine as well.

But can I do that?

She would want more—of my time, of my attention, of my secrets, of my vulnerability. She would worm her way into the blackened, shriveled remains of my soul, and her love would die there, malnourished and broken and neglected and abused.

No.

I need to see Pugli pay for his crimes against Nico and so many others. I need to deliver him into Nico's hands so the man can finally know true freedom.

I have to make sure Brys returns to her life as CEO of Bennett Development with her Midtown condo, her curated life, and her beautiful heart.

Some man, someday, will recognize the priceless treasure that is Brys Bennett, and he will snap her up and make her his—and in so doing, become hers.

I cannot stand in the way of that. I will not.

So, I must stay alive and seek my moment. Make Pugli pay. Be the bait in the trap—Nicolae is far too canny a warrior to fall for Pugli's obvious ambush. My only goal now is to make sure the trap is sprung—with Pugli the prey.

My survival is irrelevant.

I died once, but this time, it's going to be for real.

As long as my Arrows are free and Brys is safe, it will be worth it.

Stay alive, Brys. Don't do anything foolish.

Your life will be your own, soon.

I'll make sure of it.

CHAPTER 13

PART OF A PATTERN

BRYS

"So..." my mind is racing and spinning as Nico weaves his improbable tale. "Let me see if I have this straight. You live and work in a nightclub. But not just any nightclub, a secret, exclusive nightclub in a hidden location somewhere in Las Vegas, and you can only get in via invitation from someone else who has been there. This nightclub has a secret underground MMA cage-fighting venue, three stories of bars and dance floors, a more secret and even more ultra-exclusive brothel where the hookers are contract employees who lease space from Jakob, who is your boss, whom you've never met, never spoken to, never even seen, but you're sure he exists despite having zero evidence. And also by the way, I'm not sure if his name is Jakob or Caleb or something else entirely." I frown, tapping my chin with a fingernail, thinking, trying to keep straight everything he's told me so far. "What else? Oh, right, we can't forget your buddies, who are all super badass special forces dudes, except three brothers, two of whom worked for a super secret organized crime gang called The Syndicate, and the other for the CIA. You all had some sort of betrayal or super deadly enemy who wanted to kill you, and Jakob, via a woman named...shit, I forgot. Something with an I..."

"Inez. But her name is Sophia, now."

"Right, right, because half of you changed your name for some kind of ritualistic reason." I wave both hands to slow him down before he can plow onward with more insanity. "Just...just hold on. Let me put it all out there so I can try to process it. You all took a vow to never kill again, and you sealed that vow, despite your training to the contrary, with a fucking *brand* as if you were *cattle,* and then fucking *tattooed over it*? But you still go on Tom Clancy rescue missions all over the globe, taking down cartel bosses, Syndicate assassins, doomsday militia preppers, Indian billionaires, petty drug dealers, a psychotic warlord cartel kingpin whacko who was also Inez's forced-arranged-marriage husband—and we certainly can't forget everyone's favorite supervillain, this Roberto Pugli fuck-face who seems to be invincible, invisible, and unkillable. And as you guys do *all this,* you *also* have time to find true love with equally fascinating and badass women? Do I have all that right?"

Nico scratches his jaw. "Hmmm. Yes. You have summed it all up rather succinctly." He glances at me. "It does sound somewhat...unlikely, put as you have."

"*Unlikely*?" I stare at him. "If I weren't sitting in this seat with you, having experienced everything I've been through over the last...? God, is it even seventy-two hours? I don't know." I shake my head. "I would have you committed to a loony bin."

Nico chuckles. "I understand your skepticism. It is warranted and entirely valid."

"You killed those men back there," I point out.

He nods. "I did. For reasons which have never been entirely clear to me, I was exempted from the vow against taking lives. I think somehow The Boss…Jakob…knew we would need a…what is that phrase? A jack in the box?"

I snicker. "No, I think you mean an ace in the hole."

He nods. "Yes, indeed—that is what I mean. An ace in the hole. I have spent much of the past few weeks in Europe speaking other languages, so my mind is not yet fully readjusted to English."

"How many languages do you speak?"

He rolls a shoulder with suspicious casualness. "A dozen or so, depending on your definition of fluency."

"Good lord."

"So…not that I'm ungrateful for having met you, but…are the rest of your crew of killers-who-don't-kill going to join this little party?"

He eyes me. "That is uncertain."

I frown at him. "Can I ask why? Jakob, your boss, the man who saved all of you from your respective fucked-up pasts, gave you a place to live, a job, and a found family…he needs help. He's injured, possibly dying, and has been taken by the man you've all been alternately chasing and running from for weeks now, if not months—and in your case fucking *years*."

"He only called for me. It is I who has suffered the most at Pugli's hands."

I splutter my indignant disbelief. "Who the fuck cares who he *asked* for? HE NEEDS YOU ALL! This is not the time to honor his self-sacrificing wishes, Nicolai. It's time to rally the goddamned troops, call in the fucking cavalry, and rescue the man who has given all of you your fucking lives back!"

"Self-sacrificing?"

"*Yes*, self-sacrificing! He redeemed you, right? That was *your* word. Not just you, but your brothers. The women who are in love with you. He finances your entire existence. And now he's the one in trouble, Nico. What was the vow you took?"

"Once you're in, there's no going back. Never take a life. Loyalty to the brotherhood above all."

"I'd think the man who created your little club would be the number one brother in the brotherhood, the one most deserving of your loyalty. Which I'm not doubting, Nico. What I'm questioning is why you're the only one out here helping hunt down this vicious motherfucker. He's threatened all of you, and now he's using *Jakob* as bait."

Nico seems stunned. "Perhaps you have a point." A beat, a slow breath. "I have operated alone for so long that it is difficult to consider other strategies. Hunting Pugli is..."

"A group project. So call the boys, Nico."

He reaches over me to open the glove box and withdraws an old school flip phone. From his hip pocket, he produces a SIM card—he ejects the battery, puts the SIM card in place, replaces the battery, powers it up, and hits a saved speed dial number without putting it to his ear; it rings three times—tinnily, distant—and then clicks to dead space. "Operator," Nico says. "Roll call—laser, alpha, sedition, calculator. Time of recording is—" he glances at the dashboard clock. "Sixteen-twenty-four Echo Sierra Tango."

After that mouthful of nonsense, he claps the phone closed, removes the battery and SIM card, tosses the SIM card out the window, and then tosses the battery and phone into the cupholder near the dash.

I eye Nico. "Are you going to explain what that was?"

"A coded messaging system. It notifies my people that I'm reaching out."

"Why not just call them?"

His expression doesn't say I'm stupid, but it suggests that I'm probably missing something obvious. "Pugli has resources you cannot imagine. Tapping and tracing phone calls is easier than child's play. That is reason number one. But more to the point, none of us has a cell phone. Not like you, or other people whom you would consider normal citizens. Cell phones are the single easiest way to track a person. The phone doesn't even have to be engaged in a call—with the right software and expertise, one can triangulate a cell phone's location as long as that device is powered on."

"So, but..." I frown again, shaking my head. "You took the battery out and threw away the SIM card. How will they be able to reach you?"

"They do not reach me; I reach them. Sophia will receive a notification, power on a specific device, and wait for me to call again within a specific window of time."

"And that window of time is what?"

"Seven minutes and thirty seconds from the end of the coded message."

I glance at the dashboard clock. "Three minutes have elapsed."

"I know." He opens the console between our seats, produces a plastic card containing multiple SIM cards, punches one free, and hands it to me as the dot representing the car Jakob is in leaves the freeway, a few miles ahead. "Put that into the phone, if you would, please."

"Um, sure." I reassemble the phone, but do not power it on.

Nico watches the dot closely, taking the same exit and remaining several miles back, well out of sight. When he's sure they're continuing down the state highway, he indicates me with a flicked finger. "Power it on, if you please, and then give it to me."

I do so, and he dials another pre-saved speed dial entry. This time, he puts the phone to his ear as it rings. "Sophia, hello. Are you with the whole crew?"

He listens, glances at me, and then puts the device on speaker. "Sophia, you are on speaker. With me is Brys Bennet, who has been… traveling…with…Jakob." He pauses before he says the name again, as if saying it were strange and unnatural.

The voice that greets me isn't exactly cold, but it is cool and professional, faintly Hispanic-accented. "Miss Bennett." I think she intends this as a greeting. "When Nico says traveling, I assume that means you have been unwillingly drawn into our ongoing web of difficulties involving one Roberto Pugli."

I snort. "Ongoing web of difficulties," I echo. "That's one way of putting it. But sure, yeah, call it that. Jakob literally ran into me, tried to act like we were just a couple making out in an alley, and now people are shooting at me. I've seen the contents of not one but two men's skulls. I've been chased, shot at, and pulled out of cars. But yes. Ongoing web of difficulties is certainly one way of putting it, Sophia."

The silence that ensues is thick and tense. "He kissed you?"

"To distract the killers pursuing him through the streets of Manhattan, yes."

Another pause. "Jakob Kasparek...*kissed* you."

"That's his real name, huh? Jakob Kasparek? Not Caleb Indigo?"

More stunned silence. "Where did you hear *that* name?" It's whispered.

"The fat ugly fuck who pulled me bodily out of the car and almost killed me before Nico sprayed his brains all over the garage door."

"She fought like a trapped lioness," Nico says. "And he was a very large, very ugly, very frightening individual. He shot out her window, cut her seatbelt off, and threw her out of the car. She did not go quietly into that good night."

I glance at him. "Dylan Thomas, huh?"

Nico shrugs. "There is a surprising amount of downtime when one is crisscrossing the globe hunting a deranged psychopath. Poetry is a guilty pleasure of mine."

"I'm not sure you fully comprehend the meaning of 'guilty pleasure' there, buddy," A deep, rough, male voice says.

Nico frowns. "Then please enlighten me, Rev."

"Gentlemen, not the time," Sophia interrupts, very much like a teacher settling a squabble between kindergarten boys. "Let us move on to the reason you reached out, Nico."

"There has been a development, and not a positive one, I fear." He glances at me, for some reason. "Jakob has been taken by Pugli, and we suspect he has been shot. That is the bad news. The good news is that he is alive, last we saw, and I was able to place a tracker on the vehicle he is in." He pauses again. "We all owe him far more than merely our lives, which Miss Bennett has pointed out to me. I know he was very clear in not wanting us to interfere, but Miss Bennett has made an excellent point: we owe him more than just gratitude for saving our lives. I do not need to enumerate the many ways he has shown us generosity and loyalty. He redeemed us all from our various personal hells. Now it is we who must rescue him from his. We swore an oath—loyalty to the brotherhood above all, yes? He is our brother, even though none of us have ever seen or spoken to him. Loyalty, in this case, demands that we disobey his wish to handle this by himself. He did not let any of us deal with our demons alone. He will not, either."

"Nicolai," a woman's voice says—soft and quiet and accented—again, I can't place it, but that is not surprising, I suppose. "My love."

Nico's face positively melts at the sound of her voice. He answers in...who knows—some other language. God, I feel like an ignorant American around this man, who speaks a dozen languages better than I speak one.

They exchange words for a few minutes, and then there's a sense of farewell in the way he speaks, in the lingering softness in his eyes before his expression hardens once more.

Sophia's voice returns. "I thought you'd need a touch of home, Nico. Motivation, as it were."

"I did, indeed, Sophia. You are most thoughtful." A pause. "I will send coordinates, but our current location is outside of Rochester, New York, heading southwest."

Another hard, powerful male voice comes through the phone. "We got the jet spoolin' up, Nico. Be there just as fast as that fucker can go."

Another, different voice. "Try not to have all the fun without us, would you?"

"Wait!" This is a female voice, again, not the same as Sophia or Nico's wife or whatever she is to him. "Brys?"

I take the phone. "Yes, hi, this is Brys."

A giggle—several giggles. "We have a question we're hoping you can answer."

"Girls." Sophia's voice, scolding. "Not the time."

"Oh, hush, you. The men are still getting all their guns together. We have a second, right, Nico?"

"A moment or two, yes. We are driving, and they are not showing signs of stopping anytime soon. Ask your question." He looks at me. "It will likely be rather invasively personal."

"Would I ask an invasively personal question, Nico?"

He snorts. "Yes, Terra, you would."

"Fine, I would. But she's one of us now, so she's gotta get used to our ways."

One of them?

"Um?" I say. "I'm not sure I qualify as one of you."

"You hooked up with the mysterious Boss-Man. We wanna know what he's like."

"I—" Not wanting to lie, but also not wanting to betray Jakob's confidence, since he seems like a very, very, *very* private person, I hesitate as to how to answer. "I wouldn't say we hooked up," I say, eventually. "Terra, is it?"

"Yep, that's me!" She's chipper, energetic, with a thick Boston twang. "Nosy ass bitch extraordinaire."

"I don't know him well—we met under extreme duress, and it has only been a matter of days. But I can say pretty confidently that he is a private person. I do not feel comfortable discussing those kinds of personal details… especially over the phone with someone I've never met."

"I mean, I ain't askin for dick pics or a description of how he fucks. None of us but Sophia has ever even laid eyes on him. We only heard his name for the first time a few days ago. We're curious. You met him. You gotta give us *something*. Please."

"I have spoken to him," a new male voice says, this one accented as well—Spanish? Brazilian? "He is educated, intelligent, articulate, and insightful. He cares about Sophia very, very much—as a sister, he told me. He cares about all of us. He is also rather tall."

I snort a laugh. "He is all of that, yes. Including tall."

"This isn't enlightening at all," Terra says, annoyed. "No sordid details what-so-fuckin'-ever. You *suck*."

I laugh—I can't help it. "He is the best kisser I have ever met, and it's not even close."

Sophia clears her throat. "Terra."

"Soph?"

"You can interrogate Miss Bennett at a later date, although I have a feeling you will have limited success."

"Yeah, yeah. You're no fun." A sigh. "Fine. Brys, I can't wait to meet you. None of us know Jakob, but a man who can do all that he's done for the guys? He's gotta be quite a man."

Another woman's voice joins, now. "And a woman who can grab the attention of a man like that is our kinda gal."

There's a chorus of feminine agreement to her statement. How many of these people *are* there?

And why is Sophia assuming I'll even be around later to be interrogated?

"Keep your distance, Nico," yet another new male voice says, this one so deep, so powerful, and so...big...I wonder what the owner of the voice must look like. "Don't gotta tell you how dangerous fuckin' Pugli is. You know he doesn't go nowhere without a fuckin'...what's the word? Bunch of butt-lickers who follow him around like ducklings."

"Yes-men? Entourage? Retinue?" One of the other male voices chimes in. "Butt-lickers works for me, though."

"I was thinkin' retinue," Big Voice says. "Cuz I think that fucker thinks he's some kinda fuckin' king or some shit."

"Butt-lickers with fuck-off big guns, though, I'm guessin'."

"Nic? Any word on what kinda hardware these bastards are carrying?"

"Unknown for certain," Nicolae answers, "but assume at least some automatics and mainly sidearms."

"Armor?"

He looks at me. "The man who accosted you. Was he wearing a vest? Did he have a weapon other than his handgun?"

"No vest, and only the pistol. But pistol feels like a misnomer. That thing could have been featured in *The Guns of Navarone*."

"Referencing the deep cuts," someone says. "Knows poetry *and* classic films?"

"Sax, shut the fuck up. You don't know how to fuckin' read, you dumb lunk. And your idea of a classic film is fuckin'...*Ace Ventura*."

"'That's what turns me on about'cha,'" I quote, "'your attention to detail.'"

"Fuck me. She can quote *Ace Ventura*?

"Do you need a minute, Si? Some lotion? A Kleenex?"

I shoot a look at Nico, because I can't keep up with whatever the hell this banter is.

He just shrugs, grinning.

"Gentlemen, enough." I clear my throat into the silence. "My point is that the man who assaulted me was wielding a handgun the size of a howitzer. But he did not have a rifle or a bulletproof vest. But I *can* say that most of the *other* men who have been pursuing Jakob and me thus far have worn bulletproof vests and have been carrying machine guns. So, if it matters for preparation, I would prepare to fight off an army of well-armed and well-trained soldiers. They all had the air of former military, if not former special forces, such as yourselves."

"Sorry to be pedantic, Miss Bennet," this voice is new, again, and smooth, deep, rich, articulate. "But when you say machine guns?"

I sigh. "I don't know anything about guns, Mister…?"

"Solomon."

"I know less than nothing about guns, Solomon. They were not rifles in the sense of hunting rifles, or the kind of rifle my new friend Nicolae here used to kill that guy who was about to kill me. They had clips, straps that clipped to their vests, and they shot a lot of bullets very fast."

"Assault rifles," Solomon corrects. "Mags, and body armor. Assault rifles have magazines, and bulletproof vests aren't a thing. Bullet-*resistant*—"

"Sol, bruh, the lady don't need a terminology lesson, bud. Save it."

"Thank you, whoever you are," I say, humor in my voice.

"Name's Saxon. Sol is my older brother. The twit who thinks I don't appreciate classic films is our other brother, Silas."

"Pardon," Nico says, cutting in. "I hate to break up this very amusing exchange, but our quarry is slowing. We must be attentive, now."

"Go," Sophia says. "Stay out of sight until we arrive and can formulate a plan to end this shitshow once and for fucking all."

"Hear! Hear!"

"Amen to that!"

"Fuckin' right!"

"Byeseeyousoonnewbestie!" Terra says it all in a rush, too loud, as if she snatched the phone and yelled it into the microphone right before the call ended.

Once the call is over, Nico again removes the battery, tosses the SIM card out the window, and tosses the phone back into the cupholder.

"I have a question," I say.

Nico eyes me with a quirked eyebrow. "Yes?"

"If *that*," I point at the flip phone, "is what you use to make calls, and you discard the SIM and eject the battery after every call, then what's going on *there*?" I point at the smartphone in the holder clipped to the vent next to the steering wheel.

"Oh. Yes." He indicates the glove box. "There is a third-party wireless hotspot in there, providing Wi-Fi for that device. It does not have a SIM card, and thus cannot make or receive cellular calls, and therefore cannot be traced or triangulated."

"Geez. So you're a tech wizard special forces badass

who speaks a dozen languages, and, not for nothing, you're pretty damn attractive."

He shrugs. "I do what must be done. I have lived my entire life off-grid, as they call it. I am no tech wizard, but I do know my way around some technology. It isn't so impressive."

"Maybe not that, but the rest is."

"You are very kind, Miss Bennett."

"So, how many of you are there, anyway? I caught a few names, there—Sophia, Solomon, Silas, Saxon, and Terra."

"The full roster is: Rev and Myka, Chance and Annika, Kane and Anjalee, Silas and Naomi, Saxon and Terra, Solomon and Scarlett—Maria, now—myself and Tatiana, and Inez, or I should say Sophia, and Lorenzo."

I blink. "That's a big family."

He nods. "It is. We are very fortunate to have found each other."

"My next question is...what is Terra's deal? She's acting like it's a forgone conclusion that I'm gonna be... like...I dunno. I dunno! It's weird and presumptive, and I don't understand."

"You are part of a pattern. We get in trouble, go on the run, try not to die, meet someone who ends up being drawn into the situation, fall in love, and they then become part of the family."

"And she's assuming I'm next? Like me and Jakob are...?"

"Well, he *did* kiss you."

"Why was Sophia so surprised? She didn't seem to believe that he'd kissed me."

"I could not answer that, as I do not know. He is very,

very reclusive. If I had to guess, I would say that it's rather out of character for him. Which means you must be special to him, somehow. Perhaps in a way neither of you yet understands."

"Oh."

Special to him?

God, I wish. I wish I were special. I wish that what we'd shared was the beginning.

I know I shouldn't think that way. He doesn't want that. He can't give me that. He made that pretty clear.

Doesn't mean my heart doesn't want what it wants, anyway, though.

And my heart wants Jakob Kasparek. Or Caleb Indigo. I don't care what his name is. I just…

I want him.

It's stupid.

Dangerous.

Foolish.

And true.

Chapter 14

Check The Fucking Perimeter

JAKOB

LAUGHTER FEELS PARTICULARLY AND PERSONALLY insulting in this context.

Pugli's six goons sit around a tiny folding card table—gotten from who knows where—playing poker for bullets. They speak a rapid, overlapping mix of Bulgarian, Czech, Russian, and English, and it isn't immediately clear whether they all understand each other. There's a lot of yelling and cursing, which isn't unusual for these mercenary types, but it seems to me like there's a hint of tension between some of these guys. Rounded, lifted shoulders, narrowed eyes watching every movement, snapped answers, a folded hand tossed down a little too angrily.

Makes me wonder if I can use the tension to my advantage.

Pugli is always on the phone; he has three of them—one in his right hip pocket, one in his back left pocket, and one in the inside right pocket of his suit coat; he speaks English into the first, French into the second, and a pidgin of French, English, and Bulgarian into the third; despite his name, I've never heard him speak Italian. I'm not sure what any of it is all about, though, as he tends to wander while talking on the phone, pacing, gesturing angrily, rarely listening for more than thirty seconds at a time before interrupting with commands or questions.

We are, in a rather humorously clichéd turn of events, camped out in an abandoned, dilapidated, dripping old manufacturing facility in the middle of a field in the middle of nowhere. There's nothing but open fields in every direction as far as the eye can see, rolling hills, and the occasional stand of trees. We bounced along a rutted two-track for miles, approaching the facility from the rear; a cracking, crumbling asphalt road leads away from the facility, weeds growing up from the cracks, dislodging chunks of asphalt.

Let me tell you, that was the most painful car ride of my life.

Now, I'm tied to a metal folding chair, watching Pugli's goons suck at poker. When we first arrived, I was in remarkably bad shape. Losing blood, weak, and incoherent. Unfaked, also. A battered old F-150 arrived a few minutes after we did, the bed capped by a veterinarian's mobile clinic insert. A tiny, wiry old woman climbed down from the cab, her hair a chaotic silver bottle-brush exploding in every conceivable direction. She wore coke-bottle glasses that made her eyes look enormous.

When we pulled into the huge, drip-echoing building, I'd been unceremoniously dumped onto the dirty concrete floor and left there to soak in my own blood as it oozed through the makeshift bandage these hacks had slapped on. When she arrived, the old vet had tsked in disapproval, snapping something in Bulgarian—I recognize the language and know a few words, but I do not speak it or understand it. They'd found a tarp from somewhere and rolled me onto it, and she'd set about tending to my wounds, muttering to herself under her breath as she tilted me onto my side to examine the exit wound, then let me flop painfully back down…only to shove her blue rubber-gloved finger into the entrance hole and wiggling it around. Which felt personal. Like a violation of some sort.

"Very lucky," she'd grumbled, half to me, half to herself, almost but not quite under her cigarette-stinking breath. "Is what we call a soft tissue wound, no bone or organs hurt. Right through, no damage. Very painful, but okay."

"Lovely," I'd muttered. "Doesn't feel okay."

"Getting shot will never tickle, big man. I am only paid to make sure you do not die yet."

"Yet," I'd snorted.

She had only shrugged one thin shoulder. "He pay me very well for come see to you." Her accent was thick, but her English was excellent. "Is not a hard choice: make money or watch a video of your favorite cousin in Bulgaria get shot in the head. Is easy, hmm? I am sorry to you. But I do what I must do."

"I…" I had trailed off with a groan as she had indicated for the goons to tilt me onto my side while she stapled my exit wound shut, irrigated it, applied a salve, and taped a clean bandage over it. "Fuck me, ouch. I do not blame you, doctor. I understand how Pugli operates."

She did not staple or suture the entry wound, only cleaned it out and applied the same salve and a clean bandage. "You will be fine. Movement will cause discomfort for quite some time, but so long as you are cautious, you are in no danger."

"Assuming I survive him," I tilt my head toward Pugli, "How long till I'm back to normal?"

"Easy and gentle movements within two weeks. Three months as a rule for total healing."

"Treat a lot of gunshot wounds as a vet, do you?"

She rolled her eyes at me. "I was a medic in Kosovo. Now I treat animals. They do not curse me for saving them. People are ungrateful."

"Well, I am grateful," I said. "Thank you."

She'd snorted. "I am afraid if he has his way, I have fixed you only so that he may kill you later."

"I am aware," I said. "But he has his plans, and I have mine."

She'd nodded as if I'd said something particularly sage. "Do not we all have our own plans, hmm?"

She'd tossed a glance over her shoulder: the goons were engaged in a shouting match over what sounded like someone cheating, and Pugli was on the far end of the building having a conversation of whispered intensity in rapid-fire French.

"I was a doctor of people first," she said. "I took the Hippocratic Oath, which means honor demands I must help you. I can do nothing about his intentions for you, and I do not have to like any of this, but I cannot let my cousin die. What can I do, hmm?"

"I understand. Really. Pugli is a master of manipulating situations to his advantage. You are doing all you can."

Another shrug. "Perhaps." Another surreptitious look around, and then she presses a pill against my lips. "Here. Swallow. For the pain."

I press my lips together. "I was a heroin addict, many years ago. I do not like opiates."

"I only can offer you acetaminophen, then, which will help only a small amount."

"Better than nothing and better than a relapse. It is unlikely, I admit, but I refuse to take that chance."

"With such things, the pain is a better demon to face." She pressed several med kit-sized packages into my hand. "Every few hours."

"Thank you, doctor."

"Do not thank me." She pressed something else into my hand. "My card. If you should need further...repairs, on a cash basis. You understand?"

"Yes." A pause. "Your name?"

"Doctor Petra Georgieva."

"I am Jakob."

A glance at Pugli had her features hardening; she gathered her things and rose to her feet, accepting a thick envelope from Pugli before departing.

Once she was gone, they had—-again, none too gently—wrestled me onto a folding chair, zip-tying my wrists and ankles to the chair in such a way that I am unable to move. I had managed to vanish the card and Tylenol into a hip pocket before they bound me to the chair. How I'm going to get a hand loose to take the meds, I'm not sure.

That's a problem for later.

For now, the problem facing me is the pounding agony rippling through my torso. For "just a soft tissue wound," it hurts like a bitch.

Throbbing, throbbing, throbbing. The blood loss has me dizzy and weak. The pain is making me nauseated and, frankly, angry. The more time that passes, the angrier I get.

The goons play cards. Pugli paces and jabbers on his three cell phones. I suffer.

An hour passes. Two.

Finally, irritability replaces prudence.

"Jesus fucking Christ," I snarl, throwing my weight to make the chair jump and slam against the floor with a crash, drawing attention. "Are we just going to fucking *sit* here? If you're not going to kill me, then let me go. But one way or another, stop wasting my *goddamn time*!" I lift and slam again, and discover that the action causes the zip ties to shift and twist, which means I might be able to wrench them hard enough to snap. "I am not a patient man. Make a move."

Pugli, across the building, ends his call and strides over to me with the slow ambling pace of a man seeking to make a point by appearing laconic. It is an utterly transparent ploy. He produces a Walther PPK from under his jacket and presses the barrel to my forehead. "I would not be in such a hurry to die, Caleb Indigo. Your death is on its way. I would enjoy these last minutes of life."

I feign indifference—I do not want to die. Not yet, at least. Not until I'm sure it will have value, until I'm sure my death will serve its intended purpose.

"Enjoy what? The amazing view?"

Pugli sighs as if I am particularly stupid and he has no more patience for it. "Being alive. Drawing breath. It is a privilege I shall soon withdraw." The man's hubris is breathtaking.

I decline to answer, because there's no point.

Pugli glances at one of his hench-goons. "Check the perimeter."

The man frowns, blinking. "Um, but boss, is all open. No perimeter. Is why we pick this location?"

Pugli's face betrays a glimpse of a simmering rage bubbling away just beneath the surface. "Go out and fucking *look* with your fucking *eyes*. When Lash comes, location will not matter. *Go out* and *look*! All of you!" He gestures with the pistol at the gathered mercs. "Spread out. You cannot underestimate the danger our enemy presents."

Hmmm. Now *that* is an interesting statement. And what it tells me is that Pugli is scared shitless of Nico.

Which is valid. I would be too, if he weren't on my side. And I might be a little afraid of him anyway, even though he is on my side.

"Yeah, best go keep watch." I jut my chin at one of the hench-goons—the one who was winning all the hands. "He was cheating anyway. He's got an ace up his sleeve."

My comment has the intended effect—instead of dispersing to do Pugli's bidding, they devolve into a nasty, loud, and rapidly escalating argument. Pugli attempts to calm them, but they ignore him entirely, and it swiftly turns into a physical altercation. I watch with unrestrained glee as fists are thrown, noses are head-butted, guts are slugged, and jaws are elbowed. Pugli, trying to break it up, has his nose bloodied, which has the delightful effect of ruining his custom-tailored suit.

BAM!

The cheater staggers backward from the scrum, clutching his belly. Another goon swaggers after him, grabs his right wrist, and yanks at his sleeve. Vindicating me, not one but several cards flutter to the floor.

Cheater drops to his knees, blood seeping from his belly. The one who shot him, his pistol still in hand, scoops up the cards, finds the ace, slaps it against Cheater's forehead…and blows his brains out from point-blank range, sending the bullet through the center of the spade on the card.

Pugli, predictably, loses his shit, going on a tirade in

four languages, most of it incoherent French, sprinkled liberally with "fuck" in English.

By the time he runs out of steam, I'm cackling out loud—or rather, trying not to because it hurts worse than actually getting shot did; that felt like a giant fist slugging me in the stomach, knocking me backward and smashing the breath out of me. The real pain didn't come till a bit later, after the initial shock wore off.

He stomps to me, face a rictus of hate, all of his megalomaniacal calm erased. "You! You fucking—" and here he trails off into more incoherent French cursing and ranting.

"What?" I ask, innocent as you please. "He was cheating. I watched him."

Pugli's left eye twitches, and a vein in his forehead pulses. If we're lucky, he'll just have a heart attack or an aneurysm and just drop dead right here.

"Any pain in your left arm?" I ask, hopeful. "Shortness of breath? Numbness or tingling in your fingers?"

"What?" he asks, puzzled. "No. What are you on about?"

"Oh, I was just hoping you were having a medical emergency. That vein on your forehead is really going crazy."

I must be delirious from blood loss. It's the only explanation for my behavior. I have not spoken so casually in my entire life. My tutor punished me mercilessly for speaking—in any language—like a "plebeian peasant." My family is ancient, you see, on both sides; I descend from a long line of wealthy, landowning merchants on my father's side and from the tribe of Levi on my mother's. Thus, I was expected to comport myself as such. Which meant speaking with eloquence, elocution, and elegance.

He snarls at me wordlessly, whirling away. "Take care of him," he gestures at the dead man. "Then, if you please—*CHECK THE FUCKING PERIMETER*."

Two of the goons drag the dead man out of the building by his arms, leaving a gory smearing trail in his wake.

They drag open the large double sliding doors at one end of the facility—we're in what was the warehouse section, where goods were once stored.

Daylight lances into the dim, echoing space in a widening slice. They drag the corpse out into the sunlight.

Two steps.

Three.

And then all hell breaks loose.

Chapter 15

A Hill to Die On

BRYS

NICOLAI AND I HAVE SPENT THE LAST SEVERAL hours bored out of our minds.

Pugli left the freeway and cut an hour and a half into the countryside, and then another twenty minutes rattling to pieces down a two-track trail over swelling hills and down into gently sloping valleys before we crested one last hill and spied our target: a massive, sprawling manufacturing plant in the end stages of dilapidation surrounded by endless acres of yellowing, waist-high grass.

"Fucking Pugli," Nico had snarled, letting the truck roll back down from the hill so we aren't skylined, although the plant is a half-mile away at least. "No cover. An old building with basements and subbasements and all kinds of places to hide. The evil bastard is too damned smart."

"So...now what?" I asked.

He shrugs. "Reconnaissance. A fancy word for sneaking and watching and being very bored."

"What can I do?"

He eyed me. "A good question. What *can* you do?"

"Well, I have zero military training or experience, and I've never shot a gun, but I'm coordinated and not a total moron. And I've seen heads blown off already and made it through that, so..."

Nico smirked. "More than most can say." He stared out the window for a few moments, thinking. Then, he looked at me again, serious and steady. "You will not be content to remain here, I assume."

"Not a chance, buckaroo. That man down there..." I shake my head, unsure of what I was even going to say, only that sitting in this truck doing nothing was not an option. "No. Whatever happens, I'm a part of it. I'm not, like, jonesing to shoot anyone, but I will if it puts an end to this once and for all. For him," I gestured toward the building where Jakob was being held. "And for you. So I'll do what has to be done."

Nico had nodded. "Very well. Allow me a few minutes to conduct initial reconnaissance and formulate a plan. I shall return." He patted my hand. "I am only looking and thinking. And we cannot assault them on our own anyway—we must wait for the others."

"How long will it take them to get here?"

He grinned. "Oh, not as long as you are thinking. Jakob has access to some rather fascinating aeronautical technology."

"Meaning?"

"Meaning a Roth jet."

My mind had wobbled a bit—those are the most expensive private aircraft on the planet, and beyond mere expense, they only make a handful every year, so they are nearly impossible to get ahold of, even if you could afford one.

"Oh."

"An experimental, unreleased Roth jet."

"That's..." I trailed off, at a loss.

Nico shrugs. "That's the boss. He can do things, find information, find people, and procure things that should be impossible. And it is not merely a matter of money, either. Money cannot buy everything."

"It's still weird to me that you work for a man you've never met," I said.

He shrugged. "Loyalty is a strange thing." Another pat on my hand. "Now. Stay here, if you please. We do not know if they have patrols. I think not, but it is best to be safe. I shall return in a few minutes."

He had left, sniper rifle on one shoulder, walking parallel to the ridgeline, just below the crest.

A few minutes became ten, then thirty, and then he finally returned. "I bear good tidings, Miss Bennett. I know where he is being held, and I have seen him. They had what appeared to be a veterinarian attend to his wound."

"Why would they do that?" I asked.

"If he died of blood loss before he could be of any use as bait, the entire effort of obtaining him and transporting him here would be wasted, and Pugli would not have any leverage to draw me in."

"You must have some serious dirt on the man."

He nodded. "Oh, I do. Or I did. I turned it over to a German military intelligence officer who was—is—part of a multi-country, multi-agency task force investigating Roberto Pugli."

"So...did it help? Your evidence?"

He shrugged. "I do not know. The wheels of justice grind ever so slowly, internationally especially so."

"And you're not content to wait for legal justice to be meted out," I guessed.

His eyes glitter like chips of obsidian. "No. There can be no justice. Mere death is not justice, no matter how slow, agonizing, and protracted it may be. Torture is not justice." A shake of his head. "No, there is no justice for his crimes. But removing him from this earth with my own two hands is the closest thing to closure I will ever get."

"Revenge, eh?"

"*No.*" His tone is intense. "Not revenge. The man forced my eyes open and burned my wife and infant twin children alive in front of me. Killing him is not revenge. Revenge would be dissecting his grandchildren while he watches. Revenge would be carving apart his wife. Revenge would be making him watch as I dissolved his daughter in a vat of acid."

"Jesus fucking Christ, Nicolae," I whisper, stomach twisting.

"No. I do not wish for revenge. His wife and family are innocent. He must pay for his crimes, and..." he ducked his head, gathering himself. "I will not find peace in this life until he is dead, and the only way I can know for sure that he is truly dead is if I put the blade into his heart myself."

"I suppose that makes sense."

"I would never and have never done those awful things to anyone, Miss Bennet. I was making a point."

I nodded. "I know. I...well, it's tempting to say I understand, but I know I can't. I just...I understand that you were making a point."

He looked away. "I am a killer, make no mistake, but I only deal death to armed combatants, never unarmed innocents, and never women or children." A pause, a tilt of his head. "If a woman were attempting to kill me, I would protect myself, however."

"I think that's fair."

We spent the next few hours talking. He told me the long, fascinating, and wildly improbable tale of how he met Tatiana, his lover. I'm not sure of their marital status, and it doesn't feel like my business to ask. He gave me the loose outlines of the others' stories, but he insisted the real telling belonged to those involved. It all just sounded so…crazy. Treks across the Brazilian rainforest, gunfights, blown-up drug palaces, midnight rescues, everything was just so intense.

Yet, that phone call was still replaying in my mind. They cared about each other. They were a family—a real, true family. They teased, joked, and poked fun, but it was obviously all in good humor.

I don't have that.

I've never had that.

I've always been Brys Bennett, Lawrence Bennett's only child, heir to the BDI throne and fortune. In the world of Manhattan's wealthy business elite, I was royalty. My friends were chosen by my mother when I was young. My schools were the best prep schools. Everything was just so.

And then Mom died, and I was The Sad Girl. I was the kid whose mom died. No one knew how to talk to me. I had no friends—I am not a naturally outgoing person. I'm quick-tempered, sarcastic, and can be kind of mean sometimes. That doesn't make you a lot of friends. I was part of the cool clique in the silver spoon academy I went to for high school but only because my dad was Larry Bennet and funded the PTO for a year with a single check, and we lived a block from the school and had a pool with a slide, a movie theater, and a pantry full of every kind of snack food and junk food you could think of.

I suppose all that isolation and friendlessness only intensified my...prickly personality.

The shit that happened to me my senior year at Yale is why I'm unable to trust anyone. But we're not going there, not even in the confines of my own mind. I have never spoken of it. To anyone. Ever. I doubt I ever will.

How could I? How do you put a nightmare into words?

Nicolae did, and rather succinctly at that. So it can be done, I suppose.

A strange noise fills the air; Nico and I are lounging in the truck bed, talking occasionally, and waiting. I have always been comfortable with silence, so sitting in my own thoughts is no hardship, and Nico seems to have plenty of his own thoughts to occupy him, so much of the waiting is passed in oddly companionable silence. Now, the silence is broken by the strange noise—a kind of low, quiet, dense roaring.

"What is *that*?" I ask, sitting up.

"The jet," he answers. "My people." He pointed at a dot on the horizon, low and moving fast.

Really, really fast. Like, it's a dot one second, and then I blink, and it's recognizably an aircraft, and then it's flaring like a helicopter fifty feet above the ground and descending for a landing. The noise of the jet engines is...dispersed, somehow. I don't know how to put it. We're not that far away, but the sound seems...muted. Scattered. I doubt the people in the building on the other side of the hill will hear it at all, or if they do, it will be unrecognizable for what it is.

"Some kind of proprietary technology," Nico says, answering the question that must be on my face. "Apparently, even the US military-industrial complex does not know how Roth has managed that trick with the engine signature, and he is neither telling nor selling."

"It's incredible. The sound is *there,* but…" I shrug, at a loss for words, "dispersed, somehow."

"It is. And very useful." He slides to his feet and rolls his shoulders, twists to stretch his broad back. "Ah, and here is the crew."

I watch them approach, and at first I wonder if my eyes are playing tricks on me, or if there is some weird perspective thing going on, because the one guy looks like he's…

Oh, no. He's just that big.

Jesus.

These guys are…

Jesus.

I sit down, rather involuntarily, onto the truck bed's gate. There are eight figures approaching, each one dressed in black fatigues and body armor—bullet-*resistant* vests, I suppose. They're armed to the teeth, all of them.

And they're fucking hot as hell, each one of them.

Including the two women. I'm straight, but I can recognize a gorgeous woman, and these two are goddamned stunning.

The men, now. The men.

Whoo, boy. The men.

Where to start?

The tall brown-skinned god with the short mohawk? The shorter powerhouse with the badass blond beard? The seven-foot-tall Polynesian behemoth? The Brazilian beefcake? The brothers who could be triplets, each of them hotter than the last, regardless of which order you put them in?

I need a fan. Or a cold plunge.

"This is ridiculous," I mutter. "Do you guys have a calendar?"

Nicolae frowns at me. "A calendar? Why would we need a calendar? I do not understand your question, I am afraid."

I snicker. "No, like...the firefighter calendar? They do them to raise money? The firefighters get their photos taken in various states of undress, like only wearing turnout pants or with a helmet covering their junk." I feel myself going red in the face. "Never mind. Forget I said anything."

Nico is grinning as he swaggers to meet his brethren, exchanging back-slapping hugs with the men and gentler, "she's one of the guys, but she's a girl" hugs with the women. "Miss Bennett was wondering when we are going to do a sexy calendar."

I blush so hard you could fry eggs on my cheeks. "Traitor."

One of the brothers—he bears a wicked scar on his face—raises his arms and flexes like he's competing against Columbo and Schwarzenegger. "I'm down. That shit would sell like hot cakes. We could do a whole merch line. Like a li'l gift shop. Plushy version of us."

The entire group turns to stare at him.

"You're a real dumbfuck, you know that, Sax?" This is one of the other brothers—a Robert Redford look-alike. "That's the stupidest fucking thing I've ever heard. Do you ever stop and think before you open your fuck-tarded mouth?"

"That's offensive, Sol," the behemoth says—Big Voice. "Can't say shit like that."

"What? Fuck-tarded? What's wrong with it? It's not the R-word."

"It's close enough. No." Behemoth Big Voice pronounces "no" with a booming finality; the topic is closed.

Sol shrugs. "Whatever. Fine. But if anyone deserves to be called a fuck-tard, it's Saxon. And that's a hill I'll die on."

"Sol?" Big Voice's rumble is a warning.

"Alright, alright."

Saxon, when his brother turns his back to him, flips him off with both hands—the double bird also includes a hip-thrust. "*You're* a fuck-tard."

Big Voice turns on Saxon, now, then addresses the group at large. "Next person to say that word is gonna be pickin' their teeth outta their turds."

"Yeah, Sol," Saxon says, sticking out his tongue.

"Are you people ever serious?" I ask.

"No." This is from everyone, in unison.

"I see," I say. "Well, your boss may want you to, like, lock in a little so we can rescue him. Need I remind you, he's been *shot*?"

Solomon approaches me. "Brys Bennet, I'm Solomon Cabot." We shake hands, and he steps back and stands with his hand hooked in the neck of his vest. "I assure you, despite the shenanigans, we *are* taking this *very* seriously. Humor is how we cope. I promise you, the constant jokes don't mean we're not the best in the business at exactly this."

"I dunno, man," the short, stocky, bearded one says. "Alpha One does some damn fine rescue work. I wouldn't wanna tangle with those cats."

"I'll take us over them any day. They're all old now, anyway." This is from the brown-skinned one with the mohawk—a hairstyle I've rarely seen work, but on him, for some reason, it just looks badass.

"As fun as that theoretical matchup sounds," I interrupt, "can I get some introductions, or do I have to guess as to who is who?"

Nico stands beside me with a friendly hand on my shoulder; he points at each man as he names them. "Rev, Kane, Silas, Chance, Saxon, Solomon, and Lorenzo." He points at the women, next. "Scarlett—sorry, Maria, I am still getting used to that. And Sophia, also known as Inez."

"Nice to meet you all," I say, mentally repeating each name a few times, trying to pin the name to the face; I've never been good at remembering names, although I never forget a face.

"So, Nico, Brys." Solomon breaks the brief silence. "Sitrep."

Nico answers for us, obviously. "They are holed up in the south end of an abandoned manufacturing or bottling plant just under click over that ridge. There are six soldiers, plus Pugli, each of them armed with MP5s and sidearms."

Solomon frowns. "Only six? I don't like it."

I eye him. "Isn't that a good thing?"

"If you believe there's only six of them to our ten, then yes."

"Eleven," I correct. "Don't think I'm gonna be sitting in the truck twiddling my thumbs while you guys rescue Jakob."

Sol opens his mouth to argue, but a glance at Nico has him clicking his mouth closed again. "Fine. Just…follow orders, okay?"

I grin. "I'll try. That's not something I typically do very well with."

"What, taking orders?" he asks.

"Yeah," I answer. "I have a serious case of 'fuck authority.' "

"I bet that goes over well with Jakob," Sophia/Inez says. "That man has one setting—command."

"It has been a point of contention between us a few times, yes," I say, trying to keep the blush off my cheeks.

Sophia's eyes narrow at me; she knows. Shit. I don't know how, but she knows. She approaches me, scrutinizing me closely. "You and I are going to have to find time to speak in private."

I scrutinize right back. "Oh?"

Her eyes are dark and hard and cold, and the stare she gives me is icy and venomous and threatening. I bet it makes lesser mortals—namely, men—quake in their boots. I'm stepping on her territory, I think, somehow. I doubt she and Jakob are or ever have been a thing, and I know she's with the Brazilian hottie who has yet to speak. But I still get the sense that she doesn't like the fact that I'm encroaching on what she considers her territory.

I hold her gaze without flinching or looking away, and give her my own Ice Queen stare-down.

Saxon steps between us, pushing us away from each other as if we were moments from coming to blows. "Okay, okay, ladies. Enough of that. Keep staring at each other like that, and you're gonna start a nuclear winter or somethin'."

Lorenzo pulls Sophia aside, murmuring in her ear in Spanish or Portuguese or both, and Nico pulls me aside as well.

"She was his first...project," he says to me. "She cares about him quite intensely, in a platonic sort of way. Also, I should warn you, she is not someone you wish to get into a pissing contest with."

"Takes big brass ones to get into a staring contest with La Víbora," I hear someone mutter—I don't see who said it, however.

"La Víbora?" I ask, loudly.

Sophia/Inez whirls out of Lorenzo's embrace. "I am *not* her anymore," she snaps. "All those stupid names. No more. Please. No more."

"I feel like there's a backstory I'm missing here," I say.

Her gaze is droll when she turns it on me. "You don't say."

"Well, how am I supposed to know? Nico told me his story, but yours are yours to tell, not his."

Her gaze softens. "True." Her eyes shut, and she seems to soften, just a touch. "You are right. I apologize. I just...I am worried for Jakob."

"As am I."

She exhales slowly, eyes closed, chin to chest, and then straightens and meets my gaze. "We want the same thing, here, Brys. It's just...Jakob is..."

I take one of her hands and squeeze. "I know. I mean, I think I can fathom, at least. Almost three days in extremely close quarters, going through trauma together, you learn a lot about a person in a short time." There's a short silence, and then literally everyone bursts out laughing, leaving me more puzzled than ever. "What did I say that was so funny?"

Nico pats my shoulder. "You have just succinctly summarized how literally everyone here met their lover."

"Dude, no. Lover just sounds weird." Saxon is frowning like he tasted something sour.

"Perhaps," Nico replies, "but even though Tatiana is not my legal wife, to call her my girlfriend feels insufficiently adult and serious. It is more than that. For all of us, no? What other term applies? Significant other? Partner?"

Saxon's frown only deepens. "No, you're right, but…I dunno, man. Lover just feels weird and wrong in my head for reasons I can't explain."

Solomon snaps his fingers several times and hisses. "Shut up! Everyone shut up!"

He creeps up the ridge, lies down on the crest, and remains motionless, watching and listening. After a full minute, he slithers back down and gets to his feet.

"There's an argument down there. Big time. Shouting, fighting. This is our moment." He points while snapping out orders, and everyone listens without question; this guy is the leader, then. "Chance, Rev, Kane, close in from the east. Stay low. Nico, Silas, Brys, you're overwatch from the ridge. Maria, Inez, Saxon, and I will take the frontal assault." He stares at everyone in turn. "This is it, folks. No prisoners. No fucking games. Pugli dies, here and now." He looks at Nico. "I know you want to be the one to end him, Nic, but if any of us has a shot, we gotta take it. We can't risk him getting away again."

Nicolae nods. "I agree. If anyone has a shot, take it. End him. His death is all that matters."

Sol claps his hands once. "Move out."

I find myself clutching a handgun in two shaking hands, jogging between Nico and Silas, who both carry rifles—Nico's is the sniper kind, while Silas's is an assault rifle.

I glance back at the place where we were all gathered just moments ago, but it's empty. Everyone is gone as if they were never here.

My heart pounds in my chest as I jog after Nico as he follows the ridge, angling south.

A few minutes later, I'm gasping and sweating as Nico bellies down on the ridge crest with his rifle. Silas goes prone beside him and sets up a weird-looking scope-thing, and the two men mutter to each other. They're speaking English, but it's gibberish to me—windage, drop, this many meters, stuff like that.

Silas glances at me. "Your job is to make sure no one sneaks up on us. Pugli is a crafty, sneaky motherfucker. We know this is a trap, but we don't know what's gonna happen when we spring it. So just be ready for anything and keep your eyes peeled."

"I hate that phrase," I mutter. "How does one peel their eyes? And why does that mean 'keep a sharp lookout?"

Silas frowns, thinking. "Huh. Never thought about that. I dunno, to be honest."

"It matters not," Nico says. "Focus. Brys, just keep watch in all directions. If you see anything amiss whatsoever, speak up immediately. It does not do to underestimate our enemy."

There's a distant report of a gunshot, then.

"Who fired?" Silas demands. "Report in."

"That was from inside the plant," Nico answers. "Assault teams, hold position."

I'm in a position to see shapes moving through the grass—dark figures in waist-high grass. At Nico's command, every figure vanishes, dropping to their bellies a few hundred yards away from the target.

There's another gunshot report, carried with a faint rolling echo over the hills.

"What do you want to bet those shots are the work of Boss, somehow?" Silas mutters to Nico.

"I am not a betting man," Nico answers, "But I suspect you are correct."

"He is exactly that infuriating, so I'm with the two of you," I say.

Silas cuts a glare at me, as if I'd denigrated his mother.

I can only laugh. "You guys are sure protective of someone you've never laid eyes on."

Nico sighs. "You act as if that is the strangest thing you've ever heard."

"It is!" I answer. "You didn't even know his real name until a few days ago, you said. Yet he's responsible for your lives? It's weird!"

Silas frowns at me. "You need to stop making so much sense. It's confusing me."

I snort at that. "Sorry, no can do." I point at the target. "Now focus on your little scope thingy."

"It's a spotter's scope," Silas says. "It's for—"

"I don't care," I say—well, snap. "Just get to work. Whatever is going on down there is the distraction we need."

"Yes, ma'am," Silas growls. "Not one, not two, but *three* hard-ass bitches giving us orders."

"Excuse me?" I snap. "Bitches?"

"He means it as a compliment," Nico cuts in.

"Do I, though?" Silas mutters, just loud enough for me to hear.

"If you value your testicles," I mutter back, "then yes, you do."

The shapes in the grass have continued moving, creeping through the waving stalks from two directions.

Nico presses a finger to his ear—listening to the voice in his earpiece, I assume.

"Movement spotted," Silas growls. "Doors are opening."

"Down, down, down," Nico snaps. "Tangos are moving. Hold position."

Again, the shapes in the grass drop. Nicolae's entire body language shifts, tension dropping away from his shoulders as he exhales slowly, nuzzling his eyes to the scope, adjusting his grip on the weapon, and wriggling his body into a better position.

"Two spotted," he mutters. "Dragging a deceased third ...yes, I have eyes on Jakob. He is bound to a chair in the middle of the space. Pugli is near him...No, I have a narrow field of vision. The door is only open a few feet." He listens. "I should be able to, yes. Give me a second. Silas, range?"

"Eight hundred and...twenty-three meters," Silas answers, and then gives another number—windage; and another—drop. I don't know what any of that means.

Nico adjusts something on his scope as Silas reads off the data, and then mutters again. "Ready. On your mark." I watch him curl his finger around the trigger.

"Mark."

CRACK!

"One away."

The report jolts me, a sharp boom that rolls across the landscape like thunder; a figure standing just outside the plant jerks backward and topples over.

CRACK! Another report from Nico's rifle.

"Shit. Miss," Silas mutters. "He moved." Then, louder, intense. "He's on the move! Running!"

There's another boom, but this one doesn't sound like a gunshot, although I'm far from an expert.

"Ohhhh...*fuck* me!" Silas snarls. "He hit a mine! Fuck me, he's in pieces. Jesus."

"All hold!" Nico shouts into his microphone. "The field is mined. Hold, hold, hold! Repeat, the field is *mined*."

"There's the twist," Silas says to Nico. "You know there was one coming."

"How—" I swallow hard over my tightening throat. "Now what? If the field has mines in it and his own goons don't know where they are, then how are our guys supposed to get closer?"

"Exactly the problem," Silas answers without looking at me. "We have no idea how many mines there are or where they are. It's a miracle none of our people stepped on one. But they have to stay where they are or risk ending up in pieces like that poor bastard." He chuckles—it's a dark sound. "I mean fuck, the dude's legs went one way and his upper half another."

"Thanks for that vivid description, Silas," I murmur.

"Welcome," he answers.

That's when an overlapping barrage of gunfire erupts from the plant, answered by our guys in the grass.

The only problem is that the bad guys have cover, and ours do not.

And just like that, things have gotten seriously complicated.

Chapter 16

Delirium

JAKOB

I WATCH THE WHOLE THING UNFOLD FROM THE CHAIR I'm tied to.

I hear the rifle report a half-second after the guy's head explodes. The second goon takes off running—into the field, for some reason, rather than back into the relative safety of the building. Panic makes you do stupid things, I suppose.

He takes off sprinting for who knows where, but he only gets a dozen or so steps before an explosion crumps the air, rattling the building and making the dust on the floor underfoot jump. The goon is blown to literal pieces, his legs essentially disintegrating while his torso flies in another direction.

The other three henchman, in the process of heading for the door, stop and whirl on Pugli, snarling at him angrily, pointing at the pieces of their compatriot.

You neglected to tell us about the FUCKING MINES! I can imagine they're saying.

Pugli answers calmly, in English, once he's gotten them to stop shouting at him. "I may have forgotten to mention the mines, yes." Something in his eyes tells me he didn't forget anything. "But it's in our favor. They can't get any closer very soon, which means their greater numbers mean nothing." He points at the catwalk, a good twenty feet up, which goes right past the bank of windows a third of the way up the wall. "One of you up there, two of you at the doors. The mines are all outside, so as long as you stay in here, you will be fine."

I wonder about that, but stay silent. I watch one of the three remaining henchmen scramble up to the catwalk while the other two approach the open door from opposite angles.

Catwalk henchman opens fire; I hear the concussions of my team returning fire, their rounds stippling the ceiling with holes that stream narrow beams of daylight. Below, the other two are opening fire now, and receiving it turn.

Hands grab my shoulders, and something sharp and cold touches the skin behind my left ear. "Not a sound. Do not even breathe, Caleb Indigo." Pugli's voice is hot and close. "Did you feel hope, for a moment?"

The zip ties around my ankles snap free as he slices through them, but he doesn't free my wrists. "Up. To your feet."

I'm forced to keep my hands behind me, the chair dangling an inch above the ground, hanging from my wrists by the zip ties. I can walk, but it's awkward, and I'm certainly not going to be making a break for it like this, wounded or not.

Clever bastard.

Although…the chair might just stop a bullet. Something to think about. For now, his knife pricks the middle of my back between my shoulder blades. "See that door over there?" A free hand points over my shoulder, and I follow with my eyes.

In the dim recesses of the vacant, echoing warehouse, a door —a hint of silver gleaming in the gloom—leads deeper into the facility, which must cover tens of thousands of square feet. Once we're in there, all bets are off.

Shit.

The knife digs into my back, loosening a trickle of blood down my spine. "Walk. No sounds."

I should have known he'd have a better plan than… Whatever I thought he was going to do with six guys against my entire quiver of Arrows. The poor henchmen were nothing but a distraction.

I have to admire his cunning, even as it fucks things up.

I stagger into the shadows, the folded metal chair banging against my calves and heels at each step. Each time my foot hits the ground, my wounds jolt and scream in protest. I have no choice but to bear it in silence, however—Pugli wants me as bait and as a shield, but he'll drive that knife in just to make a point if he has to.

I'm just going to have to trust my arrows to find me and save me.

I hope Brys is somewhere safe, but if I've learned anything about her in our brief time together, it's that she never does what you'd expect. Which means she's likely out there with the guys, finding a way to be a part of this shitshow.

We reach the door, and Pugli leans past me and yanks it open. Behind us, the henchmen fire in short bursts, the reports overlapping and echoing and dopplering until it sounds like there's a hundred men out there instead of three.

I don't expect them to last long, but it'll be long enough for Pugli to get away with me.

I'm not even bleeding anymore, so it's not like I can leave a trail for them to follow.

Pugli shoves me through the door and lets it close behind us—quietly. We're plunged into darkness—my other senses take over for a moment. I hear dripping somewhere, louder now, a steady *plink...plink...plink...*; something scuttles underfoot, and I don't want to know what it was; I smell mold and rot and damp and mildew and dust and age. Things crunch underfoot with each step, and some of those things may have been moving when I stepped on them.

"Where is it?" I hear Pugli hiss to himself behind me, and then he curses in French. "Ah. There it is."

A spear of white light lances through the darkness, illuminating a narrow, seemingly endless tunnel writhing with pipes overhead. At each junction, the pipes leak, drip-drip-dripping onto the pitted concrete floor below.

The crunching underfoot is a carpet of dead insects, scuttling spiders of all sizes swarming in dozens, rats the size of chihuahuas bolting this way and that, and pausing to sit, hunched, and stare at us with beady, glowing eyes. Also, bones. Lots and lots of bones. Something uses this hallway as a depository for its kills. The rats? A snake? The spiders? A pack of feral cats?

When Pugli's beam flicks to life, the various living things vanish in an audible clatter of clicks and scuttling scrapes and angered chittering.

"Well, this is horrifying," I slur, dizzy and sluggish. "As far as first dates go, Robby-Bobby-Boy, this is not your best work."

There's a long pause, and then the knife-point pricks deeper, hitting bone with a sharp pang. "What on earth is wrong with you? Did you hit your head?" Pugli sounds legitimately puzzled.

"Aww, Robby-Bobby-Boy is concerned."

My head swims. My mouth seems to be operating on its own. Can blood loss make you loony? Or do I mean loopy? Loony or loopy? Loompy. Loonpy? I don't know.

"I was shot, Robert. *Shot.*" I sound strange. It's hard to make my legs work. I'm so tired. "I did not hit my head. I don't think."

"Walk."

"Poke me too hard in that spot, Robby-Bobby, and you might paralyze me." My brain wobbles. "That would be bad."

"What?"

"What?"

"You said something, but it wasn't English."

"I *said* that would be bad. Please do not paralyze me."

"That isn't what you said. It sounded like Czech."

Oh.

"Hmmm. Interesting." I shuffle forward, and he points the flashlight—one of those one-billion lumen super flashlights that can shine on the moon from earth—past me, which only serves to illuminate the crawling, scuttling horrors ahead.

"Why is that interesting?"

"Because I have not spoken Czech in...oh my. Decades. I thought I'd forgotten it all. Apparently not."

"Czech?"

"I was born in Prague, Robby-Bobby."

"You are delirious."

"Yes, I suppose I am. And whose fault is *that*, Robby-Bobby?"

"Stop calling me that. Just fucking walk, whoever you are."

I snicker. "Whoever I am. Oh, Roberto. You have never said such an accidentally and ironically accurate thing. Whoever I am. Do you know? No, you don't. You don't know who I am, Roberto. You're just...just an angry little boy with a big gun. Very silly."

My legs feel like tree trunks—wooden and inflexible. Each step hurts like a demon. My head is fuzzy, hazy, thick.

"You are far more palatable when you are not delirious. This version of you is immensely obnoxious."

I snicker again. "And whose fault is that, *Robert*?"

"You are going to drive me to murder just to get you to shut up."

"Is that not your plan anyway?"

"Timing, Caleb. Timing is everything."

"Caleb, Caleb, Caleb," I sing-song, unable to keep my mouth from its antics. "Caleb is dead. Caleb died in a car bomb ten years ago."

"Oh, come off it," he snaps, irritable. "You may have convinced the world, but you never fooled me."

"No," I admit. "I suppose not." I trip over a rat that doesn't seem inclined to move out of the way—oh, it's dead. Lovely. "How much longer is this hallway of horrors, anyway?"

Drip, drip, drip.

"Just keep walking."

The chatter of automatic gunfire is distant, a cacophony of echoing rattles and crackling. And then there's only one gun chattering and half a dozen answering, and then silence.

"Uh-ohhhh," I whisper. "Just us chickens, now."

"Silence, Indigo."

"Indigo," I echo. "An inspired choice, was it not?"

"*What* are you on about?" Pugli snaps.

"Indigo, Indigo, Indigo. Who is Indigo? Who was he? A captain of industry. And now? Digital ashes on the funeral pyre of obsession."

"You are mad."

"But poetically mad!" I exclaim, and then my legs give out.

My knees crush crumbling exoskeletons and old bones, and my trouser legs absorb whatever filthy liquid is on the floor.

"Damn it, man, on your fucking feet," Pugli snarls.

He transfers the flashlight to tuck it under one arm and yanks me roughly to my feet, then shoves me forward. "Walk."

"I am shot, Robert. *Shot*. Be reasonable. I have lost a *lot* of blood, you know. Also, wherever we are going, I do not want to go. I know I am dead, but I do not want to die."

The knife needles into my side. "Shut up and *walk*, damn you."

I stumble forward, dizzy and wobbly. "I'm trying, damn you."

"I will leave you here for the rats, if I must."

"That does not sound like an enjoyable plan. But then, I don't think my enjoyment is your primary intent."

"You are maddening."

"You are going to die, Robert. You know that, do you not?"

"Death comes to us all. You first. You and Lash."

"Cute. It's cute that you think you will win."

This time, the knife doesn't just dig, it sinks into flesh. I twist away and drop to my knees, groaning.

Pugli is beside me, and the knife edge is at my throat, either hot or cold at my Adam's apple. "I have had enough of your delirious ramblings, Caleb. I have plans for you, but they don't require your tongue. So please, keep talking." The flat of the knife blade rests on my lower lip. "I would quite enjoy cutting your tongue out of your fucking mouth."

"Mmmm," I hum, not daring to move my lips. "Mmm-hmm."

I hear something in the distance—voices. Familiar ones. To cover, I cough, lurch to my feet, and slap my soles noisily against the floor. Distract, distract.

Tricky when he's about to cut my tongue out.

It is only a slight exaggeration to trip and stumble from one side of the endless hallway to the other, careening off walls like a drunkard, and the groans of pain at each impact of my shoulder send agony lancing through my wounds.

It has the intended effect, though: Pugli snarling in annoyance, hurrying after me. "Stay on your damned feet, would you? Just walk."

"You..." I fight the fuzziness, and whatever I was going to say is forgotten.

"...ahead..." I hear an echo of a voice, and I slam into a wall again, and the chair Pugli has had me dragging around clangs and echoes in the narrow, low-ceilinged space.

"Did you hear that?" Pugli says, stopping behind me. "I heard someone speaking."

"The rats, perhaps? They are large enough. I saw one wearing robes, I believe. Perhaps it was Master Splinter." I hum the *Teenage Mutant Ninja Turtles* theme song.

He only snarls wordlessly.

Ahead, the darkness takes a different shape, a different quality—darker. Solid. A door. He yanks it open and shows me through. I stumble and hit the ground, rolling and landing on my back, the chair awkwardly and painfully stuck beneath me.

"Can we dispense with the damned chair?" I grumble.

Pugli is silent. And then the flashlight sweeps over me, illuminating yet another massive, echoing chamber. No drips here, and no light. The beam sweeps along a section of wall, and then stops on a door—a huge one, from the quick glimpse I got.

Pugli yanks me to my feet, shoves me forward a dozen or so steps, stops me, kicks the chair open, and slams down into it. Zip ties around my feet again, binding me to the chair once more.

I watch with curiosity as Pugli sweeps the light over old hunks of machinery, now long dead. Wires, cords, and cables lay tangled in serpentine knots. It lands on a gasoline generator—a new one. Pugli yanks the starter a few times, and then the machine rattles and chugs to life, and a lightbulb overhead flickers to life.

I'm on a pedestal of some sort. A giant hydraulic press? I look up: yes, I'm sitting inside a god-sized industrial hydraulic press.

This doesn't bode well.

Pugli locates the control panel—to which the

generator is connected—and presses a button. Above, the press grinds to life, lowering and lowering and lowering slowly, millimeter by millimeter.

Oh, that's nefarious.

But...

Voices and footsteps echo, nearer.

"It *was* them," Pugli says. "Tricky bastard. You heard them and were covering, weren't you?" A soft laugh. "No matter. All part of the plan, just a little sooner than expected."

The door slams open and beams of light sweep the space, land on me.

"Roberto Pugli," Solomon shouts at the front. "Hands up!"

He's standing behind me, not on the pedestal, which is just wide enough for the chair to rest upon. The knife is gone, replaced by that little Walther. "Ah-ah-ah, not another step, not another word." He gestures up. "You have a few moments at most."

I see the plan, and it is nefarious indeed. The press will crush me in another minute or two—it's descending slowly but inexorably closer to my skull. The generator powering it is behind us, so they can't just shoot it and stop the power. If they don't comply, I die. And they have a hard time limit to comply, or I die. And I assume the demand will be to trade Nico for me.

Devious bastard.

I see Inez putting it all together, too.

I see her dark eyes shining with worry, fear, fury. Behind her, the whole crew; lost in shadows.

"Lash." Pugli gestures with the barrel. "Gun on the ground, walk to me. Hands on your head."

Nico complies, eyes hard and glittering. When he's close enough, Pugli crabwalks toward him, grabs him by the arm, and yanks him backward so his back is to Pugli's front, shoving the gun against the back of his head.

"Finally, I have you." Pugli is triumphant. "Finally, you die."

A gun goes off.

CHAPTER 17

THE HALLWAY OF HORRORS

BRYS

NICO LEAPS TO HIS FEET, AS DOES SILAS. "Report!" Nico shouts. "What is happening?"

He listens, head ducked, eyes unfocused, and then snarls, yanking the earpiece out. "Comms are down. They cannot penetrate the facility." He's in motion, scrambling over the ridge

Silas grabs Nico's arm and pulls him back. "We're overwatch, Nico."

The glare Nico gives Silas could strip paint. "*He* is in there. Right now. Jakob is in there. Our people are in there. We do not know the situation within—the six I saw could have been a decoy to a much larger party."

"We'd hear gunfire, though." Silas looks at the huge building, squatting in the distance like a beetle's carcass.

"Silas. . . ." Nico shoulders his rifle with a sigh and a shake of his head, then tosses it to the ground and draws his pistol. "Stay if you wish and provide overwatch for no one. Pugli dies this day."

Before Silas can answer, Nico is jogging up the incline. By the time I reach the crest, he's flat out running down the hill toward the facility.

Silas sighs. "Fuck." He glances at me. "I don't like this."

"Who does?" I ask. "I'm not waiting around up here. I'll go nuts."

Silas and I follow Nico down the hill and through the grass—carefully following the trails left behind by the passage of the others through the minefield.

We reach the two-story sliding doors and enter: three bodies lie motionless in spreading pools of already-cooling blood. Silas flicks a switch on the barrel of his gun, and a beam of light engages from under the barrel. "Stay behind me."

"Yes, sir," I answer. "I am one hundred percent a-okay with you taking the lead."

He sweeps the massive space—roughly the dimensions of a football field, with a roof soaring at least three stories overhead. I can't even begin to guess what this place used to be.

"There." His beam fixes on a door, propped open by a chunk of concrete stuck through with a length of rusted rebar.

We reach the door, and what I see illuminated by Silas's beam of light will haunt my dreams for all eternity. Brain matter has nothing on that fucking hallway. Freddy Krueger himself would have nightmares about that hallway.

"Fuck. Fuck no." I shuffle backward. "Rats and spiders? No, no, no."

Silas whirls. "We don't have time for that shit, woman. C'mon. For Jakob, right?" He grabs my wrist and slaps it onto his shoulder. "Don't move that hand. You move when I move. Got it?"

"Got it." My voice is small and shaky. "Don't let the rats eat me. Please."

"Just hold onto my shoulder and don't look anywhere but your feet."

I manage this for a few minutes, but then I hear a chittering behind me and can't help but crane my head around. "They're following us, Silas," I breathe. "The rats."

Silas swings around, and his beam illuminates a brief but horrifying tableau: a swarming huddle of rats—dozens of them, maybe even hundreds—crawling all over each other, following in our wake. As the light hits them, they scatter with a chorus of squeaking protests.

A shudder of revulsion shivers down my spine. "Fuck, fuck, fuck."

We won't discuss the spiders.

Not the ones I see over Silas's shoulder, scuttling through the beam—if the rats are the size of dogs, then the spiders are the size of rats. I swear to god, I saw one that could moonlight as a Shelob impersonator.

We won't talk about the spiders that I feel crawling down my back, or the tick-tick-ticking of legs on my pant legs as they crawl up me. I keep one hand clawed into Silas's thick, hard shoulder, and with the other I brush constantly at my hair, my neck, my arms, my chest, my butt, my legs...I make contact multiple times, and I have to stifle a scream each time.

"It's for Jakob," I tell myself in a whisper. "It's for Jakob."

Why, though? I should have stayed up on that hill. Shit, I should have...I don't know. Done anything other than follow Nico into this horror movie labyrinth. Even for Jakob, this is...

Even for Jakob?

What does that mean?

I let my thoughts distract me as Silas creeps down the endless nightmare hallway.

Even Jakob?

He matters to me, I realize.

His eyes are sad. Lonely. It's only now, being apart from him with fresh memories riffling through my mind, that I understand. That I see the truth.

The control is armor. A weapon to keep the enemy at bay—and the enemy is…everyone. The whole world.

His mother died unexpectedly, and his father killed himself. That will leave life-long scars and trauma in its wake all on its own. But the last thing he said to me before he entered that house rings in my skull like a multiplying echo. *I was a victim of sex trafficking and forced into prostitution as a teenager.*

I can't imagine Jakob as a child, or even a teenage boy. I try to picture him gangly and lean and awkward, with his legs a little too long, skinny calves and wrists, and floppy black hair always in his eyes.

But then the image of gangly, teenage Jakob shifts, and I see him on a thin cot, waiting as someone enters. I see fear and resignation in his eyes as the shadow looms closer.

I know my imagination cannot come close to the horrors of his reality, but that alone is nauseating.

I can see how ultimate control over every aspect of his life would become paramount. Especially during sex.

I wonder what else he has endured that he hasn't told me about. I know he has more secrets—many of them. Dark ones.

If you were to know the truth of what manner of man I am, you would take your chances with the killers in there.

What does that mean? What could he have done that

was so awful? My mind flips from one horrible act to another, but I can't see him doing any of them. Despite the hardness in his eyes, despite the control, there is a core of goodness to him. Perhaps buried deep, but I've seen it. He has shown it to me.

He has shown it to these men and women.

Ironically, that's when Silas slows, and my attention is drawn forward past Silas—the whole crew is clustered together on this side of another door.

"Pugli is just ahead," I hear someone say.

"You know what's behind us?" I whisper. "A fuck-ton of rats so big I could ride them into battle."

"And yet," a woman's voice says—Inez/Sophia, "the largest rat of them all is on the other side of that door."

"Do we have a plan?" Nicolae says. "Or just go through and hope for the best? Either way, I am not waiting. I have not been this close to him since..." he trails off, growling a sigh.

"We have no idea what's on the other side of that door," Big Voice says—Chance. "Could be just Pugli and Boss, could be a whole fucking army, could be nothing at all."

Nico shoves through the crowd. "Enough delay."

Solomon grabs his hand before he can open the door. "No. Not like that. Be smart."

Nicolae growls, but stands aside. Solomon gestures at Saxon and Rev, who move up with him. Rev grabs the handle, standing so he can open it without standing in the opening. Saxon shifts his grip on his rifle, tucking the butt tighter against his shoulder, and nods at his brother. The two stand shoulder to shoulder for a beat, and then nod at Rev in unison. Rev twists the knob silently and then slowly eases the door open; a dim orange-yellow glow fills the widening gap.

Solomon peers through the opening from opposite Rev, seems satisfied he won't be filled with holes, and ghosts through the opening with Saxon on his heels; Rev follows Saxon and shifts to the side as soon as he's through.

Rev gestures for the rest of us to come through—Solomon kicks the door wide while flicking on the flashlight under his barrel. "Roberto Pugli! Hands up!"

I've always wondered why cops shout at criminals to stop when they clearly have no intention of doing so. Why waste your breath? Stop, stop! Right. Because *that's* ever worked.

And here, too—Solomon tells Pugli to put his hands up. But obviously, Pugli isn't going to do that. So why bother?

My brain fumbles off the tangent when I assess the situation in front of me.

Jakob is zip-tied to a folding chair, on a thick iron pedestal barely wide enough for the chair to fit on; above, a matching metal cylinder…which is descending. It's dim in here, but even in this low light, I can see that he's wan and pale, eyes heavy-lidded and heavy, forehead wrinkled in pain.

Pugli is standing behind Jakob with a gun pressed to the back of his skull as the cylinder above slowly grinds downward toward Jakob.

"Ah-ah-ah," Pugli says, "Not another step. Not another word." He gestures upward. "You have moments at most."

We all freeze.

"Lash." Pugli's voice is cold and ugly with hate. "Gun on the ground, walk to me. Hands on your head."

Nico sets his pistol on the ground and puts his hands on his head, stepping slowly through the cluster of killers.

Jakob groans.

Nico moves toward Pugli, and when he's within reach, Pugli snags him by the arm and shoves his gun against the back of his head while backing away.

"Finally I have you," Pugli purrs. "Finally, you die."

Fuck this.

I couldn't begin to tell you what comes over me. I just...I have to do something.

I feel my body moving, but I have no control over my limbs—over my arms as they raise my pistol. I put the iron sights on the naked light bulb.

No one is paying attention to little ol' me.

I squeeze the trigger.

The gun barks, making my ears ring, and it jerks in my hands.

Chaos ensues as we're all plunged into darkness.

I hear shouting, wrestling. A grunt.

Bang! A gun goes off, a dull orange flash illuminates a vignette—Nico on the floor, wrestling with Pugli; Jakob lolled to one side, peering up at the descending cylinder, now less than a foot from his head.

There's a distant *ping* of the bullet ricocheting off something overhead.

Bang!

I hear the chair slam. I drop to my knees and crawl forward toward Jakob. I hear Pugli and Nico grunting as they wrestle on the floor, but my focus is on Jakob.

"Jakob?" I whisper.

"Brys?" His voice is faint. "Hey. Heyyyy. Hi. You're here too? Fancy that."

I follow his voice, patting the floor—grit, dust, filth, hard-shelled creepy-crawlies wriggling under my hand. I shudder in revulsion but keep patting and searching until my hands find the lip of the pedestal.

I hear commotion—a beam of light sweeps the space, several of them.

"No!" A voice snaps. "You'll hit Nic!"

No one can do anything.

I hear a soft grunt of pain, then a loud yelp. A beam of light shows Pugli on top of Nico, whose head is half on the pedestal. Pugli is throttling Nico with both hands; Nico has a knife in his side, hanging and waggling as he thrashes, trying to dislodge Pugli, who, despite being older and far less fit, is nonetheless big and strong enough to give the wounded warrior a real fight. Pugli is bleeding from several places, the severity of which I can't determine.

I can tell the others are trying to find a shot, but Pugli and Nico are thrashing and writhing too much for a clear shot.

The cylinder above grinds lower and lower, the top now inches from Jakob's head—he's slumped over as far as his bonds will allow, buying time.

I scramble onto the pedestal but quickly realize I have no way of cutting the zip ties, and there's no time to find anything.

"PUSH HIM!" someone shouts.

Jakob groans again, low and weak—the press is touching his head, bending him slowly in half.

I'm out of time. I grab the nearest part of the chair and throw myself backward. The chair's feet scrape on metal, and I hear Jakob growl a pained sound, and then the weight of the man and the chair topple off the pedestal—not far, perhaps eighteen inches or two feet. Metal clangs on concrete.

I catch another split-second glimpse: Nico has dislodged Pugli, but they're both rolling around on the press platform, tangled up and impossible to figure out who is who. I see Nico's hand flash, yanking the knife out of his side, flash again—Pugli shouts, a tense gurgle of agony, and then Nico is rolling away as the press lowers and lowers, now less than a foot above the platform.

Pugli isn't so fast.

I hear something crunch, and a scream, but my view is blocked by the press. I hear a gun go off, an automatic rattling, a short burst—*ping-ping-ping*. "GET HIM!" Nico screams. "FUCKING *KILL* HIM!"

I lose track of what's happening as I scramble across the floor, still on my hands and knees, toward where I saw Jakob fall.

I find flesh—cool, clammy. "Jakob?"

"B-Br..."

"It's me. Hi, hey. You're okay."

"Deh...debatable."

"Are you...Are you *joking*?"

"Ow." He mutters something, but it's not English.

"Jakob?"

"Chair. I don't like the chair anymore." His voice is so faint, so muzzy and pained—delirious.

"Help!" I shout. "I need a knife!"

A massive hand appears, wielding a huge folding knife that looks like a toy in the giant paw. The blade flicks through the plastic zip ties like butter, and Jakob's hands flop to the sides.

"Oh, nice," he mumbles. "I like my hands."

"He's delirious," I mutter to Chance.

"Lost a lot of blood. We gotta move him. He needs a transfusion." The mammoth man scoops Jakob's limp bulk in his arms as if he weighs nothing.

"P-Poo?" Jakob mumbles. "Pool?"

"I dunno, Boss. You're safe, that's what matters. We'll getcha fixed up."

"Nicolae."

A grunt of pain. "Here, Boss. I'm alive."

"Pugli?"

"Got away. He is badly…" a pause, a grunt. "Badly wounded. I stabbed him several times, and something was crushed by the press."

"How…get away?"

The beams of lights swipe and sweep in disorienting, coruscating patterns, but I can't see anything.

A hand grabs my elbow. "It's Silas," a quiet voice says, close by. "This way."

"Not the tunnel of terror," I whisper. "Please. I can't do that again."

Something bangs loudly, off to my left—a tiny square of light appears. A door?

"There he goes, the slippery bastard," someone growls.

"Nico, no."

"Let go—Pugli—I have to—"

"You've been fucking stabbed *four goddamn times,* Nic. You need medical attention. We'll get him. And you got him good, Nic. He's bleeding worse than you are."

"Missed…organs. May bleed out, but…" he trails off. "*Fuck!*" It's quiet but viciously intense.

"I can go after him," another voice says—I do not know these people well enough to ID them by voice.

"No, Sax. Nic is fucked up, the Boss is fucked up, and the women are home with only Fonz and Toro to keep watch. I don't trust Pugli not to send more of his fucking army after them while we're out here. We have to regroup and try again."

"Fucking god*dam*mit."

We form a bizarre parade, then, trooping across another vast, echoing space, with only the light from half a dozen gun barrels to illuminate our way. We reach the farthest end after a ridiculously long walk.

"Heavy goddamn doors," someone—Rev?—says.

"Here, lemme set Boss down," comes Chance's gravelly rumble.

Jakob groans, and I shake Silas' hand off my elbow and shuffle toward the sound of his voice. I find a foot, follow it up, and kneel beside him.

"Jakob?"

His hand finds my thigh. "Brys. Thought about you a lot."

"Oh yeah? Care to share with the class?"

"No." A grunt of pain, a sigh. "Why are you inside me?"

I can't help but giggle. "That's my line."

His hand tightens. "No, no. Serious."

"Jakob, what are you asking?"

There's a chorus of snarling male voices shouting in exertion, and then the giant doors slowly grind open, inch by inch.

"Okay, break," Solomon pants. "Fuckers are rusted shut."

"And also weigh a goddamn ton," Saxon says. "That don't fuckin' help."

Hey, I'm picking up who's who.

The fading light of day reveals Jakob's eyes, fixed on me, searching. "Beautiful."

This is ridiculous. Why is my heart squeezing like this at the tender sound of his voice? No, no, no, heart. Harden. Don't let him in. Not any further. Bad, bad, bad. Warning, danger. This man is dangerous.

Not to my life, not to my body—in the murdery sense, at least. He's dangerous to my heart. He won't let me in. There's too much scar tissue around his heart.

His hand finds mine. "Brys."

"I'm here, Jakob. You're going to be fine."

"Hurts."

"I know. I'm sorry."

His head lolls side to side. "No, no. Not that." His eyes are intense, the squeeze of his hand on mine stronger than it should be. "Needing you. It hurts."

The men have the doors open wide enough to let everyone out, and Chance scoops up Jakob again. "C'mon, Boss-man. Let's get you to a doctor."

Jakob groans again as he's lifted; he still has my hand in a death-grip, so I shoot awkwardly to my feet and follow him out the door and into daylight.

It's weird that it's still daytime, after what feels like an eternity in that foul darkness.

I blink into the dying light as we cross the field—again, carefully treading single-file along the safe paths through the minefield.

Jakob refuses to let go of my hand for anything, even as we bundle into the absurdly sleek, minimalist, monochromatic interior of the one-of-one stealth jet with the weirdly quiet engines; I'm too worried, freaked out, and traumatized to enjoy the experience.

Who am I to deny a wounded man comfort?

All I can think about, after that, are his last words before the delirium turned to quasi-consciousness and incoherence.

Needing you, it hurts.

Why are you inside me?

Oh, Jakob.

I try to chalk it up to delirium, but a tiny voice in the pit of my soul whispers that sometimes that's when the deepest, rawest truths emerge.

Chapter 18

Truth Will Out

JAKOB

My eyes open slowly, and the world resolves by degrees—a hazy wash of light, then whiteness, then a blurry slice of the world, and then I can see a hospital room. A chair, empty; ceiling tiles. The weird stuff on the walls that does who-knows-what. A window, the blinds closed, daylight peeking through the gaps.

A hospital?

I'm in a hospital? What happened? It's all vague and fuzzy. I have hazy impressions of things—a long walk through a tunnel filled with giant rats and spiders, which is surely a figment of my imagination; a giant press, gunfire…

And Brys.

Her eyes on mine, soft and afraid and worried.

"Brys," I mumble.

"Hey, I'm here." I hear her voice from my right side, sleep-thick. "I'm here."

I turn my head on the pillow, and there she is. Honey-blonde hair has come free of the braid to drape in a wavy cascade down her shoulders and chest. She's absolutely filthy. Her jeans are ripped and caked in dirt and bits of...bone? Her T-shirt is similarly soiled, caked with dirt and blood and god-knows-what. She has dirt and grime and blood smeared on her cheeks and forehead. Even her lovely hair is begrimed.

Yet she's here, in this hospital room with me, passed out in a hard plastic chair. After going through a hell I cannot imagine.

"You—" I break off with a cough, my throat dry and scratchy.

"Here," she mumbles, nudging the rolling tray-table-cart-thing over my lap, on which is a Styrofoam cup and straw. She sits forward and holds the cup for me. "Drink."

I want to guzzle and gulp, but I know better from heroin detox. You vomit and vomit and vomit and shake and shiver, and you're so fucking thirsty, but you can barely manage to keep a single sip down. So you take a mouthful and let the roof of your mouth, your teeth, your gums, and your throat soak up the water, swish it around until it's warm in your mouth, and *then* you swallow it. Quenches real thirst far faster than gulping ever will—gulping will only make you feel worse anyway. Sloshy belly feeling, anyone?

Life pro-tip: don't do heroin. The high is like touching God, the crash and subsequent cravings are the most miserable existence you can imagine, and detox is even worse.

When I've sipped and swished and swallowed to satiety, I let my head fall back against the pillow. "Thank you, Brys."

"Yes, Jay—" she breaks off, blushing. "Sure, of course."

I laugh, which hurts like a bitch. "Oh god, don't make

me laugh, please. Oh god, ow." I catch my breath. "I know what you were about to say."

Her blush is scarlet and endearing. "Jakob, don't."

"How can I not?"

"How are you feeling?" she asks.

I let her change the subject for now. "Kind of a silly question, is it not? I was shot, Brys. That's how I feel."

"You lost a lot of blood. Like, a *LOT* a lot. The wound itself wasn't that bad, apparently, but you lost so, so much blood. Like, close to forty percent. Over forty percent is irreversible, or so I'm told."

"Well, the so-called bandage they slapped on wasn't much better than a band-aid, and the drive to that hellhole was pretty long."

"I don't want to talk about that place, Jakob." Her voice is low and shaking with intensity. "It was worse than..." she shudders all over. "I'd rather have brains blown out in front of me—or *on* me—than go anywhere near that fucking nightmare ever again."

"*On* you?" I ask

She tells me about being dragged—or rather thrown—out of the car, the fight, and almost being shot in the face before Nico saved her.

"I'm sorry, Brys," I whisper, shaking my head, dropping my gaze to my lap. "I am so, so sorry. For everything. For running into you in that alley. For using you as a distraction. Pulling you into all this. You don't deserve any of what's happened—none of it."

"You couldn't have known what would happen."

"Yes, I could have. I should have. I should have known better."

"You want to make it up to me, Jakob?"

"Of course. But it's impossible. I've totally derailed your life."

"You're giving yourself too much credit, buster." She pauses, glances away for a moment, and then back to me. "You *can* make it up to me, you know." She smirks at me. "No, not like that."

"That isn't what I was—"

"*That* is a whole separate conversation," she interrupts. "Tell me."

I frown, confused. "Tell you what?"

"Everything."

"Everything about what?"

"You." She pulls the chair closer to me, takes my hand in both of hers. "You said twice that if I knew what kind of man you are, I would take my chances with Pugli and his gaggle of murderers. Well, let's assume that's true. What do you have to lose, Jakob? If you can't or won't open up to me, what point is there in you and me trying to...?" She trails off, shrugging, as if she can't even finish the thought. "So then I'm gone. And if you do tell me, maybe you're right. Maybe it will be more than I can deal with. But what if it's not? What then, Jakob? What if I *can* understand? What if I'm capable of...of...I don't know what, Jakob, because I don't have a clue what you would tell me."

I close my eyes. Search myself, physically and mentally. I'm in pain, but it's distant and dull. My head is foggy, my thoughts hazy and hard to pin down, sluggish and oozy.

"Am I...?" I peer up at the IV pole. "Am I on opiates?"

She frowns. "I...I'm not sure. Why?"

I fumble for the nurse call button and press it several times. A nurse bustles in. "And how are we feeling today?"

I tug on the line at my forearm. "Get me off the opiates. Right the fuck *now*."

"But sir—"

I give her a look of unadulterated fury. "I will not say it again. If I have to rip the I-V out of my arm, I will."

"Jakob," Brys says, "I don't understand what—"

The nurse, however, does, her face paling. "Oh—oh no. You're in recovery?"

"Just get me off of them, please." I do my best to sound less capable of murder.

She stops the drip and removes the bag. "I'm afraid without that, the pain will be—"

"Better than heroin detox," I finish for her. "Just get me some aspirin or Tylenol or Aleve or anything that's not a fucking opiate."

"Of course, sir." She leaves and returns moments later with a dose of plain old Tylenol.

When the nurse has left again, silence lingers between us.

"Jakob," Brys starts, her voice just above a whisper. "Talk to me. Please."

I know it's mostly in my head, but I can feel the pain returning—I tell myself to welcome the pain. It means I'm alive and not risking getting hooked again.

"One for one," I mutter. "I'll tell you a secret, but you have to tell me one."

She nods while sighing. "I agree to your terms." A pause. "But to be honest, I'm not agreeing because it's your terms. I'm agreeing because..." she trails off, shaking her head.

"Why, Brys?"

"Because I *don't* want to. Because I want to..." she

looks at me. "I want to trust you. I don't want to keep everything inside anymore." Her eyes shimmer. "There are things I've never told anyone."

"And you want to tell me?"

She huffs. "God no. I'm terrified. But I...it's festering, Jakob."

"I know how that feels," I whisper.

"So let's not make it an agreement, or terms of a deal. It's you trusting me and me trusting you. I'm scared, Jakob, and I know you must be, too. But I...I'm choosing courage anyway." She leans forward and presses her lips to the back of my hand. "Will you do that with me?"

"Why?" I can't help but ask. "Why trust...*me*?"

"You protected me. Fought for me. Killed for me."

"You wouldn't have needed any of that if it wasn't for me."

"There is zero R-O-I on blame-casting, Jakob."

I let out a breath. "I was born wealthy. Very, *very* wealthy, from two very old and very important families. I was educated by private tutors—and when I say my education was classical, I mean that I was taught Latin and Greek, fencing, horsemanship, diction and elocution, mathematics...I was raised like a prince of old, Brys. In Prague. My name really is Jakob...Jakob Kasparek. But that person, the Jakob Kasparek who was born in Prague and emigrated to the States...he died a long time ago. Well, he vanished." I sigh. "I'm getting ahead of myself."

I tell her all about my childhood. My nanny, my beautiful, quiet, poised, elegant mother. My stern, arrogant father.

I tell her about coming home to find my parents gone and our housekeeper in an unintelligible panic.

The hospital—my mother's still, thin form caught up in a spiderweb of tubes and lines, my father hunched over her bed, unmoving, for days.

Her death and my reaction to it

My father's violent expression of grief against me.

Following him home, watching him shut the door in my face. The short silence punctuated by the awful finality of a single gunshot.

I tell her about being sent to live with my father's cousin in Harlem with my inheritance that he stole. How he left me on a sidewalk in a terrible section of the city, far, far from anything I knew, which was very little to begin with.

I tell her about being homeless. Walking the streets all day and all night, being beaten up by old homeless men for prime sleeping spots beneath overpasses, digging in dumpsters for scraps.

I tell her about being taken in by Miss Amy. How she fed me, bought me clothes, and gave me a room to sleep in. How at first I thought she was merely kind, wanting to help a lost young man out of the goodness of her heart.

Brys's expression betrays her understanding of what happened before I say anything further. "Oh god, Jakob," she whispers.

I clear my throat, swallow hard. My eyes burn, and my throat is tight. "This is hard to talk about. I...in fact, I've only spoken of this period of my life in any detail one other time-when I told Isabel."

Brys's gaze is thoughtful. "I have a lot of questions about her, but I suppose that's part of the telling."

I shrug. "I suppose so, yes."

She shifts on the seat. Waits in silence, watching me.

There's no getting out of this—and I realize that just maybe…I don't want to get out of it. I don't want to change the subject or shut down the conversation.

Telling Isabel was agonizing, like pulling teeth sans Novocain. Like ripping chunks of my skin off. I'd begun to realize the depths of my depravity, by then, how badly I'd wronged her. I understood that I owed her those truths.

This is different.

As Brys said, my many secrets are rotting inside me, festering and ingrown. They require excision.

Isabel listened to my tale with curiosity, skepticism, anger, and blame—all of it justifiable. Brys, on the other hand, listens with openness and curiosity, as well as compassion. Concern. Care.

I find enough courage to start again. "It wasn't all at once, you must understand. I wasn't just thrown into a room with horny women. It was a lobster in a pot being brought to a boil." I swallow hard. "If you have not experienced true starvation, then you cannot understand the power of hunger. When you have fought off rats for a nibble of stale, moldy bread dug out of a dumpster, you will do quite literally anything to never feel that way again. Just like…" I swallow, shake my head. "Well."

"Heroin," she whispers.

"Yes. But hunger was her first tool." I fix my eyes on Brys to remind myself that I am here, I am now. "Miss Amy brought…a *friend*…over to visit. This friend was very wealthy and very important. A politician's wife, I believe, but I do not know for sure. I barely spoke English back then, remember—I was a lost, starving Czech orphan." Pause for breath, for courage. "Miss Amy told me that if I wanted to have a bed to sleep in and clean clothes to wear, a roof over my head, and food to eat, I would accommodate her friend, no matter what was asked of me. *No matter what*—she repeated that several times. If I made her friend happy, she told me, the gravy train would keep on rolling."

"God, that's evil," Brys breathes.

"Oh, that was only the beginning, Brys." I look away. "I was a virgin until that day. I'd never even held a girl's hand. My life had been very sheltered, you see. Isolated and lonely. No friends, no sports, just my nanny and my tutor and my lessons, all day every day, until Mother and Father died and my cousin stole my inheritance. Miss Amy's friend, she…Miss Amy left us alone. She took me to the bedroom—my bedroom. There was no pretense of it being anything else. She instructed me to take off my clothes and…she…she just…admired me, for a moment. And then she touched me. My body responded—I was sixteen. She played with me. It wasn't…it wasn't really about sex for her. She didn't want me to do anything to her that first time. She wanted someone she could…toy with. Order around. Have control over. She made me… her favorite game was edging me. Get me to the point of orgasm and then stop. She would take a phone call. Step out of the room. If I failed to control my release to her satisfaction, Miss Amy would withhold food from me until the next time. Not all food, just enough to drive the point home. I had to have enough strength to perform, you see. I'm sure it was a delicate balance to strike—enough hunger to punish without leaving me too weak to function.

"She would slap me. Not for the infliction of pain—she was a tiny, weak woman. Even at sixteen, I could have snapped her like a twig. But the specter of the streets, of hunger, of eating moldy bread and begging for coins? No,

I dared not. I obeyed. I let her slap me. I let her slap my face, my buttocks, my penis."

"She slapped your *penis*?"

"That was her favorite thing to do to me as punishment—as a test. I couldn't protect myself, couldn't flinch, couldn't cover, couldn't make a sound. If I didn't, she would 'reward me,'" and here I use heavy emphasis for sarcasm, "with pleasure. Everything was a game to that woman—a game of power and manipulation."

"Oh, Jakob."

"For a while, it was just her. And then soon it was a different friend, in addition. This friend had different tastes. She wanted me to make her feel all the things her husband couldn't or wouldn't. She would make me perform cunnilingus until my jaw gave out. There was no talking. Just service. Again, and again, and again. This wasn't a by-the-hour thing. They had me for as long as they wanted. There were no rules other than not leaving visible marks on my body—no damaging the merchandise. They could do whatever vile sins their depraved minds could conjure, as long as my body was left unblemished.

"And then there was a third friend. She was unremarkable, and my favorite client for that. She just wanted to be fucked hard and frequently. She otherwise left me alone as long as I serviced her well."

Brys's eyes burn and shimmer. "Jakob." My name catches in her throat.

I have to look away—I cannot tolerate her compassion. It cuts deeper than any razor blade.

"I began to suffer after a few months of this. I couldn't sleep. I had nightmares. It was impacting my performance, so Miss Amy had to find a fix. The fix came in the form of a little white pill. Just half of one at first, and eventually the whole pill, and then a whole pill every few hours. It took away the nightmares. Took away the nausea that would leave me in agony on the floor before a client. The world was brighter. Sensations were…different. Sharper. More intense. The pills were the only way I could get through a client session. But the more pills I took, the more I needed. And then the pills stopped working, no matter how many I took, and that's when she introduced me to the needle. The rush was…god, I still remember the way that first hit felt, Brys. There is nothing like it on Earth. But the price you pay?" I close my eyes, shake my head. "I pray to every god there is that you never know, Brys."

Several minutes pass in awful silence before I can continue.

"The needle was how I coped, after that. It allowed her to sell me not just a few times a week, but a few times a *day*. As long as I was doped up, I would do whatever was asked of me." I close my eyes. "I made her a wealthy woman. She already was, but I…I was her golden goose. She put me up in a loft in Tribeca. She would come by every day with my medicine. She would tie the tube around my arm and put the needle in my vein, and her clients would arrive, and I would service them. Men, women, couples, throuples, I did it all. Why? Because she proved quite effectively what would happen if I complained. It only happened once, the first time she sold me to a male client. I protested. I didn't want to do it—even drugged, I didn't want that. Well, it didn't matter what I wanted. When he was done with me, she threw me out. Changed the code and the locks, and left me out on the street on my own for two weeks. The craving, the hunger, thirst, the withdrawal? It's every worst kind of misery you can imagine, all at once."

She can only shake her head, eyes dewy with unshed tears. "How did you get free?"

"A car accident, of all things. Miss Amy was crossing the street and was struck and killed by a distracted cab driver. I…" here, I trail off, breathe, start over. "This is a truth I have never spoken aloud. I was with her. We were returning to her condo for an appointment—some of her high-status clients preferred to meet me there rather than at my loft. I…I saw the cab coming. I saw that Amy was distracted by a billboard or someone down the street, I don't know, don't remember." I swallow hard. "I was high. I was always high. I don't remember deciding. I just…the cabbie wasn't looking, Amy wasn't looking. I tripped. Bumped into her. And she…she toppled into the street, and the taxi hit her and killed her instantly. I saw—I saw her go flying like a rag doll. Saw her land, saw her limbs snap, her head explode. I went to her. Pretended to be upset, but in reality, I was stealing her keys. I slipped away in the chaos as the police, fire, and EMS arrived. I let myself into her condo, and I tore it apart looking for the medicine." I shake my head, laughing derisively. "Medicine. I knew I was addicted to drugs, but I never knew what it was she gave me. I just knew I needed it. I ransacked that place, Brys. I tore open every cushion, every pillow. Looked in the toilet tanks, inside HVAC vents. I never found it. I had no money. I sold as much of her stuff as I could to pay for my drugs, but eventually I ran out of her jewelry, purses, and shoes. I tore the condo apart again, searching. This time, in a fit of craving-induced rage, I smashed a hand-carved wooden jewelry box. Which is how I found her Rolodex of clients.

I knew, even in the state I was in, the value of that client list. I also knew I was in no state to do anything. I knew the demon of the drug was killing me. So I decided to quit."

Brys recoils in horror. "Jakob. People have *died* from heroin withdrawal."

"I know that now. I didn't then. Remember, I was a very sheltered child. I pawned her stereo and stocked up on water and food and barricaded myself in with a stack of books." I shudder, which hurts. "The tunnel, Brys? With the rats and the spiders. Was that real?"

She nods, tears spilling down as a shudder wracks her. "Yes. All too real."

"That is an excellent picture of heroin withdrawal. Spiders in your skin. Centipedes crawling down your back. Rats chewing on your toes. Except on the inside. Every worst nightmare made real. I vomited until I didn't even have bile left. I clawed myself bloody. I didn't eat for days and days. Forced myself to drink just so I didn't die of dehydration. I should have died, going cold turkey like that. It is a miracle I did not, and it is no credit to my constitution or willpower. Merely luck…or some higher plan, perhaps, if you believe in such things."

"Dear lord in heaven."

"If there is a god, he or she or they did not deign to visit me in my detox. I suffered alone. When I emerged on the other side, I was a skeleton. My skin was like parchment. I had not eaten for weeks and had been subsisting on just enough fluids to keep my kidneys from giving out. But I had Amy's client list. I just…her clients paid for an impressive male specimen, not a frail, gaunt, withered ghoul covered in my own vomit and feces."

She covers her face with both hands. "My god. My god. What did you do?"

I am silent for a long while, summoning the courage to speak. "It was meant to be a stopgap measure until I could entertain clients myself. It was... Fortuitous, I suppose, is an accurate enough word. I stumbled across an emaciated teenage girl in an alley, begging for food."

Brys's expression changes. "Oh, Jakob. You *didn't*."

"Oh, Brys, I did." I harden my heart against the hate that will soon be all she feels for me. "Hold your judgment, however. The worst is yet to come." I breathe, steel myself. "I was evicted from Amy's condo and the Tribeca loft, but not before I found the keys and title to her Mercedes, which I was able to sell for enough for a deposit on a walk-up in Astoria. I brought the girl to the apartment. I clothed her. Fed her. I did to her what Amy did to me. Used hunger as a whip. But I... I was smarter than Amy. Instead of one girl operating out of my apartment, I leased several apartments across various neighborhoods and boroughs throughout the city and put my girls up in them. They worked out of their home. I checked on them. I kept them off drugs because I could never, ever do that to anyone. I would not wish heroin detox on anyone, not even Pugli."

Her gaze is troubled. "God, Jakob." This utterance is different. Harder, sharper—bubbling with acidic judgment.

"Yes," I whisper. "Now you see. But wait—I have not finished. There is worse to come."

"No," she breathes.

"I made a *lot* of money in a very short amount of time. That is where I differed from Amy. I diversified. I bought a laundromat. The laundromat was profitable enough that I bought a gas station, and then a car wash. I hired managers to run them for me hands-free, as it were. And every time I got a new stream of income up and running, I freed one of my girls. I bought them a condo and got them a job, if they wanted. Some didn't—some stuck with the sex work."

"Why?" she asks. "Why would they keep doing that?"

I shrug. "I have often wondered that. I told you of the brothel I run in my club—Hel. Every girl who works there does so because she chooses to. They are not beholden to anyone, and they are not addicts; they choose sex work for their own reasons, which are none of my business."

"I find it hard to applaud that, Jakob."

I shrug. "I understand, Brys. I really do. There is a stigma around sex work that has always clung to the profession, no matter how *woke* our society may become. But like hunger or addiction, you cannot understand it from the outside, and I do not say that in judgment. It is merely reality."

She nods. "I suppose I get that."

I blow out a breath. Keep going—into the hardest part. "I bought business after business, and eventually, I had no more girls and more businesses than I knew what to do with...and two new addictions almost as toxic as heroin: money and control."

"There's more?"

I nod. "Oh yes. I was still lost, you see. I had a penthouse condo in Midtown, a Bentley with a driver, a stock portfolio earning interest, a diverse portfolio of successful businesses...and the respect of no one. Because to anyone who was anyone in this town, I would never be anyone but the junkie whore. No amount of money could erase that. And worse, *I* knew that's all I was. Just a junkie whore in a tailored Brooks Brothers suit.

"I needed something more, I just didn't know what. I didn't drink or do drugs, obviously, because I knew the danger of losing control to a substance. So I searched for the outlet I needed to find some kind of peace within myself. The only place I ever found it was in sex—but only under certain circumstances. It was difficult to find a partner who could give me what I needed—absolute obedience. Not just sexually. In every aspect of life. And the girls I was finding to date, so to speak, could give me obedience in bed but not in life, or vice versa, or not at all."

I go silent for perhaps thirty seconds, counting my heartbeats on the monitor.

"And then," I say, whispering, "I met her."

Chapter 19

Truth, Lies, and Damnation

BRYS

HER.

Isabel.

It's hard to process all that he's told me, and he's not done yet.

"The control soon became my drug of choice while money was merely the tool that got me what I needed." He stares at nothing, seeing the past. "I burned through girlfriends, whores, subs, everyone I could, but no one and nothing could sate my need for control. It is an addiction, truly. I could not function if every aspect of my life was not ordered and in my control. I lived a very regimented life. But the partner? She eluded me. I needed someone who was pliable—pliant to my will. Someone I could mold and craft into what I needed. But what did that look like?"

He's silent for a moment or two, and then resumes.

"I met Isabel at a cafe. She was sitting outside in the sun, in this delightful, alluring little sundress. Her hair was black as night, and her eyes bright with intelligence. She was sixteen and nothing like the starving, desperate girls I used to lure into prostitution. She had parents, a family, a future. She was happy." He frowns, glances at me. "I never touched any of the girls that worked for me—never. And yes, many of them were underage. I make no excuses for that. I could claim truthfully that I kept them off drugs and kept them from starving and from being homeless, but that doesn't absolve me. There is no penance I could ever pay that would be enough, and I know that." Another pause. "But this girl? Even now, I don't know why...what it was about her. I fixated. I became obsessed with her. I followed her from home to school, watching her. I bumped into her once to prevent her from being hit by a car. I killed a man who would have mugged and raped her. She never knew. All she ever knew was that we saw each other at that cafe a few times a week, and we'd talk. She was learning English, and I knew how that felt, so I let her practice her faltering English on me. I had never touched her at that point. She was just a girl, sixteen, seventeen. Too young. But I was obsessed. I lost myself to it—to her.

"The only thing I could do to break the hold was vanish. So I did. I sold off everything I owned, every business, everything. Liquidated it all and went back to Europe. Lived incognito for months, trying to get her out of my system. Nothing worked. I even thought about trying drugs, but I couldn't bring myself to do it, not even to get her out of my mind, out from under my skin. I craved her. I don't know how to put it so you can even begin to comprehend, Brys. I wanted to know her every thought. I wanted to know every inch of her body. Every sound she made, waking and sleeping. I needed to *own* her. To make her mine and no one else's. And no matter what I did, I couldn't get her out of me.

"I liked that Jakob was gone. It was freedom. I could be anyone. So I invented a new persona—Caleb Indigo. A good old American success story, rags to riches, self-made. Rising from the ashes of poverty to be a billionaire. And that was true, to a degree. I wasn't a billionaire at first—I had about fourteen million saved. Not a fortune, but a lot."

I snort. "To the vast majority of the world, Jakob, that *is* a fortune."

"When you've had billions, it feels like nothing." He shrugs, continues past that. "I tried to stay away from her while I built my empire as Caleb Indigo. But I just couldn't. I kept finding myself standing in the shadows across from their apartment, watching her through a window. Even seeing her sitting and reading or watching TV was a thrill. To be close to her? To hear her voice? I dreamed of it every night." He sighs, shaking his head. "Then one day, everything changed. I…I saw it happen. Her father was driving. They were all together in their car. They'd gone to a movie and dinner. I followed, watched the movie, and her, from the back row. Followed them home in my car. They stopped at a red light. Went through on the green, but a cube van blew the red. Smashed into the driver's side. Her father was killed instantly. The car flipped and spun too many times to count. Her mother was killed, and Isabel was ejected. I watched it happen. I watched the car spin, flip, and tumble. Watched the metal crumple. Saw the blood smear and splatter. Saw her body fly out of the car and hit the pavement—so hard. So hard. It was…god, it was a nightmare. I was first on scene. A good Samaritan. We were only a couple of blocks from a hospital. I picked her up and carried her to the ER. There was so much blood. Her head was…" he shakes his head, voice shaking. "Her head was…" he trails off, voice broken. "I can't. I can't."

Jesus. She still has so much power over him.

I wait, watch. His hand shakes under mine. My emotions are all over the place. I don't know what to think, what to feel. For now, I put the reckoning of emotions aside for later.

"It's alright, Jakob," I murmur.

He shakes his head. "It's not. It's not. It's not okay. She had a severe T-B-I. She was in a coma for four years, three months, and six days. I spent the vast majority of that time in her room. I paid her hospital bills. Took care of my business from the room as much as I could. I sat in that room and willed her to wake up. And then, one day, she did." He pauses, his voice so soft I can barely hear him. "She lost all of her memories. Total retrograde amnesia. No clue who she was. Not her name, not a single memory. Nothing."

"So by the time she woke up from the coma, she was legal," I say.

I snort. "As if that was my concern. At that point, sex was the last thing on my mind. I saw the opportunity for what it was—a chance to..."

"She was a tabula rasa," I whisper. "A blank slate."

He nods weakly. "Correct. And I utilized it. I lied to her. I took her home and carefully, slowly, and—I must say—artfully crafted a new person out of the remains of who she was. An elegant woman. A powerful woman."

"And you whored her out."

"No!" He snaps it so intensely he doubles over, coughing. "No. Never. She was *mine*. No one could have her like that. No one but me." Softer, then, quieter. "I *did* sell her services, but not for sex. She was..." he spends a few moments considering. "I had many clients—of my many legitimate businesses—who were...uncouth, shall we say. And many of them remarked to me on a number of occasions that they wish they could learn how to be more…elegant. Refined. Sophisticated."

"More like you," I supply, my tone wry and more than a little arch.

He rolls a shoulder. "Essentially, yes." A soft snort. "Well, not essentially—precisely that. False modesty is not one of my shortcomings. A wave of his hand dismisses the topic. "I told her I didn't know her name or who she was. I took her to an art museum once, and she was captivated for some reason by John Singer Sargent's painting Madame X. So she chose that as her name—Madame X."

I gasp. "Madame X?" My mind whirls. "I have heard of her. Rumors only, but from reliable sources. I was told that a friend of a friend's cousin—or something similarly absurd—had been a client of hers. According to my friend who related this story, he was a mess. Clumsy. No social skills. Vulgar. Just an all-around embarrassment to his socialite parents. After a few months working with Madame X, he was like a new man."

He nods. "That was the business, and she was amazing at it. She could see people for who they were, and help them become who they could be."

I shake my head. "You *created* Madame X? Dear lord. And…and when she wasn't tutoring boys in manners, she was…what? Your sex slave?"

"More than that, and nothing so trite or vulgar. My ownership of her was not merely sexual, Brys." His teeth click together. "Brys, I…it is quite difficult to not defend my actions, I must admit. It is true that my obsession was far more than merely sexual. But it was still an obsession. I still lied to her for years. Used her for my own ends. Kept the truth of her past from her. Kept her…captive…

essentially, for my own purposes. I would never have let her go, but fate intervened. Brought her to Logan, who opened her eyes, bit by bit." He swallows hard. "Even in letting her go and giving her the truth of who she was, I lied to her. I…I couldn't make myself tell her the whole truth. I told her so many lies mixed with truths and half-truths that I didn't know how to untangle it all. So when she confronted me about who she really was, I told her…a *version* of the truth. In part to give her…peace, I suppose. Closure. I know her husband, at least, suspected I was lying. I think he thought I somehow fabricated her accident. I didn't tell her I'd come back as Caleb just to find her. I don't think I realized that that is what I was doing at the time—it wasn't conscious at the beginning. But I went looking for her the day my feet touched New York soil. Everything I did was bent toward…her. Everything I did to become Caleb Indigo was to be the man I thought she…" he shakes his head, as if unable to finish formulating the thought.

A long, tense silence envelops us both, then.

"And then Caleb Indigo died," I prompt.

He shakes himself out of the reverie and nods. "Yes. I…as Isabel and Logan fell in love and she left me and learned the truth and found her own life without me, I…I couldn't…I couldn't cope. It is tempting to say the wool was removed from my eyes, but that would not be accurate. I was never deluded or delusional. I knew what I was doing and did it with intent for years. But when she found herself and her freedom outside of me, I saw…" A hard swallow. "I saw that she was happy. She was happy with Logan. She was happy without me. And that…it cut deep. It drilled holes in my psyche. But I saw that she was…glowing…with life. She had children—twins." He stops, swallows, and looks away. "A boy and a girl." Another swallow. "She named the boy Jakob."

I feel my eyes fly wide, hear my breath catch. "Jakob?"

He nods. "Heterpaternal superfecundation. It just means—"

"I know what it means," I interrupt.

He nods, skips over that. "She and Logan know, but I don't think the kids do, or ever will."

I snort. "Jakob, I *saw* him. He looks nothing like either of them, yet he and the girl do look alike, and they do look like her. He will have questions, someday."

He shakes his head. "He cannot know me. He won't. I…no. No."

"That isn't your choice, unfortunately. You will just have to trust Isabel and Logan to handle that as they see fit."

He stares at nothing, ignoring this. "It became obvious that I couldn't stay in New York. But I…" A long, harsh sigh. "I had to cut myself out of her life. I had to…it was the only thing I could think of—the only permanent solution. As long as she thought I was alive, she might find me. She might have questions. Or the child might. The only permanent solution was to disappear, to die." Another pause. "I did consider making it…real. Actually—ahhh, removing myself from the earth. And I…I couldn't. My entire being revolted from the idea. So I faked it."

"The car bomb," I say.

He nods. "Nothing left to find." A shrug. "It worked. Although Logan knows I am alive. But as long as I keep my distance…" he trails off.

"And you started over again."

The longest pause yet grows out of my leading statement.

"No." His eyes slide over mine like same-polarity magnets drawing too close. "No, I never started over. I gave her fourteen billion dollars in my will. I kept...ohh, a hundred million or so. Enough to start over comfortably," he glances at me. "Business-wise, I mean. Which I did. Eventually. But personally? No, I didn't start over. I...hid. I have spent the last ten years as a recluse, living alone above the Club. I went months at a time without human contact."

"Jakob," I breathe again; so many times, I haven't known what to say except his name.

"Inez—Sophia—has been the only human contact I have had for over a decade. Until Pugli discovered my existence and began hunting me, at least."

"How do you know Pugli?"

"During the time I spent in Europe between the vanishing of Jakob and the appearance of Caleb, I encountered him. I ran in less than savory circles—arms dealers, drug dealers, mafia bosses, sex traffickers. When you're underground and off-grid, your options for human interaction are severely limited. We did some business together—vanilla stuff, mostly. I facilitated some product transportation for him—cocaine and small arms, I believe."

I wait, and he continues after a moment.

"I do not take people at their word, typically. Criminals especially. I may have been, technically speaking, a pimp, but I never thought of myself as a criminal. So when I was facilitating a shipment for him, I inspected it. And I discovered that one of the containers, which supposedly was carrying crates of guns, actually held human beings. Not women, *girls*. Ten, eleven, twelve, thirteen years old. The oldest couldn't have been sixteen. I know I—" he shakes his head. "They were *children*. I make no excuses for the things I did. I turned starving, homeless teenage girls into prostitutes. I deserve all the judgment and hatred you…" another shake of his head. "I know who I am and what I have done, and I make no excuses for any of it. I ask for no forgiveness. There can be no absolution. I know that. But Pugli? Girls who hadn't even gotten their period. One of them was still clutching a Barbie doll as she cowered in the corner of the lightless, barely ventilated container in a pool of her own…" he trails off, still shaken by the memory, all these years later.

"Dear god," I breathe. "Dear god in heaven. How can anyone…?" I can't even finish the question.

"I don't know," he murmurs. "I have long asked myself that same question. I have never found a satisfactory answer beyond the evils humankind is capable of. I, as much as anyone, but even I draw the line somewhere. Pugli does not."

"Jakob, I am not excusing anything, but…" It is hard to find the right words. "Packing a shipping container full of little girls is an evil beyond the pale."

"Made worse by the manner of their procurement," he says, his voice thin and distant. "He would send bands of armed thugs into villages throughout Europe, find the poorest villages, and buy them from desperate parents. And if they would not sell their children, those men would simply murder the parents and any siblings that were of no use, and take the rest to be sold as chattel."

"Jesus," I breathe. "Jesus Christ."

"Indeed," he said. "By the time any kind of report made it to the nearby authorities, they were gone. And those local yokel policemen couldn't have done a damn thing. Those bands were ex-military, armed with assault rifles and wearing armor. A few squad cars of policemen trained to do little more than write speeding tickets and wrangle the occasional drunk? They would have been slaughtered. He still does that, as a matter of fact. I saw a report just a few months ago about a village in southern Romania—six families were wiped out. Murdered in their homes by a dozen armed men. They just kicked in the door and shot everyone but the girls under eighteen."

"He's specifically and intentionally targeting and trafficking little girls?" I ask. "That's what Pugli is doing?"

"That is only one of the horrors that can be laid at his feet. Would you like to know more about his operation?"

I shake my head. "I would not, no. I'll have enough trouble sleeping at night as it is."

"I'm sorry," he whispers. His eyes finally find mine, and they are aching with sorrow, with guilt, with regret, with self-loathing. "I'm sorry I dragged you into my awful world. You are a wonder, Brys. You are still here, still listening to me. Why? Are you a masochist, that you should inflict me upon yourself yet more?" I open my mouth to reply, but it is clear he is not done, and I am not entirely certain he's really even speaking to me. "I shall treasure the hours we spent together in that hotel room, Brys. That you shared your beauty with me...it is enough. It must be enough. It is enough."

Again, I want to speak, but...say what?

He winces, grimaces, sucks in a breath—the pain returning in full force, now. "Ah, Brys. I wish I were a different man. I wish forgiveness was a commodity one could buy. I wish redemption was..." a shake of his head. "Nearly bleeding out does something to a person. Makes one think."

He stares at nothing again, and I remain silent, gut

churning and heart twisting, sinking, rising, burning, aching.

"Who am I, Brys? Jakob Kasparek? Who is that? An orphan, homeless and unwanted? A heroin addict? A whore? A thing to be passed around and traded and bought and sold? A vessel to be used? A plaything of wealthy women and powerful men with dirty secrets? Is Jakob the fledgling businessman? And Caleb Indigo? What of him? The titan of industry, the billionaire with an eye for a profitable gamble? He is dead, and Jakob vanished. Did I start over? No, I hid. I became no one. A voice over the phone, an entity behind encrypted emails. A faceless presence squatting in the shadows, manipulating events from afar." His eyes shut tight. "I wish I were the Jakob you think you know, Brys. But like all else in my life, he, too, is a lie."

I feel shattered, inside and out. Tears stream down my face. My throat is clogged with razors. My chest is clutched by a vengeful god's angry fist. "Jakob. I…I don't—I don't know what to—"

He sucks in a sudden, sharp breath, eyes opening and lasering in on mine. "There is nothing to say. It isn't over—Pugli is still out there, but he is badly hurt and on the run. My people will find him and put an end to this vulgar charade." The sorrier he feels for himself, the more poetic his speech. "I will hire security for you. A dozen armed men to accompany you everywhere you go. To stand watch outside your door. To drive you to work, home, to the bar, to a liaison with a handsome young lad from the temp pool. It is what I should have done from the start. Packed you off to a safehouse in Connecticut with an army of guards to watch over you. Instead, I was selfish. I wanted to be the one to protect you. I wanted—" he shakes his head. "I thought I could have—"

"You thought you could have what?" I ask, my voice a wet whisper. "Don't you fucking dare clam up on me now, asshole."

He huffs at my words. "What my Arrows have found. For a few moments of time, for a few precious hours, I thought perhaps I could have what they have."

"And what do they have, Jakob?"

He shakes his head, lips sealed tight and trembling, eyes wet and narrowed against the fall of salt, jaw as hard as granite. "Do not make me say it."

"Well, I am," I snap. "I *am* going to make you. Say it, Jakob. Say it and be damned."

"Love," he whispers. "Acceptance. Redemption. Forgiveness." A long, deep silence. "Love," he whispers again.

CHAPTER 20

CARDS ON THE TABLE

JAKOB

I CAN'T BRING MYSELF TO LOOK AT HER. I AM TOO weak to bear her scrutiny, her judgment, her hate.

I have come to the end of myself.

I could not protect Brys—when the moment came, I failed. I was shot. I walked into an obvious ambush, and it was up to others to take care of her and to rescue me.

I had no control.

I have never had any control. It has all been an illusion, a fiction I convinced myself was true.

"I need—" her voice is so quiet I can barely hear her. "I need some time to process all this, Jakob."

"Yes," I say, forcing a strength I do not feel into my voice. "I suppose you would."

"I'm not…I'm coming back."

I offer her a smile, which I'm sure is sad and self-pitying. I know how I must sound. I no longer care. "Yes, of course." I shake my head. "Let us not lie anymore, Brys. This is goodbye. I'll make the call about your security detail after you have left. They will meet you in the lobby."

"Jakob—" a sigh, a shake of her head. "You're

impossible. You're not listening." She stands up, presses her palm to my jaw. "I'll be back. I just need time to think."

"Okay," I tell her. She needs to think I believe her, so she can make her escape.

She rolls her eyes. "Jesus, you're impossible, you ridiculous, arrogant, self-centered, beautiful, delusional man. If I were going to run away from you, don't you think I would say so? When, in the time you've known me, have I ever held back what I really thought?"

"Beautiful?"

She cackles. "Of course, that's the one you ask about." A sighing shake of her head. "Good lord, Jakob. Just lay there and figure out how to get over the self-pity bullshit while I take a few goddamn minutes to process the fucking insanity you've just dumped on me."

"That's a lot of curse words," I point out.

Brys nods, laughing. "Right? Growing up, my father always got on my case when I swore. He insisted that cursing was the mark of a small mind. And then, as a woman in business—and one combating both the accusations of nepotism *and* the fact of it—I had to be twice as good as the men around me to get half as far, which meant everything I did, wore, and said was scrutinized and put under a microscope. But now? I like cursing. I'm a grown-ass woman. I'm the CEO of a multi-billion-dollar company. I can swear as much as I fucking want."

"You know that's false, don't you?" A voice says—Sophia. "The whole adage of cursing being a mark of a small mind bit. Science has proven that having a wide vocabulary of curse words is a sign of creativity and high intelligence. Science has also proven that shouting and cursing measurably and demonstrably reduce pain and speed healing."

Brys meets Sophia's eyes, and something passes between the women.

Brys leaves the room, and Sophia stands at the foot of my bed for a moment, just staring at me. "Weird seeing you there."

"Not as weird as it is to be here," I admit. "I have never been in a hospital bed before."

"Why does that not surprise me?" Sophia moves around and takes the seat Brys recently vacated. "You got lucky."

"Did I?"

She nods. "You did." A flick of her finger at my wound. "I don't mean that."

I frown. "Then to what are you referring?"

She jerks her chin toward the door. "Her."

I shake my head. "Lucky is hardly the word I'd use."

"Oh?" Her tone is sharp, as only she can make it; a lesser man would quail at the acid in her tone. "Do tell."

I open my mouth to answer, but she cuts me off.

"She is a hell of a woman, Jakob. You know it was she who shot out the light? If not for that, I think both you and Nicolae would be dead. She stuck by you every step of the fucking way, my friend. When she could have stayed back where it was safe, she crossed a goddamned *minefield* for you. She traversed that tunnel of fucking nightmares—for *you*. She faced death—*for you*. She still has brain matter in her hair. She sat by your bedside in this—" she shifts, "*intensely* motherfucking uncomfortable chair for almost two days."

Discomfort burns in my gut. "Sophia, I…"

She holds up a hand. "You listen to me, now, Jakob." I snap my teeth shut and nod once; satisfied that I'm listening, she continues. "None of us deserves a goddamn thing. All of us, this entire island of misfit toys you've created—all of us are deeply, deeply fucked up. I slaughtered thirty-two people, most of whom were innocent. Rev, Chance, Kane, Saxon—Jesus, Jakob, the man is known as the Bloody Viking, for fuck's sake. *All* of us have closets so full of skeletons they won't even close. We've all got demons. No one can absolve any of us of our sins, Jakob. I'm not sure we *should* be. And to be honest, if it's absolution you need...shit, pick a church."

"Some pep talk, Sophia."

"Shut up, I'm still talking." She smiles, gentling the delivery; it is truly weird to see a smile on her face. "Call it tough love, if that helps. And it *is* love, Jakob." She swallows hard, blinks harder. "I love you. As a brother, as...a friend? I don't know if there's a word for what we are to each other." She looks up at the ceiling. "Do you remember when I offered myself to you?"

"Of course," I say, my voice thick and gruff. "You thought it was expected."

"It was so confusing to me, how angry you were. But that? You refusing me and getting angry that I'd done that... that's when I realized I could trust you. I have worked for you for over ten years. I have never balked at any of the tasks you've assigned me. I've helped you build Club Sin. I helped you find the Arrows. I...I hope that I have earned your trust in return."

"Do..." It feels like swallowing knives. "Do you really have to ask?"

"Yes. It's time to put all the cards on the table, Boss."

"Yes. You have earned my trust a hundred times over, Sophia."

She takes my hands in hers, squeezing so hard it hurts. "Then trust me when I say that if you let Brys walk out of your life, you will be the biggest fool this world has ever seen." Her grip tightens until I think she means to break my fingers. "You will never, *ever* meet someone who could deal with the events of the last few days the way she has." She allows a hint of mirth to glitter in her dark gaze. "I know something happened between you two, Jakob. And if I know you, you made it one thing in order to avoid letting it become something else."

"Say what you mean, Inez—" I shake my head. "Sorry, Sophia."

"They're both me, I'm realizing. I can't just go back to using my birth name and think all the things Inez has been and done are just in the past, any more than I could use the name Inez and think all the things Sophia did were in the past. It's *all* in the past. The name you use is irrelevant. Jakob, Caleb, they're both you. And maybe *neither* of them is you, just like I'm both and neither Inez and Sophia. I'm just...me. I'm a killer. I've done terrible things. But I am a good person, too. I am a good friend. I am a lover—and I love my man well. I know what he needs, and I try to give it to him. I let him give me his love, and that's hard to do, sometimes. Especially when you've been and done and seen and suffered the things I have."

I shake my head. "Soph, I..."

She grins. "Soph. That's the first time you've ever used a nickname for me. I like it."

I close my eyes and try to sort through the chaos of

thoughts and feelings tornadoing inside me. "I don't know how to..."

"Of course not," she fills in, when I trail off. "I didn't. Fuck, I still don't. I still shut him out sometimes. Just the other day, I was having a bad day. I don't know why. I just...I woke up thinking about the past. I was having flashbacks of the wedding. The massacre. I couldn't get out of it. Instead of going to Ren with it, I locked myself in the bathroom and sat in the tub for four hours, thinking he'd be better off without me, because how could he love a monster like me?"

"What..." I clear my throat. "What did he do?"

"Took the knob off the door and climbed into the cold bathwater with me, fully clothed, and forced me to tell him what was wrong."

"Forced how?"

She smirks at me. "Some details are private, Jakob."

Of all things, I blush. "Oh. I see."

"Letting him in is the most terrifying thing I have ever done, Jakob. It is less frightening to face a dozen armed men, naked." She lifts an eyebrow. "Which is a claim I can make based on fact, as I have done exactly that."

"I know."

"No, you don't, I haven't told you that story."

"Well, now I'm curious."

A roll of her eyes. "The short version is that when I was my father's second in command, he was trying to work out a deal with another cartel. The negotiations weren't going well—they wanted concessions we weren't willing to give, and my father didn't take that well. So on his command, I stripped naked and walked into their compound, right through the front gate. I think they thought my father was offering me to them. Which, to be honest, wasn't that crazy of an idea, on their part. He would have, if he thought it was necessary. They surrounded me, took pictures, started talking about all the things they wanted to do to me...and then my father's men stormed the compound while they were distracted and killed every man, woman, child, and animal. And I helped." A pause. "I was seventeen."

"Jesus," I breathe. "Insanity."

"Yes, it was." She shakes her head. "You're getting sidetracked from my point. Which is that I had to make a conscious choice to trust Lorenzo with myself. And I know this may be TMI, but it was much, much easier to trust him with my body than my heart. I'm sure you can relate."

"All too well."

"But..." she looks away, searching for the right words. "It's different, now, Jakob. Between us. Sexually. After committing to him and trusting him with my heart, truly and fully, I...it's...we're..." she shook her head. "It's different."

"How so?" I hesitate. "If you care to answer, that is."

She looks away, thinking. "God, I...I don't know how to answer that." She turns her eyes to mine, and her gaze is frank and open—I see softness, tenderness, love, a sweetness I would never in a million years have thought to see in the eyes of Sophia Bruna Santos de Silva; it is not directed at me, it is not for me or about me, and I feel privileged to witness it. "It is deeper. More meaningful. It isn't about an exchange of fluids or pleasure. It is...it is the most intimate expression of vulnerability there is. Which is why it is so terrifying, the first time."

"But not the second?"

"Oh, no. It is still scary, but…Now I know the wonder of it. In time, it will not be scary at all. Only wonderful. The fear is…it's imprinted on me. It will be the work of a lifetime to undo all that instilled in me such fear of everything. But Ren deserves it, and so do I. What we have is worth the fear *and* worth the work of unlearning the fear."

"But what if…" I close my eyes, try to find the courage to ask the thing I fear the most. "What if she won't accept me? What if she can't—what if I'm not…" I snarl. "Fuck!" I snicker. "That *is* cathartic. Fuck!"

"Get it out, Jakob. Ask the question you fear most."

"How could she ever come to love me? After all that I have done…why would she sign up for that?"

"Because," Brys says from the doorway, "I'm a crazy woman."

Chapter 21

The Breaking

BRYS

"AND ON THAT NOTE, I'M GOING TO LEAVE YOU two alone to talk." Sophia rises and crosses the room, stopping in the doorway beside me. "He does have a heart in there, I promise. I'm hoping you're the woman to help him find it."

"How is Nico?" I ask.

She winces. "Out of surgery and resting. He'll make a full recovery, but it'll take time."

"And Pugli? Any word on him?"

A shake of her head. "No. He's in the wind. Sol went back and found tire tracks. He'd stashed a car. Sol followed the tracks to the road but lost them at the blacktop."

"Lovely."

"We will find him. It's only a matter of time, now." She squeezes my shoulder. "Be patient with him."

I grin. "I'm here, aren't I?"

"Yes, you are." She smiles, squeezing my shoulder again before moving on. "And I'm glad."

With Sophia gone, I take the seat. Jakob is watching me intently, curiously—and with trepidation. "You're back," he says.

"I told you I was coming back."

He nods, but seems to find it hard to speak. "I know."

"Do you have any more secrets?" I ask.

He shakes his head. "No. I...no. No more secrets."

"Then it's my turn." I am utterly terrified, and it's hard enough to let myself show him that, let alone say everything there is to say.

"Brys, you don't have to tell me anything."

"I appreciate you saying that. But I do." I pause, shake my head. "No, that's not true. I don't *have* to; I *choose* to."

"Why?" His voice is low, rough. Not at all his usual smooth, velvety, dark tone.

"You want to get into that first, huh?" I sigh, nod. "Okay, fine. Because you challenge me. You scare me. You confuse me. You make me feel safe. When I was with you, when we were running for our lives together, I was so scared. Obviously. But you...you made me feel safe." I have to shut my eyes to find the rest. "Why? Because I've never met anyone like you. You understand me. You're not intimidated by me. I'm...I'm a strong woman, Jakob. I'm loud. I'm opinionated. I'm powerful. I'm wealthy. I wield a lot of authority. No other man I've ever met has been able to accept that I am all of those things and not..." I let out a breath, hunting for the right words. "And not get intimidated, not—not feel like I threaten their masculinity. Just the wealth aspect alone is too much for most guys I've dated. I don't give a shit about money. It doesn't impress me. I don't care about a stock portfolio or investment profile. You're not going to impress me with your knowledge of financial products, how many houses you own, or how many hypercars are in your garage. But then again, I *am* used to a certain lifestyle. I care about appearances. I care about first impressions. I'm not easy to impress, to be honest." I clear my throat. "The brutal truth is that I don't like most men. I do like Charles, though, my ex. He's the only man I've ever dated that I've come to respect."

"Then why is he your ex?"

"We aren't suited, romantically. He…we…" I let out a breath. "I had a whole speech laid out, dammit, and you're derailing it."

"I'm sorry. I'll be quiet and let you speak."

"No, I…we broke up because I need someone who can take charge without shutting down who I am, and that's not Charles. He liked that I'm bold and in charge. He liked that I instigated sex. Sorry, that's—"

"No apologies," he says. "Just the truth."

I nod. "That's the truth. I was unsatisfied. I loved him, emotionally. I suppose some part of me still does and always will care about him. But I…we weren't…." I cover my face. "It feels shallow to say this, and I never did say it to him, but the honest truth is that I was unsatisfied sexually." I cackle, a hand over my mouth. "God, it feels good to admit that out loud. I've never told anyone that."

"Brys," Jakob whispers, his voice ragged. "I…"

"You had your turn," I say. "Don't make this about you." I touch his hand and smile to take the sting out of it. "There's so much for me to get out—so many things I've never even tried to put into words."

"Trust me, I know."

"I know you know," I tell him. "That's the only reason I'm even able to sit here and try. You understand. That's my point."

He watches me in silence as I regather my thoughts.

"I suppose I should start with the hardest thing," I

mutter, as much to myself as to Jakob; I look at him, hold his gaze. "Why do you find it hard to trust people?"

He looks away, thinking. "Because I've…because I know I cannot be trusted. I am a liar, so I assume others are, too. I am devious, manipulative, and selfish, and I assume others are too."

I nod, sighing. I have to close my eyes and breathe in and out slowly a few times before I can make myself speak. "It was never supposed to be me."

"What wasn't?"

"BDI. The life I'm living. It was never supposed to be me."

"Then who was it supposed to be?"

"My sister," I whisper. "Britt."

I see him process this. "Sister?"

"Older by six years," I say. "*I* was an accident; *Britt* was the chosen one."

He doesn't ask the obvious question.

"My father was grooming her to take over for him her whole life. And it's what she wanted—it's *all* she ever wanted. She wore power suits to high school. Accelerated classes. College credits her senior year. Interned for Russel Dempsey, dad's VP of operations, every summer during college. She was the golden child. Did everything right. Perfect grades, perfect behavior. Never snuck out, never got drunk, never had any pregnancy scares, just…perfect. All the time."

"That never goes well, in my experience," Jakob says. "Which means I don't like where this is going."

I acknowledge him with a nod, but that's it. "I was always compared to her. 'Why can't you be more like Britt?' they'd ask me. If I fucked up, they'd point out that Britt *never* fucked up like that. And what sucked the most about it was that *she* never rubbed it in. Never lorded it over me. She was an amazing older sister. Looked out for me. Let me tag along with her friends."

It takes a few deep breaths to get going again.

"I wanted to be just like her. I started working at the office when I was fourteen. Sorting mail in the mailroom, stuffing and stamping mailers, delivering intra-office mail, and packages. I have never worked anywhere except BDI. I dressed like her. I snuck into her room so I could organize my closet like hers because I saw how she did it, and it was so cool. I…my first boyfriend was her boyfriend's younger brother. She didn't like that very much." I laugh, remembering, then sober, shaking my head. "I knew the big chair was never going to be mine. I was happy with VP."

"But?"

"My senior year at Yale, things were really taking off for the company. They were expanding, investing in exciting new fields. Things had been happening at a breakneck pace for a few years by then. Britt was Dad's assistant—on paper, she was his PA, but in reality, she was essentially a junior VP. She had a lot of leeway. He gave her freedom to use her judgment. Let her take the lead on some big pitches and handle some big clients. And as always, Britt came through. Everything she touched turned to fucking gold. She invested four million into a startup no one had ever heard of, some niche little product that she just had a hunch was going to break out. The board didn't like it and wanted to cut back on the slack Dad was giving her. But Dad figured fuck it, it's only four mil—he could put that back into the accounts from his pay package in a worst-case scenario." I snort. "In less than two years, that company went public for over half a billion dollars. Our investment was returned with *significant* interest. She had the Midas touch. The board agreed with Dad, and they took off the training wheels. Put her on the board, made her the youngest voting member by a good thirty years." My voice wavers, shakes. "She was destined for greatness. I know that sounds melodramatic or whatever, but it's true. And then, in February of my senior year, she took her own life."

"Oh god... *Brys*."

"There are no words for the shock. Initially, it was... we would have been less shocked to find out the moon really is made of cheese. I don't know. There were no indications. She was dating a great, great guy. He was planning to propose in a couple of months. She'd had a string of wildly successful investments and pitches. We all had dinner together at this place way uptown that Mom loved. Mom and Dad stayed to drink wine and talk. I left to meet some friends at a bar, and Britt went home. The last time I saw her alive, she was taking the keys to her car from the valet. Her car, god. She loved that thing more than just about anything. She bought it with cash. It was a 1989 Porsche 911 Targa 4S, in Porsche red. Mint condition, all original. Just beautiful. I mean, that's how fucking cool my sister was. She didn't just drive a Porsche, she drove a *classic* Porsche."

My eyes burn, and then sting, and then go hazy.

Jakob shifts on the bed, grunting, and then takes my hand. "I'm here, Brys."

I sniffle. Squeeze his hand. "I watched her take the keys from the valet, and god, he was starstruck. You'd think she was Nicole Kidman, the way he was looking at her. I mean, I get it, though. She was gorgeous. Same height as me, but the fat ass gene skipped her." Another pause, swallowing hard. "She drove away, and I never saw her again. No one heard from her that night or the next day, so Mom went over to her place to check on her. Found her in her garage, in her car. She'd run a hose from the tailpipe. She'd written 'I'm sorry' in the fog on the window."

"For what?" he asked.

"Exactly what we all went crazy asking ourselves. Dad went haywire. Spent hundreds of thousands of dollars keeping it out of the news. We weren't, like, nationally famous to any degree, but around the city, we were pretty well known, and he—it was something he could do, I guess. Because no one could understand why. It hit Mom harder than anyone. She found her, and...Mom never got over it. But that came later. I'm the one who figured it out. I was the only one who could stomach the task of going through her stuff, packing it up, all that. I had to go through her personal information—her finances. And that's when I found out what had happened."

"God, Brys. That shouldn't have been on you."

I shrug. "Who else? A stranger? Some assistant from the office who didn't know her? Mom was catatonic, and Dad was running all over town handing out hush money to keep our shame out of the news cycle." I wince. "That's not fair. He was protecting our privacy. Anyway. It could only have been me."

"What did you discover, Brys?" Jakob prompts.

"A bad investment."

When I say nothing else, he frowns. "And?"

"A really, really big fuckup. She gambled and lost, that's the long and short of it. But she lost big...really, really big. Catastrophic. Dad had given her an account she could play with. She'd grown it over the years from an initial seed of ten million into over two hundred million. He bragged about that all the time. Well, she heard a pitch that sounded like a winner, and invested. Just a little bit at first. But then they faltered and needed another cash infusion. And then the markets had a bad day, and a bad week, and then a bad month, and they needed more. She was already in for a ton of money, and she couldn't bear having to admit that she'd made a bad investment because she was the golden child, the wunderkind, the girl with the Midas touch. So she just kept propping them up even after it should have been obvious they had no product, no real talent, and no future. She should have known at any one of a dozen points to cut her losses and admit she had failed for the first time. But she...she didn't. She should have known better than to keep dumping good money after bad, but she didn't."

Jakob hisses through his teeth. "Fuck."

I grin at him—it's weak, but it's there. "Swearing, right?"

"Who knew?" he teases.

The humor fades fast. "She must have panicked. Moved money from the corporate accounts to cover her losses and kept propping them up with infusion after infusion, spent her lunch breaks visiting their headquarters, trying to force them to success on her own. She nearly succeeded, I think, through sheer force of will. She reorganized their leadership, streamlined their roster, simplified their short-term goals, and restructured their finances. She had to have been working eighteen hours a day, because no one knew how much time she was spending there on top of her usual duties at B-D-I, which were not insignificant."

"She hid it well, huh?" Jakob says.

I take his statement as rhetorical and keep going without addressing it. "The day she killed herself, she'd found out that the company had folded, taking with it everything she'd invested, which, when all was said and done, was nearly half a million dollars."

"Oh, Jesus."

"Yeah." I shake my head, blinking away tears. "Dad would have forgiven her. He would have called it a very expensive lesson. The company...it was a hit, but we survived. We had to sell off a few assets to replenish our cash flow, but we survived it. If she'd just...*told* someone... if she'd felt less pressure to be perfect. If she'd...I don't know. I've gone over the what-ifs so many times over the years. I just..."

"Tell me, Brys." His hand crushes mine. "Tell me the thing you've never told anyone."

How can he see it?

"I'm angry at her!" I yell. "I'm furious! I...I can't forgive her for it—for *any* of it. Like, was she stupid? Four hundred and eighty-six *million* dollars? Into a gamified fitness app? *Really,* Britt? And...how did she not see that it was built out of nothing? I took the most cursory of glances at the package they showed her, and I could tell it was all bullshit. They had no talent behind the app—the coders were high school kids. Which isn't necessarily a problem; I've invested in companies staffed by young talent. But these kids weren't...god, it sounds bad, but they *weren't* talented enough. And for a fitness app, especially back then, when apps like that were a novelty? You need a name, and they had no one. Just some buff guys and gals that no one had ever heard of. It was obviously someone's doomed dream that didn't merit her time, attention, or money. And she should have seen that. It bothers me to this day that I still can't see why she was duped, what she saw that convinced her to put so much into it."

"When you have the touch," Jakob says, "it gets easy to think you can't fail. Your sister was charmed, it sounds like. She likely felt like not only couldn't she fail, as in she never had and never would, she also felt like she *couldn't* fail—as in wasn't *allowed* to."

"That tracks," I say. "I...yeah. I'm angry at her for just being so *dumb*. I'm angry at her for hiding it. I'm angry at her for ab—for..." my eyes fill, my throat goes thick and hot and tight. "For abandoning me. She abandoned me. She—she took the easy way out. Left me the mess to deal with. Left me with a shattered mother and a devastated father and a family business that was suddenly on the hook for five hundred million dollars. I looked up to her, idolized her. Wanted to *be* her. And then the first time in her life that she messes up, she kills herself? It's cheap, and it's weak, and it's selfish, and I *fucking hate her* for it!" I screech the last part, my voice cracking and breaking.

"Of course you do," Jakob murmurs. "How could you not?"

"She was my sister. How can I hate her so much?"

"It's easier to hate than to be sad."

I look at him. "I suppose." Now that it's started, I can't seem to stop crying. "It broke my mother, Jakob. Just broke her. She started drinking and couldn't stop. And then it was drinking, *plus* sleeping pills and painkillers. And then one day, a bit less than a year after Britt died, Mom just...didn't wake up. An accidental overdose of a mixture of things, and her heart just stopped."

"Dear lord, Brys."

"Dad hung on until I'd graduated with my MBA, and then he trained me to take his place. And then he had a heart attack." I can barely get words out, now. "I'm alone. My entire family is gone. They all left me. They all abandoned me. They all abandoned me."

I look at Jakob through tear-smeared eyes, barely able to see him through the salt haze. He lifts his hand, touches my jaw. "Come over here, Brys." He shifts to the far side of the hospital bed.

"No, you're hurt."

"Brys. Come here." It's The Voice—silky, dark, liquid, rich, smooth, humming with authority.

I hesitate, but then a lightning bolt hits me: why am I resisting? Why am I holding back? What I want more than anything is to just let him hold me while I fall apart.

So I climb onto the narrow bed beside him, careful not to put any weight on the wound site. His arm wraps around me, and he tucks my cheek onto his chest, and his hand smooths my hair.

For a moment or two, it's deliciously comforting.

And then it all hits.

Everything.

Fucking *everything*.

Britt being the favorite. Never being able to match up to her impossible standards. Her suicide. My anger over it. My sense of betrayal and abandonment. The sadness at the loss of a brilliant young woman, not just my sister but my friend, someone I looked up to—a bright light in a dark world snuffed out way too soon. That's a sadness I've never let myself feel. I've been too busy being angry and denying that I'm angry—too busy pretending I don't feel anything about it at all, because I've spent so long afraid of exactly this: the breaking.

And I know why, now: I've never had anyone I trusted to hold me when I broke. Charles was wonderful. Kind, supportive, romantic. But he had no emotional depth. He couldn't have handled me breaking like this. It would have been the end of us.

But Jakob?

He just holds me through it and lets me break. I'm safe with him. He's a hard place I can break against, and the soft place I can land when I'm done.

I cry for Britt. I cry for Mom—the same confusing mixture of sad and angry. For Dad, who died of sadness. For myself, for being the only one left. For all the times I've wondered if I should just join them.

I cry for all the awful things I've seen over the last few days.

And when I'm finally done weeping, I look up at him, and I know one thing for certain:

I love Jakob.

Chapter 22

Unbreakable and Brittle

JAKOB

It's hard to breathe.

Because, underneath all the shock and sadness I feel surrounding Brys's story, there's something else simmering inside me. An emotion I've never dared name, never had the courage to face head-on.

Yet, it's guided and shaped my every decision.

Anger.

But as my Zoom therapist once explained to me, Anger is a secondary emotion. It comes out of something else. We use anger as a displacement because anger is easier to cope with than what's really beneath it.

In my case, only now that Brys has put it all into words do I truly understand my own emotions.

"I feel you stewing up there," Brys says, after a strangely comfortable silence of several minutes, in which she rests against my chest.

"You have helped me understand myself," I tell her. "I'm trying to process that."

She waits for me to speak, her fingers dancing in slow, idle patterns over the print of the hospital gown from chest to shoulders to stomach, always cognizant of the tender area where my wound is.

The physical pain is a constant, sharp throb under everything, but it's tolerable. Every time it starts to creep up on me and I feel tempted to ask if it would really hurt to let them hook up the IV again and pump me full of opiates that will take the pain away, I put myself back in that room, shivering on the floor in a pool of vomit and shit, hallucinating and craving and hating myself and stuck in an endless hell of misery.

This pain is far better than that.

"You asked why I don't trust," I say, eventually. "My answer was true. But...I...you made me realize that the deeper truth is that I can't trust anyone for the same reasons as you: Everyone who was supposed to love me abandoned me. I know...I know my mother's death was no one's fault. She didn't choose it. But I can't quite grasp that. I don't know how else to say it. Physically, I was sixteen when she died, but emotionally, I was much less mature than my size or years would indicate. I was a sheltered, spoiled little boy. I'd never been told no. Never experienced lack or loss or hardship. My mother loved me. Even my father, as stern and hard and serious and reserved as he was, loved me too, in his way. And then Mother was just... *gone.* I had no answers, no explanation. Cancer? Aneurism? Heart attack? I don't know. I will never know—the hospital where she died was destroyed in a fire, along with all their records. She was alive and well one day and gone less than a week later, and..." my eyes burn. "My father hogged all the grief."

"Jakob—ohhh, Jakob."

"He never moved from her side. I never got to sit with

her and talk to her, or say goodbye. I was out of the room with my tutor or nanny—I don't remember which—when she died. I never…I never got to say goodbye. I never got to touch her hand. Father, he pushed past me, and I followed him. It felt like I was supposed to follow him. I barely understood that she was even dead. I tried to talk to him on the walk home from the hospital, but he didn't answer me, didn't even acknowledge me. He marched inside without so much as slowing down, slamming his office door literally in my face. Less than…what? Not even thirty seconds after shutting the door, I heard the gun go off. Mother flatlined, and Father shot himself less than twenty minutes later."

Brys's tears soak my shirt. "Jakob, I'm so sorry."

"For what?"

"No, that's—god that annoys me. I'm not apologizing, I'm expressing sympathy, you big goof."

"Oh."

"It's just so awful. To lose one parent is awful, but to lose both? And so close together?"

"Don't cry for me, Brys."

She hums the chorus of "Don't Cry For Me, Argentina" before answering. "Why not, Jakob? Why can I not share in your grief?"

That cuts me to the core. "Why would you want to?"

This has her sitting up on an elbow and looking at me in disbelief. "You really don't know, by now?"

I wrack my brain for what I'm supposed to know, but come up empty. "No. No clue." She doesn't fill in the empty silence I so helpfully leave. "Brys?"

"I'm not ready for that yet," she whispers. "Just let me be sad for you."

"Okay. Alright."

She nuzzles back onto my chest. "We're a hell of a pair, aren't we? Two broken, fucked up, abandoned orphans with trust issues and more money than sense."

"I never let myself realize how angry I am about it," I admit eventually. "Mainly at my father." It takes a while for the next truth to percolate up from the depths of me and find its way to my lips. "I think...I think my father loved my mother too much. He adored her to the point of madness. He loved her so much he stifled her, sometimes. She was the only person he ever showed any kind of softness or affection to. He loved her too much, and when he lost her, he couldn't cope. He took himself away from me. He abandoned me and left me alone in the world. I was helpless, defenseless, and clueless. He loved her too much, and it broke him." Saying the next part feels a bit like vomiting: awful, impossible to stop, and you feel better once it's over. "I think that I have refused to let myself...feel that kind of..." that's the bile trapped at your teeth before it spews free. "I have spent my life unable to trust or to let anyone love me or let myself love anyone because I am terrified of ending up like my father." Shamefully, a sob sucks the oxygen from my lungs and forces its way out. "I'm terrified of letting someone in and losing them. I lost Isabel. I...created Madame X to be the perfect companion. She was elegant and wise and sophisticated and intelligent and educated. She was conversant in classical music and classical fiction, in art and history. She was voracious for knowledge, and I fed it to her. I controlled every aspect of her existence so that I would never lose her. I kept her locked up in my tower like a raven-haired Rapunzel, because that way nothing could ever harm her and nothing could ever take her away from me."

"And yet," Brys whispers; it is a gentle, brutal prompt.

"And yet I lost her anyway. I clung to her as tightly as I possibly could, and I lost her anyway. Not to death, but to..." I laugh at the irony. "To life. I clutched her too tightly, and I lost her to life. And myself to death. In faking my death, I did die, in a way. Not physically, but in every other way. And yet...and still..." I shake my head, as if to dislodge stuck thoughts and trapped words. "But now, having come so close to death? Sitting trapped in that chair, feeling the press come down on my head, knowing Pugli was going to kill Nicolae or both of us, I...it should have been me, not him. I was helpless. I couldn't even speak. I was... so weak. I'd lost so much blood, and I was so dizzy and disoriented, and in nearly dying, I finally feel like I've...like I've come through something. Like I've burst through a membrane, and on this side of it...I'm really alive for the first time."

"Can I ask you something, Jakob?" I can barely make out her words.

"Of course. Anything."

"When I told Sophia that you kissed me, she seemed stunned. Why?"

"The one tiny fragment a whore can hold back is a kiss. It's more intimate than fucking. My clients never wanted to kiss me, and I refused the few who did try. It's a common rule, I think. I just...kissing is...I don't kiss."

"Did you kiss Madame X?"

"No. And when I finally did, it was at the end, when things were falling apart, and my feelings were beginning to be unavoidable."

"You loved her."

I shake my head. "No, not—no. I don't think I loved

her. I know I didn't. Love doesn't do what I did to her. I felt powerful emotions for her, yes, but they weren't love. It was obsession. Infatuation. Need. I was..." I laugh. "I spent thousands of dollars on therapy and got nowhere near any of this, and you get it out of me in minutes. I was desperately trying to fill the void, to...create something that would fill my need for..."

When I fail to form the last word, Brys lets out a sigh. Twists so she can gaze up at me with green-brown eyes ringed in stunning azure, eyes filled with the word that sticks in my throat like too much peanut butter. "Look at me, Jakob." Downy feathers aren't as soft as her voice in that moment. "Please."

I do; it hurts, but I do. "What." It comes out flat.

Her fingers are small and slender and clever, and they trace the hard line of my jaw. "Say it."

I shake my head. "I can't." I know what I'm supposed to say. I know it's true.

"Yes, you can. You've built not one, not two, but *three* empires. You've survived the loss of your parents, homelessness, addiction, being sexually trafficked and forced into prostitution. You built your Club and changed the lives of your...what do you call them? Your quiver?"

"My Arrows. My Broken Arrows."

"Why that name, of all the macho shit you could have called your macho men club?"

"Because if you melt a sword into a plow, it's no longer a sword. If you take a gun apart, it's no longer a gun. But if you break an arrow, it's still recognizably an arrow. I... it sounds kinda stupid now, but that was the thinking at the time. They were weapons of war, those men. But they were broken—by life, by war, by what they went through and did. But they were still...them. Once a sword has been broken, you can never reforge it into what it was. But an arrow? You can put the fletching and arrowhead on a new shaft and have a new arrow. It's like the Ship of Theseus—is it the same arrow, or a new one? It doesn't matter, I'm just saying. That's why I called them Broken Arrows."

"Because you plucked them from the battlefield and made new arrows of them." She touches the tip of my chin with a fingertip, gazing up at me, and my god, I do not deserve the tenderness in her eyes. "I think it's a beautiful thing you did for them."

"That's just it—it was for *me*. I hoped that if I could save others, do something selfless, that I'd...I'd somehow find redemption for myself. I don't regret doing it, but it didn't work."

Her laugh surprises me. "Of course it didn't. That's not how redemption works. You can't earn it, Jakob. You could do it all over again a hundred times, the whole Broken Arrows thing, and never find the redemption you seek."

"Then...how?"

"You have to forgive yourself."

My turn to laugh. "Is that all?" I sigh. "The irony is that they all found redemption. *And* love."

"You can't see it, still?" The warmth in her eyes shakes me to my core.

"Don't look at me like that, Brys." My words are wet.

She looks at me like that all the more. Unwavering. Blazing with intensity. Afire with...

Love.

Her thumb captures the dot trickling down from the corner of my eyes. "There he is."

I turn my head away to hide my shame. "Don't. Fucking—don't. You can't."

"Jakob, trust me."

I'm on fire. My skin burns. My gut pulses with nausea. Everything is tight and hot and sour. I can only shake my head. "You can't." It barely counts as speech.

"Why not, Jakob?"

"I'm not worth it," I whisper around the knives still caught in my throat. "Whore. Addict. Killer. Liar. Traitor—I betrayed Isabel. I'm a user; I use people. I'm a taker." I squeeze my eyes shut as tight as they'll go, but the tears fall anyway—I haven't cried since the day...no. Not even then. "I never cried for her."

"Trust me with it."

"Why do you want it?"

"Because I love you."

I should say it back, but my breaking is too violent a thing. She says those words so matter-of-factly, so easily—when I know it's not easy for her at all. And I just...shatter.

And all of a sudden, I'm a sixteen-year-old boy in a hospital room who has just been shoved to the ground by his father. My mother is still and thin under a scratchy white blanket, and her once-lovely features are lit by the harsh fluorescent lights, which make her ugly, when in life she was so beautiful that men would stop on the sidewalk and stare at her. Her hair, once a storm cloud of black, dense curls, is lank and thin. The only part of her I recognize is her nose, that proud Jewish nose. I don't have it—I have my father's. For a long time—to my shame—I was glad I didn't. Now I wish I did.

There's a steady tone, an awful, unending beep.

I'm sixteen, and my mother is dead, and in a short time, so will be my father.

I'm slumped on the floor outside my father's study. The gun has just gone off. I heard the *pop*, a terrible silence, and then the slump of a body. And I know.

I'm alone on the streets of New York City. I do not speak any English beyond "Hello," "my name is Jakob," "please," and "no thank you." Why my parents and the tutor thought it was more important for me to learn fucking Latin instead of English is still a mystery to me. My father's cousin has pushed me out of the car and driven away. I may be naive, but I know what has happened. That I am alone. That I will starve.

I am walking and walking and walking.

I am on a bed, face down; I have just been fucked by a man; he was not gentle.

I am in the corner of the bathroom, jonesing and tweaking for a hit. Miss Amy will not give it to me because I would not submit to the man who violated me. She locks me in the bathroom with a bottle of water until I come out. She calls Douglas. Douglas comes over and has his way. I get my shot.

I am standing over Amy's wrecked corpse. There is an ocean of blood, and her arms and legs and neck are all bent the wrong direction. Her purse is still across her slender chest, her keys right on top, visible in the open purse-mouth. I cast a glance around—there is a crowd. I crouch and pretend to check her pulse even though her eyes stare sightlessly at the leaves of a towering maple tree. I take her keys and wallet. I killed her.

I am detoxing; even in this wild hurricane of cathartic, overdue grief, I cannot relive that.

One hell after another flashes through me, as if I am dying, but instead of seeing a highlight reel, I see every moment of sorrow and horror and pain.

I am watching Isabel say, "I do," to Logan; she is looking right into my eyes as she serves me stew and does not recognize me.

In all of this, I never once wept.

Not a tear.

It all just…crushed me. Ground the crushed pieces into dust. Compressed the dust into obsidian—all razor angles, unbreakable and brittle at once.

It all comes due, now. I can't stop it.

She doesn't coo and cluck and hush. She lays her head on my chest and traces my jaw and the shell of my ear. Her lips touch the underside of my chin. My cheek. Tastes my tears.

I hear the door open. I sense the lights dimming. The door closes.

The pain is too much. Physical, emotional…it's all too much.

My eyes are heavy. It's all heavy. But as the grief and torment and sorrow flow out of me, I begin to feel a lightness within me.

"Brys," I whisper. "I—"

Her fingers touch my lips. "I know, Jakob." Then it is her lips on mine. "Later. Just rest."

"You know?" She nods. "What I…how —?"

"Yes, Jakob. I hear it. Just rest."

I shake my head. She deserves to know. "I…"

She huffs in frustrated, amused laughter. "Jakob." Her lips quest against my cheek. "They're just words. I *know*."

"But they hold power. I have given them power. Words have meaning."

"Jakob, it's alright. We have time."

"My mother had time. Until she didn't." I force my eyes open and find hers wide and clear and infinite. Looking into her eyes gives me courage. "I love you, Brys."

Chapter 23

Airplane Conversations

BRYS

"I can fucking walk," Jakob snarls. "The wheelchair is entirely unnecessary."

Now that he's decided to swear, he does so frequently and floridly. Like the rest of his Arrows, he has fixated on the many various forms of "fuck" as his preferred curse word.

"It's hospital policy, sir," says the enormous, soft-spoken Hispanic nurse.

"Policy," Jakob grumbles. "Bullshit policy. I was shot in the gut, not the fucking leg."

I touch his shoulder. "Jakob, he's just doing his job. Stop it."

He sighs. "Fine. Sorry."

"Happens every day, sir. It's alright."

He has spent the last few days being monitored and going crazier and crazier at being cooped up. At this point, he's nearly feral. We also haven't had a moment alone since our giant tell-all; the Arrows decided what was needed was some "family togetherness," which apparently means Chance ignoring the protests of the doctors and nurses as he pushed Jakob's bed down the hallway to Nico's room.

When the doctor arrived and tried to exert his authority, Chance merely stood over him, mammoth arms crossed over his mammoth chest and stared down at the diminutive doctor in glaring, threatening silence. Eventually, the doctor threw up his hands and walked out, snarling something along the lines of "at least wash your damn hands."

And that's how we spent the next few days—twenty people crammed into a single hospital room. Visiting hours were totally ignored. Saxon somehow snuck in two fifths of high-end scotch, and Terra snuck in a bag of weed gummies and passed them out to everyone like they were Certs.

It was wild. The hospital couldn't do a damn thing about it, either—they tried. The hospital security showed up, took one look at the crew of men—each of whom radiated lethal energy—and fucked off back to their booth. Since we weren't doing anything but being noisy, the hospital decided discretion was the better part of valor and didn't call the police on us.

Now, finally, Jakob and Nico have both been discharged, Nico against medical advice. They wanted him to stay a few more days for observation, but he was having no part of it. He was in a lot of pain and was barely able to move, but insisted he would heal better at home, and either they could discharge him or he would walk out on his own anyway.

A long black bus of the type that typically sees bachelorette parties arrives, and the troops tromp up onto the bus; forty minutes later, we're loading onto the same absurd jet.

This time, I'm able to appreciate it more.

It's incredible. The seats are all captain's chairs that rotate 360 degrees, but each one is its own high-end massage chair with heating and cooling functions, the ability to recline totally flat and transform into a bed, and built-in speakers that can sync to either a personal device or the projector screen television that slides down from the ceiling between the cabin and the cockpit. The walls, floor, and ceiling can be turned into screens that reflect what's outside—making it feel like you're sitting in a glass tube fifty thousand feet in the air, going several hundred miles per hour.

Ask me how I know: Saxon turned the feature on while I was dozing, and I woke up to discover I was scudding through the air, seemingly supported by nothing—the neatest trick is how the effect makes the seat beneath you seem invisible too. It's wildly disorienting.

Jakob and Nico take seats side by side in the back and huddle together—plotting Pugli's demise. Which leaves me with the women.

I am not a girl's girl. I have never had many girlfriends. In high school and college, I had a circle of friends, but it was all relationships of proximity and convenience, nothing deep or meaningful. Once I took over after Dad's death, I gave up the pretense of trying to have friendships.

So, I don't know how to be around them. I feel awkward and new. They have stories. Shorthand. Inside jokes. They whisper and giggle. I sit and watch and listen and wonder what's wrong with me.

"Excuse me?" I'm startled out of my self-pitying reverie by a soft, quiet voice.

I look at the woman who has settled in beside me: tall, lean, and willowy, with auburn hair. "Hi. Ummm... Naomi? Sorry, I'm not great with names. You're Silas's... ummm..." I trail off, hoping she'll fill in the rest.

She does. "Wife is close enough. We don't stand on legalities and technicalities." A gentle smile. "And yes, Silas is my man."

I blink. "Your man."

She nods. "Yes. My husband, although, as I said, we are not technically married. We are in every way that counts. But..." she shrugs. "I don't know. He's my man."

"I've never even thought the phrase, 'my man' before," I admit. "I'm far too independent for that."

She shifts in her seat—when two seats are arranged side by side facing the same direction, they're close enough to feel almost like a bench, which means when she crosses her ankles under her thighs, her knees nudge into my personal space. It's weirdly intimate for someone I just met, but pulling away feels rude, so I tolerate it.

"You are uncomfortable with us." It's not a question.

I nod. "Yeah, I...I'm not—I don't have a lot of friends. Or any. I...I work too much and, well, the honest truth is that I've been too shut down to let anyone in far enough to be a friend."

She casts her eyes around the group of women; it somehow serves as a gesture. "We are all like that. Myka ran away from an overbearing family and a bad relationship. Anjalee was the spoiled heiress to an Indian billionaire's fortune and ran away from an arranged marriage. Tatiana's father is a Croatian gangster. Annika was an Olympic volleyball player whose career was ended by a car accident, and then she got addicted to drugs. Maria is an operator like the boys, and the hell she went through is a whole story in itself. Terra was sexually abused as a girl and was homeless for a long time. Sophia was the daughter of a Brazilian warlord and was trained from childhood to be an assassin."

I choke. "Wait, *what*?"

Sophia rolls her eyes, having overheard. "I wasn't an *assassin,* Naomi. I was my father's right-hand man, woman, girl, whatever. Being a druglord-kingpin-warlord-whatever-you-want-to-call-him, that meant threatening, hurting, and killing people, it is true. But an assassin is a specific thing. I was the one who hired the assassin, not the one who did the assassinating."

"Oh," Naomi says. "I see."

Sophia indicates Naomi. "Her father is a militia-prepper-type. Beat her mercilessly. Used her like a slave when her mother died. Sold her to his buddy, a man twice her age, as his wife."

I stare around at the women, each one in turn, absorbing what I'm being told.

"My father left my home in El Salvador to find work and never came back," Maria says. "My mother tried to bring my brother and me to America for a better life, but she and my brother died in the Darién Gap. I made it to the border but ended up in a brothel. I escaped, eventually, and was discovered by a CIA agent, who recruited me into black ops."

"Um." I shake my head. "I…I don't…"

"Brys," Naomi says. "My point is that none of us—not *one* of us—has lived what anyone could call a normal life. We are *all* messed up. We've *all* been through hell. We may not know your personal story, and we may not know what you've been through, but I promise, we understand."

I shake my head—my eyes burn, for some stupid reason. "It's not that. I…I just don't know how to be friends with women."

There's silence, and then every single one of them bursts into laughter.

Naomi slings an arm around me and squeezes. "Oh dear. Oh my." She rests her cheek on my shoulder. "We aren't *friends*. We're…"

"Sisters," Anjalee says.

"Comrades-in-arms," Annika says.

"Every time the men go out on another mission to save one of the others, or one of us, or whatever, we're how we get through it. We're a little band of soldiers' wives." This is Terra, with her thick Boston twang and her bright scarlet hair. "We're family."

"I don't have that either," I say.

"Neither do most of us," answers Annika. "This is found, family."

Sophia doesn't say or do anything, but somehow, all the women turn to her as if they know she's about to speak. It's weird and impressive. "Brys, listen to me. I know exactly how you feel. I held myself apart from them for a long time because of it. I didn't think I knew how to interact with them, didn't think they'd want to. One of the nicknames my father's men gave me was 'La Reina de Hielo.' Do you speak any Spanish?" I shake my head. "It means the Ice Queen. I was also known as La Víbora—The Viper. That should tell you what kind of a person I was."

"The *Viper*?" I echo. "Really, that's…honestly, that's pretty fucking badass."

She just shrugs. "You just have to let us in. Let us know you."

"And really, you don't have a choice," Terra says. "You're stuck with us."

"Isn't that just endearing?" I deadpan.

Tatiana speaks for the first time. "I was so concerned as you were when Nico introduced me to the others. And I suppose you may understand, hmm? I saw them laughing, and how close they are. I had friends back in Croatia. But I was Stjepan Juric's daughter. The friendships were… it was hard to know if they were genuine, no? Do they like me for me or because my father is who he is? How do you know? I thought these ladies would not like me or think I talk stupidly, because of my accent. Or—oh, I had many fears. But now we are family."

I nod, absorbing, and then glance at the men. They're all clustered in the back around a tablet—plans, maps, who knows. Men stuff, I suppose. "And them? You're family with the other men?"

"Oh yes," Tatiana says. "I trust all of them with my life. Truly. If any one of them asked me to…Oh, I do not know. Jump off a building, let us say. I would."

I boggle at this. "No questions asked. Just…jump?"

She nods immediately. "Yes."

"How? How do you trust them like that? The men who aren't Nico, I mean."

"Nico trusts them." She shrugs, as if that says it all. "They have saved each other's lives many times. They are closer than brothers, as only men who have combatted together can be. But I have been out there with them." She waves at the wall, meaning the world at large. "I have seen them fight. I have fought with them. If they asked me to jump off a building, I know they would not do so without a reason and without a plan."

"*You* fought?" I ask.

She nods. "The man you encountered, Pugli. He and

Sophia's ex-husband sent a small army of their soldiers to kill and kidnap us. We fought them off."

Damn.

These people have been through some *shit.*

"I..." It's hard to find the right thing to say. "I can try. I want to. I want to be a part of..." I look around at the jet, the people in it. "All of this."

"Good news," Terra says. "You already are."

Oh.

But...I have a life in New York.

My god, New York. I just vanished. The board, Charles, Celia, my assistant, and Dorothy, my secretary. Lonnie the door guy at my condo.

I just vanished.

I think about New York, then. My life there, my career. My condo. The Met. Brunches with the Uptown set.

And I find myself wondering if I really want to go back to all that. I watch Jakob, still conferring with Nicolae; he winces now and then, touching his wound and tentatively stretching it.

I pull my gaze to the window once more, although "window" is a bit of a misnomer; seeing as the entire interior of the aircraft's cabin is some kind of giant screen, what I see as "window" to the world beyond the walls is actually just a program making it look like a window. Curious, I angle toward the wall, hoping to hide the potentially embarrassing thing I'm about to try. The "window" looks identical to any airplane window: small, oval. There's even a 3D illusion of depth, although the illusion falls apart if you touch the wall. Glancing to make sure everyone else is occupied and not watching me act like a dingus, I put a finger at the top-right and bottom-left corners and use a "pinch and zoom" gesture to try to make the window bigger, like I would on a touchscreen. The window flickers, although that's not the right word. It...well, it blips, like it's reacting to an invalid command. I try tapping the top-right corner; it blips again, but differently—a shorter blip. Sorry, I'm not a coder, so I don't know all the technical terms. You'll just have to deal with "blip". Next, I simply tap and hold the top-right corner; the blip is sustained—meaning the outline of the window darkens and stays that way as long as I keep touching the corner. Dragging my finger on an upward diagonal—an "expand" gesture for those digital natives out there—I succeed in making the window taller. By repeating the gesture in reverse using the bottom-left corner, I make the window wider. Just for shits and giggles, I test the limits of the window size; when I've reached the extent of my arms' wingspan, I figure it's probably as good as infinite, within the confines of the available space.

This is when my experimentation draws the attention of others.

"Wait, what the fuck?" This is Saxon, and he sounds almost irate. "You can fuckin' *do* that?"

And suddenly, there's a giant blond man half in my lap, leaning all up in my personal space as he plays with my "window" like a two-hundred-twenty-pound toddler.

I push my fingertips into his chest. "Do you fucking *mind*, Gigantor? You have your own window. Go play with that and get out of my space."

Terra snickers, reaching out and yanking him backward by a belt loop. "Sorry, sweetheart." She addresses Saxon in the tone you'd use to address a puppy. "We're still working on respecting personal space, aren't we, baby?"

Saxon flops into his own chair and goes to town,

expanding his window, minimizing it, moving it this way and that. Soon, everyone whose seat is on the window side is playing with the effect, resulting in windows of a dozen different sizes and shapes.

Jakob stares at me with an annoyed expression, and I just shrug and give him an "oops" look.

"Sorry about that," Terra says to me. "He's kind of excitable." She pats his beefy thigh. "But that's what I love about him."

Saxon, after sitting for roughly sixty seconds, is up again and across the cabin, pestering his brother Silas, who is trying to nap.

Alone with Terra for a moment, I ask a question that's been banging around my head since last night. "How long did you know Saxon before you knew you were in love with him?"

She splutters sarcastically. "Oh, fuck. Like...ten minutes?" She shakes her head, snorting. "For real, though, it was a matter of days. Granted, those days were intense, action-packed, terrifying, and absolutely bonkers. It was like two months packed into less than a week. I just..." she trails off, looking at Saxon, who has deposited himself on his brother's lap and is trying to stick a finger in Silas's nose. "God, he's impossible when he's bored."

Silas drives a thumb into a pressure point in Saxon's underarm, eliciting a howl...I tune out the now-bickering brothers and re-focus on Terra.

"I guess I just knew," Terra finishes. "I hate having to answer like that because it's a bullshit answer and I fuckin' know it. I...I wasn't looking for it, Brys. I didn't think I even wanted it. After what I'd been through, what had been done to me by men, it's a wonder I'm still straight. Like, I get it. Being with a woman would be easier, I sometimes think. Like, I just don't fuckin' understand his ass *at all,* most days. I did experiment with girls a couple of times when I was wasted, but I just like dick too much. And Saxon?" She wiggles her eyebrows at me. "Man's hung like Priapus."

I splutter and then laugh out loud, hand over my mouth. "Terra!"

She cackles. "Oh, honey, we're a wildly inappropriate bunch. I hope you're not a prude or anything."

"I'm not a prude, I don't think, but—"

"Hey, Saxy baby!" Terra twists in her seat, yelling over her shoulder.

"Yo!" Saxon replies in kind without turning around. "What up, queen?"

"Why am I not a lesbian?"

"Because you love my cock!"

The exchange is shouted; no one else bats an eye.

"This feels...I feel like I should be offended by this conversation," I say. "Or like someone should be."

"But you're nooooooot!" Terra singsongs the last word. "Are you? Because it's all just jokes. We're all allies here."

"No, I..." I shake my head. "Can we go back to how it seems like it should be impossible to feel as strongly as I do about someone I've only known for a few days?"

As if they had all received some sort of cue or signal, the women surround me again, leaning over the backs of chairs, sitting cross-legged on the floor between seats that have been turned to face inward; Tatiana is perched on Terra's lap while Terra idly braids the other woman's hair.

"We've all had this conversation," Annika says. "I

think that's part of why we're so close. I mean, we live together in close quarters, it's true, but we've all been through something no one else can understand if you haven't been through it, and the only people who have are on this jet. We all know firsthand how you can fall in love with someone you barely know. Like, I still have conversations with Chance where he tells me something about himself that I didn't know. But those are just facts, right? Like, history. That stuff is important, and I'm not saying it's not. But Chance just *gets* me. We're both addicts. Like, rock-bottom, should be dead, 'there but for the grace of God go I' meth-heads. We're drastically different in a lot of ways. We disagree on some big shit. But when it comes down to brass tacks, Chance knows my fucking soul. He's inside me—who I am as a human being. I knew I loved him when I faced the prospect of going about the rest of my life alone, without him, and I just couldn't do it. He brought me to the Club and introduced me to everyone, and that was it. I knew where I belonged." She casts a look around the group of women. "And it's as much these women as Chance, in some ways. They're my support system. They get me in ways even Chance can't."

Anjalee addresses me, then, in her lilting accent. "If you are wishing for a test by which to know if Jakob is the right person for your future, try to imagine returning to your previous life without him. Try to really sit in the feelings. Waking up in bed alone. Going to bed alone. Going on dates with other men. Sleeping with someone else—and I do mean sleep, as well as sexually. If you think you can go back to your life without Jakob in it, then perhaps he is not the right person, or it is not the right time yet."

The other women continue in that vein, but my attention wanders away.

I picture myself in my condo:

My alarm has just gone off. It's 5:45 in the morning. I'm alone in bed. I crack my eyes open, slap the alarm into blessed silence, and sit up, peering out my floor-to-ceiling windows at the Manhattan skyline. After sitting and stretching, I roll out of bed and shuffle to the bathroom. Pee, wash my hands, shuffle to the kitchen for a cup of coffee.

Jakob is already there, mug in hands, steam swirling up from the rim. He's shirtless in a pair of tight running shorts, sweat dripping down the cleft between his bulging, anvil-hard pecs. He's breathing hard, his powerful torso swelling and contracting with each breath.

Wait. How did he get there?

Try again.

At work. In my office, lights low, classical music playing softly, cruising through a pile of reports from various departments, sipping from a sweating bottle of Dasani from the vending machine in the breakroom. It's after eight in the evening, and I'm the only one left on the floor, except for a janitor pushing a large gray rolling trash can from cubicle to cubicle.

Too bad all the temps went home—the new guy is pretty hot, in a fit-but-nerdy sort of way. I bet he'd be an eager beaver eater.

I hear a rustling from the doorway and assume it's the janitor coming to empty my wastebasket—I set mine on my desk without looking up.

"What am I meant to do with that?" His voice is low and amused and dark with erotic promise.

I look up at him. He's in a three-piece suit, or the remnants of one—he's removed his jacket and tie, vest buttoned, and top shirt button undone; the jacket and tie are folded and draped over one arm. He's so fucking gorgeous I just want to eat him all up, devour him, crawl inside him and stay there—

Good lord.

I suppose that must be a sign of some sort, if he's showing up in my imagination.

I feel a prickling sensation and pull my gaze over to Jakob. He's staring at me, his dark eyes glittering and intense and full of arousal.

Nico is reclined in a seat with Tatiana beside him—she's holding his hand in hers, kissing his knuckles, murmuring to him.

Saxon has Terra on his lap with his hands under her shirt, playing with her tits. Just, like, in front of everyone. Cool, cool.

Annika is resting her head on Chance's shoulder; he has her cane in one hand with the butt on the floor, and he's spinning it idly, gazing out the window. His other arm is around her shoulders and slung over her waist.

Everywhere I look, it's the same. Cozy, affectionate couples stroking hands and murmuring sweet nothings to each other, silently enjoying each other's company, and gazing at each other with saccharine adoration.

Part of me is irritated by this garish display of love everywhere I look, but I am self-aware enough to recognize that this feeling is most likely rooted in jealousy. I'm uncomfortable with it because I have never felt about anyone the way these people feel about each other. I have never gazed at anyone like he hung the fucking moon in the sky just for me. No one has ever held my head on his lap and petted my hair while I doze like Maria with Solomon four rows forward. Maria, the badass black ops bitch who crossed the Darién Gap on foot as a child, survived a brothel, escaped, and can murder a dozen men with a toothpick in less than sixty seconds. Cozied up on her man's lap.

It has never once occurred to me to rest my head on a man's lap. If it had been suggested, I'd likely have responded with a not-quite-a-joke about biting his dick off.

I've never whispered sweet nothings. Like, what do you say? What happens in those whispered conversations?

And PDA.

They're all so openly affectionate—openly sexual. No one is outright fucking, but I'm pretty sure Saxon has Terra's bra unhooked, and from this angle, it sure does look like Maria's head is moving, so maybe it's less of a cute head-on-the-lap thing and more of a sucking-his-brains-out on-the-sly thing.

I feel the uneasy prickling of Jakob's stare again; I find his gaze.

He crooks a finger at me. *Come here,* he mouths. *Now.*

Oh.

Oh fuck.

Okay.

I get to my feet and prowl toward him, putting extra sway in my hips. Stop in front of him.

"Yes, Jakob?" I pitch my voice low, just for his ears.

"Sit." It's a command. I sit in the seat beside him, glance sidelong at him. Wait for the next command. "Not there."

Oh.

His lap.

I swallow hard. No one is looking, but they will. Do I want to let them see me on their boss's lap? What am I giving up by submitting like this in public? In private is one thing. It's fun. It's hot. It's sexy. Only he sees me like that. But here?

"Jakob," I whisper. "I..."

He takes my hand. "Trust me, Brys."

I don't want to.

But...I also do.

I'm scared. It's stupid, I know. Scared to sit on Jakob's lap. It's innocent. It's simple. It's easy.

Then why is it so terrifying?

I swallow hard, feeling my eyes burn. To obey him like this, in public...to sit on his lap in front of his crew? It's a statement. For him, for me, and for us.

I stand up, heart hammering in my chest, pulse pounding, breath coming in shaky exhales and trembling inhales.

Hesitate.

Let out one more breath.

Everyone is watching.

Absurdly, horrifyingly, my eyes burn and sting, and I know everyone can tell. My mortification is complete.

It feels, for a moment or two, like I'm giving up some vital part of myself by acquiescing to this public display. I wouldn't balk in private. He could command me to my knees and come on my face without warning, and I would take it and like it.

But this?

Can he even begin to fathom what he's asking of me?

I deposit my bottom onto his knees and perch there, spine a ramrod from C1 to coccyx. Knees together. Hands on my thighs, shaking.

So, so stupid. I'm so stupid. This is stupid. Why am I

sitting on his lap? Why am I acting like he's asked me to…I don't even know. Get naked and parade myself down the Las Vegas Strip.

My eyes meet Sophia's, and I see understanding and compassion there. She rises to her feet with lithe grace and floats down the aisle to the back of the cabin. Stands in front of me, smiling.

"Breathe, Brys," she murmurs, crouching and taking my hands. "I know what you're feeling."

"How?" I whisper. "How can you?"

"I was raised in a world where weakness of any kind was seized upon and exploited. There was no softness in my life. Ever. At all. No kindness. No affection. Do you have any idea how fucking hard and scary it was for me to soften for Lorenzo? To…to hold his hand in public. To let him kiss me in front of everyone. And forget about me showing *him* that stuff. That was totally off the table. I could barely tolerate his affection. Even his kind words, even him telling me he loved me was hard to hear."

Jakob's hands frame my waist just above my hips. "Talk to me, Brys."

I grit my jaw until my molars ache, wanting to leap up and flee. Instead, I forcibly pry my jaw open and focus on breathing.

"I wasn't raised in a drug cartel or by doomsday militia preppers or whatever," I say. "But I…I was twenty-six when Britt killed herself. Twenty-nine when I graduated with my MBA, and thirty-one when Dad died. I was thirty-one and CEO of a company worth eight billion, in charge of thousands of employees. I was—I *am*—in a position of authority over men thirty and forty years my senior. All of them were waiting for me to fail. Every decision was second-guessed. What I wear is still scrutinized. Too much cleavage? I'm dressing slutty for attention. Wear too severe a powersuit? Sexless bitch. Jeans to work on a Friday like everyone else? I don't take my job seriously. Dress up on Fridays instead? I think I'm better than everyone; I'm inaccessible. Too fashion-forward. Have a bad day and snap at an employee for fucking up? On my period. Emotional. Hormonal. Just a bitch. Too friendly with a male employee? Probably letting him fuck me. I can't show any weakness. I can't...I can't ever relax into my job. I have to be perfect in what I wear, what I say, how I walk, who I talk to, and the tone of my voice. Everything I do, I'm held up against my father and found wanting, if only because I have a vagina."

I swallow hard. Blink harder.

"Sitting on your lap in front of your employees—your *friends*," I turn my head to one side, stiffly, turning my upper body as if I have a crick in my neck, and glance at Jakob. "It goes against literally everything I have trained myself to do and to be in public settings. I must always be in control. Don't give away too much. Don't say the wrong thing. Don't laugh too loud. Don't bend over too far and let a male employee see down my shirt, or bend over to pick up something off the floor and present my giant ass to some guy in his cubicle."

His lips brush my ear, his breath wafts hot on my neck. "Your ass is *not* giant. It's fucking perfect." He breathes this so quietly that I feel the words on my ear as much as hear them.

"It's gargantuan."

"Stand up."

"After all I went through to force myself to sit

down, now you want me to stand back up?" I huff. "Fine. Whatever. Fickle jackass."

I stand up, tense all over.

I flinch violently when his hands palm my ass, squeezing each cheek in a hand. "Jakob!" I dance out of reach

"You can sit back down," he says. "Just checking."

I sit back down on his thighs; this time, it's easier. I'm less tense and rigid, and a little farther back on his lap. Still shaking all over, though. "Checking?" I ask. "Groping my ass is not *checking* anything."

"Sure it is. I groped your ass to check how giant it is. My determination is that your ass is just right."

"Did I hear someone say giant ass?" This is Terra, half an airplane away.

"Brys thinks she has a giant ass," Annika says.

Terra moves toward the back, pushing past Sophia to stand in front of me. She peers at me, frowning. "Stand up and turn around."

I throw my hands up in exasperation. "Stand up, sit down, stand up, sit down. Jesus, you people."

Nonetheless, out of morbid curiosity if nothing else, I stand up and turn around, presenting my giant ass to Terra for examination. I look over my shoulder at her—she's peering at my backside as if scrutinizing a painting at The MoMA, hand on her chin, head tilted.

"Nope. Not giant. A good size, to be sure. Nice and plump and round." She gives one cheek a little pat. "A good jiggle..." a squeeze, "yet nice and firm, too." She glances at Jakob over my shoulder, then meets my eyes. "You wanna see what a giant ass looks like?" She shoves her leggings and underwear down to mid-thigh, grabs her own ass in both hands, and shakes it. "Feast your eyes! *This* is a giant ass."

Jakob's head rears back in surprise, and then he looks away. "A little warning next time, Terra?"

"Oh, faff," Terra says. "It's just a butt. Don't tell me you're squeamish about seeing my big pasty Irish ass."

"I am uncomfortable with it, yes."

"Saxon!" she shouts.

"Yo!"

"Your boss doesn't want to see my ass!"

"His loss!" Saxon has a six-inch-long fixed blade survival knife out, and he's balancing it by the point on his middle fingertip. "Bring that Jell-O over here where it can be properly worshipped as it deserves!"

"Jell-O?" I echo. "Terra, he just—"

She winks while shaking her ass at me again. And, to be fair, there is a certain gelatinous quality to the movement. Something, I...ummm...recognize. Mainly because I see it in the mirror every morning when I check to see if it's shrunk at all since the last time...which it never has.

"My man loves my big jiggly ass. What can I say? If the man likes Jell-O, who am I to complain?" She tugs her pants back up and faces me, serious. "I spent my whole life wanting to shrink myself to fit the expectations of others, Brys. Literally. Starving myself. Running until my tits ached."

"So, two steps?" I quip.

She eyes my chest. "Yeah, exactly—you get it, Tits McGee." She cups my cheek in a small hand. "Until I met Saxon, I *hated* my giant ass. But *he* loves it. I thought it was a joke at first, like he was playing it up to be nice to me or something. But no. He really is attracted to this big ol' caboose of mine. And that feels fuckin' *amazing*, sweetheart." She glances at Jakob over my shoulder. "If the man says he thinks your ass is perfect, don't argue. Just say thank you and show it to him every chance you get. He'll appreciate it, and you'll eventually believe him." She lifts her chin at Jakob. "Now. Show him your hiney."

I bite my lip. Can I? My heart pounds. I sat on his lap and it was fine. These people are crazy, though. So…mooning the man when he's been down my throat shouldn't be a thing.

It's the audience that's holding me up.

I swallow hard and bite my lip and hold my breath… and then push my borrowed leggings down, baring my backside to Jakob.

When I find the courage to look at him, his jaw is tight, and his eyes are blazing.

"Pull the fucking things back up, goddammit," he snarls. His voice drops to a growled whisper. "Unless you want me to fuck you in the airplane bathroom."

I hurriedly obey, and the instant the leggings are in place, he yanks me backward onto his lap. Fully onto him, this time. My back to his front, my ass firmly seated on his crotch—and I can feel the evidence that he really is capable of following through with that threat.

"Having you on my lap is fucking torture," he breathes in my ear. "Do you have any clue how badly I need you?"

I shake my head. "No, I don't."

"That ass," he murmurs. "The things I want to do to it?"

"Jakob," I whisper, an admonishment. "Not here."

"I won't do anything here," he answers. "But I'll tell

you what I *want* to do." A pause. "What I'm *going* to do the second we're alone."

I can't breathe. Terra has gone back to Saxon, Sophia to Lorenzo. We're alone back here. No one is looking anymore.

I don't want him to tell me what he wants to do. Not because I don't want to hear it, though. Because I *do*—so badly. I want to hear more than that. I want him to do all of it. Now. Here. In front of everyone.

Not really.

But my arousal is an inferno inside me—feeling his erection against my buttocks has set me off. Hearing that snarl in his voice. His hands on my hips.

Oh god.

I need him.

"What, Jakob?" I breathe. "What are you going to do?"

He grinds his erection against me. "Put you on your hands and knees," he huffs in my ear, voice a silky soft whisper, midnight dark and shivering with erotic promise. Or threat. Either works. "Spank this big beautiful ass until it's pink all over." His voice drops yet further until I have to strain to hear him, even with his lips against my ear. "Yes, I said big. I fucking *love* your ass, Brys. You are not allowed to do *anything* to make it smaller or change it in any way. Do you understand me? This ass is mine. It's big and beautiful and perfect—and *mine*. Are we clear?"

"Yes, Jakob," I breathe.

He means it.

Invisible shackles loosen. Open. Fall away.

"Good." He nips my earlobe. Nuzzles the side of my

throat. "Once I've properly spanked you, do you know what I'm going to do?"

"N-no?"

"Fuck you from behind." He pushes against me, and the thick ridge of his erection nestles against my backside; I have to open my eyes and look around to remind myself that we're not alone, or I'd have him inside me within ten seconds. "And when I say fuck you, Brys, I mean *fuck*. Hard. Fuck you so hard your ass will shake until it hurts. And while I'm fucking you, I'm going to put a finger inside your tight little asshole."

"Jesus, Jakob!"

"Has anyone had you there?" he asks.

I shake my head, feeling faint. "N-no. No. No one. Never. Nothing. Never been touched back there."

"Then I'll be careful and gentle. I'll fuck you hard and finger you gently." His voice is...oh god. It makes me drip. "Do you want that, Brys?"

"Yeah," I huff. "So bad."

"Yeah?" he demands. "Is that it? That's all you have to say? *Yeah*?"

"Yes, Jakob."

"Better."

His erection is nestled between my butt cheeks. I can't stop myself from grinding on him, dragging my ass against him, feeling him slide against me. Imagining him inside me.

God, that cock...I fucking want it. I want him. I need him.

"When can we be alone?" I whimper. "I need you, Jakob."

"What do you need, Brys?"

"You?"

"You have me right now."

"Your cock."

"What about it?"

I grind harder, faster. I feel him tense. "I need it."

"You need my cock?"

"Yes, Jakob. I need your cock." I twist on his lap and breathe my words directly into his ear. "I need it inside me."

"Where inside you?"

"Everywhere," I answer, squirming. I've forgotten that anyone else exists. "In my mouth. In my pussy. In my ass. I just need you."

"Ladies and gentlemen, we're making our approach into Las Vegas," a male voice says from everywhere and nowhere at once. "Please reorient your seats and buckle up for landing."

"Guess you'll just have to wait a bit longer then, won't you?" Jakob answers, lifting me onto the seat beside him and buckling me in. "But not for long."

Chapter 24

The Next Adventure; Jake

JAKOB

I have never cursed traffic as viciously as I am right now. Mostly in my head, but an occasional snarled curse of frustration shoots past my teeth.

Beside me, Brys is sitting prim and proper, one knee folded just so over the other, back straight. Her cheeks are pink, though.

Almost is as pink as her ass is about to be.

It took every ounce of restraint I possessed not to rip her clothes off and take her right then and there on the jet in front of everyone.

She has no idea who she's dealing with, presenting her bare ass to me like that. She'll find out, though.

I bite my tongue to stop myself from yelling at the bus driver—it's not his fault. Our group is big enough now that we need a full-size party van—or, as Saxon calls it, the Fun Time Party Barge. The others are having fun—booze flows, cannabis smoke swirls, bags of gummies are passed around. There are card games. Saxon, Terra, Annika, and Chance are playing something like Charades, except no one can guess what anyone is doing, there is too much hysterical laughter.

Only Nicolae, Brys, and I are tense and serious.

Even my raging arousal is dampened upon our arrival at Club Sin—I haven't been back since I left weeks ago.

Now we're back—I'm back, and I don't know how to feel.

I'm not the man I was when I left this place.

Beside me, Brys leans across me to peer out the window at the club. It's a huge black cube; the upper few stories are black glass. Club Sin is written across the top around all four sides in fifty-foot-tall letters designed to look like dripping blood.

The bus pulls alongside the private entrance around the side, parks in a hiss of brakes, and then the bi-fold doors rotate open. We all troop off, stretching and yawning—none of us has slept much in days.

Sol pays the driver with a stack of cash, and the bus trundles away in a smelly cloud of diesel exhaust, and we're standing in the parking lot in the baking Vegas sun.

I gesture at the door. "Well? Are we going in?"

They all stare at me.

"You're…coming down with us?" Silas asks, surprised.

I shrug, nod. "Yes. The need to protect my identity is over. You all know me, now." I pause, let out a breath. "And, to be honest with you all, I don't want to go back to being a recluse." I glance at Brys, smiling. "I realized recently that while this," I sweep a hand at the building, "is Club Sin. "This," I gesture to the whole crew, including myself, "is the *real* club." And I want to be part of it."

Chance steps forward. "Then you need two things, Boss."

I frown. "Those two things being?"

"The brand and the vow."

I grin savagely. "I absolutely agree." Roll a shoulder. "The brand may have to wait until after I'm healed more, though?"

Chance smirks. "I suppose that's fair." He ducks under the lintel and inputs the code into the keypad; the door lock clunks, and he tugs the door open, holding it for everyone. I'm last, and he stops me. "You really want to take the brand, Boss?"

"Can't very well be part of the club without it, can I?"

"It's not just a club, sir."

I shake my head. "No more, Boss, no more, sir. I'm just...Jakob."

"It's a brotherhood, Jakob." His eyes are dark and serious and wise. "You've more than earned a place with us. You created this brotherhood. You don't need the brand to be one of us—you already are."

There's a hot lump in my throat. "Thank you, Chance."

A squeal of brakes draws our attention—a trim figure in black leather stands straddling a sleek motorcycle; an opaque black visor shields the figure's features. "Nicolae Dragos?" The voice is of indeterminate gender, muffled by the helmet; it could be a soft-spoken male or a woman with a deep voice.

Chance has a handgun out in an eyeblink, the figure gripped by the jacket, the gun shoved up under the lip of the helmet. "Who the fuck are you and what the fuck do you want? You have five seconds to answer before I turn your skull into a soup bowl."

Moving slowly, keeping their hands visible at all times, the figure pulls something from inside their leather jacket using two fingers—a manila document envelope. "For Nicolae Dragos."

"I am here," Nicolae says, shuffling slowly back up the stairs and out into the sun. "Easy, Chance, my brother. This person is merely a messenger. Yes?"

The rider nods once. "Correct. I am unarmed." They produce a pen from the inside pocket, and a crumpled, much-folded piece of paper—an invoice. "Sign, please. Anywhere."

"What is this?" Nicolae says, signing the paper with a scrawl. "I am not expecting anything."

"I don't know what it is. All I know is that I was contracted to deliver this package to these coordinates. I received it one hour ago."

"Do you know who sent it?"

The figure unfolds the paper Nicolae just signed. "Ahhh...a Major Lisel Neufeld. It originated from Ramstein Air Force Base."

Nicolae's eyes widen. "Thank you."

"Of course. Have a nice day." The rider guns the engine and is gone in an eyeblink.

Nicolae is still just standing there staring at the document envelope like it's either a bomb about to explode or the most precious item in the universe.

"Let's take it inside, shall we, Nicolae?" I suggest.

He nods. "Yes. Yes."

Downstairs in the newly-renovated Arrow quarters, we all cluster in the common area around Nico as he pinches the metal tabs together and opens the flap.

"Are you expecting anything from your contact, Nic?" Solomon asks.

Nicolae shakes his head. "No. I have not heard from Major Neufeld since our meeting in Germany. I had not expected to for some time, if at all. The wheels of justice, as we all know, grind rather slowly. Internationally, most especially." He hasn't withdrawn what's inside, yet. He lets out a breath and does so, slowly, gingerly.

Photos. 8x10, glossy, high definition.

The top photo was taken with a telephoto zoom lens—Pugli in the passenger seat of a battered red Lada Niva from the last century. His right hand is wrapped in a red-soaked bandage...and by hand, I mean stump; there is no hand—that must have been what got crunched by the press.

Nico passes the photo to me, his face impassive.

The next few photos show Pugli in various activities, all taken by the same zoom lens from a great distance. Eating awkwardly with his left hand. Crossing a street, the stump held against his stomach. Gesturing angrily at a henchman. Riding in another car—a silver Peugeot, newer.

"So we know he's in Europe," Solomon says. "Let's get that jet spooled up again."

Nicolae literally gasps when he flips to the next photo. "That appears to be unnecessary."

I take the photo from him, an odd and overwhelming mixture of emotions rifling through me at what I see.

Pugli.

Dead.

It's a police photo of his home in Lyon. The front doors are wide open, showing the expansive marble foyer and the suits of armor and authentic Greek and Roman busts. Pugli is on his back on the foyer floor in a pool of blood.

It's a disturbingly gory image.

His throat has been cut from ear to ear, his tongue pulled out to hang down from the open flap. His eyes are gouged out. He's naked. His cock and balls have been sliced off and stuffed in his mouth.

Cash—I see Euros, US Dollars, Brazilian Reals, Colombian Pesos, Romanian Leu, and more—have been dumped out and scattered around him, soaked in blood, sticking to him.

"Jesus," Sophia breathes. "*Jesus.*" It takes a lot to shock the daughter of a cartel kingpin.

Nicolae is clutching the photo in trembling hands. His face is stony and impassive.

"My love?" Tatiana whispers, touching his jaw. "Speak to us."

"He is dead." It's flat, emotionless.

He flips to the next photo—an autopsy photo, gore-free, the corpse cleaned and draped with a sheet up to the shoulders. It is unequivocally Roberto Pugli.

The last photo shows a message inscribed on the floor of the foyer next to Pugli's body, written in his blood, in Romanian Cyrillic. He flips the photo over—the translation is written in blue felt tip pen: "For our girls. Rot in hell."

After the photos is a single sheet of printer paper with a short, typewritten note and a signature.

Dental records, facial recognition software using the official Interpol dossier, and fingerprints all confirm that the decedent is Roberto Antonio Pugli. Power to the entire block was cut for 10 minutes. Local authorities got a hit on a black Sprinter van leaving the area, but quickly lost track of it. Between you and me, Lieutenant Dragos, no one is looking for his killers. My team's best guess, based on interviews I personally conducted with the residents of the village his men recently hit, and the message written in Romanian, is that the village was protected by someone very powerful in the world of Romanian organized crime. As your American friends would say, he fucked around and found out.

Nils shared some of your story with me, Nicolae. You did not deliver the killing blow, and perhaps this is for the best. He is dead, and he suffered. Justice has been served, I think.

I hope you will know freedom.

Your friend,
Major Lisel Neufeld

"He is dead," Nicolae repeats.

Silence.

His eyes lift; he releases the letter; Solomon catches it, scans it, and passes it around.

Shocked, Nicolae staggers backward, a frown scrunching his brow, and sinks onto a nearby bench. "I…I cannot believe it. I have…I have hunted that man for so many years. I have dreamed of the moment I…" he pulls a knife out from a sheath secured horizontally to his belt along the small of his back; the black blade is long and serpentine and wickedly sharp. He stares at it. "I have dreamed of the moment I plunge this very blade into his heart and watch the life bleed out of his fucking eyeballs."

No one speaks.

Even Tatiana doesn't seem to know what to do or say. She dares not even get too close. None of us does.

"What am I meant to feel?" Nicolae asks, holding the knife flat on both cupped palms, as if he's about to offer it up to someone in a ritual. "Should I be angry that my vengeance has been stolen? Relieved that he is dead? His throat was cut last, you know. The blood—his testicles were removed first. They left his eyeballs so he could watch them do it. Then they cut his eyes out. And *then* they gave him the…what is it called?"

"A Columbian Necktie," Sophia supplies.

"Yes, yes," Nicolae murmurs. "Columbian Necktie." A long pause. "He is truly dead."

"Feels a little…anticlimactic, to be honest," Solomon says. "All that, hunted and chased all over the fuckin' world? Gunfights, sleepless nights, fuckin'…all the hell we went through because of that fucking man. And we get a goddamn *envelope* with some goddamn *pictures*?"

Nicolae nods. "I agree. It is…" he curses in three languages. "It is damnably anticlimactic."

"I am glad." This comes, unexpectedly, from Naomi, in a firm, confident voice.

Everyone stares at her. Nicolae turns his gaze onto her very, very slowly. "Please explain, Naomi."

Tall, quiet, willowy Naomi, who has been through so much pain, kneels in front of Nicolae, covers the knife and his hands with hers. "You would never have known peace if you had been the one to kill him."

Nicolae's head jerks up at this. "I disagree most intensely. It is what I have lived for."

"Exactly." A pause. "You have tried to move on, Nico," Naomi says in her soft, sweet voice. "You have tried to let go. To frame it as justice and not revenge."

Nico nods. "I…yes. You are right, in this. I have."

"But you haven't been able to, have you?"

"How could I, when the monster still roamed this earth? What peace could I know when the man who murdered my wife and infant children was still free and alive?" His voice cracks, breaks. "Tati...Tati?"

Tatiana falls to her knees in front of him—Naomi slides aside to make room. "I'm here, love."

"I thought—I thought I had let go."

She cups his face and kisses his cheeks and his mouth and his eyes. "I know. I know."

"But I couldn't," he whispers. "The hate. The hate..."

Tatiana's thumbs sweep under his eyes. "Do you think I did not feel it in you, my love? Do you think I did not know when you woke up from a nightmare? Do you think I did not know what the dreams were of? I *love* you, Nicolae. I love you despite the hate you bore for him. But I feel as Naomi does. I am glad you were not the one to murder that man. Now you are truly free. His blood is not on your hands. It is not on your conscience. This is...I know you may not see it yet, but this is the best thing that could have happened."

He just nods slowly—acknowledgment rather than agreement, I believe. For a long, silent beat, he stares at the knife on his upturned palms. Then, by infinitesimal degrees, he tilts his hands away, down; the knife rolls, rolls, and clatters to the ground at his feet. His head hangs. His shoulders shake. Tatiana frames his face and kisses his forehead. Scoots away, glances around at the men, his brothers. Her meaning is clear: go to him.

They surround him, a brawny ring of arms wrapping around him, clinging to him as he breaks.

When he has recovered, scrubbing his face, he pushes free of the group of men and picks up the photograph of Pugli dead on the autopsy table. He stares at it for a long time. His fingers slip under his sleeve and touch his tattooed brand. "Once you're in, there's no going back," he whispers. "Loyalty to the brotherhood above all." A razor-sharp pause; his voice hardens. "Never take a life." The change in order changes everything, coming from him.

He straightens, staring at the photograph. Draws a deep breath, holds it, and lets it out slowly, eyes closed. When he opens them again, his gaze is clear and strong. He gathers the photographs and the letter, stuffs them all back into the envelope, and hands it to me. "The case is officially closed."

I accept the envelope, finding it hard to wrap my head around the news. "Yes, so it is. The world is a better place, now that he is gone from it."

Nicolae nods. "Yes, so it is," he says, echoing my words. "I think…I think I must rest."

Tatiana is at his side in an instant, tucking herself against him, propping him up, whispering to him in Croatian. He replies in kind, sounding weary and worn… but free.

"We must all rest. It has been a long fight for everyone." I look around the group. "I am proud of each and every one of you. Of us. Of how we have grown—as individuals and as a group." I clear my throat, again feeling emotional. "It feels disingenuous to include myself in that statement. *You* grew—*I* hid. You have each taught me courage. Resilience. Strength—mental, emotional strength. When—" I clear my tight hot throat again, in vain. "When I created the idea of this experiment, this group, I did so thinking that in helping each of you overcome your pasts, I would…I would find redemption and rehabilitation for myself. By proxy, I suppose. But I have discovered that it doesn't work that way. You had to find it for yourselves.

Not find—*take*. Make. Create. And *you* did. Now I must follow your example. So I must thank you." I look at each face in turn—Rev, Kane, Chance, Silas, Saxon, Solomon, Lash, who is now called Nicolae, Lorenzo, Myka, Anjalee, Annika, Naomi, Terra, Scarlett, who is now called Maria, Tatiana, and Inez, who is now called Sophia; and last, Brys. "You've each shown me the way forward. We are no longer slaves to our pasts. We have no more enemies. No reason to hide. You are free from your oaths to me. Not to each other, but to me, to this place, this life. What comes next is up to you. But first, if you would indulge me one more time."

I step forward and hold out my hand to Brys.

She takes it without hesitation.

"Follow me, please, everyone."

I led them up to the security floor. There are three floors above the security floor—Sophia's former quarters, which occupy one floor, and mine, which occupi two.

At least, that's how it used to be.

The crew, after the firefight here, rebuilt the Arrow quarters down below and now call it the Quiver. Appropriate enough. They knew I had additional work done on the floors above the club—after Sophia moved out with Lorenzo and into a rented apartment ten minutes away.

What they don't know is that I totally gutted and renovated all three floors. There are full suites for each couple: two bedrooms with en suite bathrooms, a living area, and a gourmet kitchen, all designed around floor-to-ceiling electrochromatic windows. There is now an additional common area on what was solely the security floor—I condensed the various rooms for servers, monitors, and such for security to make room for it.

Now, there are several individual seating areas for conversation around the perimeter, a central electric pass-through fireplace, a theater-sized projector screen with concert-grade surround sound, and a kitchen area. The usual entertainment features abound—foosball, pool, a professional card table, gaming systems, and anything else I could think of. The elevator is now programmed to the keycards as well as individual biometrics.

The crew looks around in confusion.

"What's this?" Solomon asks, glancing at me.

"The new common room." I let out a breath. "I…my hope was that you would all stay on, for a while at least. Maybe help me train a new crew of Broken Arrows."

"So, if there's a new crew going in down there, and this is *our* common room," Silas says, slowly, putting it all together, "then…where are our rooms?"

I grin. "So glad you asked, Silas." I indicate a pile of keycards on the mantel above the fireplace. "The cards are numbered. On the three floors above, there are ten apartments. Nine of them are identical except for position within the building." I sort through the pile until I find the one I want and show it to them, my grin widening, becoming a little arrogant. "Seeing as I paid for it, I've reserved the corner suite on the top floor for myself. It is a little bigger than the others. You know, because I'm the boss and all."

"Apartments?" This is from Rev. "When you say 'apartments'…?"

I gesture at the keycards—heavy black metal inscribed with a scarlet numeral in the same font as the club name on the outside. "See for yourselves."

Brys is smiling as if this whole thing amuses her or

something. She leans against me, watching the others excitedly grab keycards and head up to explore.

"C'mon," I tell her. "Let's go see the—my—our…" I swallow hard. "Not sure how to put it. I don't know—we haven't—"

Her lips touch mine, silencing me. "*Our*. The word you're looking for is 'our', Jakob."

"But…New York. BDI. Your life—"

"Was planned for me from the day I was born. There was never a question that I was going to work for my father. I…I obviously never expected to be CEO, but it was a foregone conclusion that I'd be an executive of some kind, someday. I always assumed I'd be Britt's VP." She shrugs. Looks around. "I…I want this life with you, Jakob. These people. I don't know what it looks like, but that's part of the adventure. I've…I've never traveled, as an adult. We did a lot as a kid, but then college and career took over, and…" she shrugs again. "I've already decided I'm going to step down as CEO and sell my shares. Maybe even sell the whole company. I'm ready for what's next, and I'm hoping you'll let me spend what's next with you—all of you. Whatever it looks like. I'm ready for an adventure."

"Let you?" I echo, my tone reflecting my stunned disbelief. "*Let* you? Brys, I was prepared to beg you to spend every other weekend here with me."

She grins up at me, fingers dancing over my crotch. "You can still beg, Jakob. Just…for other things."

"Perhaps we should go explore our new home."

She looks at me with such love that my soul could explode from the intensity and wonder of it. From the shock that she could see me that way. Want this with me. So easily just… accept me.

Again, my stupid eyes burn.

She lifts up, frames my face, pulls me down, and kisses each of my eyes. "None of that, if you please, sir."

"Sir, is it?"

"Yes, sir." A breathy, erotic whisper. She slips her hand inside my borrowed sweatpants and clutches me. "Command me, Jakob. Please."

Feral, blazing hunger for her ignites within me—held at bay until now. "Let's go."

I drag her by the wrist to the elevator, tap the keycard against the reader. When the door closes, I pivot, slam her back against the wall, and take her mouth.

Slash a hot, demanding kiss across her lips, steal her tongue, devour her breath. "God, I fucking love you," I growl.

She whimpers, and her knees give out. "Jake...Jakob. Oh god."

I catch her, hold her up, pin her to the wall with my hips. "What did you just call me?"

"Jakob?" I kissed her momentarily, stupid, I think.

"No, before that." He sounds angry.

"It was...I stammered. I said Jake—like...I didn't mean—"

"Say it again."

Her exotic eyes find mine. "Jake."

I shake my head, laughing. "Jake."

She wrinkles her nose. "I don't know."

"Maybe just in private, for now." I kiss her again, until she breaks away, panting. "When I'm making you come, you can call me Jake."

"Yes, sir."

I huff a laugh. "Fuck, I love that."

The elevator dings, announcing we've reached the top floor. I drag her down the hallway to the correct door. Tap the card. Shoves open the door.

She has no interest in a tour. "Bed." She's already tearing at my sweatpants, shoving them down. "Bed, *now*."

"Try again." I grab her wrists, pull them away, trap them against my chest with one hand, and pull her against me by her ass with the other.

She tosses the card onto the narrow table near the door. "Take me to bed. Now. Please...*sir*." Her blue-ringed eyes are damp with desire, tears of...I don't know. Joy? Need? Pure, overwhelming love? All of the above. "Please, Jakob. *Please*."

"As you wish."

She cackles breathily at my reference. "*Princess Bride*? Really?"

"I watch movies. I was a recluse for ten years. What did you think I was doing? Knitting?"

"Mysterious supervillain shit, I imagine."

"I was *not* a supervillain."

She quirks an eyebrow at me, takes the card from me, and shows me the dripping-blood font. "Oh no?"

I smack her ass as I lead her to the bedroom. "Well, maybe a *little* supervillan-y."

She walks backward into the bedroom, pulling me after her. "If I'm not orgasming in the next sixty seconds, we're fighting."

I close the door behind me and cross my arms over my chest. "Then you'd better take off your clothes."

"Yes, sir," she breathes. "Right away, sir."

Chapter 25

An Ending

BRYS

My heart pounds with anticipation. Jakob is between me and the door, strong arms crossed over his heavy chest. His eyes blaze with arousal, and he breathes deeply and slowly, brow furrowed, jaw ticking as he stares at me.

I peel off the shirt first, toss it to my feet. Push down and step out of the leggings. Reach for my underwear.

"No," he barks. "Bra first."

"Yes, sir." God save me, but I feel such a wild thrill in this. In knowing I can submit to him safely, willingly, eagerly. Give him all the decisions, all the control.

He loves it just as much—knowing I *want* this. He's not taking anything from me; I'm giving it. All he's doing is accepting.

Serendipity.

Puzzle pieces made to fit perfectly together.

I strip the bra off, watching him watch my breasts bounce free. His cock swells behind the gray cotton of the sweatpants.

And now I get it.

You see those memes about gray sweatpants doing

for women what a skin-tight pair of yoga pants does for men. And I never got it.

Now I do. I *really* fucking get it. Because fucking hell, the gray sweatpants. The outline of his huge cock behind them. The way I can see it swaying as he moves. The way they cling to his taut, hard, round ass.

Fuck, yes.

"You need to wear those more often for me," I say.

He glances down. "Ratty old gray sweats?" He sounds adorably confused, maybe even a little offended.

I grin, and I know exactly how it looks—wild with arousal, positively primal with it.

"Yes!" It comes out a soft snarl.

He smirks. "If that's what does it for you, sweetheart." We both go still. "I…I've never used terms like that before."

"Me either." I shake my head, throat tight. "Use them all. I want…" I blink. "I…I want—"

"I know what you want," he says. "Now come over here, Beautiful."

I come over there, in just my panties—Terra's, as she's the only one with a big enough ass to lend me her underwear. Good news is they're kinda sexy. Black lace cut high on the hips to bare my ass cheeks and a narrow triangle covering my puss.

I don't own sexy underwear. If I want to seduce a man, I put on my silk kimono. But I admit, this feels…hot.

His eyes burn with barely restrained need; his hands shake with it. When I'm a foot away, he holds a hand up. "Stop there."

I stop. Stand waiting, breathing, eager for his next command.

"Turn around."

Swallowing hard, I turn around. What is he going to do? Spank me? I've long fantasized about that. I told him as much. But I'm also scared of it. Not the pain—he told me doesn't get off on pain, and neither do I. What am I scared of? Trick question—it's not fear. It's…anticipation, desperation.

"Take them off. Slowly." I glance over my shoulder, but he nudges my head around. "Don't look at me. Just do as I say. Take off the panties, now, slowly."

"Yes sir, Jakob."

I'm panting shallowly, shaking all over. Slowly, I shimmy my hips side to side as I wriggle the lace down past my buttocks. As they reach my thighs, I bend at the waist, little by little, pushing the underwear down.

When they're pooled on the floor around my feet, his voice stops me with his next order. "Grab your ankles."

Good thing I'm flexible.

I hold onto my ankles, feeling more exposed and vulnerable than I ever have in my life. A rough hand smooths gently down my spine from my shoulder blades to the small of my back. Fingers dance over my left buttock. A single fingertip traces the circumference of one cheek. The other. I gasp when the fingertip brushes the tight knot of my asshole, and I remember the things he promised he'd do to me, there, and I stop breathing.

"Spread your legs a bit." I shift my stance wider. "Good girl. Thank you."

This is new; thank you?

I shiver at the praise, the thanks. I don't understand why I react this way, and frankly, I don't give a single, solitary, flying mother-fuck. I like it. I want it.

"Ask for it."

"Spank me, Jakob."

"Say please."

"Please, Jakob?" I'm so excited I can barely breathe, so turned on that my arousal is dripping down my thighs, literally. "Please spank me."

"Stand up."

Disappointment slithers through me, but I obey anyway. "I asked," I protest. "I said please."

His lips ghost against my ear. "Fuck, honey. You *really* want to be spanked, don't you?"

"Yes," I whisper. "So bad."

"Why?"

"I don't know."

"Why?"

"I don't know!"

"*Why,* dammit? You *do* know. Just admit it."

"I just want it!" I cry. "I don't know why. I don't want it to be, like, hard, so it hurts. Or...or not much. Just... god, Jakob, I *don't know*! It's..." the truth topples out of me, and I'm glad I'm facing away from him so he can't see my face when I say this. "I want to surrender completely to you. To trust you to know how hard to spank me so I like it. It's about trust, Jake." The new nickname just slips out on accident. "It's just about trust."

"Step forward to the foot of the bed." His lips are on my ear, the words growled, trembling with...it sounds like fury, but it's not. The proximity of it to fury, though... the knife-edge of danger, knowing his power, his strength, fuck. So hot.

I'm burning up all over, dripping with arousal, shaking with need.

I walk with slow, measured paces to the foot of the

bed. Stand naked and wait, not daring to look at him. If I disobey, he won't give me what I want, and I fucking *need* this. More than my next breath, I need this.

His lips touch the shell of my ear, and I shiver. "Touch your pussy." His chin rests on my shoulder. "Let me watch you."

"Yes, Jakob." I slide my fingers down my belly to the apex of my thighs. Slip my middle finger down my seam and inside myself, and I whimper.

"Are you wet for me, darling?"

"Yes, Jakob."

"How wet?"

"Dripping."

"Dripping?" He sounds skeptical.

He nips my earlobe and sighs into my ear as he drives his palm down my ribcage, avoiding my breasts, down my side, over my hipbone, over my quad to the inside of my thigh.

"Open for me." I spread my thighs apart so I'm standing with feet shoulder-width apart. "Good girl." Fuck, fuck, fuck, my pussy trembles at the praise. He trails his fingers up the inside of my thigh, smearing my essence. "Ohhh my fucking *god*, Brys. You *are* dripping for me."

"Yes, Jakob. I'm dripping for you."

I hear him suck his fingers clean. "Jesus, you taste so fucking good." He rests his forehead against the back of my bent neck, sucking in deep breaths as he slides a finger through my seam, gathering my juices.

I hear him pop it in his mouth and suck it clean, grumbling his pleasure. "Sweet as honey."

My hair has been in a braid since the short, cold shower in the hospital; he tugs it free of the braid and skates his fingers through the kinked waves, then wraps the whole mass around his fist. My pulse goes frantic in anticipation.

"Please, please, please," I whimper, not pretending or faking or exaggerating.

He presses me forward by his grip on my hair until I'm bent in half over the bed. "Close your eyes." I close them, panting whimpers. "Do you trust me, Brys?"

"Yes, Jakob, I trust you."

"Ask for it again."

"Please spank me."

He bends over me, lips to my ear. "As you wish."

Smack!

I cry out in shock, spasming forward in a visceral reaction. My left ass cheek stings terribly, a hot burning across the flesh where his hand connected, hard. Before I can process that he's actually spanked me, his palm cracks across my right cheek, and I cry out again, jerking almost upright.

He isn't touching me, then. "More?"

"Y-yes, p-please."

"Then bend over the bed." I obey, and his hands cup my ass, smoothing and soothing in soft, gentle, loving circles. "Good girl. Ready?"

I nod. "Y-yes. Yes. More. Please."

"Grab the blankets. Hold on tight." His voice is close, hot, dark with arousal, vibrating with pleasure. "And feel free to scream as loud as you want, honey. I had these apartments soundproofed. No one can hear you screaming."

Oh, oh god. Oh god.

Crack! His hand slaps my right cheek again, and then my left without pause or warning. I cry again at each smack, louder.

"Touch your pussy, Brys." He bends over me, fits his fingers to my sex, slips a thick digit inside me, smears my juices over my throbbing clit—I scream, then, as I quake on the cusp of climax from the one touch. "Touch your pussy while I spank you."

The next time he smacks my ass, I grab the blankets over my head with one hand and fit my fingers of the other to my sex, and then wait—the next smack comes unexpectedly, and I flick my clit with my fingertips in time with the spanking.

A lightning bolt strikes me, searing through my belly and core first, spreading up to tighten my nipples and down to make my ass cheeks flush with a rush of blood. I scream out loud as the initial rush of orgasm smashes through me.

Jakob growls as I lurch forward with the climax. "Fucking hell, Brys. You're coming already?"

He spanks me again, left… right… left… right; now hard enough to make me cry out in shock, now soft little taps, and then he doesn't spank at all, just pets my bottom, smoothing the bruised flesh. And through it all, I finger my clit in ever faster circles, and my climax crests and recedes, breaks me, and then fades.

That's when he keeps his promise.

I'm shaking through a wave of climax when I hear him spit, and then saliva-wet fingers touch my asshole. I tense, gasp.

"Trust me, darling."

My legs shake, and then threaten to give out.

"Jakob, I…I can't…" I feel my knees dipping. "Jakob—"

"Trust me."

I sink against the bed and force myself to relax,

breathing and softening myself for him. He hums a low, aroused growl as he smears saliva over my asshole, spits on his fingers again, and smears again, until I'm dripping with hot, wet spit. Then, he presses a fingertip against me. I whimper. Pressure, and I…at first, I don't like it. It feels unnatural and intrusive. But I let out a breath and soften again, release tension. I gasp as he slips that finger deeper, and then deeper.

"Touch your pussy, Brys. Finger your clit."

"Yes, Jakob."

I obey, and now his finger pulses inside me, pushing deeper inside to the rhythm of my circling fingers against my clit, to the rhythm of my gasps as heat billows through me, pressure swells and expands and crushes. Deeper, and deeper, and then I feel his knuckles press into the soft give of my ass cheeks, and I'm coming, screaming, knees dipping as orgasm rips through me, and he's spanking my ass with his free hand and fucking my asshole with his finger.

"That's so beautiful, honey," he snarls. "Fucking beautiful."

I can only whimper helplessly as my legs quake, jellied. Another wave of climax crests inside me and leaves me shivering, weak-kneed, and on the verge of collapse. He catches me before I fall, and I'm held in his arms, bride-over-the-threshold. His mouth is on mine, and he's kissing the breath out of me, taking my breath and giving me his all at once.

I sling my arms around his neck and clutch him to me and open my mouth to him and whimper my greed for his kiss, receiving a rumbling snarl in return.

We're moving, and the bed is under me, and he is over me. "One sec," he whispers, and he's gone, and I'm shaking like a leaf, and I hear water running as he washes his hands, and then he's back and over me again and cupping my face and kissing me as if he'll never stop.

I spread my legs open for him, and his fingers find me and touch my clit and make me twitch and jerk, and then his fingers are inside me and pumping in me, and I have to fuck, have to move.

"Jakob," I whine, "oh god. Please, I..."

"What, sweetheart? Tell me."

"You." I reach for him, find stupid cotton in the way, shove at it, dig my hand under it, find his erection. I grip him, pump his length. "This."

He kicks at his sweatpants, going from one knee to the other, and then I feel his hard, hot thighs on mine and his belly on mine. His shirt is gone, I don't know when, don't care. He's naked and all mine. I clutch his cock with zealous greed, bite his lower lip, and caress his thick length until he's snarling.

"Please, Jakob," I breathe, lips moving on his. "Please. Please!"

"Please, what, Brys?"

"Fuck me," I whimper. "I need your cock inside me."

He wedges his hips between my thighs, and I curl my legs high around his hips. His mouth touches mine in a tease of a kiss, and he nuzzles my seam with the tip of his cock. Then he's whispering in my ear. "What if I said I don't want to fuck you, Brys?"

I keen my sorrow at this news. "I *need* you. I fucking—I *need* you. *Please*, Jake."

He hunches over me at the nickname. The hot, soft, fleshy head of his cock nudges my slit; I hold absolutely still, waiting for him. "What if..." His strong arm curls under my neck, and he tilts his hips against me, nuzzling his tip just between my lips, "I said that I wanted…" a little deeper, now, so his cock-head is splitting me open, "to make love with you instead?"

I meet his eyes, and I know mine are wet from the effect of his words. I palm his ass, hook my feet together over his back. Stare into his eyes without blinking. "I love you, Jakob."

He fills me.

I scream at the ache of it, head thrown back against his forearm, and he bends to kiss my throat as I scream, and he growls, hunching as he slowly eases himself inside me.

Inch by inch, he splits me apart, filling me with himself. Buries himself inside me to the hilt, and he's so big, so hard, so hot, so thick, so long, so perfect. I can't breathe for how glutted I am, every synapse attuned to him, every nerve ending fused to his, reacting to him.

"Jakob, ohhh—oh god. Oh my god, Jakob, my love."

He shudders, burying his face in the hollow of my neck and shoulder. "Brys." He sounds utterly broken. "How can you love me?"

I move, tilt my hips against his. Take him deeper. "Would you ever hurt me?"

"No."

I thrust against him again, ripping a ragged groan from him. "Would you ever betray me?"

"No!"

Another thrust. "Will you lie to me?"

"Never."

Another thrust, and he shudders, feathering a soft thrust to meet mine. I rest my lips where ear meets cheek, breathe my question to him. "Will you try to control me? As in my life, who am I, what do I do, or where do I go?"

"No. Never. I love who you are. I don't want you to be anyone but exactly who you are."

"*That,*" I whisper, giving him another gentle thrust, "is why I love you. I know who you are. You're my Jakob."

He arches, snarling, driving deep, and then withdraws, hunching, his forehead on mine all the while. "I don't deserve you."

"And I say you do."

"Everything I've done—"

"Is in the past. We're looking forward, Jakob."

He shudders above me. Trembles helplessly, overcome, wracked and wrought. "Brys," he breathes.

I roll him to his back, lose him in the process. But that's okay—I want this part. I settle astride his thighs. He's panting hard, brow furrowed. He's unsure about this, my ever-in-control Jakob. "My turn," I tell him, smiling so hard it hurts.

I sit tall on him and stare down at him—all brawny power and rippling muscle. His chest is thick and heavy, his abs hard and dense, his hips lean and narrow, his thighs bunched and massive. The bandages are white squares on his torso, front and back; I know the wounds must hurt him, but if they do, he's showing no sign of it beyond an occasional tightening of his brow.

And then there's his cock, my god. Slick and glistening with our commingled desire, lying flat against his belly, standing hard and proud and ready.

I cup his face. "Do you trust me?"

He's terrified. He has never, ever given anyone this side of him before—he doesn't have to tell me for me to know it to be true. He nods, jerkily. "Yes. I...yes. I trust you, Brys."

"Then let me make love to you."

He relaxes a little, and his hands—once fisted into the blankets at his hips—now come up to frame my hips. "Please, Brys."

My hair drapes around my face as I lean forward and bend over him. "Touch me." I dip to kiss him. "Anything. Everything. You have all of me, Jakob."

I slide up, dragging his cock lengthwise between my lips, brace my hands on his chest and balance, lean forward, lifting my hips. "Look at me, now, Jake." I grasp his length and touch him to me. "Watch us."

His eyes flick to our union, watch, rapt and unblinking as I slip him inside me and hover above him, just the tip of him between my lips. "Brys, fuck. I ache. I can't—" he drives against me, trying to get deeper. "I need you. Please. I need—"

"What, honey?" I breathe, teasing away from him, never letting him out of me but not letting him any deeper. "Down. Hold still."

He drops to the bed and goes still. "I need to be inside you."

"Like this?" I sink onto him, give him one, long, slick, wet stroke, bottoming out on him so my pussy smears against his body and roll on him, swiveling my hips around in a wide circle. And then slide back up his immense length and hover over him once more, almost out of me.

He shudders. "Fuck—oh god, fuck, yes, Brys. I need that. Please." He's shaking, gasping, and I feel him throbbing inside me. "I'm close, honey. I...I need to come."

I bend over him and drape my breast against his mouth. "Suck."

I throw my head back and groan like a cat in heat as he suckles my tit, and then he's greedy and hungry for me, gone for me, his hands grasping and squeezing my breasts, guiding one to his mouth and then the other, and he pinches and rolls my nipples until I'm frantic with arousal and lightning is searing inside me.

"You want to come, Jakob?" I demand.

"Yes, Brys," He snarls around a mouthful of my nipple. "I need to. I can't hold it back much longer. I ache to give myself to you."

I rip my breast away and replace it with my mouth, guiding his hands to my ass. Show him that I want him to lift me up and drive me down. "Then *take* me," I snap, slamming down onto him all at once. "Take it from me."

He grips me by the ass and drags me up his cock until he's almost out of me and then drives me down in one hard thrust, fucking up to meet me.

"YES!" I scream as he buries deep. "Jakob!"

"Brys!" he moans. "Oh god, honey. Fuck."

There's no control, then. No one is in charge. I'm taking, and he's giving; I'm giving, and he's taking. It's what I've always craved—the play of power, the chance to let go and trust someone totally, and find myself in him as he finds himself in me.

We move together in perfect synch. Stars burst behind my eyes as I come apart around him, and he whispers my name like a song. I scream, and I cry, and I come, and I come, and I come.

And the more I come, the harder he fucks me, and I know he's desperately holding back, I feel him trembling with the effort, sweating, gasping, but he won't give up, can't let go.

"Please, Jakob," I breathe, stretching myself along his body. "Come for me. I want you to fill me. Let go, honey. Please."

"I can't," he snarls. "I don't want this to end."

I nip his earlobe and writhe on him, take him in slow, sinuous thrusts. "I'll never, ever leave you, Jakob." He snarls at this, drives up into me, hard and deep. "I'll never leave you. Never abandon you."

"Brys," he whispers, voice ragged and wet. "Stop. I—I can't."

"Let *go*, Jakob," I whisper. "I've got you. Now and forever."

"Can't. Can't." He's so scared to let go—to break, to let himself shatter under me. To show me the last piece of himself—the piece no one, ever, has seen: physical and emotional vulnerability.

"You *can*." I tremble as I move on him, take him in thrust after thrust, aching and pulsing, shivering on the edge of a climax that honestly scares me, too. "Please. I'm begging you, Jake. Please." I kiss him. "*Please*, just let go and trust me."

His eyes are bright and damp on mine, seeking, searching. He scours my body with his hands, cupping my breasts, lifting them and letting them drop heavily, and then my hands and his are tangled, and he lets me press his hands up over his head, and he groans raggedly as we move in unison, bodies meeting in waves of slow, rolling collision.

His thrusts falter. "Brys," he gasps. "Oh god."

"Trust me," I whisper, riding him faster. "Give it to me."

He meets my thrusts, then, finally, and his eyes leak tears, and he grunts like a bear with each powerful thrust, and he yanks his hands away and grasps my ass and holds me in place so he can fuck me as hard as he can.

"YES!" I scream, wailing wordlessly as he pounds into me, harder and harder.

I sit high on him and pile my hair on my head and ride him for all I'm worth as he fucks me with everything he has, finally giving me every last piece of himself. "Jakob! Yes!"

"Brys, oh god, I—I fucking love you, Brys. Jesus, I love you."

"I love you, Jakob. Don't stop!"

He bellows, then, and I feel him come inside me. It's hot rush of cum filling me, exploding through me, and it unleashes my own final climax, and just like the last time I was with him, this last nuclear-hot orgasm shreds me to pieces, and I feel something break open inside me and he's fucking me as hard as he can, my tits shaking wildly, my ass clapping against his thighs as our bodies meet, his cock smashing inside me, plunging his cum through me, and I feel the breaking become shattering. I'm screaming and wailing and I can't move anymore, can't breathe, can't do anything but hold on to him, fall forward and let him grab my ass in both hands and brace his feet and fuck me even harder, coming and coming and coming, and then white light bursts over me and through me and the shattering becomes the hot wet rush of an orgasm splintering into something more.

I feel myself let loose all over him, squirting all over him and myself and the bed as he fucks me into oblivion.

His thrusts slowly subside to stillness.

We breathe raggedly together.

He opens his eyes—still damp, red. "Brys."

I lift up, exhausted now to the point of delirium. "Jake."

He rumbles a laugh. "Yeah, honey. I'm your Jake." He cups my face, making me look at him. "Thank you."

I kiss him in answer. "Thank *you*."

I hear him gulp. "I never knew it could be like that."

I summon enough strength to look up at him. "It's what I always fantasized it could be."

"Thank you for loving me. For showing me…" A charged silence. "Everything."

We pass out in each other's arms, in a wet spot, tangled up and happy.

THE END

ALSO BY
JASINDA WILDER

Visit me at my website: **www.jasindawilder.com**
Email me: **jasindawilder@gmail.com**

If you enjoyed this book, you can help others enjoy it as well by recommending it to friends and family, or by mentioning it in reading and discussion groups and online forums. You can also review it on the site from which you purchased it. But, whether you recommend it to anyone else or not, thank you *so much* for taking the time to read my book! Your support means the world to me!

My other titles:

Forbidden Fruit

Wild Ride: Biker Billionaire

Delilah's Diary

Big Girls Do It:
Big Girls Do It
Married
On Christmas
Pregnant
Rock Stars Do It
Big Love Abroad

The Falling Series:
Falling Into You
Falling Into Us
Falling Under
Falling Away
Falling for Colton

The Ever Trilogy:
Forever & Always
After Forever
Saving Forever

From the world of *Wounded:*
Wounded
Captured

From the world of *Stripped:*
Stripped
Trashed

From the world of *Alpha:*
Alpha
Beta
Omega
Harris
Thresh
Duke
Puck
Lear
Anselm
Sigma
Gamma
Delta

The Houri Legends:
Jack and Djinn

Djinn and Tonic
The Madame X Series:
Madame X
Exposed
Exiled

The Black Room (With Jade London)

The One Series
The Long Way Home
Where the Heart Is
There's No Place Like Home

Badd Brothers:
*Badd Motherf*cker*
Badd Ass
Badd to the Bone
Good Girl Gone Badd
Badd Luck
Badd Mojo
Big Badd Wolf
Badd Boy
Badd Kitty
Badd Business
Badd Medicine
Badd Daddy
For a Goode Time Call…
Not So Goode
Goode To Be Bad
A Real Goode Time
Goode Vibrations
A Very Badd Christmas
Badd Apple
Badd Baby

Dad Bod Contracting:
Hammered
Drilled
Nailed
Screwed

Fifty States of Love:
Pregnant in Pennsylvania
Cowboy in Colorado
Married in Michigan
Christmas in Connecticut

Billionaire Baby Club:
Lizzy Goes Brains Over Braun
Autumn Rolls a Seven
Laurel's Bright Idea

Club Sin:
Rev
Kane
Chance
Silas
Saxon
Solomon
Lash
Inez

Blood Heir
Blood Heir
Blood Rising
Blood Bonds
Blood Reign

Three Rivers
Into the Light
Light in the Dark
Light Up the Night

The Cabin:
The Cabin
Christmas at the Cabin

Standalone titles:
Yours
The Parent Trap
Wish Upon A Star
Big Hose
Too Pucking Old for This

Non-Fiction titles:
You Can Do It
You Can Do It: Strength
You Can Do It: Fasting

Jack Wilder Titles:
The Missionary

JJ Wilder Titles:
Ark

To be informed of new releases, special offers, and other Jasinda news, sign up for Jasinda's email newsletter.

www.ingramcontent.com/pod-product-compliance
Lightning Source LLC
LaVergne TN
LVHW050926080826
845145LV00001B/223